WORLDSHAKER

ALSO BY J. F. LEWIS

Grudgebearer

Oathkeeper

WORLDSHAKER

J. F. LEWIS

an imprint of Prometheus Books
Amherst, NY

Inquiries should be addressed to
Pyr
59 John Glenn Drive
Amherst, New York 14228
VOICE: 716–691–0133
FAX: 716–691–0137
WWW.PYRSF.COM

21 20 19 18 17   5 4 3 2 1

Library of Congress Cataloging-in-Publication Data

Names: Lewis, J. F. (Jeremy F.), author.
Title: Worldshaker / J.F. Lewis.
Description: Amherst, New York : Prometheus Books, 2017. | Series: The Grudgebearer
    trilogy ; book 3
Identifiers: LCCN 2016047508 (print) | LCCN 2016055240 (ebook) |
    ISBN 9781633881853 (softcover : acid-free paper) |
    ISBN 9781633881860 (ebook)
Subjects: | GSAFD: Fantasy fiction. | Occult fiction.
Classification: LCC PS3612.E9648 W67 2017 (print) | LCC PS3612.E9648 (ebook) |
    DDC 813/.6—dc23
LC record available at https://lccn.loc.gov/2016047508

To all the dads out there . . . but I'll be honest, this one was mostly for me.

CONTENTS

PART ONE

AN END TO WAR

"When King Rivvek stepped through the Port Gate with his volunteers, the Unforgiven, the Eldrennaic remainder, those unfortunate elves the Aern would not accept. . . . It was easy to believe they would share a fate similar to that which befell the Lost Command for which they vainly sought: to be relegated to the murky mists of mythological speculation, lost forever to infinite unknown and unsatisfying ends.

General Kyland, a Soldier and Elemancer whose might and legend among his people would be surpassed only by the fame of Wylant, his daughter, had stepped forth into history as a noble sacrifice. Who could imagine otherwise for King Rivvek, the scarred, the hated, the only elf I ever called friend? How could any survive the Demon Realm of the Never Dark for a day, much less many centuries?

We should have had more faith in both of them.

It is never wise to underestimate one's foes. Why then do we so often make the same mistake with regard to our allies?"

From *Dimensional Exiles: The Triumphant Returns* by Sargus

CHAPTER 1

THE END OF A BEGINNING

Child tucked firmly against his chest, Striappa ran, his sharp black talons gouging furrows in the tile floor. Chaos erupted about them in a tortured reflection of the battles raging in the Guild Cities, outside the walls of the Long Speaker's tower. The manitou's fur-covered ears rang with the clamorous din within and without, raised voices combining to form another voice, a meaningless babble of aggression and fear . . . the dying, the injured, and the aggressors all becoming one cry. Music, he imagined, to the war god's ears.

Clutching Caius Vindalius, the winged little son of the crystal-twisted young woman Kholster had entrusted to the Long Speakers' care, even more tightly to his feathered and furred chest, Striappa shivered both at the tickling touch of the babe's tiny hands on that warm band of thick fur where breast feathers met belly feathers and at the recalled sharing of his grandmatron. His surroundings, the sound of them, drew out remembered tales of the great wars before most manitou left the lands of the shape-locked and founded the Gathering Isles, far off to the west in the grand expanses of the Cerrullic Ocean, away from the violence of those melded sounds.

Noona shared the vibrations of this third voice, taught the clutches of her family and those who nested with them to recognize it, and, when they heard it, to migrate home. "The voice of war is one the manitou no longer wish to hear," she'd told Striappa and his siblings as they'd curled near the fire pit, snatching at the flames with their claws to harden them and to learn the strength of the fire, how to resist it, how to let it move through them, how to feel the way it changed and flowed and perhaps apply that to their shapeshifting, if they could.

"But fighting is glorious, right, Noona?" Striappa had asked.

Noona's face had morphed from the friendly beaked and feathered visage that had spat scrumptiously softened foods into his maw when he had been too young to hunt for himself to a spiny face of leathery skin, a mouth of sharp fangs. Great curling horns had erupted from her brow, as tusks had sprouted from her morphing muzzle. The bands of alternating fur and feathers of her body had flattened into bony plates of armor, jutting spikes rising up from the ones she chose. Talons had become claws and seized him, forcing him down, head close to the flames. Solid black eyes like those of a shark had glared at him from a face no longer warm or comforting, making him ill inside.

"Am I glorious or terrifying?" Noona had growled, in the harsh tones of a non-avian throat.

"Both," he'd answered squawkily.

"Yes." She'd smiled, still ghastly in her aspect. "Both is right, my little one." Releasing him with a grunt, she had turned her back to the flames, leathery wings stretching out to take flight.

"Where are you going, Noona?" Clohi, one of Striappa's sisters had asked, but Striappa had known, even before Noona had spoken the words.

"To hunt, my lovelies." The barb at the end of her long tail caught the light as she flew. "All change has its price, and most amount to blood in the end. I'll be back soon."

*

"Run, Striappa," a grizzled voice snapped in his ears, "or fly or whatever it is you manitou do the quickest."

"I am running, Master Sedric," the manitou squawked back at the hazy smoke-formed image of the Elder Long Speaker. Sedric might know everything there was to know about Long Speaking—Striappa certainly could not send his mind out across hundreds of miles as a being of smoke—but he knew more about shapeshifting than Sedric ever would, and it was hard to move quickly and change at the same time. Sedric was right, though; if Striappa was going to get Caius to safety, he knew he was going to need his wing-arms free at some point, so he was trying to create a belly pouch to hold him. "Pouches are hard."

"You weren't thinking about pouches, child." Sedric's smoky lips pursed. "You were brain-fogged by tales your Noona told you as a cub."

"Hatchling," Striappa corrected, before he could stop himself. He darted for the open doorway through which Sedric's smoky sending had emerged, but Sedric waved him off toward the far stairway.

"Too much fighting that way; you'll need to fly out of here." Sedric groaned, then vanished, eyes ablaze with inner light, a ball of burning, crackling red manifesting at the center of his brow. He reappeared when Striappa paused halfway up the stairwell to get the pouch right. It had to be easier for girls, or surely they would never bother. Striappa kept losing the opening or making something more mouth-like, into which one would not want to place any infant one wanted to keep.

"Oh for Torgrimm's sake, Streep. Why are you stopping now?"

Streep. Striappa's hackles rose at the barb. Even a single-shaped human as enlightened as Master Sedric thought it was okay to drop in a nickname, despite how insulting that was to—

"I know exactly how insulting it is," Sedric said with a sigh. "You keep stopping, and I can't guide you much longer. The fighting at Castleguard is getting worse, and Cassandra and I—"

"Then shut your changeless maw, 'dric, and let me finish!" Striappa growled, beak giving way to fang-filled muzzle. The anger, the desire to prove Sedric wrong, gave Striappa the extra bit of inner energy needed to complete the change, and he slid the quiet, almost contemplative, baby into his belly pouch. The weight took a brief adjustment to muscles and bones, so he wouldn't be off balance when he flew or, Gromma and Xalistan both forbid, if he needed to fight. He let the start of a barbed tail begin to sprout . . . just in case.

"Master Sedric," Striappa began.

"Yes, yes." Sedric waved away his comments with hands of wispy smoke. "We're both sorry for insulting each other. Well, you regret insulting me in any case. Now move!"

At the top of the stair, the manitou looked out into the hallway. Near the top of the spire now, close to the Apex Chamber, there were supposed to be guards: at least one Far Flame and a Long Fist, plus a Master Long Speaker. Striappa was none of those things, just a Long Speaker, and a weak one by human standards, though quite strong when compared to the scant gifts most manitou Long Speakers possessed.

Two screams rang out, preceding a female Long Speaker in master's robes, who poked her head down into the stairwell that opened up in the center of the chamber above.

"Striappa?" She ran down to meet him. Her face was wide and strong and well-fed. "I'm Arin. Master Sedric said I was to allow you access to the Overview."

She held her hand out, calloused palm up so he could scent her if he wanted. Or was he meant to take it? He did, impressed by the strength of the muscles coiled beneath her skin. Exceptional for a human.

"What happened to the other guards?" Striappa asked, as he followed Arin up the stair and out into the Overview. From inside the walls of the vaulted chamber a thinly applied layer of mirror-smooth Aldite crystal allowed initiates of the Guild a panoramic view of the city below and granted them the option, if necessary, to focus and amplify their abilities . . . a secret the leaders of the surrounding cities had, in the opinion of the Long Speaker's Guild Leadership, no need to know . . . and exactly the reason why no Long Speaker (or Far Flame, in particular) was allowed unaccompanied access to the Apex.

On a normal day, the top of the spire served as the point from which the strongest Long Speakers relayed messages from other Long Speaker schools and outposts, acting as hubs of information, collecting, recording, and relaying data as needed. A single door broke the seamless expanse, allowing access to a circular balcony where two more guards should have stood.

Striappa spotted the interior Far Flame and Long Fist guards, his neck feathers ruffling at the sight. They lay dead at the exterior doorway, each with a knitting needle poking out of their skulls. One still twitched, prompting Arin to kneel next to him with a gentle clucking of her tongue as she adjusted the angle of her knitting needle and stilled him forever.

"Poor things," Arin explained, when she noticed his gaze lingering on the bodies. "I hope whomever is the god of death today is kind to them. They were loyal to the city rather than the Guild . . . and Master Sedric insisted there wasn't time to argue the point with them."

Striappa eyed her, still studying her scent, tail barb twitching.

"Come. Come." She straightened with a limberness better suited to a manitou her size than a human and gestured at the open exterior door.

"Hurry along now." Arin shooed him. "I can't take my full attention from the transmission flow, or I'll miss something and risk a resend."

"Don't resends happen all the time?" Striappa asked.

"Not when I'm on duty." Arin's eyes sparkled with pride and, perhaps, a trace of gentle madness. Or was that loyalty? It could be hard to tell with humans. "I have a perfect transmission record."

"Ah." A movement at Striappa's belly drew his attention. Baby Caius peered over the pouch edge, looking at the dead men with inhuman blood-red eyes.

"Oh." Arin beamed, eyes alight with delighted appraisal. "What I wouldn't give to have an apprentice come to me with a look like that in his eyes."

"You could take him," Striappa offered. "You have a Matron Guard's scent about you. You could—"

"He has no outward reach," Arin told him. "He has gifts, but he's thrifty with them, keeps them all directed inward. His body will be his weapon and his mind its architect. Reach out to him. Can you feel his thoughts?"

"No," Striappa answered. "I thought it was because he was so soon out of the egg and my abilities are not very—"

"I can feel them." The large woman reached out to the child and cooed at him, but the child's eyes followed hers, ignoring the hand as if it were of no import. "But give him a few years and a little practice and to those of us with the Long Ways, it will be as if he doesn't exist." Her smile did not falter when she added, "We should kill him."

"But Master Sedric told me—" Striappa bared his claws.

Caius laughed.

"Put your claws away, little manitou." Arin laughed, too. "I'll abide by Sedric's will because I am so sworn. But you mind what I said. That one should have never been brought here. He's a little sponge and they took him to the center of the Guild Cities where all manner of knowledge could slip into his mind and stick there. What seeds have been planted in that fertile brain amid all of this bloodshed, I shudder to think."

At a loss for words, Striappa squawked a challenge at her, but Arin made no move to impede him. Fluffing up his feathers, the manitou walked out onto the scant balcony. The cities of Loom and Lumber were burning. Rioters streamed through Commerce, the central city. The standing guard of Warfare could be seen deploying throughout the conjoined Guild Cities, working in tandem with various members of the Long Speaker's Guild. Bridgeward, the great Southern Gate stood closed, its walls manned by Dwarves and the Aernese Token Hundred. Even if the Guild Cities fell, the Bridge would stand fast.

Mason, to the southwest, seemed quietest of the embattled metropoles, so Striappa flew in that direction. Once he was clear of the city, he could find a tree or a cave and sleep until dusk. He preferred traveling at night, particularly at the rising and setting of the suns, when he was more comfortable and his sight was better. He wasn't alone in the sky. Bat-like Cavair swooped from place to place in the city, some assisting the guard, others taking part in the looting. Ignoring them as best he could, Striappa flapped toward the strong stone walls of Mason. As he drew closer, he could see the massive ever-open gates had been secured. Archers manned the arrow-slitted walls, taking shots at any who drew too near.

Turning circles in the sky, Striappa surveyed the flow. He didn't like the look of those bowmen, and flying too high might endanger the baby. Humans did not do so well at high altitudes. Still . . . A few more revolutions took him higher and higher until he felt certain he was out of bowshot. It would have been stupid to die in the open having already escaped the Long Speaker's tower and the violent divide that had, in the Guild Cities at least, spread even to those of the Long Talents. Initiate versus initiate in the absence of Master Sedric. *How fared Sedric?* he wondered. *If Master Sedric and Mistress Cassandra fall at Castleguard, what will become of the—?*

Bands of multicolored light filled the air, blinding him mere heartbeats ahead of the explosion. The mind lash accompanying it nearly took the thought out of him. Protected by his weakness in Long Speaking, Striappa felt the gift burn out (not for good, he hoped) and fade, rather than experiencing more drastic results. Striappa dropped a double handful of wing-lengths in the air, but flapped, beak bloody, back to a safer altitude soon thereafter, concentrating on the feel of the infant breathing in his pouch to ensure they did not travel high enough to cause him harm.

Striappa looked back long enough to watch the spire fall in a flicker of slow motion, fading in and out of sight as if—

No. There was no time to speculate.

Master Sedric had given him a mission: get the child out of the city. Get the child to safety. Await further instructions once the child was safe. And so he flew and tried not to think of the body he'd seen in the afterimage, arms wide, amid the wreckage and the falling chaos, eyes closed in concentration as she kept the transmission river flowing on the swift trip down.

*

Burned out and abandoned, the farm looked safe enough to the young manitou. The dead—and there had been dead—lay cold in the ground, yet no rebuilding had begun, and the barn seemed vacant enough despite the smells clinging to it. Best of all, it was out of the rain. Water falling from the sky did not bother Striappa. A manitou of his clutch could easily shift from feathers to leather wings if flying lightly-boned, but the lightning disconcerted him. When his Long Skills were functioning he would have risked it, but the infant didn't like flying through it all, and though the child did not cry, Striappa was mildly concerned about keeping the boy warm and dry.

So, once the water had risen too much for him to shelter under the small, well-built bridge he'd found (and he didn't much like sheltering that low to the ground in any case), he'd circled back to perch in the loft of the barn.

Striappa had not meant to doze, but he had been tired and not entirely certain the bloody beak and the fading of his powers was not a sign of a head injury. He was surprised to hear little Caius's burbling coo.

Pain came next, sharp and sudden, burning him through the back and lungs.

He slashed back reflexively, talons catching a dirty ragged shirt instead of finding purchase in the meat of Striappa's killer. Shifting into a more land-friendly form hurt, but he had to defend Caius against—

"Name's Hap," spat the hard-looking human with murder in his eye. He wore a coat of plates, with a layer of rags sewn over the top to make it look less like armor. Angry hanging-scars at his throat burned red from recent exertion. Little Caius hung in a sling looped under the coat, but over Hap's shoulders. In either hand, Hap held cruel-looking daggers. Both bore blood. "My boy's name is Caius. Where's his mother?"

"Hap?" Striappa squawked numbly.

"Happrenzaltik Konstantine Vindalius." The man gave a slight nod.

"I have been your murderer this evening. Now where is Cadie? Slight little thing, three-colored hair. A crystal twist. Burned down that house fighting whoever killed my crew. She wouldn't have left the child behind, and you're here with the child. It doesn't take a scholar to know one sun rises right after the other."

"Murderer?" Shifting came too hard. Things which should have melded together ripped and tore.

"Shifting won't do you any good now, you dumb squawker," Hap snarled. "I cut you nice and proper cross your core muscles. What you're doing will only make the wounds hurt worse and you die faster."

"Why?" Striappa managed, as the world began to blink in and out of focus, field of vision narrowing.

"I was hoping you could tell me where the boy's mother is. Cadence Vindalius." Everything went dark, and Striappa felt himself drop to the dirty straw. "And barring that, a man has to eat."

*

Striappa gasped as the pain vanished and he found himself back in the family nest he had missed since the great storm had wiped it away when he was little and they'd had to rebuild. When he'd been a hatchling, there had been no warsuit-clad Aern standing in it. Removing a helm that bore the likeness of a horned lion's skull, the Aern looked down on him with a stern face, made less frightening by eyes with black sclera and jade-rimmed amber-colored pupils, which, though unusual, possessed and conveyed a sad understanding.

"You're an idiot, but you're a well-meaning one, and you died in the keeping of an oath, so I have no particular disdain for you." Kholster, the new god of death, ran a hand over his red hair, his forearm bending his wolf-like ears down each time he did so. "Do you want to go back and try things again, or do you want to be judged by the Bone Queen?"

"I'm dead," Striappa said, more awe in his voice than fear.

"Yes." Kholster bared his teeth, showing off his upper and lower doubled canines in a sarcastic grin. "And you aren't the only one who will be dying tonight. If it helps at all, you seem a nice enough soul to me. Minapsis will not likely find you wanting."

"What will happen to the baby?" Striappa asked.

"*I* don't know, and you never will." Kholster's tone sang to Striappa of barely constrained impatience.

"Is something wrong, sir?" Striappa asked. "You seem to have greens down your gob about something, if I'm using that phrase correctly."

"Yes." Kholster held out his hand. "There are a great number of things going wrong right now. Come along. I fear one of me will be required in some tunnels very soon now, and if I'm needed I would like to go myself."

"You were mortal until recently, weren't you?" Striappa obediently took the god's hand. It felt like he had taken the hand of a statue that had decided not to crush all of the bones, but only just.

"I was."

"The people who might need you, in the tunnels, were they friends of yours?"

"One was," Kholster said, as the world went all to stars and Striappa felt himself begin to flow from one place to another. "The others are friends of my daughter."

CHAPTER 2

TUNNELS AND TERRORS

Another blast of fire shot past Tyree's head, scorching the stone beside him as he spun away from a freshly sizzling reptilian corpse. His mouth watered at the smell of cooking meat, proving that the human body doesn't always have the best sense of timing or propriety. Worse than his body's reaction to the scent of flaming Zaur was that the reptile in question kept moving toward him. It had lost all of its left foreleg but rose steadily on its hind legs to compensate before continuing in his direction.

Farther along the tunnel, more dead Zaur and Sri'Zaur, their larger and more dangerous cousins, crept, crawled, and lumbered forward, their various fatal and post-mortem injuries illuminated sporadically by the inconstant light of a lady who equally appealed to and concerned Captain Randall Tyree.

Even sweating and covered in lizard gore, Cadence Vindalius put ideas in his head which were of absolutely no use in a tunnel filled with the animated dead. Cloak forgotten, her cotton tunic clinging to her form, she conjured fire with her mind, sending off waves of power Tyree hoped would be sufficient to the task at hand. If she were a crystal twist, as he assumed (one of those Long Speakers who enhanced abilities by crunching god rock), Tyree could only imagine what Cadence might have accomplished if she'd had some of the crystallized deific essence handy. She was right deadly without it.

"Either there is a lot I didn't learn about these guys when I was their prisoner," Tyree said, backpedaling away from his current opponent, "or I'm willing to bet something, somewhere has gone terribly, terribly wrong."

"It's happening at Port Ammond, too." Kazan's voice came from just behind him, and Tyree turned to see the Aern, the only one of the young male Aern traveling with him who seemed completely unharmed, unsling his warpick. "No reports past the Parliament of Ages."

"How do you—?" But Tyree cut off his own question as the Aern brought the warpick down on the head of the reptilian corpse, crushing its skull.

"Some Armored Bone Finders saw it happen," Kazan grunted, as he jerked his warpick free and turned to face another corpse, "and it isn't hard to know that no Aern past—"

Tyree laughed. Bone Finders. Of course. Obviously if the Aern knew what happened so far away, there were other Aern at the Eldrennai capital to relay the information. Were they still at the capital, or had they left? The distinction might be important.

"So was this Bone Find—" Tyree rolled back further, eyeing one of the moving reptilian corpses, looking for an opening.

"Alysaundra, Teru, and Whaar—" Kazan's head jerked back and stared at the rocky tunnel wall as if his gaze could penetrate it. "—were the Bone Finders, and they were at Port Ammond. Save that arrow for a moment, though. Do you know why the humans in the Guild Cities and at Castleguard have started fighting in the streets? They—"

"Castleguard is too far away to care about right now," Tyree said. "So are the Guild Cities. We humans fight for all sorts of reasons. I remember one time—" He feinted at the corpse with his dagger, but it didn't take the bait. "when I was off the coast of—"

"No one cares where you were," Cadence broke in, as she shoved past the Aern and Tyree both. The purple ends of her tricolored hair flared as she drew on the Far Flame to set more moving corpses ablaze, scales reflecting the light, wounds painted in tones of black reptilian blood. "Do you know how to kill them yet?"

Not yet, beautiful, Tyree thought, mostly to see if, even amid the confusion of combat, Cadence could pick up the stray thought.

I can only hold them off so long, Cadence thought back at him.

He grinned. The first in the long list of things Randall Tyree knew he needed to accomplish in order to survive was get out of the tunnel and, promptly thereafter, away from the dead things. The second was to get the beautiful woman to smile at him. Even if a smile was all the affection he ever got from her, it would be worth the effort. Such thoughts twisted his lips upward because he knew the need was only partly his own.

He might never be a full Long Speaker like Cadence, but, with even his meager empathic gift, she transmitted her emotions too loudly to miss. She had a use for him. He felt that much . . . and though it did not appear to be the more intimate sort of encounter he might prefer, he was quite curious to know what she wanted and whether she would ever bring herself to order or ask him to do it.

A dreadful wound that distraction would have bought him was avoided by years of training and instinct, as Tyree caught the sharply angled Skreel blade thrust at him by the quadrupedal Zaur corpse he'd been watching. He plunged both his daggers into its throat, cutting the head free of its thickly muscled neck with a deft application of butcher's skill and brute strength belying his size.

"See?" Tyree shouted. "Now why do some of them use their weapons while others are all claw, claw, bite? Am I missing something?" He threw his hands up in irritation. Reptilian gore, black and rotting, covered his hands and arms up to the elbow, staining his once-billowing sleeves. Nothing seemed to stop the cursed things. True, they could be diced fine enough that the wriggling pieces weren't much of a threat, and they seemed to need their heads, if not their eyes, to see well, but, no matter what, they kept coming.

I'm beginning to regret having ever worked for you, General Tsan, Tyree thought to himself.

Who is General Tsan? Cadence thought at him.

Somebody who owes me a ship, Tyree thought back. He looked around for the wide-brimmed hat he'd bought scant days before and spotted it impaled in the ribcage of a semi-bisected corpse. *And a new hat.*

Kazan tackled two corpses, bowling them over and continuing his roll across and beyond the prone reptiles. He came up gripping his bone-steel warpick in both hands and used it to pulp one skull and then another, before a bipedal Sri'Zaur corpse with black scales sunk its teeth into his shoulder. Igniting as it flew backward, its fang ripping free of the Aern's bronze-colored skin, the corpse slammed into a group of mostly intact Zaur, knocking them down like gruesome pins in a game of Dwarven bowling (minus the tricky row of five at the back). *Dwarves!* Eleven pins to avoid a composite number, when nine would have so obviously been—

He had started forward to assist the Aern when a surge of emotion registered in his mind before the resultant sound reached his ears, and Tyree froze. His horse, Alberta, neighed loudly, farther back down the tunnel, an urgent, though not threatened, feeling of summons accompanying it.

"Yes, ma'am," he called back to the horse. "Quick as I can."

It didn't seem fair that one of the Aern in the tunnel with him (M'jynn, wasn't it?) got to ride on Alberta and stay so far down the tunnel. Not that life was fair . . . and, yes, M'jynn was missing a leg, but wasn't a one-legged Aern supposed to be the equal of ten men? Tyree was sure he'd heard that somewhere before and, if not, he resolved to start that rumor as soon as possible to avoid any similar inconvenience in the future.

Of course, if fairness were a consideration, fighting a patrol of seeming dead reptiles in a tunnel was a situation in much direr need of adjustment on the scale of injustice. Hadn't some warrior or another already gone through the trouble of killing them all once? Shouldn't Shidarva be looking into this? Not that there was any sign of the goddess of justice and retribution showing up to even out accounts. Not that Tyree expected her to actually appear. Gods, in his estimation, were rarely where you needed them and, if they were, they seldom shared your opinion on matters.

More heat buzzed his cheek and then Cadence, of the tricolored hair and beautiful eyes, was at his side blasting the closest Zaur with her Long Flame. Tyree had never been envious of another's mental abilities before, despite his only-minor touch of Long Speaker talent, but he'd have traded it then and there for even half of Cadence's power.

"Go back with the others and see if you can help find a way out," she said, as she summoned another burst of power, this time the Long Fist, hurling a mass of shambling Zaur back.

"The Aern can't remember how we came in?" Tyree laughed. "I thought they were supposed to have perfect memories."

"We do," Arbokk shouted, his mostly bald head gleaming in the light of Cadence's flames as he ran back up the tunnel to take Tyree's place. "But we were hoping there was a faster path to the surface." There were still bits of charred hair clinging to the Aern's scalp in places, but no sign of the multitudinous cuts and abrasions Arbokk had received in the last clash they'd had with the Harvest Knights before taking to the tunnels. Tyree still did not know all of it, only that the young Aern would have all been dead if Cadence had not somehow sensed their danger and arrived with Tyree to reinforce them at just the right moment. Tyree felt he had acquitted himself well, too, but none of that would matter at all if they died together in these blasted tunnels.

Tunnels.

Tyree ran through the tunnel system in his mind. An unwilling guest of the Sri'Zaur until he'd helped Wylant and Rae'en escape (or been rescued by them, depending on whom one wanted to believe), he didn't know every inch of the Zaur tunnels under-running the Eldren Plains and the Parliament of Ages, but he'd seen enough to develop a firm understanding of the reptilian mindset that had been applied to their creation.

"Give me a moment . . ." Tyree took off at a run, reaching out with his meager empathic gift to see if there were any other sentients in the surrounding area. Did his gift detect the corpses? He spun back in their direction. Anger hit him in a wave so strong he fell, landing palms splayed and bleeding on the stone. Not multiple minds, but one horrific torrent of hate and death and—

"Angry dead guy," he yelled, as he shoved the mind away from him. "Angry dead guy in my head, Cadence!"

"But the spirits of the dead can't accost the living," Kazan said, blinking.

Tyree tried to open his mouth to ask what that had to do with anything, but found himself able to do nothing more than strain against the clawing, grasping mind that was trying to seize the depths of him. Vast and ancient, it loomed over his consciousness, and if it had not been touching so many minds at once, Tyree doubted he could have put up even a token resistance.

"Kholster wouldn't let that happen," M'jynn said.

Joose, another of the young Overwatches, opened his mouth to speak, but Tyree couldn't listen. He had to run away from that mind, but he felt like it was chasing him.

Cadence, he thought. *I can't pull free. I—*

A wave of fire scoured his thoughts. The being's hold on him snapped with a twang and, as he dropped away from it, he saw it clearly for an instant, a skull with bone metal teeth cackling in the ether. Tendrils reached out from it in all directions, taking root wherever they found purchase.

Tyree? Cadence's voice filled his mind, but instead of an answer he thought her his best idea for an alternate route to the surface as he fell face-first toward the stone, hoping someone had the presence of mind to catch him before he broke his nose or, worse yet, chipped a tooth.

*

Catching the man up with her mind, Cadence Vindalius had to wonder which god it was who found it so amusing to continuously force her to rescue so many able-bodied and presumably competent males who should have been able to look after themselves. If the god in question was Kholster, then he was welcome to whatever small amusement this provided. Without his merciful insight, she would have been either dead, dead and in his daughter's belly, or still under Hap's control until she'd crunched so much god rock that she'd burnt out her abilities or her body completely and he sold her off or left her for dead. If one of the other gods were behind her increasing number of rescues, Cadence hoped the deity in question got to experience a full divine arvashing at Kholster's earliest convenience.

The air, dry from Cadence's constant use of her Far Flame, stripped the moisture from her clothes as she struggled to carry her unconscious fellow human and hold back the Zaur dead. She did not know if it was the increased body awareness from her studies with Sedric, headmaster of the Guild Cities' Long Speaker's College, or that being forced to go through god-rock withdrawal had just left her hyperaware, but she noticed when she stopped sweating.

She loosed a sharp bitter hiss of a laugh as the Aern around her asked questions and shouted; Cadence didn't have any extra attention to give them. Were all males this stupid? Most. Yes. And yet . . . another of the visions she had been having over the last few days hit her when she considered leaving them all, Tyree in particular, behind and just running. She believed she could escape without them, could make it all the way back to the Guild Cities and to her son, but if she did . . .

Flashing images, disjointed and dismaying, battered her mind's eye. Image after image slammed into place, each replacing the other imperfectly, like the wall advertisements in a Midian back alley: one sign slapped down over another, bits and pieces sticking out behind, paint sloshed over, signs creating a collage of unwanted information. In them, she saw her infant son, Caius, currently—she hoped—safe in Sedric's care, in a varying array of futures and ages. When Tyree, a man she'd only known for a few days, was present in those images of tomorrow, Caius's destiny made her smile.

In the premonitions without Tyree, Caius's hands dripped blood, none of it his own. Wielding an array of weapons and wearing any number of guises, sometimes with his leather wings intact, full-sized, and functional, other times with one or both of them missing, Caius the man stared out at the world through the eyes of a creature whose greatest skill was to take the life of his fellow mortals, with the blank expression she'd seen only in the worst of men, the ones who did horrible things not because they had dark and evil desires, but because no one else was even real to them. They were worse than Hap's eyes, which had seemed to delight in the torment of others because, even blade-deep in the throat of his enemies, the Caius without Tyree's influence felt nothing.

What was so special about that man? Until she knew that or the visions changed, Cadence decided she would just have to—

Fancy a little bit of that wastrel, harlot? Hap's voice rang in her mind. Not the real him, of course. In actuality, Hap possessed no more capacity for Long Speaking than a hornet. He'd put his words in her mind like the poison in a serpent's fangs, injected by years of abuse, verbal and physical, tearing her down until he need not even be present for her to hear his venomous talk. *He'll just leave like I did. Find something fresher and—*

"Enough!" With one sweep of her Long Fist, she seized the Aern between her and the dead, shifting them to the lee of herself, grinding her molars together as if she were crunching god rock to twist crystal. Molars that weren't her own, transplanted from Kholster's own jaw when he'd been mortal, to replace her own badly broken teeth for reasons Cadence still didn't truly understand. Story and legend described Kholster in tales of diametric opposition: The Beast, the Savior, the Immortal General, the Merciless, and yet mercy, perhaps even salvation, was what he had shown her based only on a chance encounter . . . because he looked in her eyes and recognized what he saw.

Why? As she asked, she felt the bite of her power, that point where, were she twisting crystal, she would have known the artificial boost was fading. With just a little training, she had learned to feel that same bite when she reached the edge of her power's, to quote Sedric, "naturally abundant store," She didn't have any god rock, but that just meant the power she wielded beyond that limit had to come from her own body, eating up her body's reserves, dehydrating her, sapping physical strength in exchange for . . . power.

"There will be a lot of smoke," she called over her shoulder as she turned to face the dead. "You will have to carry us."

With a second sweep of her mind, Cadence wrapped a blanket of warm thoughts around Tyree's mind, protecting him from further contact with whatever creature had sought to infect him . . . A skull with teeth not only similar to her own, but from the same source . . . A monster wrapped in borrowed flesh, dead flesh that moved beyond the natural dictates of corporeal life. A name . . . You led? No. Uled. It came to her in ancient symbols of High Eldrennaic, a language she did not speak, but linked even briefly with that inhuman mind she knew its name, its—his—dreadful need to inflict his will upon all of Barrone, the whole world, even the gods.

Touching my *mind, you wretched little cow?* Its grating voice found her, tried to catch her with barbs of spirit. *How dare you commit such an affront to me? I have conquered death and life and bear no fear for either. I am transcendent!*

For a heartbeat she was no longer conscious of the tunnel, only of Uled's horrible touch, of the flow and ebb of his tendrils reaching out from a wrecked throne room somewhere to the north, in the mountains, in the dark. She thrust him away, thankful for the distance that weakened his grip as he clawed her mind but found no purchase. Then she was back in the tunnel with such suddenness she almost fell.

More words from the Aern: protestations, gratitude. Cadence was drawn too tightly within the core of herself to interpret. Silent, calm, and sure, at the center of a storm of power, she waited for the words to come. Even without Uled, there was always Hap to taunt her. Sedric had told her it was a sickness of the mind not uncommon among the most powerful Long Speakers, particularly those who had needlessly abused god rock.

Needlessly. The corners of her mouth quirked at the word.

Oh, you think you're impressive now do you? Hap's hatred spewed in her mind. *Now with a little god rock in you or late at night with—*

Fury rose in her chest, a meat hook lifting her into the air. Say one thing for Hap, real or imagined, he always had known the fastest way to wake her rage.

*

A single syllable passed Cadence's lips, and Kazan wasn't sure whether it was a curse or a denial, but, whatever it was, the air between the slight woman and the dead wavered like the air over the Guild Commerce Highway on a hot day, working the mortal remains of the reptilian dead in quivering unreality. Before, when he had seen the purple ends of the human's tricolor hair glow, they had shone with a dim light, a dry pine needle used for kindling, but now her hair blazed, leaving chromatic spots in his vision as he averted his gaze. An afterimage of Cadence, arms outstretched even as she sagged, swam in relief over his vision.

Are you well? Eyes of Vengeance asked. **Your vision is impaired, let me . . .**

His vision cleared immediately, enough so that he could bear to turn back and grab the unconscious form of Captain Tyree still floating in the air. Weight returned to the human male as he took him, but Kazan had no eyes for the man just then. Past Cadence, the walls of the tunnel suffused with a fiery glow. Rock walls flowed in a molten mass, the bodies within the tunnel hissing and smoking before bursting into flames. A black and billowing smoke issued forth from them, so thick it quickly filled the tunnel, stopping a step beyond Cadence's outstretched hands as if pressed against a wall of glass.

Take him, Kazan thought at his Overwatches—not the ones serving Rae'en directly, off at Fort Sunder, but the ones nearby: Joose, M'jynn, and Arbokk, who, like him, had been Elevens with Rae'en, and who, unlike he and his kholster, would likely never be Armored. Which meant that while he could stay behind and attempt to rescue Cadence, relying on his warsuit, Eyes of Vengeance, to heal him from afar, to breathe for him, or safely hold his spirit until his bones could be reclaimed if need be, the others would have to get far enough away to avoid suffocating in that smoke once Cadence ran out of whatever fueled her astounding display and the cloud of black rolled over them.

Aern didn't feel most extremes of heat or cold, but they had to breathe just like any other mortals.

Take him and get out of here, Kazan ordered as Arbokk relieved him of his burden.

But, Kaze!

Now, Kazan hissed in Arbokk's mind. *And when did I become Kaze? I'm Prime Overwatch and I'm kholstering this situation. Move!*

In the upper right quadrant of his mind, he watched their positions relayed, even in their aggravation with him, to apprise him of their progress along the tunnel route. He didn't know how they could expect to make it back to the air vent in time, but they were every bit the soldier any Aern was, and they'd do their best or die in the attempt.

Move, he thought at them. *Faster!*

Advancing on Cadence even as he urged the others on, Kazan took up a position just behind her floating form. He was short for an Aern, but he could still peer past her at the luminous smoke, the scene reflected in the jade-rimmed amber pupils swimming in the sea of black that were his eyes.

It sounds like the biggest bonfire I ever heard, Joose thought at him.

I expected a sizzle, M'jynn ventured.

Oh, they are past sizzling, Arbokk thought with a laugh. *Remember those plague fires they had outside Darvan when they had that outbreak of the weeping reds? That had smoke like this.*

The guttering flame leapt unmindful of name to consume flesh both wrinkled and taut, Joose quoted in the shared conversation. *Each garment and thread that was worn by the dead did burn whether stolen or bought.*

Why does Irka compose stuff like that? M'jynn asked.

Who knows, Arbokk ventured. *I prefer a well-woven memory myself. Too much time among non-Aern, maybe?*

Some kholsters preferred their troops to keep it more orderly than this, particularly when dealing with soldiers like Glayne, who were capable of being an Overwatch but had more rank and file leanings. With Overwatches, it was much scarier if they got too quiet.

Cadence's hair abruptly dimmed, blinding Kazan momentarily as his eyes overcompensated, growing cold at the base to facilitate seeing in the dark, then warming as his ocular system settled on the mere expansion of his amber pupils.

A whispered curse died on his lips. Yes, he could see the tunnel better, but he wanted to keep track of Cadence and the molten rock beyond. Cold crept back into the base of his eyes as he switched over to thermal vision. There she was! Cadence stood out in relief against an outline of reds, yellows, and white, the heat differential so great she seemed a living shadow when compared to the heat down-tunnel. Kazan was already moving as Cadence dropped, carrying her low in a run after his fellows, her face pressing in against his neck.

Estimating distance from the affected area and updating your internal map, Eyes of Vengeance told him. **Run faster.**

How long could she hold back the force she'd unleashed behind them? How long before they were swallowed by the black . . . and, beyond that, how long before Cadence suffocated on the ashes of their enemies?

I can breathe for you, Kazan, Eyes of Vengeance's thought reassured him, accompanied by the sensation Rae'en had felt as Bloodmane had breathed for her when, searching for the bones of her father, she had thrown herself deeper and deeper into the Bay of Balsiph.

I know, he thought back. *I'm Armored, but—*

Kazan hit his warsuit with images of M'jynn, Arbokk, Joose, Tyree, Cadence, and even the horse, Alberta. *They're all still mortal, Eyes.*

As are you, the warsuit intoned, conjuring the memory of his previous occupant's injury by a Sri'Zauran assassin wielding a shard of the Life Forge. Pain punctuated by silence and aching void of disconnection both from Vander and from the other warsuits, truly alone in his mind for the first time in the whole of his forging.

Doom came heralded by the scent of char in the dank tunnel air. It had a sound as well, something Kazan couldn't describe, the hissing breath of suffocation.

We might as well be trying to outrun an explosion, Joose thought at him.

Or a tidal wave. Arbokk laughed. *It was a good run, Kaze. At least you'll make it out of this.*

I can link you up with Rae'en, Kazan thought at them.

She doesn't know?! M'jynn thought back.

I haven't bothered her, Kazan thought. *Nothing she can do about it, and she's busy enough with things the way they are at Fort Sunder.*

How could he explain to them he was only partially paying attention to all of this himself? As Prime Overwatch, his thoughts spread among the thousands of Armored and their warsuits, observing, suggesting, highlighting things he thought kholsters ought to notice. He checked and rechecked patrol routes where those at Fort Sunder scanned for signs of the assassins with the camouflaging scales and the thin daggers they wielded, so uniquely deadly to the Aern.

Part of his attention was constantly centered on his physical surroundings, grounded in his own body, but an equal portion stayed locked on kholster Rae'en. Everything left over tracked the Aernese Army as a whole, holding a current map of all their activities and whereabouts in his mind like pins in a map or trignoms on a table.

Black-scaled and wound-covered, a Sri'Zaur corpse sprang from a side tunnel in front of Alberta. Only instinct made Kazan stay M'jynn's attack. The light of intelligence burned behind its murky eyes, its paws upraised, claws unbrandished, straight, and unthreatening.

Don't kill it, yet, Kazan thought at the others.

"With me, scarbacks," the creature hissed. He pointed out a concealed side passage with one broken clawed forepaw, the black scales of his arm splayed open by a multitude of injuries. "The horse will not fit, but you will."

Kaze? M'jynn eyed the sharp slope.

Smoke does rise, Joose thought. *If we could drop to a lower tunnel . . .*

We can run faster than the river of rock, Arbokk agreed.

"Who are you?" M'jynn asked.

"I was Kuort," the dead thing hissed through jagged fangs, the set on the right side of his muzzle visible even when his mouth was closed. The flesh of his cheek had been ripped away, remnants of scale and muscle hanging in ragged strands, trembling as he spoke.

"Why are you helping us?" M'jynn asked at Kazan's prompting.

"Because I need your help in return," the creature rasped as he ducked back, vanishing into the depths. "The dead rise, and there is a mad thing in my skull."

Isn't he dead, too? Joose asked.

Just follow *him*, the three other Overwatches thought in unison. As the smoke overcame them, the Aern descended, and Alberta galloped on alone.

*

Amid the smoke and terror, one god smiled a brief smile, but not at the circumstances of the mortals in the tunnel. Their plights, though of great import to his daughter, were no longer his concern. Not until the time came for reaping and, happily, despite his earlier fears to the contrary, it wasn't time for that yet. Not quite.

"Kuort," he whispered in the dark.

Eyes glowing amber, he recalled reaping that particular Sri'Zaur. Kuort had been the first of the reptiles whose soul had impressed Kholster enough to send it on to Minapsis for judgment and, if the death god had read the reptile correctly, his reward.

"Even without your soul, you are full of surprises."

What of Uled? Vander's voice filled his mind.

Aren't you the god of knowledge now, old friend? Kholster thought back. When Vander had been wounded by a shard of the Life Forge, losing connection to his warsuit and all other Aern, slowly dying, Kholster had decided the time was right to replace Aldo, the former god of knowledge, with his old friend. It was a decision he did not regret. He hoped Vander's warsuit, Eyes of Vengeance, who had been passed to Kazan along with the responsibilities of Prime Overwatch, was equally remorseless.

Are you sure Vax does not have that title in mind? Vander asked.

I would not think so. Kholster decided to treat Vander's question as the jest he hoped it was. He understood a certain amount of concern on Vander's part. Vax was unique. When Wylant had forged their son into a shape-shifting weapon to destroy the Life Forge and defeat Kholster at the Sundering, the child had remained only partially awakened, spending six centuries being wielded by his mother. It could have damaged the child's mind, but he was strong, and Kholster trusted his children, all of his children.

Having plans and declining to explain them. That sort of secret keeping would paint Kilke as his target. An easiness of spirit slipped back into Vander's thoughts, so Kholster pushed a little to get him back on the right trail. *Or are you saying I should ask Vax about Uled . . .*

I know all about our maker, Kholster. Vander chuckled. *But understanding the mad old elf and comprehending his plan are two different things. I was asking your opinion.*

Have you seen a change in his activities?

No, Vander thought. *But if he does not find a limit to his reach soon, it will be worse than we imagined.*

Show him to me. Frowning, Kholster took a single step, transporting himself from the tunnel and the physical world into the realm of the gods beyond.

CHAPTER 3
DESIGNS OF THE DEAD

Writhing and snapping, Uled's ethereal hooks sank into the dead and claimed them. Viewing from on high, Kholster interpreted the phenomenon as thin lines of white cord emerging from a more central mass beneath the Sri'Zauran Mountains. Stretching tendril-like, the cords ran under the Eldren Plains and portions of the Parliament of Ages, but only in those areas where there were no Root Trees nearby.

One of the many of Kholster stood next to the motionless body of a dead Zaur, which lay too close to Hashan and Warrune for Uled's tendrils to take hold. Each Root Tree's magic appeared to stave off Uled for a full jun. *Perhaps*, Kholster thought, *we ought to encourage an expansion of the Vael territories . . .*

Thanks, Kholster 8972. Vander acknowledged the thought, but said little, because regardless of how much 8972 felt like he was the real Kholster, the Prime Kholster, he obviously was not. Kholster 8972 shook his head, glad it was up to Vander to sort all this out and not him.

Unlike his predecessor, Torgrimm, who had possessed the ability to enter a dimension of timelessness, allowing him to deal with each soul's departure personally, with only one body, Kholster, perhaps because of his experience as First of One Hundred, accomplished the same task with an army of almost infinite selves. The strain had nearly been sufficient to drive him mad or worse, but with his friend Vander, the new god of knowledge, standing in as Overwatch for the multitude of Kholster, things were back under control.

He couldn't help but wonder if bringing Vander in to solve the problem hadn't been somehow selfish. Still, it wasn't as if Kholster was likely to have the chance to redefine his deific role over again and attempt a more timeless and self-sufficient approach.

Besides, Harvester intoned, **Vander is already in place and growing to fill his appointed task admirably. Unless you feel you require his abilities, in which case, I have been thinking about—**

Not necessary, Harvester. Kholster 8972 shook his head. *We don't hurt Vander. Ever.*

As you say, sir.

While Kholster 8972 discussed Vander's merits with Harvester, another of him (143) examined the rotted corpses of two Zaur who had attempted to ambush him a lifetime ago, after he and Rae'en had split up upon entering the Parliament of Ages, their journey of thousands of miles which had run from South Number Nine, through Darvan, along the great merchant road, through the Guild Cities, South Gate, Midian, North Gate, Kings Guard.

He remembered when they had both fallen asleep at the feet of Torgrimm's statue on Pilgrim's Hill and missed the Changing of the Gods completely. The simultaneous blessing and curse that was an Aern's memory recalled every nuance . . . the feeling of Rae'en resting against him. He'd wondered if it would be the last time he and his daughter would ever share such a moment. It seemed likely.

Elsewhere, still watching, one step removed from the mortal world, the Prime Kholster frowned. Arms folded across his chest, wrinkling the smooth lines of his cotton shirt, the First Forged and, for millennia, the First of One Hundred, the Aern-turned-deity glared with disapproval at the new atrocity wrought by the being who had created him. His amber pupils seemed lit from within, illuminating the jade irises surrounding them and creating a ghostly second iris in the reflection of the black sclera of his eyes.

Blood spattered the cuffs of his steam-loomed jeans, spreading dark and wet across the top of his work boots. The blood was not his own. A single drop of it clung to a link of Kholster's belt of corded bone-steel.

Sir, a voice intoned within his mind, I could easily cleanse your garments if . . .

No thank you, Harvester, Kholster thought back.

When he'd first ascended by ripping away roughly half of Torgrimm's powers, Kholster had preferred to allow himself the illusion of mirrored reality when he stood apart, creating mortal environments to suit him in much the same way Aldo, the late god of knowledge, had generated a book-filled inner sanctum. Only, in Kholster's case, he had tended to duplicate the material world around him not realizing that was what he was doing. Understanding had led Kholster to either ignore the need for such things completely or to do as he did now: stand at the edge of an omnipresent precipice similar in many ways to the watch station back home among the mountains of South Number Nine, viewing the rest of the world from above, creating a deliberate divide.

Harvester, his second warsuit, a massive thing of bone-steel, paced nearby, the light breeze of Kholster's imaginings stirring the flowing red mane that decorated his helmet. Where Kholster's first warsuit's helm had been wrought in the likeness of a roaring irkanth—one of the horned lions native to the Eldren Plains where Kholster had been forged—Harvester's helm echoed Kholster's own transformation, its likeness that of an irkanth's skull.

I assume we are going to do something about that. Vander's familiar voice filled his mind, comforting Kholster not only with his presence, but, concurrent with Vander's new role as Aldo's replacement, by allowing Kholster, the Prime Kholster, First among an army of infinite selves, to endure the omnipresence required by his duties as the Harvester of Souls.

Still trying to understand exactly what Uled has done, Kholster thought back.

Ah, Harvester's thoughts broke in, **with Torgrimm's former might split in twain, he as the Sower and we as the Reaper—**

Not what I meant, Kholster thought back. *That is what he appears to have done.*

I assure you, sir—

No, Kholster's thoughts were unintentionally stern. *It is what he has accomplished, yes, but I am not certain exactly what it means or what he intends to achieve with it.*

The endgame, Vander agreed, thinking to both Kholster and the warsuit.

You think there is more to it than a return to the material world?

Vax does. And that has me thinking: if this was Uled's goal, Kholster thought, *then why are the dead still rotting?*

And— With a thought, Vander relayed visuals of a different scene. At the ruin of Port Ammond, the frozen and burned army of Zaur and Sri'Zaur poured over the rubble, clearing it as they went. *Why are they doing this?*

As they watched, the dead Zaur, Sri'Zaur, and the corpse of the dragon seemed intent on wiping the port city's ruin from the face of Barrone. With the dragon's help, it didn't take them long to reduce the port city to a field of rubble bearing only a geological resemblance to the former capital city.

"Coal." Kholster muttered the word despite himself. For hundreds of years, the great gray dragon had been his friend and confidant. For most of that time, the gargantuan wyrm's scales had been the pale gray of spent coal. At the very end of his lifespan, as Coal had saved the Aernese fleet from a supernaturally summoned hurricane, leaching the heat from hundreds of miles of ocean, the old dragon's scales had blackened again, a last burst of metabolic effort, the final stage of a dragon's life.

Coal had lived for so long that Kholster could only think of one being who remembered a time before Coal had hunted the skies over the Eldren Plain. He should have had a hundred years in his second "youth," but he'd chosen to spend it all for a last battle with Hasimak, eldest of the Eldrennai. Wizened, by elven standards, the Eldrennai High Elementalist and his apprentices had fought the dragon and won, but at the cost of Port Ammond's destruction and the loss of two of his apprentices: Zerris and Lord Stone. Zerris (also called Lady Flame) had been the head of the Pyromantic School of Elemancy and identical twin of Klerris, Lady Air, the head of the Aeromantic School of Elemancy. She and her sister had swapped robes, tricking the dragon into attacking the one of them (Zerris) most likely to survive his flame instead of her sister, who had kept the dragon from taking flight with gale force winds.

Lord Stone, the head of the Geomantic School of Magic, had died with less heroic tactical value in Kholster's opinion, but they had been the first elves Kholster, as the new god of death, had surrendered to the Horned Queen to be taken to their punishment or reward. They were Aiannai, Oathkeepers, whether they had been officially dubbed so or not. They had never held the leash and they had gone out of their way to help free their teacher, when he could not help himself—releasing slaves of one's own accord was weighty currency in Kholster's eyes.

When the Sea Lord, Hollis, had etched the grave marker and interred the bodies of Lord Stone and Zerris, Kholster had raised an eye at the inclusion of Hasimak's name upon the rough monument. After all, he could see the old mage, floating unconscious between dimensions, half way between Barrone and the Never Dark, where the Ghaiattri dwelled. Injured? Yes. Dead or dying? Kholster knew the first to be untrue and doubted the second would be likely as long as two or perhaps even one of the Port Gates from which the old elf drew his mystic might remained intact.

Sir, Harvester prompted. **I cannot discern an outline for what they are building.**

Building? Kholster shook his head. *They are eradicating. They are— Interesting.*

Sir?

Kholster narrowed his gaze, allowing Vander's capacity as both Overwatch and god of knowledge to enlarge and enhance the images that interested him. The gray and brown scaled corpses of Zaur, smaller and more homogenous than their Sri'Zaur cousins, swept in low to the ground, picking bits of shiny detritus and holding them aloft for a handful of Sri'Zaur to check. Several of the gilled Lurkers, a sub-breed of Sri'Zaur adapted for the ocean depths, moved among the Zaur inspecting their findings, discarding most, hissing with pleasure over others.

On a display in the upper-right quadrant of Kholster's vision were arrayed the various types of Sri'Zaur, displaying common variances even among a single group by injury and coloration. Most bore scales worked in dark greens and blues with stripes or mottling resembling seaweed, but two displayed pale blue scales, with dark stripes along their limbs and bright red splashes of color above and around each eye.

More numerous, the black-scaled Sri'Zaur with zigzag bands of yellow or blue also searched, while their commander, his boiled scale-covered hide burst open, cracked, and torn in a manner so thorough there was more of it hanging loose than taut, surveyed the scene from a spot atop dragonback. Had the dead Sri'Zauran Commander, with his rheumy parboiled eyes, seen what his mount was doing?

Show me that again, Kholster prompted his Overwatch.

Vander replayed the careful way the dragon's corpse plucked a melted lump of bone-steel and dropped it casually within the ruin of its own gaping chest, where it tumbled down inside the wound and froze snug against the chest cavity, out of sight beneath the garish blue glow of the being's ruined torso.

Did you see it that time, Harvester? Kholster thought.

Yes, sir, but why—?

Why indeed? And why does a similar degree of autonomy appear to have been granted to Kuort back in the tunnels with Rae'en's Overwatches and the two humans?

And how? Vander thought at both of them. *Coal is dead, or he was the last time I checked. Kholster, you didn't slip his soul back in while I wasn't looking, did you?*

Kholster transmitted the recent memory of one of him, a glowing egg-shaped soul in his arms, arriving at the home of Torgrimm and Minapsis. It was a small, unassuming farm by deific standards. The fields seemed to stretch on forever, but no wildlife populated it. Even the crops appeared to be mostly for display, edible, but planted whenever the Sower wanted to sow and harvest whenever the Harvester so desired.

"Do what you will with him," Kholster told the Sower when he found him planting corn in a newly plowed field. "He feels finished to me, but I saw no afterlife for dragons, and that's your wife's dominion anyway, not mine."

The memory ended with Torgrimm wiping dirt covered hands on his trousers before taking the soul reverently into his arms.

I didn't really mean for you to answer that, Vander thought mirthfully. *I did see it, you know.*

I know, Kholster thought back, just to tease his friend, but in his mind's eye he watched the dragon hide away the lump of bone metal and pondered. Next to the repeating image, he queued up a loop of the entire operation and watched for whatever else he was missing. *But you also saw Kuort in the tunnel.*

Yes, Vander admitted. *Contrary to the opinions of many on the matter, however, knowledge and comprehension don't always share a bunk.*

Kholster snorted at that.

You care to put me on the scent? Vander asked.

When I'm certain I have it, Kholster assured him.

What *do* you expect to find? Harvester asked.

The real reason for all this destruction, Kholster mused, as the eradication of Port Ammond played out before him. *Uled has a purpose even in events that appear to be mere vanity. I just don't see what it is yet.*

Or did he? What were those Zaur corpses doing off in the direction of the old barracks? And the others, moving down exposed stairs to the sublevels beneath the former keep? Kholster walked that way, only to find the openings covered over with stone and concealed. What had they done down there?

Should I connect you with Wylant? Harvester asked. **She and Vax—**

No, but . . . Kholster ground his teeth. Conflicting desires and emotions furrowed his brow. He wanted so much to see his wife, to spend time with her, with his sons, with Rae'en, and let the world hang, but that would be a great disservice to the Aern as whole. *Vander, do you mind showing them to me?*

*

And now? Vax asked.

Clemency, the newest of all the warsuits, stood across the practice room from Wylant, wielding a bone-steel warpick the spitting image of Kholster's current warpick, Reaper. Wylant studied the weapon for any sign of deception, but the illusion was perfect. Even Clemency's stance was a lie. Her raw bone-steel betrayed no hint that it was empty; even the leather portions visible at the joints appeared to have skin pressing against them, muscles shifting beneath.

Unlike many of the warsuits, Clemency showed no signs of decoration beyond the highly embellished helm. Lines of red crystal swooped and curled about the helm, reaching down as far as the center of the breastplate but no farther. All warsuits could adjust themselves to fit a new occupant, but ordinarily this occurred only when one Armored Aern chose to die, lending their spirit, their skills, and their memories to strengthen the whole and bestowing their warsuit upon an Incarna or heir.

She should not have found it so surprising. Most warsuits had not been forged by a half-born Aern who spent most of his time shapeshifted into a weapon wielded by his mother either.

Okay, Vax thought at her. *Now check this.*

As Wylant watched, Clemency's proportions morphed into those more suited to Kholster: thicker in the waist, broader at the shoulders, flatter in other areas. Thus altered, Clemency executed a series of attacks, straight forward, but measured and in control. Each blow screamed precision, balanced by a sheer force no human or elf could equal.

Good?

"It's excellent Vax, but it's missing—" Wylant began. Her flaming tresses, torn so recently from the scalp of the fallen goddess Nomi, moved of their own accord as she walked around Clemency to judge her from all angles.

One more phase to go, mother.

"I wanted you," Kholster's voice came from the armor, "to judge each portion in turn."

He froze, warpick held on the horizontal before slinging it on Clemency's back and walking toward her. His stride, the swagger, was subtle, but conveyed confidence and drive. Kholster walked as if no obstacle could divert him from his intended path. Clemency mimicked it perfectly.

I can't do his scent until— Vax let the last word hang. *Well, not until later.*

"Now." Her own voice came from the warsuit. "Check me and see if I have you right, too."

*

He will have you down, Vander thought. *Give him a few weeks and—*

Days, Kholster corrected.

You want to go to them, don't you? Vander asked. He joined Kholster on the cold expanse that had once been the Lane of Review, the cracked ground shifting under his feet. Vander looked at the ruin as a chance for a new beginning, beautiful in its way. If Rae'en and her people, her newly combined peoples, wanted to reclaim this place, they would not be haunted by the architecture of the past.

Yes. Kholster knelt, studying the ground. Around them, unaware of their presence, the dead worked, the dragon in their midst.

Why not—? Vander knew Kholster was going to cut him off before he even began the sentence, but the words would have their effect all the same, designed as they were to spur Kholster forward, to get him to do whatever it was he already knew he should do next. Kholster almost always knew what had to come next. In Vander's experience, Kholster's chief problem was trying to look for other ways around it, if what Kholster had to do ran counter to what Kholster desired to do.

No. Wylant and Vax have their own roles to play, and Clemency with them, Kholster cut him off. *This is mine.* He encompassed the shambling and the more fully functional alike with a sweep of his hand. *Uled is my responsibility.*

Vander nodded.

Why? Harvester asked.

"He is my father." Kholster strode a little way toward the dragon before speaking again. "I think Coal is still resisting him, too. Look."

*

Bereft of their souls, few had the power to resist Uled's grasp. Coal tried to watch the gods observing him without giving any outward sign. Uled's thoughts flowed around and occasionally through the great wyrm's mind, but the dragon responded only with great deliberation to the annoying abomination's commands. Coal, or what was left of the once-great dragon, fought the influence of the ancient evil in measured bursts: First, to warn the Bone Finders of his lack of control and then two more times, once to discreetly pluck a bit of bone metal from the wreckage of Port Ammond and another to deprive the exhausting little Zaur of a silver of the Life Forge by jamming it firmly into the tip of a foreclaw when it seemed clear he could not risk dropping the thing into his chest cavity with the bone-steel.

It had been risky enough to allow the Bone Finders, who had come to the shattered ruin of Port Ammond, the site of his glorious defeat at the hands of Hasimak and his favorite pupils, to flee. Oh, when Dryga had insisted, Coal had snapped and struck, but death (Alas! Ha!) seemed to have affected his reflexes. Other examples of the newly risen dead seemed slow and ungainly at first, so why then should he not emulate them?

It wasn't as if he were under his own control. Was it? Or not so much so that Uled could tell without Coal wishing it. When Kholster had arrived in his skeletal warsuit to claim his draconic soul, it had been like being split in twain, cold filling up the spaces where his inner heat had once dwelled. Enough to end the sentience of most mortals, true. Enough to dim even his own self-control momentarily. He had possessed Jun's breath, his destructive flame for his entire life, and being without it . . .

But I, Coal roared within his own mind. *Soulless or not. Heartless or whole . . . as long as my brain is intact, my mind is ancient. Powerful. Indomitable! I AM DRAGON!*

Wings flexing under the starlit sky, Coal's eyes blazed with inner light, the gaping hole in his chest pulsing with an energy both raw and unfamiliar, yet he could feel the workings of his gas sacks and, while they functioned, drawing in power from the atmosphere around him, there existed fundamental error in their operation. He tried to draw in heat but sensed instead the raw influx of elements from the air.

"Something . . ." He breathed frost through a maw from which only a short time past molten rock and superheated air had flowed. Now, his gargantuan muzzle was frost-rimmed, jagged lengths of ice dangling from the corners of his jaws; icicles the size of a human's arm terminating in deadly piercing points. "Something is wrong with my breath."

"We don't need it," Dryga snapped. "We're almost done here."

"Something is wrong with my breath," Coal repeated dully.

"Don't give me a running tally of your bodily injuries, Betrayer," Dryga snapped. "Just do as I command. Understood?"

How dare that insignificant little lizard speak to me in such a manner?! I—

Coal paused, partially to feign taking a few moments to process such a simple command and also to rein in his temper at the Sri'Zaur's use of the name given him by his own kind before they left him alone on the world they had once shared.

"Understood," Coal repeated.

Still quick and ready, that one, Coal warned himself. While he didn't believe it would be easy for Uled to seize complete control of him, it seemed unwise to bring Uled's lack of dominion to the wretch's attention prematurely.

Clusters of empty-clawed Sri'Zaur took their positions in columns once more, awaiting their leader's inspection. They had found all the bone-steel and Life Forge fragments they were likely to uncover, the simple wretches. It was an impressive feat, or would have been if Coal hadn't been able to scent several small caches of the precious metals that had been missed. They even seemed to have managed to complete the disassembly of the local Port Gates, which had remained in partial alignment even after the destruction of Port Ammond.

"North," Captain Dryga bellowed, Skreel blade upraised.

To the mountains or to lay waste to another Eldrennai city?

Coal found himself curious in a vague way, but most of his thoughts turned to the Aern. How was the daughter of his old friend handling the command Kholster had so longed for her to have? And up to what had the death god himself gotten? Was he still watching even now?

Yes, if Coal squinted he could still make out the deific forms continuing to observe him from just outside the material plane. He chuffed at the sight and tried to keep his thoughts from the one thing about which he had become most curious, just in case—a purely needless precaution, surely—just in case the thing Uled had become managed to pull it from his mind.

Body moving northward at the head of the dead army, Coal's mind turned to west. *How long?* he mused. *How long until Zhan comes for the bones?*

CHAPTER 4
LAST OF ONE HUNDRED

An hour before first sunset, the steady cadence of patience wed to purpose rang out from the soles of the Ossuarian's armored boots. Zhan's eyes flashed, sunslight catching his amber pupils, sending reflected light flaring brighter than usual through some quirk of atmosphere or emotion. As Zhan sped to a run, Keeper, his warsuit, opened itself to release him, the sound like the hiss of steam from a Dwarven conveyance down south in Midian. Bone-steel plates of armor split into a series of interlinked bands of metal, rejoining seamlessly as soon as its rightful occupant was completely free.

"Why the hurry?" Alysaundra bit back a whistle at the sight of the Last of One Hundred out of his warsuit. Where others of the One Hundred, and indeed most Aern (Armored or not) tended toward the same steam-loomed denim favored by Kholster, Zhan's pants were leather and more form fitting. His devotion to craft caught her, too. Few other Armored bothered to make their own clothes, much less use bone-steel for the buttons up the front. The boots were his own work as well, showing the same careful maintenance and attention to detail present in all aspects of Zhan's life.

Most Aernese females viewed Kholster or Vander as the masculine ideal, even many among the Bone Finders, but for Alysaundra it had always been Zhan—a wasted yearning given the peculiarities of his creation.

Kholster, forged first among Aern, was raw and primal, his right to kholster, his will, his everything, the essence of what it meant to be in, to use the old word for it, command. Uled had wrought that power and responsibility into him from the bones out. Vander, as the first Overwatch, had been the most mentally powerful, the one capable of the greatest connection, with the Third through Fifth of One Hundred possessing less raw Overwatch ability, each more refined, as Uled mastered the new type of Aern.

Glayne, as Sixth of One Hundred, was intended by Uled to have been the first full Soldier, but had been capable of being an Overwatch. His dual nature resulted from a natural learning step between Overwatch and Soldier, where the Seventh of One Hundred through Ninety-Ninth were Soldiers, sharp canines and well-placed strikes to their opponents' vitals, straight up fighters through and through, excellent at receiving their kholster's orders and working together with Overwatches.

Each time Uled had created a new type of being he had tended to overcompensate with the first attempt. By the time he'd turned his thoughts to Zhan's creation Uled had become an old hand at making soldiers, and it had been theorized (because who would dare ask Uled himself?) that Zhan's creation had been more of an exercise in what could be done with the connection between Aern and bone metal rather than the filling of an actual need. For the first time since Glayne, Uled had actually been excited about forging an Aern. As the Aern during whose creation Uled was most experienced, was it any wonder that—

"I do not like this." Zhan's words silenced Alysaundra's musing as he gestured to the ruin of Port Ammond around them.

The once-white towers were fallen, the Lane of Review shattered, cracked, and pitted by the battle that had taken place a month earlier. No stone lay stacked upon another, and in many cases huge chunks of rubble had been smashed apart since Alysaundra and her ex-husbands, Teru and Whaar, had been here last. The only good thing she had noticed thus far was that the dead had moved on to other purposes, and their route did not seem to have taken them back toward Fort Sunder.

"Small game is better than no game," Alysaundra muttered to Bone Harvest, then she swore as she stepped into one of the glassy tracks dragon fire had cut into the ground.

Alysaundra could almost picture it: Coal, the great gray dragon (should he still be called that when his last burst of youth had turned his scales a vigorous black again?) unleashing columns of violent heat and flame, razing the city as he slew the invading Zaur and sought to kill Hasimak, the High Elementalist, and his apprentices—the five Elemental Nobles who'd remained behind to hold off the Zaur and give both the Aern and the Eldrennai (Aiannai now?) time to retreat to Fort Sunder out on the Sundered Plains, to the safety of bone-steel plated walls and fortifications that had survived the Demon Wars even before Kholster had become the Harvester and refortified it with the bone metal of the Aern slain when Wylant shattered the Life Forge.

Alysaundra tried not to dwell on images of the dragon as she had last seen him, his breast torn open, a parboiled Sri'Zaur planted atop the great wyrm as if he were a mundane mount to be ridden and not feared or respected.

"Run," Coal had told her, "for I fear I am not my own."

And run she and her former husbands had. All the way back to Fort Sunder with what little of the melted and cooled remains of Glayne's soul-bound weapon they had been able to recover.

Below them at the splintered docks, the waves crashed and the wind howled. Zhan stood at the overlook, where once the Royal Towers had loomed, and peered down into the debris field. Cold wintery sea air riffled his short red hair, the scars on his back plain for all to see. They were not his father's scars. Like the other Hundreds, his scars were his own, the origination of the patrimonial scars borne not by his descendants, because unlike other Aern he was incapable of reproducing normally, but by all Bone Finders, because all Ossuarians were his family, whether their parents had been Bone Finders or not.

At first, to the casual observer, it was the mass of bone-steel one noticed, not the pattern of scars connecting it. Some imagined it a web, but to Alysaundra it seemed more a stylized wave, with the largest bead of metal at the center of his back, a sample of Kholster's bone metal, with each surrounding bead born by the waves extending from it as if they were rippling outward from the source of the water's disturbance, ripples caused by Kholster, by his creation, his life . . . one for each of the first ninety-nine.

"I come for the bones" was carved in clear block symbols arcing from Zhan's right shoulder to his left, accenting the bronzed flesh.

Alysaundra reached back to remember the last time she'd seen him this way. Had it really been over six hundred years? Shirtless and brooding, he was the Zhan of old, not the reserved and severe figure who favored silk shirts with bone-steel buttons, but the one who shunned all clothing save his true skin, his warsuit . . .

Holding out his open palm, Zhan tugged at the bone metal around him, pulling so hard Alysaundra took an involuntary step toward him before she could shift her weight and resist. Three tiny scraps of pearlescent metal shot from the rubble like bullets from a jun, embedding themselves in his outstretched hand.

"There is still some of it missing." Zhan turned to face her, frowning as he picked the metal from his flesh, oblivious to the orange, iron-deficient blood welling up from the wounds even as they healed. "A near-smooth nugget, the size of my thumb."

Placing the fragments in the palm of his right hand, Zhan covered them with his left, cupping them.

Alysaundra sensed what was happening even though she'd never managed it very well herself, could feel the rapidly shifting pulses from Zhan's hands as the bead of metal grew hotter and hotter. Near the end, his fingers parted, palms still close, to reveal a solid orb of glowing, white-hot bone-steel hovering between them. Shifting his stance, dance-like, twisting and turning his hands from one side to the next, he worked it into a perfectly round orb.

Once it had cooled enough to hold its shape, Zhan let the heated mass drop into his left palm, tearing a gash in his right with his canines, using the blood to cool it.

"If you were trying to impress me . . ." Alysaundra teased. But he wasn't, of course. The Ossuarian did not care for such things. His control over bone metal, the physical need to collect and retain it, so much stronger than even other Bone Finders, had rendered him effectively sterile. As a result, living Aern were of no interest to Zhan in the sorts of ways that might lead one Aern to show off in front of another.

"No." Zhan tossed the ball to her, and she felt his hold on the metal even as it flew through the air, only actually releasing his unseen grip on it once she had asserted her own. "But you always impress me, if that is of any consolation. No one could have expected this new turn of events."

"The dead rising?" Alysaundra laughed. "No, the idea is ludicrous, or would be if it hadn't happened. It's just not the sort of thing Torgrimm would allow: dead people being not, well . . . dead."

"Yes," he nodded. "It concerns me greatly that Kholster permits this, even more so if this has been managed against his will." Pivoting, Zhan held his already healed palms out to his sides, shifting them closer together, further apart, more one way, then another, until they faced northwest and up. "The missing bone-steel is in flight."

"So either the dragon has it—" Alysaundra growled.

"Or the creature on his back does," Keeper spoke, its voice deep and reverberating in a way it did not when Zhan occupied it. "Do you think the army is with it?"

"I know not." Zhan shrugged, moving to let the warsuit encompass him once more. "But it does not matter. One way or another—"

Alysaundra smiled beneath Bone Harvest's helmet. "We come for the bones."

Ossuarians know— Zhan's mind reached out, touching each Bone Finder. *—one of the One Hundred has bones in the wind. I suspect we will have to destroy a dragon who is dead yet moves, a dragon at the center of an army of quickened corpses. The Ossuary is at war.*

What did he just say? Bone Harvest asked in Alysaundra's mind. **The Ossuary doesn't wage war, we—**

The last time it happened you weren't even a schematic, Alysaundra thought back, *but I assure you, in the pursuit of his duty, I can think of very few things Last Bones wouldn't do if he felt the need. He—* A string of commands cut her conversation short, images, instructions, schematics, plans, work assignments . . . not just hers, but how her part related to the whole, its impact, its importance. Zhan was nothing if not thorough.

*

Elsewhere, Aern with Zhan's scars on their backs, many wearing skull-like helms of bone-steel, but all Armored and intent on the retrieval, storage, and protection of bone metal, began moving in ones, twos, and threes. Their paths diverged, a seemingly random scattering, like blood oak seeds at the edge of winter, but all of the Armored Bone Finders, save for the recently stripped and dipped Caz, converged on the Eldren Plains.

Noiseless and alert, Caz the Silent stood clad in his warsuit, blocking the door to Fort Sunder's Ossuary, a bone-steel long knife in each hand.

"You see what Zhan's doing?" Vander asked one of Kholster. The two stood together in Vander's version of Aldo's study. Similar in concept, a library, but one consisting of shelves of bone-steel tiles, each one containing volumes of data. It was open to the elements, lush blue-green grass forming a primitive maze between the tiles, the whole thing surrounded by a low stone railing, allowing one to stand at the edge and look down on the mortal realm below.

"I do," Kholster answered, frowning. "But it's his right. He's the Ossuarian and the Bone Finders are his. Always have been. I only hope Rae'en notices his deployment strategy in time to take advantage of the situation."

"You could always tell her . . ."

"It's not my place to do so." Kholster growled softly at the thought, even though he knew it was the appropriate course of action. "She'll have to ask him, or he will have to decide to tell her. This is a matter between the Ossuary and the Aernese Army and I, at present, am a part of neither chain of command."

Have you decided what you intend to do about that? Vander thought.

It's time, Harvester interrupted. **I believe they will not turn back from this attempt.**

A moment, Kholster told Vander. *I want to pay attention to this.*

Kholster closed his eyes, seeing through those of his warsuit. Harvester stood at the edge of a plane of human paradise. One of the loud ones, but not the loudest. The scent of wood smoke, grilled meats, and other succulent (to humans) aromas. One could find a brawl if one so desired and other more intimate amenities many of the more high-minded of Minapsis's realms omitted entirely. Marcus Conwrath stood at the edge as well, his notched ear revealing him, even in death, to be a captain in the Hulsite militia. Japesh, bald and blinking, stood a few paces back from the border of the place.

Kholster wondered how the two spirits could see it. No mark in the grass delineated the point where one dimension became another, but it was there, not at the road but several feet from it, partway up an embankment, where the grass was not more lush than in other places. It was an easy climb even for an inebriated human, or it was for the two human spirits who had dwelt with Kholster since his ascension to godhood.

A single step took the other Kholster from Vander's side to Conwrath's. Kholster's heavy boots squelched in the wet earth beneath the grass in a way the human's did not. It wasn't just the weight of him, the way any Aern weighed almost double that of an equal-sized human, but a reminder Minapsis ruled the next realm, that the horned sister of Kilke was watching.

"Going?" Kholster asked.

"We tried it, Grudger," Japesh spoke up, "but we can't hang about your realm like this, not without knowing down which trail we're meant to be hunting." He took a step, paused, and met Kholster's eyes. "I don't wish to cross you, but if I've your permission . . ."

"You have it, Japesh, though you do not require it," Kholster said with a nod. "I will not keep you here against your will."

Without looking back, the old man clambered up the rise, shedding years and cares as he went. He faded from Kholster's view as he moved past the border. Kholster sensed he could follow the spirit of the human even there, but he had no reason to do so. Whatever Torgrimm and Minapsis had intended Kholster to learn from the two old soldiers, he had failed to glean. Keeping them about indefinitely seemed selfish and—

"I'll stay," Conwrath offered, "if you think it will help. You once said Torgrimm left us with you to remind you of something, but I'll be an irkanth's dinner if I know what it is . . . You seem to have all this Harvester business well hunted, even if you are a little more raw about it than Torgrimm was when he handled both the planting and the reaping of souls." Marcus looked down at his well-worn boots, moving the grass around with the toe. "Maybe it was the balance that helped him, I don't know, but I don't know that he'd handle this Uled creature as well as you would. You'll put things to right. With or without Japesh and me, but—"

"Balance." Kholster laughed, a loud bark that appeared to startle Conwrath despite his ethereal nature. "Thank you, Marcus Conwrath." Kholster clapped him on the shoulder.

"For what?"

"I'd lost sight of the key reason Torgrimm sacrificed a portion of his power."

"What was it?" Marcus asked.

"You may never know." Kholster reached out to Harvester and made a request he knew the warsuit wouldn't like. Aloud he asked, "Are you okay with that, Marcus?"

"I am," Marcus said, as he scrambled up the hill after his friend. "Good-bye, Kholster."

Sir, Harvester intoned, *if I may object . . .*

You may, Kholster thought back. *You may do anything you want, even refuse my request. You aren't my slave any more than Bloodmane was.*

Ah. Having been granted the freedom to refuse the request, I find it seems rather petty to do so. But are you quite certain, sir?

"I need to mend the breach in the wall Uled has managed to batter open," Kholster said. "It won't destroy the dead who have already risen, but it should stop any more from rising."

Should?

Nothing is certain, Harvester. What do you think?

I think that it is possible the action you desire will merely weaken the risen dead. I think you and I should slay Uled and deliver his soul to Minapsis before even considering this course of action. Further, I say that should you ever need me, sir—

"I'll need this." Reaching out, the Aern took the warpick, Reaper, from the warsuit's back and smiled a wolfish grin.

Sir? Harvester asked.

Kholster? Vander thought at him.

You're in place, Vander. The god of knowledge is restored as god of fact and fiction and is thus what he should be once more. War will be righted soon enough as well, recast as conflict and resolution. Now I have to close a circle of my own. But what that will mean for you and me—

It will mean whatever you want it to mean, old friend. Vander laughed. *I'm too old to get used to another kholster, and I have no desire to take the reins myself.*

Then it's settled. With a single moment of intent, power shifted along the link between Harvester and Kholster. Throughout the realms, all of Kholster's multiples vanished, leaving a single Kholster and a warsuit already bearing the correct name for his duties as death god in his own right. It was much more pleasant than the way Torgrimm had surrendered a portion of his powers to Kholster, but Torgrimm had lacked the true bond between a warsuit and its rightful occupant. Torgrimm's Harvester had been a warsuit in appearance only, an affectation. Kholster's Harvester and his Reaper were a true warsuit and warpick, and bestowing a measure of his deific might and responsibility to his own creations was as simple as leaving a piece of his soul behind.

*

Marcus Conwrath looked back from the edge of the eternal city, but Kholster, the one and only, was already moving, warpick on his back. If Kholster felt strange to no longer be connected to a warsuit, he also felt lighter to have surrendered the responsibilities that came with being Harvester. He wondered how the Changing of the Gods at Oot and at Castleguard would reflect the current state of the heavens when they reset at noon and midnight.

For a moment, he considered remaining without a warsuit, but decided that link, not only between himself and a warsuit, but through that warsuit to any of the other warsuits, was an advantage he did not wish to be without for long.

He walked not toward the forge he had created in Fort Sunder, where the bone metal anvil sat in place of the pieces of the Life Forge Wylant had destroyed all of those centuries ago, but toward a divine one and the one deity to whom he had not spoken, but then he paused.

"Balance," he muttered to himself. "Of course. I almost made the same mistake Torgrimm made the first time."

Turning in the air, he let himself flow toward Torgrimm as fast as he could, gripping Reaper firmly in both hands. A new warsuit would have to wait.

CHAPTER 5

THE CLOSING
OF LOOPHOLES

Clothed in simple farmer's garb, Torgrimm worked in an ethereal garden planting fruits and vegetables he did not need to eat; but it amused him to do so, and it was something to do in between births, now that deaths and the collection of souls no longer occupied his time. Births were easily his favorite part of life. The dead needed to be consoled, addressed, handled, but the souls of those yet to be born were uncomplicated.

To most souls, one species was as good as another, and so sending them along to the right parents was almost the same as sending them to any parent at all, unless they were particularly rare sorts of beings. The rarest souls could take tremendous deliberation. Kneeling in the dirt outside the small cottage / palatial estate (which depended on whether it was his or Minapsis's turn to control the particulars of their shared living area), Torgrimm withdrew a glowing package from his seed bag.

Unwrapping the layers of silk, he lay the egg-shaped object and its covering out on the loamy earth, the ground beneath it growing alternately cold, then hot, as it pulsed. Light and bright and burning, cold to the touch, but engulfed by flames, the soul of Barrone's last dragon presented a unique problem for the deity. Torgrimm knelt over it in study, still at a loss.

He'd been wondering what to do with Coal since the dragon's death in its final battle with Hasimak, the Eldrennai Master of High Elemental magic, and the old elf's apprentices: the four elemental nobles. The combat had ended with the death of the dragon and three of the elementalists. Kholster had sent the Eldrennai and the dragon to Torgrimm to be reincarnated. The elves had been easy, but the dragon . . .

A dragon's soul would not fit naturally within a mundane body, but breaking it up into several smaller bodies did not seem like the thing to do either. The afterlife was out of the question, because Coal had long been banned from it in the aftermath of the ancient wrongs that had earned him the title "Betrayer" among his kind. Torgrimm could not send Coal to another realm, as had been done with so many of the others, because the Treaty of Star Preservation precluded the presence of more than one true wyrm in each reality, thus avoiding the same stellar depredations that had led to the construction of the Outwork and the barren emptiness that was the Dragonwaste beyond it.

And though the souls of all dragons were technically Jun's flame, Torgrimm didn't feel as if it were something that ought to be returned to the Builder. It was no longer the raw material of life, but a finished product.

Finished.

Yes. That was the root of the dilemma. Coal considered himself finished, as did Torgrimm. In the dragon's own strange way, it had redeemed itself at the end by keeping its word to the Aern and dying in a grand fashion. Its morals would have seemed strange to a human, just as Torgrimm was sure the morals of the insectoid Issic-Gnoss Queen would have felt confusing to a Dwarf or an Aern, much less a dragon.

"Min," Torgrimm called to his wife in the cottage. They had taken to playing at mortals when they were alone. When it was his turn to pick the state of the house, it was hers to pick whatever food they might eat. He could smell the sizzling meat from where he knelt, and he shook his head in bemusement. He preferred a meatless diet, and hers was a carnivore's palate, but even deific marriages were built on comprise, and so they each met the other's meal ideas with gusto and appreciation. And, in the same way, where he preferred most mundane modes of communication, Minapsis utilized more divine methods.

"Min?" he called again. A sense of being observed, of benign focus, came over him, and smiled. The Horned Queen was not one to waste words.

"What do you think I ought to do with him?" He cleared his throat, standing, the soul cradled to his breast. "The dragon, I mean."

"I've answered this." Minapsis manifested next to him, clad in a silk garment embroidered with miniature likenesses of the many afterworlds that were under her domain. Her left half depicted punishment, her right reward. The crown-like arrangement of horns on her head held the crystalized souls of her most ardent worshippers, permitted to dwell with her directly for a time until they were returned to the tending of souls in various states of redemption. To Torgrimm, no being was more beautiful than she. "Give the soul to me. He is not the only elder wyrm whose after-ending I have overseen."

"But what will you do with him?" Torgrimm asked.

As she arched her eyebrows, a second set of eyes normally concealed beneath them opened, the pupil-less orbs of violet rimmed white glaring down at him.

"I'm not doubting you, dear," Torgrimm hurried to explain. The Horned Queen did not abide meddling in her work, even from the deities she loved. Her brother, even at the height of his powers, had wilted beneath the gaze of her second eyes, the eyes with which she stared into the core of any soul. "I am concerned for Coal's essence, and I know you will do whatever is right and fair, but I can't help wanting to know."

"You are no longer the Harvester, my love." The eyes closed, and her expression softened, a feeling of love and gentle reproach washed over him in soothing waves. "And even if you were, you ask for knowledge that is not yours to possess. Either render the soul unto my care or do with it whatsoever you will, but I ask that you cease this dithering. It is unbecoming."

"No matter what you do with Coal's soul," Kholster said, manifesting near them both, "we need to revisit part of that statement."

"Dithering?" Torgrimm asked.

"No." Kholster, armor-less and clad in his usual garb, sniffed at the odor of cooking meat in the distance. Torgrimm couldn't quite place it, but his fellow god felt different. Some fundamental change had been wrought within him.

"What do you want?" Minapsis snapped, banishing the cooking smells with a wave of one set of arms. "It hasn't been more than a few hours since—"

"Since one of me was here delivering souls," Kholster said. "I know, but that was back when there was more than one of me."

"Was?" Vision obscured as his wife teleported to a spot directly between Kholster and himself, Torgrimm strained his head around to look past her.

"Please, don't." Twin axes of bone appeared in her hands, a layer of dark metal rising like mist from her skin to form a suit of brigandine. "He's so much happier this way."

"I'm not tracking either of you, but—" Torgrimm said, only to find himself perfunctorily hushed by his wife.

"There must be balance," Kholster told her. "I just figured it out thanks to an old friend, but I suspect you've known all along."

"I did." Minapsis nodded. "I hoped you would not."

"Do you have a better suggestion?" Kholster asked.

"Yes," Minapsis growled. "Reap the world. Cleanse it of all save the Aern and your damnable creator, then give all of the souls to me."

"That would give Uled quite an army." Kholster's eyes glistened, locked on Minapsis, but he made no move to don his armor or manifest a warpick.

"Have you no faith in your daughter?"

"More than I have in most beings."

Tense and electric, the air between them failed to fill with coruscating lightning or streaking streams of fire as Torgrimm felt they ought. A vague memory seemed to stir from a deep sleep in the back of his mind, some remnant from before he had been simplified and become Sower only. He could touch the edges of it, but the memory felt as if it were elsewhere, as if it had not survived the transformation he'd undergone when Kholster tore away half of his power.

"Why now?" Minapsis asked.

"Tell me a better time," Kholster said, shrugging, "and I'll come back then. After dinner, maybe?"

"No." The Horned Queen shook her head. "I would not be able to enjoy it, and my lack would ruin things for him, too. You have all you need or—"

"Most of it," Kholster said.

"Thank you for letting him have the time he did, Kholster." With a sigh, she opened her second set of eyes and studied Torgrimm briefly, before reaching out and seizing a portion of his power. Without pause or explanation, she ripped it free, a writhing mass of energy.

"Ow," Torgrimm yelped. It was hard to believe such a small portion could accomplish so much, but why would she take that piece of him away?

"Trust me, dear," Minapsis said, "it was less painful for me to do it."

"I don't understand." Torgrimm wiped his hands on his pants again, needlessly, then said, "Hey!" as she hurled the power to Kholster. "Min, why did you do that? I don't understand any of this."

You will, an echoing metallic voice intoned. Harvester manifested and engulfed Torgrimm entirely, reuniting the Sower and the Reaper, birth and death.

Balance restored.

CHAPTER 6
REUNIONS

Frowning in the morning light, Rae'en paced the edges of the balcony outside the room that had once served as the quarters for Kholster and Wylant when they had been stationed at the fortress, in the time when the Eldrennai had held the leash and her people had still been spell-sworn to obey their creator's race in all things. Rae'en adjusted her shirt of bone-steel mail, wondering how something that had been so much a part of her less than a month ago now took getting used to when she was outside of her warsuit. The world beyond Bloodmane's metallic embrace loomed too close, and she was too diminished to dwell properly in it.

"I'm too short," Rae'en whispered into her hands. Best to try and get her mind on useful matters.

Coming along okay? she thought at Kazan.

A little unexpected detour, Rae'en, but we're on the other route now, he sent back. *Nothing to worry about.*

Was there something furtive about his thoughts? Rae'en let it go, sucking in air between clenched teeth. She hated this. Not the responsibility, she'd been raised for that, but this . . . this . . . feeling.

The denim of her jeans felt raw and exposed, her thick boots too light and insubstantial. Though the cool morning air did not chill her, she still felt its touch against her skin and riffling her red hair. The scents it carried were muted and uncommunicative. With a short hop, Rae'en landed on the balcony rail, letting the connection between herself and the bone-steel hold her firmly in place despite the thin slick ice that coated it.

Rae'en growled in frustration at the scene below her, exposing the doubled upper and lower canines so distinctive to the Aern, finding fault with the chaos.

Sunslight fell on the battlements of Fort Sunder, picking out the pearlescent white of the bone-steel that coated the stone construction, and lending the massive structure that overlooked the Shattered Plains an air of unreality even greater than that which it had possessed in the all too recent past, when iridescent crystal barriers had encompassed the whole of the keep and the grounds within the walls of the lower fortifications. Frost left its mark upon the walls and on the thick grass of the training grounds, where drilling areas had been sacrificed to house the refugees from Port Ammond and from the nearby villages, whose people sought the protection of their king and, perhaps more importantly, the Aern.

Their tents, some all of a piece, others assembled from whatever materials they had managed to scrounge, were reflected in the amber-rimmed jade of her pupils, then more darkly where the irises met the obsidian sclera of her eyes. Pale white forms in worn-out clothes moved among bronze-skinned Aern and looming warsuits.

Rae'en should have been able to smell the stink of the Oathbre . . . No. Stump-eared or not, they were Oathkeepers now. Aiannai. Though, in Rae'en's opinion, few of them deserved the honor of being spared, it had all been agreed upon. Oaths had been given . . . And though she did not know whether breaking one of her own oaths would unmake her people in the same way they would have been Foresworn if her father, Kholster, First Forged, and until his death the only First of One Hundred the Aern had ever known, had ever done so, she knew that she would never give any stump-ear, Eldrennai or Aiannai, the thrill of seeing her falter like that. She would not let them see her weak.

And yet they looked so weak, weaker still so close to the center of the Life Forge's unmaking and the twisting effect it wrought upon their elemental magic. Cramped so close together, the stink and the noise of them wasn't the clash of arms or the shouts, grunts, and laughter of real fighters, but the nervous emanations of the frightened.

They had every right to that terror. Enough Zaur and Sri'Zaur were coming to wipe every last elf from the face of Barrone. And that, she was now told, was the least of her worries . . .

Her army—her people still hovered at the edge of her thoughts as they should, reassuring by their very existence. Kazan and her other Over-watches could be called upon with utmost alacrity, but they respected the boundaries of the exercise.

The exercise you are attempting to ignore? Bloodmane asked.

It's impossible to ignore, she thought back.

A glance at the candle burning back in her room confirmed what she knew deep down: she'd only been outside of Bloodmane for a hundred count and already she was stamping about like a caged irkanth bristling with displeasure.

It will get better. The armor's voice interrupted her thoughts. **The more you get used to going back and forth, spending time outside of me—**

I know, Rae'en snapped. *I even agree, but that doesn't mean I have to pretend to enjoy it.*

No, Bloodmane agreed. **I do not enjoy it either, but I have had more practice. I'm sorry I distracted you, kholster Rae'en.**

It's fine. She closed her eyes. *What was I thinking about?*

The issue with the abnormal corpses, Bloodmane prompted.

Right. Dead were rising.

Rae'en had seen the sights viewed by Alysaundra, Teru, and Whaar, the Bone Finders kholster Zhan had dispatched to the now-obliterated capitol of the technically extinct Eldrennai to recover the bone metal of one of Glayne's soul-bonded dagger. They had expected the slaughter and destruction they had found but not the army of risen dead crawling out of the rubble and forming up in neat formations around the dragon— or later the way it had been leveled utterly. Not even a dragon usually wrought such destruction.

Coal.

One cannot become friends with a dragon quickly, so Rae'en had never been very close to the ancient wyrm, but Kholster had grown close enough to the dragon over the centuries that Coal had been a regular advisor to him. Rae'en had wondered what kind of advice such a being might give until she had become First and Bloodmane had bonded with her. Whatever means Kholster had used to defeat Torgrimm, the former god of birth and death, to become the new death god himself meant his knowledge had not passed to her the way it should have. By leaving his warsuit behind, however, Kholster had granted her access to a great number of his experiences, even if they were from a more objective eye.

"What happened to his soul?" Rae'en whispered, the act of saying it softly rather than thinking it making it less likely she would actually fail the exercise and communicate with her Overwatches or her armor until the time limit set by Bloodmane had elapsed. "You could tell me, couldn't you, father?"

"Though I am loathe to interfere too much in your battle plans," a familiar voice intoned from the room behind her, "the current state of things grants me a certain latitude to tell you what I know about this new threat."

"Dad?" Freezing, not wanting to look lest she banish the phantasm that he surely was, Rae'en's pupils flared, jade irises expanding into the blackness of her eyes, as memories of her father flashed through her, as real as if she had been transported through time to experience them anew. She remembered him holding Testament, her warpick, its bone-steeled glass nigh unbreakable now that it was one with her spirit. His pleasure at her first kholstering. Being tested at the bridge when he sought to see if she could still think independently after the luxury of having Over-watches at the edge of her mind every minute for the preceding thirteen years. Racing him across Bridgeland and exchanging gifts with him. The ring he'd made of silver and bone-steel alloy from his own bone metal, which even now graced the middle finger of her right hand. Then diving into the water seeking his bones, his voice in her mind, in the mind of all Aern, declaring her First . . . his form wrought in obsidian rising from the waves at the Changing of the Gods as he took his place among them.

She had never felt so conflicted: furious at him for not answering her any of the other times she had called his name since he'd died, and yet so thrilled to hear his voice. His hand touched her shoulder, the flesh of his skin reassuringly solid on the links of her mail.

"Take your time," Kholster said softly. "I have a long walk ahead of me, but I'm in no hurry to depart."

*

"How . . . ?" Rae'en shook the rest of the sentence away, eyebrows furrowed as she considered, then reconsidered, some thought Kholster could not know. She chewed her lip, both upper right canines pressing deep into the red-hued flesh. It had taken him millennia to lose that sort of indecision, and, while he knew she loathed the way it made her feel, he wondered if she would miss it when it was gone. In place of his own similar inner turmoil and doubt (for the most part) a deliberate weight of decisiveness had sprouted. A comfort, it was not.

Being the Harvester had finally begun to feel right to him, but Birth could not remain sequestered apart from Death, not if the balance were to be maintained. Other peculiarities of Torgrimm's true role had bloomed in import with the revelation. He had been close to understanding multiple times, but, as had been his practice when first forged, he'd let his gut guide him without truly examining his instincts. Yes, they were good ones, but as he'd aged Kholster finally understood the need to examine hunches in the aftermath of battle, to see if any underlying lessons or principles could be derived from them in a way that could be shared with others.

Wylant had become a deity in her own right, killing Nomi, scalping her, and donning the flaming hair that Nomi had herself stolen from Dienox millennia earlier, a physical manifestation of a portion of Dienox's might. Kholster had tried to drive Nomi in Wylant's direction, hoping Wylant would see the opportunity and take it, but the victory had been hers alone.

When Vander had attacked Aldo, he'd done so as a part of Kholster's plan to trick the god of knowledge, momentarily blinding him with a pair of false Aern eyes forged by Irka, Kholster's older son, somewhat less damaged than Vax. As the god of knowledge had reached into his box of eyes to see through the eyes of an Aern and tried to look through them, Vander had been ready.

But it had been Kholster, as Harvester, who'd reaped Aldo's soul, in the same way he had Nomi's. With Nomi, he'd assumed he had the power to reap her because she had once been human. But when he'd seized Aldo's soul and hidden it elsewhere and neither Minapsis nor Gromma had objected, he should have seen the symmetry then. He had not, and in missing it had remained blinded long enough for one of Uled's contingencies to take effect.

He could have stopped it before it happened, but he'd completely overlooked it in his joy at Wylant's apotheosis and her relationship with Vax. Knowing that his son, if not truly awakened, was happy, too—an emotional fog of war.

He could still feel Nomi's soul where he'd hidden it. Aldo's, too, for all that he had given Gromma permission to harvest it. Aldo inhabited an ant colony, sentient, self-aware, but too small and powerless to affect anything beyond his small tunnels of earth. All of the gods were meant to possess dual purposes, to give them balance and perspective. A balance that had eroded over time.

Once he'd truly understood that, Kholster had realized what had to be done: Torgrimm had to resume his role as god of birth and death of mortal sentients. But putting the puzzle back together exactly as it had been was not an option either. Doing things that way just meant the same broken system would have been in place, even with Wylant and Vander in the mix.

Balance.

That simple word had been the key. But it wasn't a balance between birth and death Torgrimm had had in mind when he'd allowed Kholster to challenge him and steal a portion of his power. Kholster still wasn't certain he was the right Aern for the task, but that had never stopped him from finding a way to succeed before, so he had no desire to do so now.

Even as he marveled at how wonderful it was to stand in front of his daughter and breathe the same air, Torgrimm's words came back to him.

All things die, Kholster had told the god as they stood there on a plain of endless gray, which lay featureless because Kholster had never even considered the afterlife, because he presumed that he would never die.

And life continues, Torgrimm had answered, summing the whole of his purpose and existence in six words.

Bloodmane had not meant to allow him to be so terribly injured, but a Ghaiattri's flames can burn the soul, and the soul was how a warsuit and its Aern were linked.

Words from throughout his talk with Torgrimm collided and rearranged in Kholster's mind:

No soul has anything to fear from me.

I hold them when they are small and newly formed. I put them into the right body when it is time. And when they must leave, I take them safely to the next step on their journey.

I have a favor to ask . . .

Elsewhere, through Vander, he felt Harvester at the edge of his senses reaping the dead, his new occupant regaining familiarity of purpose, glad to feel whole, but saddened by the loss of freedom singularity of purpose had allowed him when he had, for a brief span, been sower only. Kholster granted them no more attention than his lungs required to draw breath.

He allowed significantly greater allotments of attention to the ebb and flow of information about his loved ones.

Peeking in on them via Vander's nigh omnipresent gaze, he spied Wylant, Clemency, and Vax practicing maneuvers. He took a deep breath, marveling at how quickly things had changed. Given sufficient time, he felt he could watch them, happy in their training time together, forever. In mid thrust, Wylant froze, arms extended, balance shifting.

Vander? Kholster thought. *Is this some sort of spell or——?*

You've stopped time, sir, Harvester, his second warsuit (now no longer truly his, but never truly not his either, it seemed) intoned.

Have I? Kholster thought back along their link. The communication felt more tenuous than it once had, more like when another warsuit had been connected to him by Bloodmane during their centuries-long separation. *I thought given my new responsibilities that sort of thing would no longer be within my purview. That it would have vanished along with the infinite selves required by my tenure as the reaper of mortal souls.*

A perception I shared, sir.

Kholster still didn't like that "sir," but if the warsuit was more comfortable using the appellation, Kholster did not think it would be right to insist on another form of address.

Am I stopping time for everyone? Or . . . ?

I only noticed because Torgrimm became unresponsive, and I found myself rendered immobile. Given that yours was the most recent alteration to the divine state of things, I decided to check in directly. I hope I haven't overstepped . . .

No, Kholster thought, sending along a sensation of reassurance and approval, *I am always available to you. Why would I be stopping time? My new role is much smaller in scope; I'm not certain that I——*

If you wish a technical assessment, I believe that, though your role has indeed narrowed, the abilities commensurate to that scope are no lesser in magnitude when the ramifications of it are considered. Does it truly seem unusual that you might, when acting in this new capacity, interacting directly with the divine rather than the mortal, not find useful the option to allow yourself moments of infinite contemplation? Harvester intoned. **A certain timeless aspect does seem to be a default ability with regard to sowers and reapers.**

Okay, but why now? Kholster asked. *Is there something requiring my intercession? I presumed I would sense if such were the case.*

It's the first time you have met your daughter face to face for millennia, from your relative temporal emotional state—

That's not a real thing, Kholster scoffed.

You missed her and now you have done what we saw many mortals do at the moment of death, when their loved ones are near.

Are you saying I'm trying to freeze this moment in time, to lock it in my memory? That makes no sense. My memory is perfect.

But you are not, Harvester said gently. If it helps, it appears to happen when you . . . well . . . when you hold your breath. And given that you don't actually require air, you—

If that's true, then if I— Kholster studied Rae'en until he knew every aspect of her, not to be recalled later, but to be experienced now, to truly appreciate the light in her eyes, the smile on her lips, and the confidence that, even in this moment of discomfort, outstripped that possessed by many . . . Kholster had let himself feel so guilty, so uncomfortable facing his daughter's conflicting emotions that he'd stopped time and let his mind run amok studying and reinterpreting the metaphysics of his recent action. He knew Rae'en had done nothing of the sort. She was confronting the now. And maybe that would forever be the difference between them. He hoped she could hang on to that.

Then he breathed.

Rae'en sprang into motion again, the wind whipping her hair behind her as she closed with him for a hug.

"I love you, Dad."

"I love you, Rae'en."

"How is Mom?" she asked as they embraced.

Kholster held his breath again.

Time stopped; this time on purpose.

*

Rae'en knew in an instant, just from the way his muscles tensed that Kholster had not even thought to find her mother. Helg's death was her most traumatic childhood memory. Few things even came close. There were times when her mother's death, seeing the rocks fall, still stopped her in her tracks: when she heard her mother's name unexpectedly or the scent in the air and the clatter of stones were just right. The only memories that came unbidden to her mind as startlingly were the collection concerning her arena battle in the Guild Cities when she'd fallen into the water below the arranged walkways and her father had been forced to rescue her with a well-timed All Recall, forcing her body to take over and rescue her based on sheer instinct. One of the only times she felt she had failed her father, and she'd done it not just in front of him but an audience. Self-awareness conjured both memories close to mind, combining with her current discomfort forging a semblance of . . . What? Anger? How could he not have gone to see Helg in the afterlife? He was the Harvester!

"Dad?" Rae'en bared her upper canines and sniffed, nostrils flared in an automatic attempt to seize olfactory confirmation of her accusation, but his scent offered no emotional cues. He smelled like an Aern, the most Aern of all the Aern if one were to think hard about it, but instead of the nuanced moment to moment variations of odor that came with mood changes, Kholster felt like facsimile of his normal aromatic palette . . . not emotionless, but unyielding calm. She pulled away from him, breath coming faster. Pupils quivering, ready to expand at least part way into the Arvash'ae.

"I am not Minapsis." Kholster's words were soft but firm, his eyes unflinching despite the guilt Rae'en knew he had to feel.

"You remember Mom though, right?" Rae'en continued the verbal assault, knowing his defense was too good for her words to make it through to score a vital hit. Then, surprised to see the blow strike home and uncover hurt in those eyes rather than reprisal, she still couldn't stop her words. Too many emotions, too much said and unsaid, too much still to say . . . Relief at seeing him. Betrayal for being left without word from him for so long when she knew that he'd visited Wylant, his Other Wife. She bulled on. "People other than Minapsis remember my mother, right? Being the Harvester doesn't preclude the memory of lost love, does it?"

"We can talk about this when I return." Kholster folded his arms across his chest. "You may find the argument more satisfying then, but I do not believe you have time for it at present."

"Dad!" Rae'en nearly caught the signs of an impending Kholsterian dismissal too slowly to stop him from leaving.

"Yes?"

"How's Wylant?"

His eyes narrowed, the amber pupils lighting from within with a light not the pale hue she had so often seen, but a harsh white cored with blue. Then it winked out again, and he was smiling at her in the way he had when she'd forged Testament, when she'd passed his test on the trek from South Number Nine to the Guild Cities, when she'd given him the smoke-lensed glasses after Midian as a part of their contest to make the race interesting once they had to speed up to make it to Oot by the appointed time.

"She is well." Kholster's voice was deep and warm. "As are your brother Irka and your half-born brother Vax."

"Irka?" She smiled, but the corners of her mouth turned down as she comprehended what he'd said. "Half-born?"

"Vander is also well," Kholster continued. "Being the new god of knowledge suits him. His ascendance saved me when I was Harvester. A mortal mind isn't meant to cope with being in so many places simultaneously. The strain was considerable, and I had trouble adapting with sufficient alacrity."

When he was Harvester? Cope? Strain?

This is all news to me as well, kholster Rae'en. Bloodmane's thoughts were tinged with longing. What must it be like to see his creator, the being with whom he had once been part of a whole, and to not be inside his head, to lack completely that sense of connection that had existed for the bulk of one's existence and say . . . nothing.

Is there anyone near Oot? she asked Bloodmane and Kazan together.

We can send— Kazan began.

No. She cut him off. *Never mind.*

"So you were busy, but you could have—"

"Peered longingly across the spiritual divide and yearned after a departed mate who has already gone on to her reward? If it helps you come to terms with this, Rae'en, I did not disturb your mother's rest even though, yes, I have no doubt Minapsis would have allowed it; nor did I look in on any of the other wives to whom I was joined before her, those whose souls were reaped by Torgrimm." He looked away. "It would have been selfish of me, and, beyond that, when would it have stopped? Wylant lives, and I can fathom why it pains you that she survived to be reunited with me, when your mother did not, but none of this diminishes my love for Helg then or now."

He makes a valid—

Oh, shut up, Bloodmane! Of course he made a valid point; he's Kholster. Rae'en closed her eyes. *Hearts don't care about logic, and feelings are what they are whether we like it or not.*

When she opened her eyes, she expected for him to have vanished, but Kholster stood right where she had left him. Still smiling. He looked weird without a shirt of chain.

"Where is your armor?"

"I worked my old shirt of chain and the bones from my body into a new warsuit, to make it real, to make it mine."

"Okay, but where is it?" Rae'en asked again.

"I suppose you could say, that, like with Bloodmane—" Kholster looked past her and, though his gaze fell on the ragtag collection of tents and refugees, Rae'en suspected he was looking somewhere far off beyond the physical world. "—I realized that I was going to have to leave him in someone else's care."

"Do you want . . . ?" Rae'en began, but couldn't finish. He couldn't want Bloodmane back. That wasn't the sort of thing Kholster would do. So what was he trying to tell her? She sent the exchange to all of her Overwatches that hadn't been directly listening, and it was Amber who coughed up: *What is he god of now? Is he still a god?*

Her other Overwatches remained silent, but Rae'en assumed there was furious conversation going on in the more private mind-space where Overwatches argued with each other, held discussions, or whatever they did when Glayne and now Kazan told them to stop bothering her.

Picking apart everything her father had said, that's what they were doing. Figuring out what he'd meant. They—

"I am not asking for Bloodmane's return, Rae'en." Kholster's eyebrow quirked down, his eyes squinting, as if he were looking through her skin and into her mind, her soul. And maybe he was.

Can gods do that sort of thing?

"Vander and Kilke can, when they are functioning properly, look into the minds and hearts of men, as can Torgrimm to a degree, even Shidarva if she is acting in the role assigned to her, but I can't see that often being a part of my duties."

"And Minapsis," Rae'en said, before her Overwatches relayed the same thought. "When she is evaluating the dead."

"And Minapsis," Kholster agreed.

Ask him, Glayne thought at her, *what his new role has become.*

He'll tell her if he wants and she'll ask him if she wants, Joose cut in. *Stop cluttering her head with—*

Enough! Kazan's thoughts shoved the others away. *Sorry, kholster, we'll keep it down unless we have something useful to say.*

A wolfish grin on his lips, as if despite his protestations to the contrary Kholster knew exactly what was going on inside her head, Kholster shook his head and gave a single barking laugh. "It will take time for them to learn to work with you as seamlessly as they did before Kazan was Second. The others know each other better. New dynamics. New strengths. New weaknesses."

Another question went unasked as she realized that of course he understood what was likely happening in her mind. He'd been First for so long, gone through changes, not of Firsts, but of others in his Prime cadre of Overwatches, Amber, etc., that he of all people could identify with the weight on her mind and shoulders. Instead of questioning it, she decided not to waste any more time. She could try to get him to explain things to her, but he wouldn't do so unless he thought she couldn't figure it out on her own.

"I'm glad to see you."

"My eyes are always on you, Rae'en." Kholster uncrossed his arms, the tension leaving him. "And the sight of you always makes me happy. And proud."

"Always?"

"Even when you are making oaths to brave elven kings with my scars on their back."

"You saw that?"

Without answering, Kholster embraced his daughter.

"Tell Sargus that our father has discovered a state neither dead nor alive," Kholster said. "He should be able to figure out what happened once he knows who is behind it."

"God of knowledge now, too, are you?" Rae'en asked.

"No." Kholster looked puzzled. "Vander is."

"Then what are you?"

"I'm Kholster." He smiled, eyes twinkling in the sunslight. "I was First Forged, though you are now First of One Hundred. I am the enemy of all deities who would play games with the lives and lands of mortals. I am your father."

"But which god?" Rae'en asked.

"I will tell you, but you won't understand," Kholster said. "I am the god who walks like a mortal and lives like one. I am the one who sees their side. I am become, by my two natures, the Arbiter."

"Arbiter?" Rae'en asked. "What? Like one of the headmen in Darvan or something?"

"I'm keeping the fullness of my role a secret for the moment." Kholster leaned forward and kissed her on the forehead. "I want to make very sure Kilke understands what I am, and I want to conceal it from Shidarva and Dienox until the time is right."

Guys? Rae'en thought.

We're thinking, Kazan thought back.

"Um," Rae'en said. "Okay, I'll have to trust you on that. You said you were going somewhere. Can you tell me where?"

"I am going to Port Ammond. And I'd like Sargus to travel with me or to join me there whenever you can spare him."

"After we finish the current fortifications." This was so disconcerting. What did a daughter say to her dad, the god, when he came to visit? Did he need sleep? To eat? "Can I feed you before you go?"

"I would appreciate it," Kholster said, "if you have meat to share."

"Meat?" Rae'en punched his arm. "Have you seen all the humans and elves running around this place?"

Kholster blanched at that, the expression giving way to a grunt of amusement as he caught her true meaning. *How did he do that?* she wondered. *And when I'm as old as he is, will I be able to read others so facilely?*

"They've been hunting, gathering, and herding nonstop since we got them settled in," Rae'en said, "to avoid that same first thought you had."

"In which case," Kholster said with a nod, "I am pleased to be your guest, kholster Rae'en."

"Tell me about this 'half-born' brother of mine." Rae'en led the way down toward the expanding territory of Fort Sunder. She had refused to surrender her parents' old quarters to the humans and elves, but they'd infested nearly every other space except for the barracks and the wall berths. They'd get used to the barracks in time, but the wall berths were a lost cause with them. "Do I get to meet him? Where is he?"

"He's busy now, but you will meet him in time." Kholster sniffed. "I had to wait six hundred years."

"How?"

"Think of him," Kholster said, "as the one Aernese child who did not go with us into exile."

"Where is he now?" Rae'en stopped at the foot of the main stair to let elves and humans notice the two of them and clear out of the way. She wondered if Kholster saw the looks in the eyes of the elves they passed. They were in awe of him, but her they . . . feared? Hated? Maybe it was a good thing she could not decide which.

"Vax is with his mother," Kholster said.

"What kind of a name is Vax?" Rae'en wrinkled her nose at that.

"His mother named him." Kholster's eyes went dark and unfocused. "She did not know he was sentient when she did so."

CHAPTER 7

A FEW IDEAS

With a single day's practice, Vax and Clemency were swapping from impersonations of Wylant to Kholster seamlessly. Transitioning still was not instantaneous, but they could manage it between blows if they timed it right and added an acrobatic roll to buy time. Around them, the practice area showed signs of abuse from their sparring. Cracks and divots marred the stone, and a particularly impressive furrow ran the whole of one wall. Vax had nearly had Wylant there.

"Very impressive." Wylant rolled her head to help ease some of the stiffness out of her neck. She reached for a towel to dry the sweat from her brow, intending to head for a bath, when she heard Vax giggle at her.

Right, she told herself. *You're a goddess now. You only sweat because you keep expecting yourself to sweat. Your muscles hurt because you think they should. Physical exhaustion is only a state of mind.*

Closing her eyes, she focused on resetting herself. Clean clothes. Clean self. Body fresh and rested. It worked.

"I will never get used to that," Wylant said to her son and his warsuit. "Now will you tell me why that trick will be so important?"

One of the ideas Clemency and I had, Vax thought.

"You mean those plans you haven't fully explained?" Wylant mock-growled at him.

If I told them to you, Vax said, *they wouldn't work. I need them to be secret so Uncle Kilke will know what to do.*

"Unc—?" Wylant stopped herself and let the comment pass. "If I don't get to know specifics, what's the next phase about which you can tell me?"

Take us to the Guild Cities, Vax told her. *It will be self-evident.*

Banishing the training room to wherever deific constructs went when they were no longer needed, Wylant let Clemency engulf her, still marveling at the sense of power wearing a suit of living armor entailed, even to a goddess. Whether it was the slight increase in height or size or having such intimate reinforcement for any task, the feeling was one of strength and safety.

Her flaming hair manifested on the exterior of Clemency, still in touch with Wylant, but, if magical flame had a penchant for the dramatic, it was echoed and amplified by the locks that signified her godhood. She took to the air, transitioning from that step beyond, where dwelt the gods, to the mortal world. She paused, hovering over Fort Sunder, pleased by the progress being made. Elves and humans crowded together like cattle, but it was working. They were reinforcing and expanding in concert with the Aern. Some looked at Rae'en with baleful eyes, but not at the rank and file Aern or their warsuits.

All of the main pathways had been trodden down, the grass trampled, and the central hub was now a sprawl of bare dirt. Even the hearty purple myrr grass of the plains did not appear to be able to survive all of the people and construction. Atop the original wall marking the boundary of the fortress, the Dwarf, Glinfolgo, argued with Geomancers, elves who represented the overseers of public works back at Port Ammond, and a group of human farmers who had been chosen to represent the interests of the scattered communities to which Wylant herself had appealed when she'd begun preparing for the expected Zaur siege of Fort Sunder.

This is not— Vax started.

"I want to see your father first," Wylant said. "Just for a moment."

Her husband sat with Rae'en at the edge of a fire pit, eating cuts of meat that had not been cooked. Kholster waved a chunk of beef liver at his daughter, and Rae'en waved it off in disgust, turning away. Kholster looked up at Wylant then and smiled when he realized Rae'en could not see her. "I love you," he mouthed, and Wylant fought the urge to interrupt the reunion of father and daughter.

I told Dad that when he goes to Port Ammond, he should find the remains of the Proto-Aern, Vax thought at her.

"Wasn't it destroyed?" Wylant asked.

If it is, then I'm wrong. But if I'm right, it is still alive, locked away underground . . . Uled has multitudinous ways to ensure his continued existence, Mom. Stop him at one step and he will return at a second. We have to get two contingencies ahead of Uled to stop him, Vax thought at her, *or one ahead and force him to make the choice we want.*

"And make that one a dead end?"

Yes, or two, but they have to be the right ones . . . consecutive ones. We have to close off the routes out of that set of options without him knowing he'll be trapping himself.

"Which amounts to the same, thing doesn't it?" Wylant asked.

He cannot answer, because he does not want to lie to you outright, Clemency thought to her when Vax did not answer.

"I don't track you there, but . . ." A pang shot through her, dappled with suspicion. What could Vax not tell her? The general in Wylant wanted to demand an explanation, but the mother in her wondered if she should trust him and let it go. "We may revisit that. You said Port Ammond and the Proto-Aern are your father's assignment. What's mine?"

Well, he thinks I don't know he feels Uled as a whole is his problem, Vax thought, *but yes, the Proto-Aern stage of things is all we need from him on that front.*

"That isn't what I asked you, Vax."

If you had taken us to the Guild Cities as requested, you would have seen for yourself, but . . . Vax paused for a hundred count. Was he waiting for her to give up on an answer and take them there? If so, he was mistaken. She wanted to go into things with some modicum of forewarning. Finally he answered: *Dienox is our part of the plan.*

"That wasn't such a hard piece of gristle, now was it?" Even the thought of his name made her blood boil and her flesh crawl. "You don't expect me to enlist him, do you?"

No, ma'am. Clemency thought. **Just kill him.**

"I like this plan," Wylant said and, with a thought, she left the skies of Fort Sunder and materialized elsewhere.

*

Below Wylant, the roiling mass of combatants left a trail of power like blood scent marking Dienox's passage. Soaring above the mobs, her fiery hair flared out behind her like the tail of a comet, Wylant sought her prey. From what she could tell, a portion of him would have been present here because of the conflict itself, but the heavy musk of his delight covered everything. He was not causing the turmoil below, but he was making it worse. Dienox's trail left a path of growing strife and mounting casualties. Blood red afterimages of him marked his progress through the streets below. Let kholster Rae'en and Queen Bhaeshal handle Uled's armies and the struggles of the north. Conflicts between the longer-lived races tended to drop down to the occasional simmer, even to . . .

Her cooking analogies ran low on her. Cooks did simmer things, didn't they? Surely there was something they did where they let bread rise or rest or . . . She knew they boiled, fried, grilled, and seared, but . . . Wylant herself could, if absolutely necessary accomplish two (three?) of those food preparation techniques. Not well.

You're letting yourself get distracted, she thought. And she was. Children crying, dying, the screams. This was no conflict between two armies on a battlefield. Innocent beings bled, died, and became forever altered. Human conflicts had always bothered her. Whenever she had stepped into them in the past she felt as if she made the situation worse. Even when she tried not to hurt them, they insisted on volatility and useless overly emotional reactions. Whether it was an innkeeper wanting to make a point and ending up maimed, or mad Captain Tyree with his need to ignite a small cache of junpowder for a distraction no one needed . . . or these people below.

Dienox had taken the existing uncertainty caused by the shifting of the pantheon and turned it into fear and blame. From there all he had needed was a spark: a fight in the right place or between the correct factions and . . . blood.

Why argue over the gods? Why do anything with regard to them unless the gods asked (demanded?) and even then, why humor them unless it also served human self-interest?

Except Torgrimm. She understood the reverence for him. All he asked was that all mortals treat each other as best they could. Even if you failed, he was calm and understanding . . . and they had him back in his former role now, so why all this conflict? Kholster had not killed Torgrimm, and their statues no longer stood at odds on Pilgrim's Hill or at Oot.

The humans would not know about Oot, but the Long Speakers at Castleguard would have seen and . . . But there was fighting there, too.

Only part of it was due to the temporary exchange of roles in which Kholster and Torgrimm had engaged. A larger percentage was due to Dienox's influence, his followers, and his desire for battle and clashing armies. Less than half. Humans were like little bottles of discord and violence waiting to be decanted and splashed upon their fellows. Even Torgrimm's followers, knowing full well their god did not support the taking of life, would kill in his name.

"You were mortal not long ago," the voice of Dienox whispered in her ear.

That is becoming tiresome, she thought at her companions. *Did you get a location on him?*

He's hiding from us, Mom, Vax thought. *He suspected you would come for him.*

I did not expect so blustery a deity to be this cowardly or good at evasion, Clemency thought in her mind.

Clemency's voice made her smile. If anyone ever wondered why she found Aernese males so fascinating . . . well, one example was the way a male Aern was not disturbed at all that a portion of his spirit might present itself as female. Wylant did not know why she had assumed all warsuits to be male—perhaps because Kholster, Vander, and the other First One Hundred had all forged armor they considered to be male—and since warsuits did not reproduce that had been the end of her thoughts on the subject until Clemency's commanding yet decidedly feminine voice first filled her mind. Yet even Kholster himself had warpicks whose spirits he considered to be female without any perceived threat to his masculinity . . .

Mom? Vax thought. *Was that thought for us? It didn't make any sense if it was and—*

It seemed to revolve around Kholster, Clemency added. **If you would like for me to connect you, I can, but we saw him quite recentl—**

No! Wylant coughed. She loved her husband, but the last thing she wanted was to have him in her head. It was weird enough to have Clemency and Vax catching the occasional unintended thought. *Sorry. No. I'll talk to him in person later, once this is all handled. Thank you, though.*

Of course.

He's not a complete idiot, Wylant thought at the two of them. *Dienox, I mean. Dienox tried to kill me, nearly succeeded, and even then I hurt him. He knows I've been given the right to kill him.*

Not that you need it any longer, Vax thought.

Your father disagrees. Wylant frowned as she continued to scan for her quarry.

He does?

His permission would be required if the gods had not already given theirs.

A little mind-quiet, okay? Wylant shushed the two of them as gently as she could. *I'm not made for all of this mental chatter like Aern are.*

The silent compliance was immediate.

Trust an Aern and a warsuit to follow orders without question, apology, or the need to explain themselves. Even her Sidearms were not always able to accomplish the same task, back when they had been under her command. Wylant focused her attention more closely on the ring of conjoined cities below: the Guild Cities. Things were far worse there than in Midian. Plumes of smoke trailed up from fires burning out of control. Lumber, and the city that bore its name, blazed, entirely engulfed, tongues of flame reaching high enough it seemed to set the sky alight: a complete loss.

Everywhere people screamed and fought, Wylant sensed Dienox's power and traced it like a feeder vine, trying to follow the flow of shadowy impressions back to the source, to the god of war himself. A taste like blood and ash, a scent like burning flesh and the sharp breath of steel, the clang of metal on metal and tearing rip of teeth in flesh, all of these were the way his power felt when used in practice. Sickening, familiar, and, in some ways, exhilarating.

"I've had enough of this," Wylant growled under her breath, as she dropped down to land on the South Gate, where the Token Hundred kholstered by Draekar manned the top of the sealed passages that led in times of peace from the Guild Cities to Bridgeland, Jun cannon and Dwarves by their sides. Bone-steel breastplate caked with blood, Draekar and his Aern had the look of hunting dogs brought to heel when they could see and smell their prey. Below them, crowds of people hammered and screamed at the gates, but the Dwarves stood firm and speechless, watching, judging.

They would help. Later. Once the fighting was over and order had been restored, the gates would reopen and the Bridgeland Dwarves would issue forth with food and medicine, to help minister to the wounded, to the sick, to the hungry, and to help rebuild. But not before. The Dwarves did not fight in the wars of other races, had only ever provided direct assistance to the Aern as far as Wylant knew.

She stood unseen among them and felt waves of disappointment flowing from them as the Dwarves watched the non-rock-eating peoples destroying themselves. It was a power that called to some deep part of her current role. They, like she, were what came after war.

On instinct alone, she expanded her consciousness, seeing, in her mind's eye, the other end of the great bridge, where the Token Hundred and the Dwarves who stood guard there held a nearly identical silence and position. No war was welcome on the Great Junland Bridge, nor fighting on this scale. They would have none of it, though, if pressed, they would fight to preserve their lands, their people, their . . . peace.

My peace?

"My peace." Wylant crossed to the nearest cannon and walked out on its round steel surface until she stood at the muzzle. Aern drew back a step when she appeared, but not a single Dwarf reacted to her presence.

"I've been thinking about this the wrong way," she told Vax and Clemency. "He is conflict and I am resolution."

Surely you already knew that, Mother, Vax thought.

Yes, we already—

"I'm chasing him around while he draws power from the conflict and breathes new life into its embers when the flames dim." Wylant drew in a deep breath, reaching out with her Aeromancy, shaping the air, prepping it to amplify her voice. The very essence of being a Thunder Speaker combined with the power of a goddess.

I don't have to fight him to combat him.

"Enough!" she shouted, the wind carrying her voice so far that miles away it could still be dimly heard. She dropped into the midst of the mob, pushing all away from her with a circle of air. "Only one of the gods wants this fighting, and in the Guild Cities his worshippers are limited largely to the city of Warfare."

Interesting. Clemency unfolded her helm, flattening it across the front and back of her torso and along her shoulders where the multiple crystals which served as the warsuit's eyes sparkled like jewels.

I didn't know you could do that, Wylant thought to the warsuit.

I could not do so until now.

Why?

I am uncertain. Then as an aside only to Wylant, **Vax was not surprised.**

"Followers of the Harvester, your deity has been restored." Wylant's flaming tresses brightened and dimmed as she spoke, increases in illumination accompanying stressed words or syllables, with an equal and opposite reaction whenever she paused. "You know as well as I that he wants no fighting on his behalf. As always, he does not command nor request his followers worship him in any way. His only guidance for those who wish to make him happy or to act on his behalf is to aid their fellow mortals, to make life easier for one another."

"What about Aldo?" several voices cried.

"Another Aern took his place. The Aern are going to conquer the land of the gods, take their places, and devour all save the Dwarves!" a soldier in blood-stained armor argued. "It's the end of Barrone! It's—"

That's Dienox, Vax and Clemency said as one.

"Dienox!" Wylant shouted, boosting the volume with Aeromancy. "Gods are supposed to make things better for people, not worse. You are out of balance and—"

"You need not shout, Wylant." Stepping forward, the soldier smiled, the tattoo of Dienox that covered his own features moving of its own accord. "You already had my attention."

Or . . . oh. A God Speaker, Vax and Clemency announced.

Sorry, Mom, Vax thought. *I'd never seen one before.*

We were not intentionally misleading, Clemency thought.

"Hush," Wylant whispered. "I know that."

"Then why did you shout?" The lips of the God Speaker remained tightly shut, all sound coming from the moving lips of the tattoo he bore.

Could he really be that self-centered? Any Aern would have realized she was speaking to the warsuit she wore, or that she was speaking private thoughts aloud to keep them from bleeding across as overheard thoughts.

"If you're so great, why did you murder Nomi?" one of crowd yelled.

"Because she wasn't keeping Dienox in check," Wylant growled.

"And you have me very much under control?" Dienox asked. "I believe I liked you more when you were my champion. Your hair was so beautiful, and when it was soaked with sweat and spattered with blood, I could—"

Vander says if you kill the God Speaker, Clemency thought, **it won't affect Dienox at all.**

Vander?! Wylant thought. *Is Kholster watching, too?*

No, ma'am. Clemency's thoughts were muted for a moment. **He is traveling east from Fort Sunder to the remains of Port Ammond at Scarsguard's most eastern point.**

Scarsguard? Wylant thought. *Do you know where he is all the time?*

Harvester does, Mom, Vax thought. *They are still a little connected. Vander knows, too, but Clemency tracks him through Harvester. And we don't know if Rae'en is really going to call it Scarsguard or not, but that's what the people you rescued are calling the area around Fort Sunder.*

"Kholster's mouth never hangs open like that when he's conversing with his armor." Dienox's image scratched its chin. "It makes you look stupid."

Dienox's image winced at Wylant's scowl.

"He was made for it, and he's had more practice." Wylant drew Vax, willing him into a utilitarian sword. "I'll work on it after you're dead."

"And you wonder—" Dienox smiled, arms crossing, a movement echoed by the God Speaker whose tattoos served as the medium for his current discussion. "—why I prefer to speak to you via proxy?"

"You're afraid," Wylant spat.

"Afraid?" Dienox laughed. "No, Wylant. What I am is busy. Besides. You can't kill me as you are now. You are peace. We are linked."

"Bird squirt," Wylant scoffed. Willing Vax to a longsword, Wylant touched him to the God Speaker's throat. A thin line of blood welled along the blade, but the man himself stood still. *No longer in control of his own body perhaps?*

"It's true," the tattoo said. "War never ends. War springs from everything: it is waged in sorrow, it is waged in anger. War is waged to defend, to seize, to control, and to set free. You cannot end war. Even peace itself is merely a war against the natural state of conflict that exists between all sentients at every level."

If he gets you to believe that, it will be true, Vax thought, *but it is not the natural order of things. His will ends where yours begins.*

"There may always be war." Wylant pulled the blade away as if to concede the point, continuing the motion and adding pivot, her speed increasing as she struck the opposite side of the God Speaker's throat. "But not Dienox."

Rolling back to avoid the blow, tattooed image and body drew a two-handed greatsword, seemingly out of nothing. Unlike the tales she'd heard, both the tattoo's blade and that wielded by the mortal appeared distinct from one another.

Either blade can cut you, Clemency offered. **Dienox is cheating. You should be prepared for him to grant the God Speaker Justicar status in the midst of the fight if Dienox thinks doing so will let him win.**

Harvester says Dienox is using his armory to allow himself access to other weapons and resupply. An array of weapons in spectral blue manifested in her mind's eye, hanging suspended in the air at waist height. Describing the circumference of the circle created when Wylant had pushed the mortals aside, they lay ready, awaiting the war god's call. *Do you want Clemency and me to make them visible to you?*

I can already see them. Wylant took the God Speaker's measure with a few easily blocked strikes. Quick with the blade and also on his feet, the God Speaker kept his range, refusing to advance or let her close the gap between them. She could already tell she was the faster of the two, even the stronger . . . though his skill was akin to one of the One Hundred, if not Zhan or Kholster.

"Nice." She spoke and he moved, thrusting with the tip of the blade, trying for a wound at her shoulder. She turned it aside and tried to close, only to find Dienox moving to close as well. Their swords locked, each countering the other. Vax shortened as she moved for a sweep and found Dienox already attempting one over which she barely managed to jump. Reversing her grip as Vax changed, Wylant slashed at Dienox's back, but he was no longer within range, his movements faster.

Justicar, Clemency verified.

Aeromancer, Wylant thought back.

"Dienox!" She spake lightning from a cloudless sky, once, twice, three times, marveling as he dodged the first strike . . . glad that she had gone for what she had thought to be overkill.

"Hardly sporting." The God Speaker's lips jerked in erratic spasms, his eyes wild, limbs flailing, as his greatsword flew into the crowd, spearing an unlucky observer in torn finery. The leather beneath his plate began to smoke, and he tore it from his body with desperate lurches, growing more controlled by the second. One eye was milky, the other unfocused. After a swift stripping, he stood before Wylant in his breeches, the lines of his nerves etched in red blisters along his skin. Black bruises and burns outlined the bones of his right arm and hand.

Even as she watched, his wounds healed.

She stopped watching, removing both head and heart out of an abundance of care. She dropped the head to her left and the heart to her right, where it beat a few more times, then lay lifeless in the street.

"There will be no more fighting," she roared at the top of her lungs. "This is foolish beyond words. Torgrimm doesn't want your deaths in his name, and I don't want them on my conscience out of some misguided confusion. The only god who wants this carnage is Dienox, because he loves it and cares not one—"

"Of course I care," came the god's voice, this time from the lips of a young woman with a spear in her hands, her armor an unusual array of enameled horn plates sewn together in rows. Dienox's form shone through despite the material's opacity, though his armor had changed to match. "Each death in battle, each casualty, whether a soldier, milkmaid, or suckling babe is sacred to me, as sacred as their souls are to the Harvester or his irritable wife."

"How many God Speakers do you have lying about?" Wylant growled. Sweat trickled down her spine, until with a thought she made her skin once more comfortable and dry.

Sorry, ma'am, Clemency intoned. **I'm still adjusting to working with an Aiannai and I keep expecting you to remember not to sweat, since . . .**

Since I don't have to, right.

"I would hardly call them layabouts." Dienox laughed, his voice and the warm sulky tones of his current host mixing in a disconcerting unity. "But if you mean in the Guild Cities . . . then hundreds. I am very popular in Warfare, and my physical requirements are a bit easier to meet than the spiritual state some of the other gods require. Exercise is easy compared to purity of heart and righteousness of soul."

Arrows rained down, and only the rapid deployment of Clemency's helm prevented Wylant from being skewered, the points of other arrows clinking as they struck the warsuit and fell at her feet.

"Saved by the helm." Dienox's current host, the pale eyebrows visible despite her helm, hinting at blonde hair beneath, raised her spear into the air waving off further fire. "If you hadn't had your son's warsuit, I'd have had you that time. She's a clever thing."

"Am I going to have to kill every last one of your God Speakers to end this war?" Wylant asked.

"You would, too, if you could." Dienox voice came out half awe and half outrage. "And I'm not certain you can, because that is expressly forbidden by the rules. Ask Aldo, or, well, ask that Aern who has taken his place."

Ask Vander about the rules, Wylant thought at Clemency.

He says that there actually aren't any, Clemency replied after a moment. **The instructions to which Aldo kept referring were a message from the Artificer to the deities in whose care he entrusted the Last World.**

What did it say?

"Be kind. Love them. Care for them. Be the parents to them that I could not be to you. Let them flourish and protect them from all external harm, even undue influence from yourselves or your fellow deities," Clemency quoted. "Let them learn from their mistakes. Guide, but never rule. Be stern, but never cruel. They have been through too much at my hands already. Do not seek me, for I am already within you and you will not find me without."

And he didn't tell them? Wylant asked. *What do they think it says?*

Aldo wrote down all the rules he invented, Clemency relayed. **Vander says the volumes would fill whole buildings. Apparently, Aldo did try to tell the other gods at first, but they wouldn't believe him. Being the god of fact and fiction, when the first did not serve he defaulted to the second. He "admitted" it was a joke and started fabricating rules as they were needed. He appears to have tried to keep the strictures thematically compatible with the Arbiter's initial instructions, but the more complicated the rule system became, the harder it was to preserve the spirit of the message.**

"Just a moment." Wylant held out a hand. "I am conferring."

"Take your time." Dienox's smile was echoed on his God Speaker's lips. "The battle may have paused here at the gate, but it continues in the rest of the city." Turning her head to face the spreading fire, the God Speaker sighed contentedly. "Is it not glorious?"

He is insane, Wylant thought to Clemency and Vax.

He is an unbalanced deity, Clemency and Vax answered.

"I can't just kill every Dienox follower in the city," Wylant hissed.

"No." Dienox's tattooed lips moved over the closed lips of his young priestess. "You could not."

Certainly you could, Clemency thought.

No, Vax thought. *Not just. Not either. Not only. Every follower.*

Vax . . . Wylant's blood ran cold.

He is conflict. Vax's thoughts held no horror at the suggestion. He thought it could be won. Most battles can only be lost . . . By one side or the other . . . And always, at least to a small degree, by both.

You are resolution. Vax's thoughts blended with the pictures in his mind and, as his words reached her, the illustration came, too. *Conflicts can be resolved with a hug, a kind word, a punishment, a scolding.* She saw Kholster hugging Rae'en after she'd forged Testament, Kholster leaning over an aged woman to let her spit in his face, having Rae'en fetch him water so she could try again when the first gob fell short. *My father's war with the Eldrennai was resolved with the death of thousands and the sacrifice of thousands more.* Elves lined up to be slain or scarred or banished.

The resolution to a spark in dry grass can be a hunter rushing to put it out, hopefully the wiser for his brush with catastrophe . . . Or it can resolved by the catastrophe itself. She saw herself forging Vax in Uled's blood upon the Life Forge before destroying the Life Forge with the weaponized body of her son. He tried to show her an image echoing his words, but that one scene reverberated, not from her point of view, from his. He'd felt it. Every blow. No blame came with it, but when he reached for an image of the greatest pain he could imagine, none other could take its place. *A forest of ashes to bring forth new life.*

A wave of nausea struck Wylant; the world seeming to blink and judder before her eyes, then return to normal, almost as if her perceptions had sped up to match the speed of Vax's thoughts, enabling the mental conversation to take place in the space of a few breaths. She had not noticed the change, focused as she was on the exchange itself, but the reversion was impossible to miss. Wylant wondered if Aern did that sort of thing in the midst of combat without even noticing.

"You want me to destroy," Wylant whispered, fighting off the nausea, willing herself not to tear up, for Vax's sake, and (*gods curse me*) because she could not take her attention off of Dienox. Any weakness displayed he would exploit. *You want me to kill all of his followers?*

You can do it, Mom. Vax's thoughts surged with confidence. The Life Forge exploded under Vax, shards of it penetrating him, wounding his soul, his form, infecting him, until Kholster had repaired him, never mentioning what he'd found wrong with their son, what he'd had to undo. *Or destroy the Guild Cities. I know you have it in you; you destroyed the Life Forge. That killed far more people. And you liked them.*

My son is pouring out his heart to me, Wylant thought, *and I cannot give him my full attention. What's worse: he would expect nothing different.*

Two sounds increased in volume, picked out and amplified by Clemency even as they were displayed at the edges of Wylant's field of vision. An attempted ambush.

"No." Wylant parried a dagger blow from her right, Vax as longsword, cutting through the axe of a second of Dienox's God Speakers while she caught the wrist of a third with her left hand and knew what it would take to get Dienox to face her or be diminished to a degree his ego would not be able to accept. "Not his followers."

"His temples." She hurled the dagger-wielding youth at the female God Speaker, decapitating the axeman without breaking Dienox's gaze.

Taking to the air, the goddess of resolution flew for Warfare, the war god's sacred city.

CHAPTER 8
KEEP YOUR EYE
ON THE ENDGAME

Vander watched Wylant fly, observing her quarry as the war god concentrated his powers to confront her. The Overwatch-turned-god-of-knowledge saw Dienox as a stylized sword, a symbol less personified than all of the gods except Torgrimm had been in centuries. Ties of power, some trickling, others like rushing torrents, raged between the natures of the two beings . . . The power, as they drew nearer to one another, a shared pool from which they both pulled.

The thought to inform Kholster about the progress on this front melted away like dew before the second sun as he spied web-like connections between Wylant and Clemency. Curious, he followed the tangle through the magical fields that drove the warsuit and gave it life, expecting to find the source centered in the warsuit's spirit. Hard to follow even for all his power, however, Vander traced a tenuous wisp reaching beyond Clemency. Like a trap line, the strand of power ran all the way back to Vax.

Did you want me, Uncle? Vax thought at him.

Kholster, Vander thought, even as he considered how to answer, *Wylant has decided to lure Dienox out by attacking the city of Warfare.* Then to Vax, *Just keeping an eye on things, Vax.*

We're not going to hurt my mother, Vax thought. Vander relayed the thoughts to Kholster, too, letting him hear the conversation, but leaving him a mute participant.

I did not think you were, but if you wanted to explain . . .

Not at this time, Vax thought.

Leave it be, Kholster instructed. *If Wylant is moving forward with her side of things, how about mine? Is it where Vax thought it would be?*

Vax's actions don't—? Vander said.

No, Kholster interrupted. *They do not. He is my son, Vander. I trust him.*

Very well, Vander thought. *As for the Proto-Aern. Yes, it was in the vicinity. Once I knew where to look it was easily found. Would you like to see?*

Show me, but please don't let me miss Wylant's fight.

Paying attention to a separate thread of information, Vander allowed his gaze to linger on the unusual pair of mortals he'd been tracking in case they became useful: a Vael princess named Yavi and her apparently intimate companion, one of the last remaining Eldrennai, Prince Dolvek. He traced their progress backward to the Sri'Zauran Mountains and their rather impressive escape from Uled, leaving a mental note to himself on a scrap of bone-steel he'd forged from a molar, the first ring of a new mail shirt, imprinting the information in the same way he and his fellow Overwatches marked the bits of bone-steel embedded in the steps back at South Number Nine. Vander allowed his attention to shift from the two and their flight in the wrong direction.

Letting his gaze slide over the mountains and across the plains, Vander plunged it through the ruin of Port Ammond and down to the source of Kholster's question, shuddering, and relayed the image without comment. The cursed thing made him want to yarp.

Do gods yarp? he mused. *Had Kholster done so?*

I have not felt the need to eat, drink, or yarp, Kholster answered. *But we can, if we so desire. All of the deities I encountered, even those who ate and drank, did not see fit to carry such tasks through to their less palatable conclusions.*

Will you? Vander asked.

Given the stance I will soon be taking regarding gods playing at being mortal, I believe I will need to set an example. Kholster paused, a sliver of bemusement coming through. *Then again, I've often felt the Aernese process of waste elimination to be much tidier than that practiced by the other sentient races.*

Now that he observed as much as he did, Vander had to agree with him there. Even a wet yarp was still just a pellet. It didn't have the excessive odor or disease component associated with human or elven waste. Still thinking about that, and marveling at the sheer volume of information now available to him on the subject, Vander routed the requested view to a display in the corner of Kholster's vision.

Alone in the dark, breathing, but not moving, the soulless body lay, not where the warsuits or even Sargus had left it, but in a hidden offshoot of Uled's long-sealed labs beneath the ruin of Port Ammond. Liquid-bearing tubes ran from both of its oversized arms, a third disappearing into the thing's left nostril. Recumbent on a stone table similar to that upon which Kholster remembered first awakening, the creature's torso and head were propped up at a forty degree angle; the table's sides were bounded by tarnished metal railings that had been inexpertly assembled despite the obvious care taken in its design. Standing, it would have towered twice the height of Kholster.

Dust and detritus covered the floor in the adjoining rooms, broken only by trails left behind by the chamber's recent visitors. Two of them appeared to have been Sri'Zaur, based on the central tail tracks. Their claw marks were precise. Another set of tracks was uneven and smudged, as if the creature had been having trouble walking.

I don't like looking at it, Vander thought. *Any clue as to why Uled would have the dead Zaur do that?*

Do you not know because you would need to research the matter, Kholster asked, *or because it is a deliberate secret?*

Secret. Which meant that Kilke would know; but the god of secrets and shadow did not surrender his treasures without a compelling reason, secrets being a quite literal currency for the two-headed deity.

I'm trying to convince myself the Proto-Aern is only a backup plan, but I wonder . . . Kholster shook his head as, in the physical worlds, Rae'en led him around—*Scarsguard?* Kholster thought to him. *Truly?*—her city and its fortifications.

Vander noted everything she said in case Kholster missed something important, but he wondered if even Kholster noticed the way he'd begun reflexively answering Rae'en's opinion questions about patrol routes and defense strategy with his own idle thoughts about extending the fortress perimeter and increasing the fortifications.

Should I tell him? Vander considered. Pointing it out to Kholster would doubtless stem the ebb and flow of data between daughter and parent though, so Vander monitored the exchange closely in case Kholster's ideas began to supplant Rae'en's, but Kholster's end of things was restricted to refinements and leading questions: the sort of guidance that seemed in the past to have fallen within the tricky area of restricted interference Kholster allowed himself when giving advice to his daughter. In a few millennia he would be able to converse with Rae'en more freely, but she was new to being First of One Hundred, and it would have been very easy for Kholster to let his counsel stunt the development of her own style of kholstering.

"How long," Vander whispered to himself, "before we have a new batch of Elevens who question that word 'kholstering' and begin to forget it is also a name?"

What? Kholster asked, as if part of Vander's thought had bled through unintentionally. But then . . . No, if Kholster had meant Vander's thought, he'd have specified: Tell me what? Not a blanket question. Which meant Kholster was letting his own thoughts bleed over into his conversation with Vander.

Two choices then: Let him continue on uninterrupted or prompt him to finish the thought. Vander starting counting to one hundred. If Kholster was going to continue, he rarely took longer than a hundred count—

Exactly what makes one First Forged, Kholster thought at Vander. Not a question. A statement. *That's what's been bothering me.*

But you're—

First Forged of the Aern, Kholster agreed. *But if properly awakened and inhabited by a soul, what is he? Torgrimm once told me that, as First Forged, my body and soul would have eventually healed from the Ghaiattri flame I endured at the Final Conjunction.*

He said, Vander quoted, *"You were made first. Even without the warsuit, your body will heal eventually, if you choose to live."*

Is the same true of the Proto-Aern? Kholster asked.

Secret, Vander responded after a brief search.

Torgrimm told me my strength came from the effect being First Forged had when combined with the nature of Aernese spirits, the way we strengthen the whole even in death— Kholster thought.

That you, Vander quoted again, *". . . have the strength of all the Aern to empower your spirit should you call upon them."*

Could he have been forged in a manner sufficiently similar to mine as to allow him to exercise the same link?

Frowning, Vander let his mind turn inward, into that part of him that was the power belonging to the god of fact and fiction, only to find a blank space where the knowledge would normally lie.

"More and more," Vander whispered into his hands, "I am coming to despise secrets."

CHAPTER 9
TUNNEL TRAUMA

Kazan followed along the low-ceilinged tunnel, eyes scanning for any sign of egress. He wondered about the dead Zaur (Sri'Zaur?), Kuort, as it called itself. Why had it saved them? Behind him, the others carried the two humans as best they could. Weight wasn't the problem, merely the cumbersome nature of unconscious adults in the restrictive space of the smaller tunnel. A stretcher or two would not have gone amiss.

They still breathing? Kazan asked.

She is. Barely, Joose answered, as the others turned their tokens black to indicate a negative. *I think the male died a little while ago.*

We might want to wait to eat him until we find out whether he is going to get up and walk around like the dead Zaur, M'jynn thought.

Leaving him here would make it easier on those of us who are actually having to carry people, Arbokk groused.

My leg hasn't grown back yet. M'jynn's thoughts were barbed with a sense of disbelief. *You want me to put him over one shoulder and hop?*

I can take another turn, Kazan put in. *And yes, we wait to eat him until the woman, Cadence, has her say. I think they were getting ready to become mates or something.*

I wasn't suggesting we break the bones and suck the marrow, Joose put in. *We'd polish the bones for her, but M'jynn could use the liver at the very least.*

No. Finally! Up ahead Kazan spotted the adit for which they had been looking. From this side of the horizontal mine entrance he could see the back of the mixture of clay, rock, and scales the Zaur had used to camouflage it. Nostrils twitching as he caught a scent other than smoke, Zaur, blood, and rot, Kazan reached out to Eyes of Vengeance for assistance.

I am better at enhancing vision than I am at picking out scents, the warsuit replied, **but, yes, there is something . . . horse perhaps?**

Better not be more Harvest Knights, Kazan thought, sharing the message and the whiff of equine odor with the others.

It's Alberta, Joose thought. *And the dead guy: Kuort.*

And a few Vael, maybe? M'jynn thought. *We should get up there and let them know not to kill our dead guy.*

OUR dead guy? the others thought in unison.

Anyone who saves me from suffocating, I claim.

Cadence is starting to wake up, M'jynn thought.

Well, let's get her aboveground first and see what she wants us to do with the male.

*

Sound stirred nothing in the mind of Randall Tyree. Smoke-settled lungs that had given up breathing were not moved by the sound of Cadence Vindalius as she shouted at him. He stood next to his body, smiling at the curve of her cheek, appreciating the lines worn deep, not in her skin but in her spirit. Hers was an old soul, quite literally.

"How many times has she been through it all?" he asked the god behind him. Torgrimm had made no sound, but Tyree sensed him as surely as he had felt mutiny in the minds of the men aboard the *Wasteless* all those years ago when he'd run away from Japesh the first time, only a handful of years after Marcus Conwrath's death.

"Many times." The voice, gentle despite the echo of the speaker's helm, was a voice any man could trust. "Some souls see so much hardship. Even when I think I'm placing them in a safe place—"

Turning his gaze on the warsuit-clad deity, Randall smiled.

"You aren't Kholster."

"No."

"You're Torgrimm." Randall rubbed the end of his nose, thinking. "When I fell overboard on the *Wasteless* . . . you're the one I met then: Torgrimm."

"Yes." Torgrimm's voice held a welcoming timber, even though it came from behind a warsuit's helm. "Yes, twice, if the redundancy is of use."

"Is it time?" Randall asked. "And do I get to fight you like Kholster did or—?"

"No," The god behind the leonine skull helm said softly. "I have promised not to allow that again if I have any choice on the matter . . . and, in general, I will have complete choice in such cases."

"Lost your first time out and decided not to play anymore, eh?" Tyree studied the armor, the way the crystal eyes shone.

It looked like Aernese armor, yet something was different.

No warpick.

"You could say that," Torgrimm answered.

"But it wouldn't be true, would it?"

At some point in their conversation, the action in the real world had stopped. Cadence bent over him, kneeling in the charred grass next to the adit through which the Aern had dragged them. Kazan and the others were motionless, Kazan frozen in the act of ripping open Tyree's shirt. Around them the forest was a blackened waste, but, even as dead as it all looked, Tyree saw spirits underneath waiting for the rain to come, waiting to start again. He even spied Alberta and a few Flower Girls looking far more militant than he'd expected.

"Do you want to die, Randall?" Torgrimm reached out for him, the bone-steel of his gauntlet opening and folding back on itself along the forearm. His touch was warm, and there was dirt under his nails.

"I don't want to die . . . or grow old, if you're taking requests."

"No." Torgrimm pulled his hand away, gauntlet folding itself back into place even as he reached up to remove his helm, tucking it under his arm. "No requests. Not exactly. But you are in a very interesting position."

"I've been passed out on my back with a beautiful woman shouting at me before," Randall teased. He knew it wasn't what the god of death meant, but if anyone needed a little gentle ribbing, Tyree figured it was Torgrimm. Who ever joked around with the Harvester? Tyree bet that, while he probably wasn't the first, joking with the death god put him in a distinct minority. Surely most were morose at best. "Or did you mean something else?"

"Birth and death are once more joined, but while Uled's abominable state persists, it would be possible—"

"No." Tyree knelt next the woman with the tricolored hair, watching the way the light fell upon her skin. From there, his gaze shifted to his own body, and the point where it appeared Kazan's fist would strike. "Send me back or take me on. I'm not scared."

"If I send you back, your body may react unpredictably. I am not convinced it can sustain you. If I send you on to my wife . . . Well, the Horned Queen would not be pleased to see you; not pleased on your behalf, that is. She is less than fond of scoundrels."

"She'll warm up to me, Torgrimm." He winked at the god and laughed. "Everyone does eventually."

"I will not send you back," Torgrimm said after a long silence, "or onward without your express consent. This, whatever happens, should be your decision. Just as you always wanted . . . to be judged or not on your own terms. That is what you always hoped, was it not?"

"One question first," Tyree asked. "Why is the Aern going to hit me in the chest? I'm already dead, and we seemed to be on good enough terms before I died. Is he just tenderizing me or . . . ?"

"They learned it from the Dwarves, though they are only attempting it because Cadence is so distraught."

"They wanted my liver for One Leg, huh?"

"I believe that figured into it," Torgrimm answered.

Thinking about what the Aern wanted from him brought to mind the fleeting thoughts of utility he had gotten from the edge of Cadence's thought.

"You don't happen to know what that one wants out of me, do you?"

"Ah." Torgrimm followed his gaze. "Only because it figures into her thoughts about death and unfinished business. She nearly died in the tunnels, too, and it was very clear."

"Can you tell me?" Tyree caught himself trying to project thoughts of trust at the death god and stopped, offering Torgrimm an almost chastened grin by way of apology. "Please?"

"She has visions of the future in which her son's life is only a good one if you are in it."

"Are they accurate?"

"Such is beyond the scope of my function." Torgrimm answered. "I only know she believes it to be true."

"But if you send me back, it might not work," Tyree said, "or things may go unpredictably."

"Yes," Torgrimm said, "or I could reincarnate you and ensure your soul arrives in a being in close proximity to the child."

"Would I remember anything?"

Torgrimm shook his head.

"Send me back down then, I guess." Tyree laughed. "To my own body, I mean, not some new one I'd have to break in. I've always been a fool for pressing my luck."

"As you wish." Torgrimm gave Tyree a gentle push, his image tele-scoping as Tyree fell toward his body for far longer than Tyree thought possible.

"Wait! One last question: Where did they learn something like that—a method to restart a body?"

"Without the warsuits," Torgrimm began, his voice growing distant even as his outline began to blur and the real world to fade to black, "unArmored Aern are mortal, so the Dwarves taught them to— Oh. That is unexpected."

"Oh?" Tyree tried to ask. "Unexpected? What's unexpected?" The rush of consciousness allowed no time for such an exchange.

*

Did you do that on purpose? Harvester asked its wearer.

"I am uncertain." Torgrimm eyed the strange assembly surrounding the human, Randall Tyree, and could not decide whether he should smile or frown, so he smiled. "And since it has never happened before, how could I have known?"

What would have happened in the past?

"Upon rare occasions, a soul has not been able to return to the body, and I have had to console the newly dead and apologize."

Apologize?

"What?" Torgrimm's smile grew broader as he watched the soul of Randall Tyree bond with his mortal body. It was a different interface, unusual in the way it spread throughout each fiber of the human's being. The spirit and the physical each in turn changing the other. Becoming something rare. "You don't think a god should apologize for anything?"

I did not believe you could accept the possibility that you _were_ wrong.

"I wasn't wrong," Torgrimm said. "I cannot recall a time when I have been wrong. Doubtful. Full of regret. Disappointed. Ashamed of what I had to do . . . even trepidatious, but apologies are not always about seeking forgiveness."

No?

"No," Torgrimm said. "To seek forgiveness and to grant it are sacred acts, but to empathize, to let a soul know you feel, in some small way, the pain they feel, and that you experience sorrow in response to their discomfort, or even because you see obstacles in their path they cannot avoid but must endure. Those are the apologies I offer."

Interesting . . . sir.

Torgrimm noticed the "sir" and welcomed it, but it wasn't something he would point out to the warsuit yet. That would come in time. Time, they would all have, thanks in part to his own actions long ago, and more recently. Trusting Kholster had been less risky than he had felt it would be at the time. His only regret was that Aldo, who had seen far in advance the road the First of One Hundred would need to walk, would not see the fruits of his choice.

Sir, Harvester told him, you said to notify you if it looked like Wylant and Dienox—

Show me, Torgrimm thought, puzzled by the amusement the warsuit found in his choice of phrase.

CHAPTER 10

FLAMEFANG AND
FAR FLAME

The fire woke first. It always did and always would until Brazz's alchemical essence grew weak and he breathed his last. Mustard yellow scales turned orange in the glow of the aged Flamefang's zig zag markings as he dreamed of conflagration. Wisps of steam trailed from Brazz's scales and the scales of the other Sri'Zaur of similar hue drowsing nearby. Some deep inner sense tracked the careful padding of a diminutive gray-scaled Zaur picking his way around the entangled cluster of darker-scaled Sri'Zaur crowded together during the sleep cycle to preserve warmth, the largest of them on the interior of the ring, more directly exposed to the heat emitted by the Flamefangs surrounding Brazz.

The first set of Brazz's nictitating membranes opened, exposing unseeing eyes still blinded by sleep, and nostrils flared at the scent of the approaching Zaur, the messenger's pheromones announcing his intentions and authority in a manner Brazz could not believe the other races did not on some level possess, despite their insistence to the contrary. As he neared the inner ring where Brazz slumbered, the Zaur began a series of sharp light tail and claw taps upon the hard-packed ground, charred and scorched in places by the Flamefangs' preparations for sleep and the occasional corrosive expectorants they drooled or spat in their slumber.

<<Brazz, sir,>> the tapping and slapping of Zaurtol told any who could feel or hear it. <<I am instructed to wake Brazz by the authorization of Glider Lieutenant Len.>>

Muted vibrations reached the edge of Brazz's dream, dimming the mass of eternal combustion that filled his nights, consuming no one item, merely existing, burning it cared not what. He Who Ruled in Secret and in Shadow was to be worshipped, but if Kilke was Brazz's deity, then fire was the Flamefang's truest companion. He felt about it the way he imagined humans cared for their wives, their husbands, their children, and their parents all in one. Fire lay in potential all around him. All it needed was the right air and good fuel . . . and most things could be made into excellent fuel given sufficient . . . encouragement.

<<Brazz, sir. Please, Glider Lieutenant Len said it was urgent.>>

Surrendering his slumber to the dreadful noise of claw on scale, Brazz's eyes began to focus, his jaw to open, readying to spew his ire upon the offending awakener.

<<Commander Brazz,>> the slight gray-scaled Zaur tapped. <<Please don't burn me, but the Gliders have found something unusual and they—>>

"Gliders," Brazz hissed sluggishly, sniffing out the Zaur's name. *Ninth Hatchling of the Twentieth Brood of Joolis? Never heard of a Joolis before who was worth the one brood, much less twenty.*

"Joolis?" Brazz angled his arrow-like head at the rounder wedge of the smaller reptile's. *Not worth burning.* "Gliders?"

<<Yes, Commander.>>

Brazz took in the trees overhead, marking as best he could the time by the passage of the most visible moon, but all it really told him amid all this scandalously unburnt forest was that he'd been woken far earlier than the dawn rousing he had been expecting.

<<So I'm a Commander now, am I?>> Brazz chuckled. <<Is that how they twist events so that it makes sense in their cold little brains?>>

<<Kuort was left in charge, Commander Brazz, sir, and, in his absence, General Tsan had instructed that command should fall to you and in order for that to happen then you had to at least be—>>

"Fine," Brazz whispered. Fumbling around for a flask of Dragon Venom, he unstoppered the container, breathing deep its fumes, letting the vapor ignite the last vestiges of black damp in his mind. "Any further signal from General Tsan?"

<<No, sir.>>

Where was he? Well, likely she *by now, but even if the Warlord had commanded her to brood, Brazz's orders ought to have come from Kuort or, Kilke forbid, Captains Dryga or Asvrin.*

"To His secret purpose, then." Brazz gave the air a taste with his forked tongue, sliding on his vest bedecked with vials of Dragon Venom. Eight out of thirteen left, if he judged the weight properly. Enough to burn the whole of the Parliament of Ages down if only the Weeds hadn't seen the truth behind the burning of their Root Tree and realized the strength and value of the Sri'Zauran Empire as allies. Given the sight the scouts had seen: the General, an Eldrennai, and a young Weed flying for the mountains . . . Well, if there was ever to be war with the Weeds, it loomed far enough in the future Brazz might never see it.

The Weeds now dwelt within the lee of time, safe within the good graces of Kilke's chosen. They possessed impressive abilities, too, and he could see their value as allies. Weaker than the Sri'Zaur of course, but then were not all Jun's creatures lesser than they?

"Well, Spawn of Joolis?" Brazz hissed at the little Zaur to nudge him onward.

"To His secret purpose?" the Zaur asked.

<<Indeed,>> Brazz thumped with his tail, <<but I meant the Gliders. Lead on.>>

*

A small contingent of Weeds (all females, Brazz assumed, from their arms and armor, but it wasn't always easy to tell) paced nervously alongside Lieutenant Len and his Gliders. Two of the Gliders perched on all fours at Brazz's elbows, ready to steady him if he lost his balance on the wide branch that they all graced. One of the Weeds, a silvery barked one with green frond-like head petals, gestured with an outstretched limb pointing something out to Len, who nodded tersely before turning to face Brazz.

Wounds of various levels of severity dotted Len's mottled scales. A long cut shone dark and angry on his shoulder. A Skreel blade, maybe?

<<Commander Brazz,>> Len tapped, exposing his throat.

<<What happened, Lieutenant?>> Brazz tapped in response.

"The fallen," Len spat softly.

"Fallen?" Brazz asked. "Ex—"

"A tremendous web of spiritual evil stretches from the north," the frond-headed Weed interrupted. "You may be blind to it, but the Vael are not. It reaches into the very heart of the dead and raises them like dolls on hooks, which dance to their weaver's will."

"A moment, noble Vael." Brazz cleared his throat. <<Who is this Weed?>>

<<Ella,>> the young female tapped with the hilt of a knife upon her armored belly, <<this *Vael* is.>>

"You speak Zaurtol." Brazz forced himself to keep his breath even. No need to let her see his surprise. General Tsan had warned some of the Vael had a limited understanding of the more common dialects. Making a mental note to himself to give the order to shift to one of the more secretive dialects, he studied the Weed, looking deep into her black-green pupil-less eyes, the unpruned dental ridges, and smooth, yet unstripped bark. She was a hardy breed, an evergreen; her scent was bright and tart like the mountain trees that survived the winters on high. Things could be worse. He could have been forced to deal with one of the more florid sort, with their acrid stench.

"Enough to know the difference between <<Weed>> and <<Vael>> when I hear it."

"We were right to desire a peace with your people." In his mind's eye Brazz set her alight, watching her burn, imagining the crackle and the wood smoke. She'd be hard to enkindle properly, but he had powders and tinctures to assist with that. He could almost hear the hiss and pop. Such a pity her people were strong enough to be allies. Then again, they were allies for a reason and, thinking on it, Brazz did not even need to come up with a false one. "Not because you understand Zaurtol. As a language, it is not all that difficult; even our hatchlings can grasp it. Appalling more warmbloods can't seem to make tongue or tail of it, really."

"Then to what were you referring?" Iella asked.

"You can see the spirits to which our cursed maker blinded us." Brazz lowered his throat to surface of the branch, his limbs catching the distant rumblings of Zaurtol from other agents. A dead Zaurruk? A cadre of dead. But, also, two humans, some scarbacks, and— No. That part could not be correct. "You will be most useful. Assuming, of course, you are requesting the Sri'Zauran Empire's assistance in dispatching this threat."

"We would, but first we want your opinion on something else."

"Oh?"

"One of the fallen has been encountered with a small group of Aern, a crystal twist with an Aern's teeth, and a human who is not quite what he seems. The fallen one says its name is Kuort. It has been asking for you."

"Kuort." Brazz narrowed his eyes, holding his breath to maximize control over his exterior expressions both obvious and subtle. He hated all of this honeyed wordplay, but—"Yes, I suppose we can spare the time to see what he wants."

*

Randall Tyree's eyes snapped open and closed again in rebellion, stinging like no experience he had ever known. His lungs burned, crackling as he wheezed. Two distinct types of pain radiated from his chest: a low dull throb and a sharper stab when he breathed in. Broken breast bone, maybe? How many times had the Aern hit him? Everything smelled like smoke, pine trees, and rotten flesh. Lizard, too?

Still. Pine was a good sign.

"Nobody hit me again," he croaked, tongue dry and raw. "The Harvester's already seen me once today."

Emotions touched him quicker than the flood of words from those around him. Shock. Surprise. Awe. Confusion. Fear. Along with a type of emotion he got from animals more often than humans, which he could describe most accurately as a sort of loyal joy.

He recognized it. *Good. Alberta survived.*

Eyes watering (surely those could not have been tears of relief—he'd only known the horse a matter of days), he tried to separate the sounds he was hearing.

Words, he thought, *definitely words.* They swam in circles around his brain but refused to make sense yet.

"Can somebody hand me a wet rag?" Cold and wet, a rough cloth was at his eyes as someone worked to wipe away a mask of soot and char. Warm hands touched his cheeks and his forehead, a heavy weight on his chest, then gone.

More words he didn't understand, at first, but they sounded gentle and feminine, so he saw no reason to complain.

Can you hear me? Cadence's thoughts hit his brain, made his ears and mind ring.

Do I get a kiss if I can?

Between the snort and the lack of lip contact, he presumed the answer to be resoundingly negative.

Worth a try. Attempting to open his eyes again, he spotted trees, but snapped them shut against the light, a miasma of colors wobbling before him even after he closed his eyes again.

"Too bright." The trees made him happy, though. Trees meant they were out of the tunnels. Shielding his eyes with his left hand, he let them slowly open once more.

Aern faces surrounded him, peering down and out at other figures that surrounded them. Alberta whinnied plaintively, drawing a weak smile out of him.

Where'd you go? he thought at Cadence when he did not see her.

Alberta snorted and stomped, not a fan of being ignored.

"I'm glad to see you, too, lady." He attempted a roll in that direction, but his body responded slowly, its complaints visceral in their agony. He had heard many people say pain was a good thing, and his opinion about those sorts of people was that they needed to feel more of it so they would stop sounding like idiots. "Give a moment and I'll—"

Rolling his head toward the sound of Alberta's whinny, he spotted a rotting Sri'Zaur carefully brushing the animal down and cooing at her in a sibilant, yet calming tone. Other reptiles with mottled scales and large membranous flaps along their limbs surrounded the Aern.

"Gliders," he whispered. Jerking back in the other direction to try to take in their number was a mistake that left him vomiting across his own bicep. *Well*, he thought, *I probably would not have been able to get all of the smoke and soot out of it anyway.*

"Captain Tyree," one of the Sri'Zaur, a Flamefang, the older one, began. Tyree did not know his name, but he'd seen the reptile once or twice during his captivity. "I expected that you would be half way to Midian by now."

"You mean this isn't Midian?" Tyree managed a smile. "I knew there seemed to be a lot more trees than the last time I was here."

"Your attempt at humor is—"

"I'm sorry Mr. Flamefang, sir." Tyree tried, eyes sparkling, to beam positive emotions at the Sri'Zaur. "But you know how it is. You come upon a group of young Aern. One of them loses his leg somewhere, so you all have to go looking for it, and then no one can find it, so you have a cookout in a cave. Somebody forgets to check the air vents and . . ."

"Brazz," the dead reptile said softly, "has never had much of a sense of humor. Have you, Brazz?"

"You talk." Brazz eyed the dead one warily. "The other corpses don't."

Not true, Tyree guessed, by the emotions coming off of the nearby Vael.

"Dead or alive, I am Kuort," the dead one said. "I serve General Tsan and have been her trusted guard and advisor. Do not lie to me, honored Flamefang. Of course the dead speak, but most of them do not speak freely, as I do. The majority are slaves to our cursed maker's will."

"Who?" The interior of Brazz's mouth began to glow. "Who is it?"

"Our maker," Kuort said slowly, taking great pains to enunciate well around split or missing fangs. "Ours, not just mine." He gestured at the other reptiles then back to himself with one jagged foreclaw.

"Uled?" one of the Gliders asked.

Hate hit Tyree from all sides. If Uled was the angry dead thing he'd accidentally touched back in the tunnels, the thing from which Cadence had rescued him, he understood the feeling. Now if only they could all hate the guy a little more quietly . . .

CHAPTER 11
THE FLAME-HAIRED GODDESS

Filled with stones and coated in flaming pitch, a barrel crashed over the wall of Warfare and down, past the angry goddess of resolution, toward the still-crowded marketplace at the center of the Guild Cities. Tornadic winds seized the barrel, kicking it back up in an arc that would return the projectile to the city from which it had been launched. Flaming hair, no longer merely an attractive quirk of magic, filled the air around the warsuit-clad Wylant in a writhing, hungry conflagration, consuming or igniting all it touched beyond the goddess, Clemency, and Vax.

Arrows burst into flames as they sought her. Steel crossbow bolts melted and blew away, drops of liquid metal spattering and setting small fires where they found purchase. Fighting forms, with tattoos of Dienox across their fronts, manned siege weapons, directing the rank and file to keep firing arrows, to try anything that might slow the advance of the end to hostilities.

It was hard not to pity them, but Wylant knew war and how to end it. With negotiation no longer an option, all that remained was the killing. Against an enemy like Dienox, one who would not or could not surrender, she had to keep coming until he actually showed up in person and lost . . . or until she destroyed every last temple and follower he possessed, robbing him of his power and leaving him helpless . . . She hoped.

It will work, Mother.

Wylant prayed Vax was right, but she did not know to whom she should send the prayers. Aldo would have been her deity of choice in the recent past, but she could not stomach praying to Vander.

He would not mind, Vax thought.

Clouds rolled in and tore apart, cutting misshapen tunnels in the sky from which fire and lighting rained. Steam rose from the Grand Arena most sacred to Dienox, the water boiling, killing the sharks within and reducing the helpless terrors to cooked meat in a wrathful stew.

"Dienox!" Wylant bellowed, "Face me, you craven thing! When I was mortal you tried an ambush and came away more wounded than I! Come and die!"

"You are acting beyond even the great leeway we have allowed you as one new to godhood." The voice, female and strong, erupted from the clouds. "Gods do not treat mortals and their habitations this way, Wylant!"

"Shidarva." Wylant spotted the goddess hovering amid the maelstrom, could feel her influence seeping into the clouds, shifting the fallout to rain and hail.

A complication. Clemency intoned. **I shall keep a lookout for Dienox while you resolve this, ma'am. He will not catch me unawares.**

Thanks, Wylant thought. *These are the rules Vander mentioned earlier, right?*

Yes, Vax answered. *But she's referring to rules Aldo wrote, not the guidelines the Artificer left behind. Most of the gods view them as irrefutable, because Aldo convinced them they were, but any god or goddess is free to do whatever they can manage without the other gods stepping in to stop them. Scary, given how fickle they seem to be.*

Sounds like we were all lucky Aldo was a good bluffer. Wylant wanted to know more, but she decided the ruler of the gods took precedence. With the same judgment that had led her to decapitate Nomi and scalp her, Wylant weighed her chances against the four-armed goddess. She had never seen the goddess depicted in this aspect. Her skin ranged from midnight blue to light and dark grays as if storm-filled skies merely echoed her own visage. Shidarva flew free of the clouds, her Altan armor falling into place as if assembled by the rain.

Eagle-helmed plate armor covered her chest, back, shoulders, feet and knees. Arms exposed, but wearing gloves of black leather, Shidarva wielded curved blades wreathed in blue flame. Two wings sprung from her back, covered in gray feathers crackling with lightning.

I haven't seen armor like that on a living person, Wylant thought at her sword and warsuit. *The paladins of Alt used to wear it charging into battle. I've seen paintings of it.* She chuckled to herself.

What is so funny, ma'am? Clemency asked.

Kholster's commentary on the armor. Wylant studied the way Shidarva held her blades. She knew how to use them, but the memory of Kholster's voice was still clear in Wylant's mind. *I thought it was strange of them to go through all of the trouble of forging that metal, then leaving me wonderful swathes of exposure to facilitate dismemberment. The wings made excellent handholds as well. Dyed feathers on a wire frame. Silly.*

Amusing as the memory was, Shidarva had donned the traditional armor worn by the fallen champion of the sacred continent she had sacrificed in order to save the world. Wylant did not know the full story, only that somehow the demons had been close to finding another way through Port Gate at the Great Temple of Shidarva, which stood at the very heart of Alt. The priests had failed to follow the correct order of destruction, as each rune on the border of a Port Gate needed to be eradicated in a specific sequence to permanently sever the link between the gates. Hasimak might have been able to prevent any incursion under normal circumstances, but at that point in the Demon War, his attention had been wholly consumed with maintaining the quarantine barrier at Fort Sunder, and even then he had required the wills and power of multiple elemancers to assist him. Neither demon nor mortal combatants could escape that barrier, but if a second breach had occurred . . . With its connection to the other gates unbroken, the Port Gate at Alt had been a potential second breach. Shidarva had seen a horde of Ghaiattri massing in the Never Dark, at the edge of her domain, preparing to force their way through, and acted. Shidarva had destroyed her own continent to sink the Port Gate far enough from its proper alignment that it became useless. One could travel through it still, but anyone doing so would arrive torn apart and inside out at the bottom of the ocean floor.

"What right do you have to judge my infractions against mortals?" Wylant asked. "Didn't you sink an entire continent? By comparison, I'm—"

"You find this amusing?" Shidarva's lips did not move, her voice omnidirectional and shaking with rage. "You mock my sacrifice and compare it to yours, you wanton—"

"You know Hasimak told me you need not have destroyed your continent," Wylant said. "You could have had them knock the stupid Port Gate over and pull it a few dozen feet out of position."

"That is a lie!" Shidarva roared.

It was, too, as far as Wylant knew.

"Not that you have any way of knowing. Oh! I know. Why don't you ask Aldo?" Wylant made a practice swing in the air, with Vax in gladius form. "Or do you not speak ant?"

"I asked him at the time." Shidarva flew nearer, framed in lightning. Lightning, which, Wylant noted, struck the ground heedless of the mortals it hit. "He said . . ."

"Did he—" A voice came from the shadows, where a tumbled statue of Dienox lay broken at the knees and bent forward across the entrance of the Grand Arena. "—tell you it was a secret?"

"That was during my angry period." Two-headed Kilke, one head bearing the curled horns of a ram, the other jutting the long horns of a bull, each bedecked in sapphires, stepped free of the shadows. Flowing after him, the darkness became a suit of plate armor, featureless and disconcerting. "You see, he did not know how to do it, and I declined to tell him. His solution worked, but, well, it lacked elegance and waxed toward . . . Excess."

"You!" Shidarva's gaze burned with blue fire, her attention locked on the god of secrets and shadows.

"Do you mean me, the letter between T and V, or are you calling for a lady sheep?" A two-handed sword, forged by shadows, so large it appeared to have been made for cutting cattle in half, filled his grip. Standing twelve feet tall, Kilke strode out among the warriors of Dienox's city. A handful turned to fight, but most ran. A single blow from his blade bisected one armored foe wielding a war hammer, continuing through the hammer as it dropped, and through a man in brigandine behind him. Four other men charged in from the side. Kilke never looked at them, spiked tendrils of black springing from his armor and piercing them each through both eyes, points emerging from the backs of their skulls before vanishing back into the depths of the shadow armor.

"Minapsis," Shidarva shouted. "Torgrimm! Sedvinia! To me."

Shidarva's twin, the goddess of joy and sorrow, rose from the blood of a dead man where the tears of an older man—Wylant presumed it was his father—struck the blood. Wearing no armor and welding no weapon, she crossed the battlefield in a dress of white silk, head bowed, the hot teardrops that fell from her eyes, mixing with the rain and leaving diamonds in her wake.

"They are not coming," Sedvinia said. "You are our ruler, but you stand alone if you oppose Dienox's punishment. I apologize, but even if I were to take up my arms and join you, sister—"

"What is this?" Kholster appeared on the arena wall between strokes of lightning, doubled canines bared, snarling at the other gods. "Wylant was granted permission to kill Dienox. We all agreed to it. Dienox refused to fight her." Kholster's warpick described an encompassing arc, emphasizing the chaos. "His cowardice brought her wrath upon his followers. This is far less than she could have done to draw him out."

"Kholster—" Wylant tried to catch his eye, but he looked down. Was he angry?

"Wylant, I apologize for interfering." She recognized the look as he spoke. Kholster thought she was angry at him for stepping in, when she would have been pleased as an irkanth stumbling across a lame elk if Kholster had killed the cursed god of war himself and any others who got in their way. "You are perfectly capable, I know—"

His fear of—what was the word—disempowering the ones he loved teetered on the edge of insufficient support. Blaming him would not help. It was even sweet, but . . .

"Kholster, you idiot." Wylant laughed. "You are my husband. I expect your help even when you know I could handle the hunt. We fell in love on the battlefield; do you really think I do not enjoy fighting side by side, spending time with you? If you start to annoy me, or become somehow overly helpful, it is my firm intent to tell you. Won't you join me?"

A weight fell from him. Wylant had seen the same wildness that rushed through him in the eyes of hunting hounds loosed from the leash or horses given their head. With one short exchange, he transformed. A predatory grin showed in the corners of his eyes, his joyous bark pure and unadulterated. "Love you," he mouthed, wheeling to face Shidarva.

"Queen of Leeches," Kholster yelled, his amber pupils glowing brightly, storm clouds and lighting strike reflected in the blackness of his eyes. "If you continue to interfere with my wife's rightful vengeance, all will not go well for you."

"You forget yourself, Kholster," Shidarva spun toward him, her swords twirling madly. "I am the ruler of the gods."

"And he," Kilke butted in, both mouths leering gleefully, "is the birth and death of gods."

Kholster growled.

"Oh—" Kilke's long-horned head's lip made a mocking O, which he covered daintily with one hand as the other head spoke. "—did I give away a secret?"

"You may think of me," Kholster said, "as an Arbiter between the mortal and the divine. The old laws of the gods may have had no teeth, but I shall lend mine." His lips drew back in disgust. "Get in my wife's way one more time on this front and I will arvash you and all who stand with you. I so swear!"

"Sedvinia," Shidarva called, but her sister had faded from sight and abandoned the field. Eyes wide, Shidarva sneered at Kholster. "I will not surrender the throne of the gods without a fight."

"He does not want your throne," Kilke's ram-horned head spat.

"But he will not tolerate your obstructionism," the other head finished.

"You will note," Wylant offered, "your sister was the only god who answered your call. Why are you standing in my way, Shidarva? Dienox is a fool! He is a petty, self-important, homicidal mind rapist. Why—?"

Ma'am! Clemency rolled, avoiding the brunt of Dienox's attack, but Wylant felt the sting of the cut, the warmth of blood on her side.

Longsword? Assuming Dienox would expect her to fly any direction but down, Wylant released her grip on the magic holding her aloft and dropped like a stone, cutting wildly with Vax in the direction she hoped Dienox might be. Only then did the blue of the war god's ethereal armor become visible. Elsewhere, Kholster shouted at Shidarva to go away, to return to the ruins of her sacred temple and play with the eels.

Again pain lanced through her, this time her shoulder. Clemency struggled to adjust, and Wylant fought the armor for control, attempting a separate maneuver.

"What are you doing, Clem?" Wylant spat between pain-clenched teeth.

Trust us. Vax and Clemency thought as one.

Please, Vax added.

"Coward, am I?" Dienox's blades hissed through the air, clanging off

Vax or Clemency or striking home so quickly Wylant could not track his movements. Each blow came more swiftly than the one before, confidence lending strength and alacrity. "We could have been such good partners!" Pain scratched down her side. "I would have forgiven you anything but this!"

Vax? Twirling so fast she could no longer clearly see, Wylant felt her body jerked in a sequence of parries and counters all twice her normal speed, all in a style matching her own, yet divorced from her mental faculty.

He has to believe it, mother. Vax's thoughts burned with an emotion Wylant had not known he could possess: Rage. Primal and fathomless, it coated his mental communications with blood. *He has to smell blood.*

"Anything!" Dienox thrust in time with the final pronouncement. Wylant saw his eyes, frozen in triumph as he saw an imaginary hole in her defense, a fatal flaw exposing her chest. The sword struck Clemency's breastplate, splitting it open. Heat and cold struck her harder than it ever had. Fire, rain, and hail battered her, the leathers she'd been wearing beneath Clemency no help at all against the warring temperatures. Warm blackness cushioned her fall, wrapping her in a protective cloak of . . . shadow?

"He's very clever," Kilke whispered in the dark, "your son."

Above them, Clemency had turned inside out, thin bands of armor splayed like the detonated cauldron of some unfortunate gnomish apprentice. Only . . . Wylant narrowed her gaze. Clemency showed no sign of true damage, as if she had opened herself to the greatest of extremes. Dienox, roar of triumph on his lips, understood what had happened a heartbeat (his last) after Wylant.

Like limbs of a dying spider, Clemency's multitudinous bands curled inward. A bone-steel shackle bearing Kholster's scars engraved upon it, Vax shone pearlescent against the ruddy skin of the war god. Eyes widening, Dienox moved to cut at the shackle, his other hand coming away ensnared in a matching restraint, joined to the first by a rod of bone-steel. He screamed, unable to flee or break his bonds, as the warsuit closed around him.

"You hurt my mother," Vax's voice echoed from within his warsuit. "You made her forge me into a weapon, and that hurt me, too. She would have rather been foresworn than do what she did to me. It still haunts her. It makes her cry! AND IT'S ALL YOUR FAULT!"

Unable to look away, unable to even process what she was seeing until the deed neared completion, Wylant stared up at the warsuit, swollen to accept Dienox's body. Before the eyes of the flame-haired goddess and the core of Dienox's most devout worshippers, Clemency shrank to more Aern-like proportions. As she diminished, a small hole opened at the base of each armored boot letting the bones of the war god fall one by one, clean and polished, from the storm-tossed sky.

The war god screamed until his ribs lay white and shining in ruination at Wylant's feet. Worshippers in the streets and forges shivered and wailed as they watched their god die. Some ran to collect the bones, of which all except the skull had now fallen, but most peered skyward at the hovering warsuit and waited. Lines of red crystal ran down in rivulets, extending the pattern from Clemency's helm to the rest of her, the color darkening to a deep maroon.

"Vax?" Kilke's midnight embrace released Wylant, the flame brands of her hair flashing intensely, as if displeased to have been dimmed briefly, even to the benefit of their host.

Thunder cracked overhead, clouds scattering as Wylant waved them away thoughtlessly. Kholster stood his ground, watching, waiting, measuring, calculating in the way of all good kholsters. How could he stand there and do nothing? Wylant took to the air, rushing for her son.

"And now," a voice whispered from within the warsuit, "you have made amends."

"Please," a tiny whimpering voice replied, "I was only doing what I was supposed to do. War is all I had left."

"There are limits," another voice (was that Vax?) murmured. "You stepped beyond yours."

Outstretching its gauntlet, the warsuit's fist opened, the skull of Dienox manifesting within. Rearing back, Clemency hurled the skull to Kholster, who caught it with a nod and a smile, then vanished.

"Father," the strange voice said, as Wylant drew even with the warsuit, "must see to Dienox's soul, but I assure you he has expressed his congratulations and his love."

Vax's disembodied voice, the one she had heard in her mind since Kholster adjusted his scars, had been a child's. Deeper now and more solid, she hoped this new voice was coming from proper lips, flesh and muscle, blood and bone metal.

"Vax . . . are you . . . ?" Wylant held out a tentative hand, blinking rapidly when the helm collapsed into a gorget of crystal and bone-steel. Impossible features greeted her: a grin revealing doubled canines less pronounced than an average Aern's, ears set high in a position more suited to a wolf—their tips blunted—each three-quarters of a hand in length rather than the full hand more typical of his father's people. Vax had her cheekbones and his father's chin. Both parents showed in his image, a more attractive combination than either of them alone.

Most striking were the eyes: black sclera and amber pupils with irises the same clear blue as his mother's. Wearing his strawberry blond hair in the close cut of a Hulsite mercenary, his skin a healthy tan, Vax stepped free of his warsuit, shirtless and barefoot, in a pair of dark gray denim jeans with bone metal buttons and leather lacing up the sides.

"Hello, Mother."

"Vax!" Wylant embraced him, tears welling up as she felt his strong arms wrap around her. "Are you . . . You look well, but are you?"

"I am unused to a proper body, but—" He pulled free of her, experimenting with his fingers, touching the fingertips on each hand to their resident thumb in the same order, then reversed, and lastly in the opposite order on each hand simultaneously. "—my time controlling Clemency was a great help. She—"

A human God Speaker with burns where her tattoos of Dienox had once been approached. Skin shifting from tan flesh to blued bone-steel, Vax faced the young woman.

"Whom do I now serve?" She prostrated herself before Vax, the new god of war, arms raised, palms slick with ash and blood.

"Do you still wish to serve war?" Vax asked.

"I live to kill."

"Killing may be needed." Vax held out his hand to her. "Tell me. Do you believe that to serve me is to kill, to fight, for no reason other than the glory of it?"

"Yes," she answered, letting him help her up.

Vax waited until she was steady.

"May I share with you a few of my feelings on the topic?"

PART TWO

A DRAGON RISEN

"The reign of Queen Bhaeshal set many precedents. She was the first female elf to rule in her own right, and the first elf of either gender to reign alongside free Aern in a peaceful kingdom without a grudge borne against herself or her people. While her subjects were ambivalent toward their absent king, they hated his brother Dolvek, the story having somehow made its way to Aiannai ears that King Rivvek's actions would not have been necessary if his brother had not broken faith with the Aern in the first place.

Her elemental focus, obvious for all to see, served as a constant reminder that the actions of the previous bloodline had not spared her. Peace with the Aern, bought so dearly by Rivvek, bestowed its gifts, meager though they may have been, upon the Queen. I wish I did not hold that fact against her. It is utterly unfair."

From an unpublished draft of
The First Rulers of the Aiannai by Sargus

CHAPTER 12
RUN FROM THE HILLS

Warleader Tsan ran through the tunnels of the Sri'Zauran Mountains, the head of her deity clutched in her forepaws. Kilke's horns scraped rhythmically against her crimson scales, his golden hue standing out in contrast, its reflective quality sending shards of light skipping across her abdomen—rills of magic riding the tide of her scales. Fear scent blocked out the more subtle odors that would have marked the main corridors of the underground highways of her new kingdom, overwhelmed only by the rising stink of the dead.

How long have we been running? she thought.

Two days? Three? I haven't been counting, just reinvigorating your little army as needed. Do you want to keep the crimson scales? One-Headed Kilke thought at her. *Or would you prefer a shade more clearly echoing my own coloration?*

I would prefer to get out of here alive, Tsan sent back, the acid in her thoughts drawing a bemused chuckle from the deity in her grip.

That much is assured; you ran soon enough, the disembodied head thought. *Even with all of the cutbacks and detours we have taken, Uled's army is no longer gaining. You finally found a route so secret even Warlord Xastix had not known about it, therefore Uled could not have learned this route when he . . . merged . . . with Xastix.*

Merged? Tsan saw it all again in her mind's eye: Warlord Xastix's flesh unraveled as the thing Uled had become knit itself a new body out of the warlord's scale, meat, and bone.

Erupted, if you prefer. Kilke's thoughts tiptoed through her mind as clumsily as a biped's, feigned ineptitude to ensure she felt his presence and could not accuse him of hiding it. *I have to make changes here as well. You and I will escape these tunnels intact even if I have to turn you into a dragon to manage it. Uled could kill and claim the whole of your kingdom and still fail to seize the true prize.*

A dragon? Tsan already felt larger and stronger than she had in any of her previous careers and the various bloodline changes that had accompanied them.

Not even that daunts you, does it? Kilke asked.

Becoming stronger? Was Kilke a fool? Did he fail to understand the workings of a true Sri'Zaur even as he worked might into her body? *Strength is an asset I have long understood.*

With Kilke's help, clearing the long-sealed escape route the Zaur had used to effect the first exile had been the work of an hour when it should have taken weeks, proper equipment, and crews of workers . . . even a Zaurruk. The sheer power of her limbs, the way her body moved . . . Each action felt an effortless inevitability the likes of which she expected the Armored in their tireless warsuits might feel.

Perhaps not even they. Tsan wondered if even an Aern evolving from mortal to nigh immortal with the forging of a warsuit, back when the Life Forge had been whole, could relate to the changes Kilke had wrought within her.

We are close enough to smell outer air, Kilke thought.

Luminescent mushrooms lit Tsan's path unnecessarily, as her new eyes drew in every measure of light, magnifying it until the tunnels felt as if they were in full sun, bringing out previously unseen details in the stone gardens and rock formations of which her people were so proud. Despite the fear scent, she could indeed detect hints of mountain air.

<<Not much farther,>> she tapped with a combination of claw and tail strikes on the cavern ceiling. Guards behind her repeated her message in unison, amplifying Zaurtol's subtle scraping percussion so that her meaning could be discerned even amid the pad of so many reptiles fleeing along the corridors of their once-home.

Tsan ducked under a stone curtain whose wavy lines were reminiscent of the splash of a rock thrown into a pond, its surface flash frozen by the preamble to a dragon's first breath when the heat leeched out of the world.

Am I still growing?

Did you want to stop? One-Headed Kilke's voice cooed in her mind. *I'm becoming fond of the dragon idea now that I've thought of it, and I sense some of Jun's primal flame has been released from its flesh. A rare opportunity exists to birth a dragon as they were in the beginning.*

Already larger than the Zaur who served under her, Tsan had increased in size beyond that of the largest Sri'Zaur she had ever known. Increased alacrity had come with the change, too, and the new stamina . . . she'd had to set one of the surviving Sri'Zauran guards to notify her when the lesser reptiles had to rest so Kilke could reinvigorate them. For three days she had slept only when others needed it, when Kilke informed her that further mystical stamina would damage her army in the long term.

Could I fight it then? Tsan asked. *The thing that took Warlord Xastix's body?*

You could fight him now, Kilke thought, *but defeat . . . I have no idea how to destroy what Uled has become. Who can say if even the Harvester knows how to deal with such a being . . .*

If it's a secret, then surely— Tsan thought.

Uled. Kilke used the name as just another proper noun, without the sense of gravitas and hate all of the mad Eldrennai's creations held for him. Tsan's gender cycle had been completed more times than she could count or recall since Uled had twisted the Zaur, taken the primitive idyllic sun-basking nomads and shaped them into the Sri'Zaur. A memory so deep as to be near instinct told her she had been among those early clutches, but the details had worn away little by little over the centuries, an erosion of the old to make way for new selves, new careers, and even the new breeds she had been forced to assume. That she had remembered the ancient route they'd taken to escape Uled so many thousands of years ago seemed a gift from the gods.

I may have helped a bit, Kilke said, *but it was still there in your mind. All it needed was a little nudge to bring it forth. Easy enough to do while keeping your most recent persona intact. Might as well shift a few other valuable nuggets from past careers in the process. Yes?*

Memory.

Tsan's skills remained bright and hot, freshly encoded in her muscles and membranes, but she lacked the perfect recollection of self-history with which Uled had imbued the Aern. Tsan suspected it was akin to the Litany wrought into the very roots of the Weeds, each knowing the names and faces of all who had offended their people but lacking the facts of each case, retaining only its gravity and punishment. At times she envied the scarbacks their memory, wished she could shut her membranes, still her thoughts, and send herself back along the corridors of her mind to relive past triumphs and injuries.

But perhaps it was for the best she lacked such talents. Tsan still could not close her nictitating membranes without seeing that misshapen wretch forming itself out of the unspooling flesh of her former warlord. Everything had been going according to plan. Kilke had demanded her warlord produce a sample of Eldrennai, Vael, and Aern blood to demonstrate Warlord Xastix's fealty. Tsan had not known the bodiless deity had done so only to buy himself time to—

Kilke? Warleader Tsan thought. *Why did you ask Xastix to gather exactly what Uled needed to complete his ritual?*

I asked for no such thing, Kilke sent, his thoughts filled with admiration at the Eldrennai's cleverness. *You must understand. Uled's is a mind unlike any others who have walked this world. I don't believe he can actually see the web of destiny, but even from down here I can feel him working to change it. All, I presume, based on deductive reasoning on his part. He has successfully theorized the grand designs of the Artificer.*

Who? Tsan asked.

The god who created the gods, Kilke thought. *When Uled was born, I wanted to destroy him at once, but Torgrimm put up such a fuss I relented. Uled's thoughts are the turning of wheels within wheels. As I mentioned, the very gear work of the universe is obvious to him and when it comes to games of strategy Uled, even as a young apprentice, excelled not so much at seeing his opponent's next move but at being able to develop a counter for all of the opponent's possible moves and setting those counters into place with speed and precision, adjusting all possible outcomes to benefit him . . . eventually.*

So, Tsan thought, *you did not do what he wanted, but rather he had a contingency in place to take advantage of such a request in case it were to be made?*

Daunting, isn't it? Kilke purred.

If he is that forward thinking, Tsan thought, *then how did he die in the first place?*

Some, Kilke answered, as sunslight became visible in the distance at one of the larger exits into Rin'Saen Gorge, *think his greatest weakness is his evil. But I find Uled's largest obstacle to be a failure to account for the ability of his creations to function beyond their intended purposes. To do so would require a sense of wonder, of love, and of compassion beyond the rudimentary emotional algebra he uses to understand the feelings others possess and he lacks.*

So an Aern killed him? Tsan stepped into the light, her claws gripping the rocky soil of the gorge bottom. A light rain was falling, the cool drops most often unwelcome to cold bloods such as herself washed over her scales like the words of alliance to a doomed lesser tribe. Mist rose off the trickling stream that ran along the gorge's base. Earthy and rich, the smell of dampening soil filled Tsan's nostrils even as the gentle rhythm of precipitation danced in those specialized organs reserved for sensing motion and vibrations.

No, General Wylant working with Uled's own spawn: Sargus.

How?

It doesn't matter, Kilke thought. *He'll not be slain by the same beings again or by any mortal.*

Then what do you suggest?

I usually rely on Kholster and his kin to handle this sort of threat. Kilke's thoughts came tinged with admiration and disappointment in a complicated tangle.

And you can't do so now? Tsan asked.

I am . . . uncertain. Do you still plan to try to kill the Aern?

I've discussed it with the current warleader, Tsan thought haughtily, *and she thinks that if the Vael want peace between the three of Uled's races, and the Aern are willing to help us kill our creator, then the need for redress with regard to certain other, more recent, grievances may be obviated.*

How enlightened of you, Kilke purred. *If only I had more accurate information about what has been happening out beyond the tunnels, I could make a better plan. How I miss my other heads at moments like this.*

Is that the first step of our plan, then? Tsan asked. *Scout out and see what we can see?*

No, Kilke answered. *Normally, yes, I would delve into the secrets available and find some juicy little piece on the board, forgotten by all but me, and play it. Likely my others heads are doing just that. They have that luxury. Who knows what complications or secrets lie ahead? I don't. Not currently. But power is always a good bet and, at present, it is my only play. So as to my plan . . .* As the rain stopped, clouds dispersing, the sunlight seemed to catch on the golden scales of Kilke's head, his horns growing translucent, filling with their own inner brilliance. *Our first move is: dragon.*

CHAPTER 13

PERMANENT TEMPORARY SOLUTIONS

Rae'en watched in silent appreciation as huge slabs of stone soared through the morning sky. Some flew high enough to chase the stratus clouds through the air, the contrasting grays rendering it hard—for brief moments when rock passed through cloud—to tell one from the other. Larger masses of stone rode across the surface of the plain like an army of uncharted statues. Slabs landed in the waiting gauntlets of warsuits on construction details or in pre-dug trenches.

Humans, and elves lacking elemantic abilities but possessed of architectural knowledge, observed and assisted, each holding relevant sections of the grand plan on sheets of thin flexible crystal produced by elven artificers under Dwarven command.

"If I had a gnome on hand," Rae'en heard Uncle Glinfolgo bellowing, "I might let him explain the math to you, but for some sections we'll need concrete and for those parts, you don't get to know why it works or how to make it. Nor do you get to help. You'll just have to accept: The Dwarf said so. Or go live in a mud hut someplace and pray Kholster comes quickly!"

Torgrimm, Rae'en corrected subconsciously without actually speaking it aloud. *Dad does something else now. Something mysterious.*

I can explain the matter to your Uncle, if— Bloodmane thought. The warsuit's voice, which such a short time ago had been a source of anger and grief, had morphed into a source of indescribable comfort and reassurance.

Leave it, she thought at her armor. *I can tell him later.*

Running her gauntleted hand along a completed section, Rae'en felt the stone against her skin as if there were no bone-steel between them. With her warsuit, Rae'en felt strong enough to unsling Testament (or Grudge, which hung on the opposite shoulder) and pound through the mass of rock like it was nothing.

Don't you think that would defeat the purpose? Kazan teased.

Rae'en sent him a burst of wordless amusement by way of response, letting her gaze turn along the extant portion of the great barrier: a wall built by elven, human, Aern, warsuit, and Dwarven cooperation. She smiled, glad to feel like she was doing something, even if it wasn't actively pursuing the Zaur or holding off their attack.

Rae'en had been expecting an attack imminently, but it hadn't come. Not from the Zaur Army. Not from the stubbornly restless dead. Not from anyone.

Yet.

Or maybe never, if the new Vael-Sri'Zauran alliance were to be believed.

Kazan showed her images of Sri'Zaur and Flower Girls fighting bands of the dead. More grievously injured corpses fought with chaotic nonsensical tactics, each attacking the nearest living thing, abandoning the careful formations the more intact dead used. A calculating mind lurked behind those battle plans. As she watched, a group of reptiles scattered in all directions only to form up again with synchronized grace in another portion of the battle, letting the squads with more advantageous positions take over their abandoned melee.

Each Zaur opponent the dead felled rose up with little or no pause to resume the battle alongside the creatures that had slain them. The newly risen fought with less martial skill than their fellows, dropping their weapons and wielding fang and claw. Fighting as they did drew attacks of opportunity to exposed flanks and ignored parries, but the dead withstood most wounds without noticing. Only severely crippling injuries hampered them and only being hacked to pieces and burned appeared to have any permanence.

Their overall strategy is like Aern, Rae'en thought.

Old ones, Kazan agreed. *Amber says they are pre-Sundering formations.*

They are setting up for a big strike. Rae'en circled a section of the battle in her mind, painting the section of the battlefield in black. *It's meant to look like normal drift, the sort of thing you can't see from within the battle.*

Setting up an Armored thrust, Kazan thought.

What's their equivalent? Rae'en asked. *Mounted Skria wielders? Zaurruk?*

"Hold it! Hold it!" Queen Bhaeshal bellowed, directing the Aiannai from the air herself, voice booming in that annoyingly impressive way

Thunder Speakers possessed, the sound jerking Rae'en back to the world around her. "Kam, reinforce him before he drops the whole section."

Kam, the youngest of the queen's newly appointed guard (once Wylant's Sidearms, now Bhaeshal's Royal Lancers) shot out under the listing hunk of rock, cloud-like familiar at his side to shore up the other Aeromancer's weakening hold.

The name "Cerez" appeared over the other Aeromancer's head, identifying him even as he collapsed atop the very stone he'd been transporting. With a yelp of pain and a grunt, Cerez rolled off the edge of the rock, only to be caught by the queen.

Bloodmane amplified Rae'en's vision enough that the wave of metal advancing along the elemancer's arm was plainly visible.

His elemental focus, right? she thought.

The gold tokens of her Overwatches—still strange to have so many of them—lit up gold in her mind indicating their agreement.

He's pushed himself too hard, Bloodmane intoned.

A pang of guilt tightened her chest. Maybe she should have found a way to have forgiven more of them. It hadn't even occurred to her that she could do so until Prince, no, King (now) Rivvek had thrown the idea in her face as he led his troop of brave fools through the Port Gate into the Demon Realm. Could it have been that easy? Her father couldn't have done it. She'd felt his rage, his desire to be able to feel other than he did, but he'd been so incapable of forgiveness for the Eldrennai that simply touching Bloodmane, who had forgiven them, was enough to burn Kholster's skin.

It no longer matters, Bloodmane thought. **We hunt the prey we are tracking now. It is irkanth for dinner or bones for the Bone Finder.**

I haven't heard that saying since I was a Fourteen. Rae'en laughed.

It seemed appropriate.

There are other Eldrennai out there, you know, Joose thought, *Unless all of the Watches were completely emptied or destroyed. I know the Zaur took some and others were ordered to pull back to Port Ammond, but do we know if they actually all got there?*

Rae'en watched as the queen sent Cerez off to rest (and to be examined by an Artificer) and Kam took his place. The twins, Frip and Frindo, took up positions closer to their queen. And so construction continued, following the plans Sargus, Rae'en, and Glinfolgo had laid out.

In an upper quadrant of her visual field other viewpoints cycled at her whim or at the suggestion of one of her Overwatches. Unable to trust the Geomancy of the elves within a few dragon lengths of the existing fortress, the new wall wended its way around the exterior of the invisible area so that Aiannai elemancers could help patrol the walls more effectively.

Within the walls, working from local supplies as well as new deliveries brought in by crews of Aern, elves, and humans, the assembled refugees worked to build the bones of a proper city. Glinfolgo had been referring to it as the Northern Annex, but Rae'en had heard the name Scarsguard bandied about by humans and elves who seemed to think the name appropriate. Scarsguard sounded good to Rae'en, too, but maybe not just for this place. Maybe . . .

She shook her head to clear the thought, not banishing it, but hanging it out to cure for a bit, to make sure it was ready. With the excess time granted them by whatever was going on with the dead, Rae'en intended to secure this place as best she could; and even if every elf and human died, Scarsguard would stand as a foothold in the Eldren Plains for the Armored and any Aern reinforcements she called forth. But how long before one enemy or another showed up to complicate matters?

Hunters ranged far and wide, bringing in meat and livestock (when possible), and every day it seemed more human families arrived. Some came with tales of the dead heading for the mountains, others with stories of being raided (or ignored completely) by Zauran and Sri'Zauran forces of varying size.

Updates? Rae'en thought at Kazan.

I think you're right about the Zaurruk, he sent back instantly. *Wylant slew one of which we know. There were mounted Zaur in that battle, too.*

Warn them.

I did, kholster, he thought back. *But it's already here.*

Show me.

Charred and with only one eye, a ghastly hole where the other had been, the Zaurruk burst up from the forest floor, sending chunks of rock and clouds of dirt in its wake. It charged and struck, scattering Vael and

Zaur alike as it thrust at the center of the assembled Zaur-Vael troops. Calvary of the dead rode out after it, trying to widen the break and scatter the living, break their formations. Twelve riders in all rode up out of the tremendous hole in the forest floor through which the Zaurruk had erupted.

But the Gliders and Vael, already in motion, leapt up and away, soaring on membranous flaps of skin or lifted by air spirits, escaping unscathed.

The Zaur felt the Zaurruk's vibrations before it broke the surface, Joose thought. *Everything is clear back here at the main Zaur camp. Do you need us to come get you, Kazan? We can bring Cadence.*

Cadence can't use her Far Flame trick like she did in the tunnels, M'jynn thought. *She's still too weak.*

What trick? Rae'en thought at all of them. *I knew she had certain abilities, but other than setting Dad on fire at one point . . .*

I may, Kazan thought, *have left some things out when I mentioned we were having a little trouble earlier.*

Such as?

Kazan told her.

Bloodmane, Rae'en thought directly to her armor, leaving Kazan out of the loop, *see if Eyes of Vengeance minds heading out there to meet my Prime Overwatch and get him back here before he omits himself or my other Overwatches into an early grave.*

He would be delighted, kholster, Bloodmane's thoughts boomed. **Eyes declined to ask, but I know he has wanted an excuse to go and retrieve his rightful occupant for some time.**

Good, Rae'en smiled. *Tell him to take ten other warsuits with him, will you? I don't want any of you running off by yourselves in case there are any Zaur or Sri'Zaur still out there with shards of the Life Forge who haven't heard about the temporary cessation of hostilities.*

Of course.

I'm sorry for not telling you earlier, Rae'en, Kazan thought, *but how could we have known we'd be heading into so much trouble?*

Trouble.

Unknown trouble.

Zaur.

Dead.

And something else. Rae'en's head hurt all of a sudden, and she could not tell exactly why, but some idea was there, like the answer to a puzzle to which she stood too close. But with just a little more perspective she felt like it could all come into focus and . . .

Kholster Rae'en? Arbokk asked.

Everyone be quiet a moment! Rae'en thought. *Except you, Bloodmane. Can you play back a conversation? Not the memory, but just the words?*

Kholster never asked me to do so . . . I believe I can, but do you not remember it all?

I can relive it and remember it all of a piece, but I can't let myself caught up in all the other distractions going on.

I understand that gets easier with age and experience. Very well, but from when?

Just pick a moment. About an hour back, the whole conversation we've been having, but without the distractions. Just give me the words.

Bloodmane did so.

Bird squirt! When Bloodmane got to Joose's statement, the one about there probably being more Eldrennai out there, it all clicked in Rae'en's mind. *The dead left Port Ammond heading north, right?*

Yes, Kazan thought. *Zhan and the rest of the Ossuary are being more quiet than usual, but Keeper and the other warsuits are relaying their data and positions. They are still trailing a large group of them north right now.*

Bones in the wind, you know? He waited for a beat, but Rae'en was silent, still processing. *Oh, and a message just came in from Silver Leaf City, Queen Kari is requesting that we not engage any Zaur we don't have to, but given what Lieutenant Ella and Commander Brazz have relayed, it tracks. I guess she sent the messenger before we met up with them.*

Silver Leaf? Rae'en stopped pacing, the flow of workers continuing around her. *When did this happen?*

A messenger came into Silver Leaf and told one of the hunters we sent out that way.

The same one we've heard from before? Rae'en asked.

An image of the Flower Girl in question appeared in Rae'en's mind map. Beautiful, like all Vael, but something about the way she pruned her evergreen head petals, the set of her jaw, and the way she held herself forced Rae'en to think of her as more than a mere Flower Girl.

From what we overheard, the messenger was Liv, Kazan thought at her, even as the image faded to be replaced by the relevant area on her mind map.

Or an evergreen who fits her description, Arbokk added. *She could fight, whoever she was.*

The hunter reported it to the human called Michael when she came back in with the load of venison, M'jynn explained. *I'm sure it will be relayed to you directly once it reaches high enough up in the Aiannai command chain, but Ambush overheard them and reported the information immediately.*

More detail than I wanted, Rae'en thought, *but thanks.*

The group that left the ruins of Port Ammond are still heading for the mountains, Bloodmane thought. **Coal is with them.**

Yes, Rae'en thought, *I know, but I don't think Zhan knows exactly where the dead are heading, and he might need to know.*

Where are they heading? Bloodmane and Kazan thought at the same time.

Rae'en felt the suppressed thrill of realization from Amber and gave her the mental nod to go ahead and one up her fellows.

To North Watch, Amber thought. *Any survivors they can kill or who died already and were buried in the rubble—*

Become reinforcements, Kazan thought. *Bird squirt indeed.*

*

Zhan, Rae'en called in his mind. *Where are you?*

He saw no need to respond. Clearly she already knew the answer to her question, was disturbed by the knowledge, and wanted an explanation. Even if that were not the case, the way she continued to act as if the Ossuary were within her chain of command was . . . irksome. In Kholster, the tendency had been understandable, even endearing in moderation, but in Rae'en—

"Bloodmane is reaching out to Bone Harvest," Alysaundra called to him. "Should I . . . ?"

Zhan ran on, frozen grass crunching under his boots where it had not already been trodden down by the army of dead reptiles traveling farther ahead of him. A day ahead of him now? Two days if the corpse of Coal kept ranging ahead of the main group. Zhan could not know yet, but that felt right based on the strength of the bone metal he felt drawing him on. He kept running for two candlemarks before answering, impressed with Alysaundra for not rushing him or offering nervous prompts as if he might have forgotten or not heard.

Of the twelve Bone Finders who ran with him, Alysaundra was his favorite and, though he possessed no true offspring and considered all Ossuarians to be his children after a fashion, Zhan considered her his replacement should he for some unknown reason depart Barrone. Kholster's obsession with a Freeborn successor made sense, after a fashion, for the Aernese Army, but the Ossuary and its members could never be free in the same way.

"Should you?" he echoed.

"Which is a 'no,'" Alysaundra said with a smirk. "She's really gotten under your armor, hasn't she?"

"No Aern can get under my armor." At the words, Zhan felt the lie in them, the memory of clashing warpicks with Kholster after the Sundering. The memory burned, not because Kholster had bested him, but—

"Has she requested information from you? First of One Hundred to Last?" Alysaundra asked.

"She called my name and asked me the answer to a question she does not need answered." Zhan felt the tug of the piece of Glayne's bone metal change direction slightly and altered course to follow. "None of this concerns the Ossuarians or me personally."

"I see."

"You disapprove?" Zhan tried to shake off the memory of Kholster's hand in his as the First of One Hundred helped the Last of One Hundred up from the ground where he'd lain in a pool of anemic orange-colored blood. The lasting injury came from the words, not the wound.

"Not my place to disagree with the Ossuarian," Alysaundra said.

A verbal barb. Letting Keeper take control of his forward momentum, Zhan played back the last few days in his mind, examining his thoughts, actions, and assumptions. While not strictly in error at any point, his behavior stood out as a non-inconsequential contributor to the divide he felt growing between the army and the Ossuary.

Do not make me question the loyalty of the Ossuary again, Zhan. Kholster's centuries-old words burned like faint embers under the ash, unfelt for so long until the right sort of wind spurred them to a bright orange heat that could start the world ablaze.

You are leaving the bones behind! Zhan's heart pounded. *My skin behind! My—*

In exchange for our unborn, Kholster had said.

Your unborn, Zhan had said in return. *Not mine!*

I am truly sorry, Kholster had said, and those words had meant nothing, but the look in Kholster's eyes, the real hurt, sorrow, and regret, the lines around those ageless eyes . . . They had kept the peace.

Do not ask me to abandon bones again, Zhan had said, the whole conversation happening in their minds, unheard by any other Aern as far as Zhan knew.

You have my oath on it, Kholster had said. And that too had softened the blow, but now, even though the bones had been reclaimed, Kholster had used them to reinforce Fort Sunder. Was it glorious? Yes. As a god, could Kholster do whatever he wanted? Zhan supposed that was how the gods worked, but the bone metal belonged in the Ossuary. Each fragment should have been entrusted to him, to his . . . keeping.

Zhan, the reasoning part of him, could even agree with the benefits of plating Fort Sunder with the bone-steel at hand, but it was not what he would have done were the decision his. It forced Zhan's hand; an Ossuarian presence would now always be required north of Castleguard. On the other track, so what, then? The army had always decided where to go and what to do without consulting the Ossuarians, but having Kholster do so and having this young—

Is it her youth that galls me so? Do I have a preferred candidate? Do I, or some part of me, believe I would be better suited to lead the army? Zhan puzzled over the thought.

No, that wasn't it. Structural compatibility did not ensure functional compatibility. Could he send an All Know? Only to Bone Finders. Could this be circumvented with warsuits? Not perfectly. Could the army adapt? Certainly. Aern were Aern, but should they need to adapt?

No. Not unless they became deprived of a First of One Hundred and, for some reason, the First failed to pass on her unique properties to a successor . . . an eventuality Zhan would go through any lengths, even the destruction of himself and every last Ossuarian, to prevent. So what was the problem? Why allow himself to drive a rift between Last and First? Was it truly about the bones? Or was it deeper than that?

Sir, Keeper interrupted. **The kholster of the Aernese Army would like to speak to the Ossuarian.**

Zhan suppressed the instinctive anger he felt, while trying his best to examine it. Was it Rae'en personally? Her lack of experience? Or could her lack of formality, her instinct to ignore the appropriate protocols, be the culprit that wrought such turmoil within him?

Another possibility stung him with its pettiness: Was it merely that she was Kholster's daughter? Could his anger at the First have blossomed on her back much as had her father's scars?

Did she phrase it that way, Zhan asked, *or have you politely reframed the request?*

I asked as she asked, Keeper replied, then, with a hint of pleasure: **Snow, sir.**

Running on, immune to the unfelt chill he knew must be present, Zhan opened his eyes, taking control back from his warsuit. What was so special about snow? And then Zhan understood, if not himself, then his warsuit; he felt the frozen water through his armor's senses and tried to open himself to Keeper's emotion. It was the first snow Keeper had touched or seen with his own eyes in centuries. His anger subsided.

It was nice, the twelve of them running together, a light snow slowly changing the world beneath their feet to a blanket of white. Others were coming; he could feel their bone metal tugging against his own. He'd summoned them. He was going after the bones, his Ossuary with him. What could be wrong? What was worth his wrath?

Sir? Keeper prompted.

I— Zhan took a deep breath, held it, let it out slowly. Very well. *Please connect us.*

Do we have a problem, Zhan? Rae'en asked.

My command's whereabouts are mine to determine, First of One Hundred. Zhan kept a polite tone to his thoughts. *If the kholster of the Aernese Army objects to—*

What are you going on about? Kholster Rae'en's thoughts felt genuinely puzzled. Which made things worse. How could she fail to understand that the Ossuary—

Is this about my Overwatches using the information from your warsuits? Keeper could have just said something if he would prefer we make only specific requests, but Bloodmane and Eyes of Vengeance told Kazan the Ossuary did not track what information the warsuits bonded to their Ossuarians shared as long as the Aernese Army shared their data as well. Which is all fair hunting to me. Aern help Aern. Or am I not tracking down the right trail?

Zhan released conscious control over his own movements again, Keeper seamlessly assuming the reins of locomotion.

You are not contacting me to ask why I have withdrawn all of my Aern from Fort Sunder? Zhan thought. *Why I am not headed to Fort Sunder?*

Kazan's guess was that you wanted reinforcements to go after some of Glayne's bone metal. Glayne says Coal dropped a portion of one of his soul-bonded knives into his chest, kholster Rae'en sent. *I thought grabbing more Armored to fight a dragon and its accompanying army of reptiles who won't stay dead was a prudent move. If I may be completely open with you, I have been wondering what the protocol is to offer you reinforcements from my kholstering. Apparently asking is without precedent, but I am not my father . . . and since you already seemed to have greens down your gob about something, I didn't want to risk the possibility you'd feel that I was questioning your ability to kholster.*

Kholster Rae'en. Zhan smiled. It did not happen often, and he was pleased no one could see it. *Why exactly have you contacted me?*

Because we know where the army of the dead you're chasing is headed and we know why . . . I thought we ought to make sure you knew, Rae'en thought.

And why tell me directly?

Why would I not tell you directly? Rae'en asked. *You kholster the Ossuary and I kholster the army. You're heading with all of your Armored into a fight that is bigger than you could have known. What am I supposed to do, just keep it to myself and hope you figure it out? Act like I'm too important to speak to you and have Kazan do it? From a structural point of view, we're equals. Right?*

Thank you for the information, kholster Rae'en, Zhan thought, *and for the offer of assistance. I do not require it at this time, but should the situation change, it is nice to know that I can rely upon your aid.*

So we're all in alignment again? Rae'en asked.

"I believe we are," Zhan whispered, before transmitting a terse positive acknowledgement. "I believe we are."

CHAPTER 14

THE DECISION
TO TAKE ROOT

Kholburran sat outside the temple of healing, listening to the sounds of injured warriors and the chants of the healers. The canopy of the Twin Root Trees Hashan and Warrune quivered, leaves shaken free falling to the forest floor still green and unblemished. Talk of the warfront filled the air, occupying the thoughts of even the least warlike. The consensus was that the Root Guard and their Zaur allies were winning, but the advance was slowing rather than stopping.

Only a handful of the Sri'Zaur Flamefangs had fallen and risen as enemies of life, but in every case they had started fires that did more damage and required more forces to fight than were readily available. Fire had come close enough to Moss Arbor and Gravid's Vale that the Root Trees had been within sight of the flames.

War had come to the Parliament of Ages with a ferocity it had not known since the Sundering. When he had been a sproutling, he would have been sure that the Aern would come to save them, yet the Aern were digging in at Fort Sunder and had offered no aid. The contingent of reptiles that had attacked and destroyed Tranduvallu as a sign of the Sri'Zauran empire's usefulness as allies, with their Zaurruk and fire-spewing Flamefangs that had only days ago loomed as a threat and a promise as sure and unmistakable as Kholster's warpick suspended above an Eldrennai's throat, were now the most useful allies the Root Guard and the Vael Defense Forces had to repel the army of the dead.

Any moment now Kholburran expected the Root Guard to come and escort him (forcefully if required) south.

I should be out there fighting, Kholburran thought. His heartwood warpick could cleave skulls just as easily as any girl-type person's heartbow.

As a royal boy-type person, however, he was doomed to be viewed as nothing more than a future home for other Vael: a home, a city, providing the raw material for heartbows and growing pretty furniture and decorations within himself. Unable to move or speak of his own accord . . . A glorified germinator to pollinate whichever of the Root Guard or other Vael were deemed worthy to—

Will I even notice? He scratched thoughtlessly at the fang-like thorns protruding from the edges of his upper and lower dental ridges. Catching himself, he stilled the nervous movement, running his fingers through his red head petals instead, scratching the bark beneath. He forced himself to stop that, too.

No one knew exactly how sentient Root Trees were after they grew beyond a certain size. Queen Kari seemed to be able to commune with them in some unclear spiritual-beyond-a-boy-type-person's-understanding sort of way, but that was a less than fabtacular mental path down which to hunt. She was a Root Wife and not all Root Trees had one. Kholburran thought of Uncle Tranduvallu's last moments—burning, screaming in a way only other plants could sense, no Root Wife to calm him or ease his pain . . . Utterly alone as his former inhabitants fled for their lives.

Plucking out a head petal, Kholburran crushed it in his fist.

Whether the Root Guard intended to try and make him Take Root earlier than intended haunted his thoughts, too. Images of running away rose in his mind. South to Castleguard and the bridge continent beyond, maybe all the way to the caves the Aern called home, where surely some Lady Aern would let him learn to fight from her, learn all the techniques Arri and the others, even Malli, had not seen fit to . . .

You thought her name, he berated himself, glaring at the temple with a look he was certain must be so blatantly lovelorn that if a girl-type person were to spot him, she would surely laugh at such a foolish display of boy-like hyper-emotionality. *Malli is healing well. She'll mend whether you're here or not.*

Thanks to Tsan, the Sri'Zauran general who'd come to them to negotiate a possible truce, they'd been able to produce the blue flower needed to treat the opportunistic fungus that had begun attacking Malli's air bladders. But the healers had missed that problem. What else might they miss?

"Rot and ruin!" he cursed, letting the mangled head petal fall to the ground.

"How long until they let you back in?"

Kholburran jumped at the stern yet understanding voice of the girl-type person who'd caught him unawares.

"It's just me, Snapdragon." Arri patted him on the head with the back of her diminutive right hand, which grew green and spindly from the full-sized stump of her right arm where she'd been forced to hack it off at the fall of Tranduvallu. This far into winter, her head petals had all fallen, her outer bark grown more thick and rough, but it was good to know that her body had decided to regrow the limb immediately. Sometimes an injury endured that close to the seasonal shift from bloom and growth to sleep and endurance would remain unchanged all winter, waiting for the rebirth of the world that came with spring.

"They only just sent me out again," Kholburran growled. "I was helping with the injured, but they said I was underfoot."

"Want me to go check on her for you?" Arri's voice was unusually gentle, despite the way she shook her head at what Kholburran assumed was her bemused disapproval of his . . . problem.

"That would be . . . kind of you." He studied her pupil-less black eyes and tried to imagine what she might be thinking. She wore her Root Guard armor, so she was not off duty, but there was a softness or a sadness that seemed to carry with her scent . . .

"Want to come in with me?" she offered, letting the back of her strong left hand rest lightly against his other shoulder.

"Really?" He felt the sap rushing to his cheeks as he smiled. His smile faded when he noticed the other Root Guards, each positioned casually distant but close enough to pounce.

If I run they'll chase me. They're really going to take me south, aren't they?

Arri nodded as if in answer to his unspoken question when he looked back at her.

"Am I saying goodbye?" Kholburran asked.

"I hope you're only explaining why she won't be seeing you for a few days, Snapdragon," Arri said. "You know how I feel about the idea of losing Malli from the Guard if she agrees to become your Root Wife, but that doesn't mean I don't want it to work out between you two all the same. Do you understand?"

Kholburran bit back an angry retort and forced himself to nod.

"I understand," he said, after he was certain he could control the tremor in his voice. "But I won't say goodbye."

Moving with purposeful restraint, Kholburran rose to his feet. Not wanting to injure Arri's sprouting hand and forearm, he delicately extricated himself from her grasp, diminutive arm first, then the hale and hearty arm. If they really were here to force him south, there was only one way he could see to forestall the inevitable. Kholburran doubted they would resort to true force, but he knew at least one way they could make an unwilling prince Take Root.

Cuttings. The word coursed like herbicide through his brain.

Malli would have never let them do it. Under normal circumstances, he doubted his mother, Queen Kari, would allow it either, but he would be far to the south and with a war on in the north. If reports were to be believed, if even Hashan and Warrune were in danger . . . He studied Arri's eyes. She wouldn't want to do it, but he could almost see the script behind her eyes, the same sort of words that were said by girl-type people to justify doing whatever they felt necessary to "protect" a future Root Tree.

When it comes down to root and earth, that is all a prince is to them: a Root Tree, more useful for a trick of gender than as an actual person.

"Gather my Root Guard," he ordered, his voice breaking on the first word but stabilizing at and strengthening on the last two words.

"We're most of us here, Snapdragon," Faulina said. She stepped forward from her position across the way from him.

"For my procession, Faulina." But his eyes met Arri's rather than Faulina's. "As Tranduvallu, Hashan, and Warrune, and other princes have before me, I feel that it is time for me to seek a proper planting."

All of them gasped save Arri. Kholburran struggled to puzzle out the meaning of her expression. She looked . . . proud? Had she arranged all of this to deliberately prod him into Taking Root, or was she merely impressed that he had done it? Had she entrapped him or been trying to help him see what was coming, to offer him a chance to take what control he could of his future, limited though it might be? Too many possibilities and none of them mattered now.

"What of Malli?" Arri asked. "How do you think she will track all of this?"

Nearby stretches of bioluminescent moss, which festooned the underside of many of Hashan and Warrune's upper branches and natural bridges, brightened. Pale green light cast an even, steady glow, replaced swiftly by the unsteady amber illumination of Warrune.

Father's watching me, Kholburran thought.

When he'd been younger, just a sproutling, he'd thought all of the lights were amber. They'd followed him everywhere he went within the Twin Trees until one evening when the green light of Hashan had appeared instead.

"Why is the light green, Mom?" he'd asked Queen Kari.

"That's your uncle Hashan's light," she'd said, a look on her face and a sound in her voice that he'd never before heard. "Your father is tired today, Kholburran."

But if Warrune was tired or world weary on this day, Kholburran could not sense it in the glow that indicated his attention; it burned brighter than Kholburran had witnessed in years, except for when the Root Tree communed with Kari. What did it mean? Was Warrune giving him his support or concerned to see one of his sproutlings condemning himself to the fate that had befallen Warrune? Regardless of the intent, Kholburran felt emboldened by the Root Tree's focus.

"Leave word with her that my procession has begun." Kholburran felt the weight of the words, but, having said them, there was no taking them back. "I love her and I want her to be my Root Wife if she will, but my decision is not contingent upon hers. I know you hate it when I mention fairness, Arri, but it wouldn't be fair to saddle her with that responsibility. It was a proposal, not a bribe required to induce me to perform my duty."

"Faulina." Arri's smile broadened, cracking the rough winter bark at the edges of her lips, bits of it flaking away and landing on the breast of her leather armor, where she brushed it off. "Ready the prince's things and alert Queen Kari. We head south—"

"North," Kholburran snapped.

"North?" Faulina asked, but Kholburran did not look at her, still focusing solely on Arri.

"Snapdragon—" Arri began.

"We need a more northern post," Kholburran's voice was almost a growl, his ridge thorns showing clearly, as if he were biting ends of the words. "Tranduvallu has fallen. I have not. So we go north. If my mother would prefer a more southern outpost, then she must grow more sons. If that outpost were to be me, I would plant myself to the far south, past

Castleguard, maybe near Midian or all the way across Bridgeland to the foothills of the mountains the Dwarven-Aernese Collective calls home. I refuse to Take Root in the Parliament of Ages . . . unless, of course, you want another dying Root Tree whose rotting protests must be hidden from the world."

"Snap—" Arri started again.

"It's my decision, Arri!" Kholburran unslung his warpick, bark squeaking against the polished surface of the heartwood as his grip tightened. He couldn't tell if he was more angry, afraid, or anxious . . . all of those feelings played off one another, his air bladders working faster in response. "My choice! You can't make me Take Root wherever you want. You don't have to stay there for centuries. I do! Long after you are all gone, I'll still be stuck there, so I'm sorry if my choice of direction is inconvenient, but my mind is made up and my intentions clear!"

A thin layer of defensive sap had begun to form on his bark when he realized Arri was simply standing there, staring at him. No one was rushing to grab him or—

"Are you done?" Arri asked.

"You won't force me to Take Root wherever you want, Arri."

"Are you done . . . now?" Arri's voice was clearer than right after she'd taken an arrow to the throat, but the subtleties of her full vocal range had been skewed enough that Kholburran had trouble reading non-dynamic tones. But she did not seem angry . . .

"What I was going to say was, 'Snapdragon, you can Take Root wherever you choose, but I hope you will listen to our suggestions and heed our advice.'"

"And if I don't?"

"Such is your right," Arri said, "and I will protect your right to choose no matter how foolish I may personally feel it to be."

"Really?"

Without answering, Arri swept his feet out from under him, jerking the warpick from his grasp with one smooth motion of her right arm. She brought it up and over in an arc, stopping it point first above his chest, before rotating the head so that the flat cheek of the warpick's head lay against him, and she let it fall with disdain.

"Really. And don't you ever brandish your weapon at me again, little prince." Still leaning over him, she cut her eyes toward Faulina. "Was there something you did not understand about your orders?"

"No, ma'am," Faulina swallowed hard, eyes not on her commander but locked like Kholburran's upon the steadily growing incandescence of Warrune's light. It grew in intensity until even Arri was forced to look up at the now smoldering moss.

"Arri . . ." Faulina started, but as she did the moss flared star-like, the scent of burning leaves filling the air as a mote of light leapt from the dead moss and scorched wood to the heartbow on Arri's back.

"Dad, no!" Kholburran shouted, unsure of how he knew what was going to happen, but clear none the less that Warrune was intent upon and capable of expressing his displeasure with the Root Guard in a far more serious manner than burned moss and a light show.

"Wha—" Arri clutched at her throat in surprise, as her heartbow wrapped around her neck and shoulders, a writhing snake of dark wood.

Faulina dropped to her knees, eyes cast down, as did the other Root Guards, save Arri, who fell against the wall, only to feel its bark crimp in around her shoulder, holding her in place.

"ROOT." A voice made of the rustling of leaves and the twist and crack of wood vibrated in their ears from the bark and wood rather than the forest air. "GUARD. PROTECT. ASSIST. SERVE. FOR ALWAYS, ARRI."

"Dad, stop!"

"HE CHOOSE. HE SURRENDER. AND CUTTING STILL IN YOUR HEAD?!" The voice grew louder, drowning out Arri's curses as her diminutive right arm vanished into the living wood of the Root Tree's wall. "STILL?! TAKE THIS GRAFT THEN. FEEL WARRUNE."

Blackening around her shoulder, the wall smoked and hissed, with the pop of green wood burning. Struggling against the Root Tree's grasp, Arri reached toward her sisters of the Root Guard, but even Faulina refused to look at her.

"Father." Kholburran hesitated, mind a whirl of ideas and emotions, all in conflict with each other. The effort this interaction was costing his father felt immense, but that it could happen at all meant there was more to Taking Root than he knew. Tranduvallu's screams filled his mind as he recalled his uncle's fall. There was a way to remain in communication with his fellow Vael, but what Warrune was doing made his sap run dry. It was wrong. "She's rough around the edges, but she has always protected me. Arri put her life at risk for mine, and she's my Root Guard now, Dad."

"Mine, Dad." He reached out, taking Arri by her free shoulder in a true grasp, fingers closing on her, gripping her, claiming her if but for the moment. "Give her back to me. Please."

"FAVORITE BOY." Warrune's voice sounded dimmer, as if his rage, so quickly roused could no longer be sustained in the face of Kholburran's compassion. "TAKE HER, BUT I WATCH. ALWAYS I WATCH."

Kholburran pulled her free of the wall, each inch hard won and where the stump of her right arm had grown green and small it came away fully formed, the color of lacquered heartwood, shot through with a knot-like whorl of moss at her forearm, which shined a pale amber at its center. Arri grunted, collapsing against Kholburran briefly, before pulling her heartbow from her neck, another matching whorl complete with gleaming amber light revealed in its wake.

Behind her, the wall slumped and collapsed, glowing embers and ash falling away from its center.

All eyes went to Arri.

Flexing the fingers of her new right hand, she turned it from side to side. Her left hand found the change at her throat, studying it with the tips of her fingers. On the ground nearby, her bow twitched back into its more usual shape and she scooped it up.

"Arri?" Kholburran offered.

"I apologize, my prince." Arri dropped to her knees. "While I do not believe that I ever would have given in to the temptation, I admit that I harbored thoughts of forcing you to Take Root where it most suited. Judge me as you will."

"Will you still take me where I want to go and protect me on the journey and when I Take Root?" Kholburran asked.

"It would honor me more than I deserve to do so." Arri looked up at him, eyes glistening with sap.

"Fabtacular then." Kholburran used one of Yavi's favorite exclamations deliberately. He held out his hand to her, thinking at first to offer it in the way of most Vael, allowing forearm to rest on forearm, altering it at the last second to the kind of grasp humans or Aern might use. She could spurn it, which might embarrass him, but he hoped she would see it for what it was: a gesture of trust . . . and if Warrune saw it that way, too, then maybe his father would understand a little better, as well, and . . .

"From this day," Arri said as she took his grip and rose, "I am your Root Guard, Kholburran. I pledge myself to the service of the new Root Tree you will become until the day the Harvester takes my spirit, Gromma reclaims my body, and Xalistan sees fit that I hunt no more."

"And I," said Faulina, kneeling. The others followed her example.

"Good." Arri nodded. "Then I'm glad you stayed. Make sure you explain the possible duration of Prince Kholburran's sojourn, will you? See if Queen Kari wants to go with a larger or smaller escort given the circumstances."

"Arri?"

The Root Guard turned to face him, Faulina darting off to carry out her captain's orders.

"Thank you."

I'm really doing this. He took one more look toward the temple where Malli lay healing and wished she could go with him. Whenever he'd thought of this moment, both she and Yavi had come with him, one last joyous romp through the Parliament of Ages with the Vael he loved and his favorite sibling. Malli would still be healing long after he had Taken Root and, unless she chose to become his Root Wife, they would never speak again. And Yavi . . . who knew where she was? Off in the depths of some reptilian tunnel making deals and securing a formal alliance with the Zaur. *At least she's safe,* he thought, *and well out of harm's way. An Eldrennai prince at her side and the whole of the Sri'Zauran army to keep her out of trouble.*

CHAPTER 15
LOOKING FOR TROUBLE

Cold clear mountain air pushed heavy snow-bearing clouds north across the jagged ridge of the Sri'Zauran Mountains into the human settlements. Light from the first risen sun crept into the shadow of the stone overhang occupied by two sentient beings for the first time in more than a century. Yavi stirred when the burnished edge of day's inevitable march found her outstretched arm. Her bark yearned for more heat, but that did not stop her outer layer from soaking up as much of the energy-abundant light as it could. Rising with a smile, she stepped out into the snow, letting her greedy yellow head petals spread as freely as they would to maximize the exposure.

She could almost imagine that she wasn't fleeing for her life or chasing after something so dangerous she ought to be running the other way.

Exactly which of those two she was doing was up for debate. Yavi liked to think it was a bit of both.

An oppressive weight, the presence of the risen dead and the solitary mad thing that controlled them, loomed ever present, its tendrils streaking the sky when Yavi opened her senses to the spiritual realm. Dark streaks of writhing energy cut smoke trails in the sky visible only to those with the gift to see them. Less thick here than they had been farther east, they still showed the advance of Uled's monstrous will.

Yavi hoped she and the prince had veered far enough from the trail to avoid any direct encounters until after breakfast. She tried to force thoughts of Uled and his risen dead out of her mind by focusing on the natural spirits within the mountainside around her, the diminished singular essence of the small rocks (noting in particular those most likely to want to be thrown), and the great spirit of the mountain, so large it could scarcely be fully comprehended, much less called upon, and the still spirits of living plants lying dormant or growing determinedly despite winter's approach.

But someone has to find out what he is planning. She shivered at the thought and the cold equally. *And we're the only ones who made it out of there alive as far as I can tell.*

151

The chill bit more fiercely beyond the range of Prince Dolvek's elemental flames. If she squinted, she could see the magic in them, though the beads of fire were themselves such a light blue they were near invisible to the naked eye. They provided enough warmth to let the two survivors of the dead thing's formation (birth?) stay comfortable, but cast a dim enough light to make it difficult for them to be spotted in the night.

How he could maintain a series of spells in his sleep, Yavi did not understand. She smiled back at his sleeping form. He had come a long way from the ignorant chauvinistic royal annoyance he had been when they first met. It was enough to make her wonder if, despite Kholster's sarcasm about warrior's blood when he had helped Yavi concoct an antidote against Zaur venom to save the prince, that maybe the Aern's blood *had* been responsible for a portion of the transformation Dolvek had undergone.

The Eldrennai prince lay with his back against the stone, still clad in his armor—who other than the Aern actually did such things?—with the light of the newly risen suns casting him in a warm glow only dawn could produce. She sniffed the air and started.

Is that smell me?

She sniffed her tunic and blanched.

Definitely me.

An aroma of roses permeated the doeskin leathers she had been wearing for the past several days. If she had known she was going to be fleeing for her life from some undreamt horror, she would have made sure to keep a change of clothes stored more securely about her person. One to wear and one to wash, anything more is wasteful dross, as the Root Guard said.

Maybe the prince could magic them clean? Yavi snorted at the idea of taking off her clothes and asking the prince to clean them for her with his elemental powers. His short, barely pointed ears twitched at the sound, a lock of raven-black hair falling across his face as he shifted.

Yavi ran her silvery bark-covered fingers across her own much longer, more than hand-length ears and shook her head, running her tongue along her unpruned dental ridges. What did it feel like to have a mouth full of teeth, like Eldrennai or humans or even the Aern? To have skin that was soft and supple in all seasons?

Dolvek had changed so much from the arrogant idiot she'd met before the Grand Conjunction. His features had been softened by the breaking down of so many years of self-righteous superiority, but instead of becoming bitter he had been gently worn down, not broken but honed.

His spirit had smoothed around the edges, its colors more subtle and its aura more open. She felt sadness there blended with resolve and a spark of hope Yavi yearned to help grow. Gathering her heartbow, Yavi turned her senses elsewhere, seeking the spirits of animals hiding in burrows beneath the snow or slinking along the rock searching for food.

By the time the prince was awake, she'd caught a fat little round-bodied rodent she found perched on a rock making high-pitched calls to other of its more discreet kin and a pair of medium sized birds that reminded her of grouse she'd seen once when visiting the more south-eastern edge of the Parliament of Ages, closer to Castleguard. Only these had whiter feathers.

"Breakfast?" she asked.

"Yes, please." Dolvek rubbed his eyes. As he did, nearby snow melted, water flowing around Dolvek and passing through the flames until it was warm and steam-chased, then flowing over and around his clothes, skin, and hair, only to be dried away in moments by heated air.

He blinked twice when she handed him one of the two grouse she'd cooked, watching her carefully before beginning to eat his own meal in the same fashion she did.

They were halfway through breakfast before Yavi realized Dolvek had never eaten meat before and hadn't known exactly how to approach the task without studying her.

"Blast," Yavi cursed. "You don't eat meat. Why didn't you say anything?"

Dolvek's laugh tickled her ears, bright and heartfelt, made all the more attractive by a sigh that sounded to her ears like resigned amusement rather than impatience or exasperation.

"I assure you, Princess, I have already mewled and whined far beyond the allotment most are granted for their entire lives. I'm attempting to let some of the other societal interactions catch up."

"Like what?" Yavi quirked a smile at him, hoping that he had not been brain addled by some hidden head injury. They had plunged straight through who knew how many juns of stone when they'd fled from Uled, and their days of tracking the leader of the dead and the bulk of his army had not been entirely uneventful.

"Gratitude." Dolvek shook his head, his lips drawing a straight severe line. "I should have offered to bathe you and clean your garments before I did so for myself."

"I didn't know you could even do that."

"Jolsit taught it to me when I was with the elves assisting Kholster's warsuits in assaulting the Zaur." He frowned. "Before I deserted my post . . ."

"Fabtacular." Yavi began to strip out of her garments.

"A moment." Dolvek breathed softly. "While I will able to provide a more pleasant experience if I can see what I'm washing, I must admit to a certain degree of . . . preoccupation with your form . . . specifically."

"It would have been hard not to notice." Yavi smiled, exposing her dental ridge. "And well, I am a Vael, so . . ."

He smiled back, she thought, half in shock and half in—, *no sign of a flinch at my unpruned dental ridge. Eyes locked straight with mine.*

"Yes." Dolvek nodded. "I . . . fear that portions of the process may feel restrictive. It's a simple exercise for me to perform the magicks on my own person because I can feel what I am doing more directly. Doing so to another is more complicated. If you like, I can construct a crude bath of sorts and—"

"I trust you." Yavi took his hand and placed it palm down on her arm.

Dolvek's fingers snapped open, an exaggerated non-grasp.

"You won't grab me unless absolutely necessary, right?" Yavi asked.

"Not purposefully, but I can't promise that by accident—"

Yavi hushed him with the tips of her free hand. "And if I want you to let me go, you will. Right?"

"Of course, but—"

"And that's one of the reasons I trust you, Dolvek." She hushed him again. "Don't make a warpick out of a finger bone. Just go ahead and clean. Okay?"

CHAPTER 16

LINES OF COMMUNICATION

They make a cute couple, Vander thought at Kholster.

Couple of what? Kholster thought back.

Vander let the matter of the Eldrennai and the Vael drop. There was only so much baiting the irkanth that was wise, even for the god of knowledge. He rolled his eyes. Only one person could have ever gotten him to even consider being a deity, and he could not decide whether it was good fortune or ill that that single being had been the one who asked.

Surrounded by books in the form of data embedded in tiles of bone-steel, Vander felt he ought to be attired in scholarly elven robes, but could not bring himself to wear the horrible things. If the world was not ready for another deity who preferred jeans, boots, and bone-steel mail, then it would have to learn to live with it or stage a deicide.

He grabbed a tile in an attempt to read farther into the available data about what Uled had done to himself, but it was all useless. His mind was too quiet to study. When there had been multiple Kholsters to coordinate and keep thinking roughly as one, he had been able to distract himself, but the lack of Eyes of Vengeance ached like an arm hacked off to use for bone metal. He could make another warsuit if he wanted; the combined knowledge he had inherited from Aldo made it clear such a thing was well within his capabilities—even a new Life Forge was not beyond him—but one such forge had been enough and no armor could replace Eyes.

You got quiet, Kholster prodded. Vander put the tile he was reading aside and turned more of his attention to the mortal world.

Our ascendancies are wreaking havoc, Kholster. Unfolding beneath the Outwork, Vander watched the news of his own apotheosis continue its spread from Long Speaker to Long Speaker. Information, when he looked for specific points of it, showed in blue, gold, silver, and red. Initial reports were golden, the information's hue altering as it left the source and changed. Falsehoods were a bright silver. Lines of red concealed hard-to-read messages designating the dangerous overlap between his and Kilke's domain, with open discussion and the muddying of fact, fiction, and opinion assuming varying shades of blue. Shades of sapphire meant more accurate data, where obscured or deliberately distorted data shifted into hues of indigo, even mixing with red to make amaranthine strands of opinions believed to be fact.

He wasn't sure about the orange yet. Aldo had obviously not seen the world in the same way Vander did. Withheld truth, perhaps? The mortals (and wasn't it strange to no longer consider himself one of them) reacted badly to the depth of change in the deific hierarchy. Torgrimm's diminished state and Kholster's rise as death had been enough to set off only the most fanatical of the Harvester's worshippers, their tongues wagging and causing the Harvest Knights of Castleguard to hunt Rae'en's Overwatches, but Vander's taking of Aldo's role and the death of Nomi at Wylant's hands had served as a large wedge in the crack, and exactly what the widening fracture would reveal was difficult to predict.

How would they handle the newest upset? Kholster had presumed they would find Torgrimm's resumption of his more-familiar role to be reassuring, creating a palliative effect upon the humans in particular, but Vander believed otherwise, though Vax demonstrated a refreshingly calming aspect as the new god of war.

Well? Kholster asked, as he stomped along the trail to Port Ammond.

Concentrating on Kholster made things easier. Vander slid Kholster's battle map around beneath his gaze without changing what Kholster saw. A small band of Zaur and Sri'Zaur tracked the ancient Aern but seemed content to observe him rather than interfere. There was no telltale link in the flow of data representing news of the Vael-Zaur Alliance and the proposed addition of the Aern to that treaty.

If they had possessed knowledge of it, Vander presumed they would keep a watchful eye on Kholster, offering no interference until the larger matter was settled. Even so, maybe they would be smart and leave Kholster alone.

Strike that. A team of twelve seemed to have gotten up the nerve. As he watched, lines of red began to mass. Interesting.

How are the humans handling things? Kholster asked.

It was at the edge of Vander's mind to point out the approaching enemy, but a flick of Kholster's eyes and a twitch at the edge of his mouth was a sure sign Kholster had spotted them on his own.

You want me to show you? Vander thought. *It looks like you're about to be rather occupied . . .*

They can't do any harm, Kholster thought, *but keep everything contained to one quadrant of perception, will you?*

Of course. Castleguard knights lined the perimeter along Bridgeland border, all traffic having been closed. The Dwarves, seeming content to leave the humans to their dispute, had sealed Bridgeland's western borders in response, withdrawing the Token Hundred within the safety of its gates, but the beginning of strife had spread with the need. Vander provided an aerial view of the bridge as if from the perspective of an arrow hurtling an impossible distance along the center of the bridge from Southgate to Northgate.

Clusters of humans fought each other, Dwarves, and the various Token Hundreds present in-between. Midian itself seemed immune to the battle, the Dwarven presence too concentrated there to allow anything more than minor skirmishes or brief riots that were put down quickly with the deployment of steam-driven Dwarven vehicles and the occasional burst of junfire.

The Guild Cities? Kholster asked.

A handful of rogue Long Speakers got the word out before Sedric and Cassandra could stop them. With the central spire down, the news of the next shift in the pantheon can't make the rounds, but—

How is Vax handling things? Kholster asked. *How is Wylant?*

Good news there, Vander thought back, *of sorts. Some are still fighting, but more and more are gathering around to hear what Vax has to say so—*

Show me.

Vander wanted to argue, to remind Kholster about the nearby Zaur and the fact that Kholster could at least shift into the realm of gods so they could not attack him, but he knew the tone of that "Show me"; it would brook no argument. So Vander showed him and kept a small portion of his attention focused on Kholster's nearby observers.

*

A rare quiet had settled over the Guild Cities by the time Vax finished speaking with his followers. Wylant listened to most of it, but the approach he espoused came as no surprise to her. At their core, Vax's values reflected the shared beliefs of his parents. Killing could happen. Not killing was preferable. Vax's own twist on the myth came across as a desire to have reasons to fight and be true to them: home and hearth, friends and family, right and wrong.

"Not everything," he had said at the last, with thousands surrounding him and vying for a better view, "can be slain with a sword or sharp set of teeth."

The Token Hundred laughed loudly at that. Draekar and his kholstering stood at the outskirts of the crowd, eyeing them suspiciously. Wylant wondered if they should have kept their position on the gate with the Dwarves. She had no intention of correcting them either way, or of doing anything but listening to Vax and watching as he addressed his . . . worshippers?

"Draekar," Vax had called to the kholster, "Aern know more about combat than many beings ever will. Can you think of an enemy one cannot fight with a physical weapon?"

"Well . . ." Draekar rubbed pensively at his bone-steel breastplate, a sign that he had been granted the honor of forging a warsuit only to have the Life Forge destroyed before he could complete it. "Stupidity."

"Stupidity or ignorance?" Vax had asked.

"Either." Draekar shrugged.

"How would you combat ignorance—" Vax turned to a young woman in the crowd, her face covered in sweat and grime, her hands thick and strong, marked with scars from smithing. "—Lori?"

"My mother always said—" Her voice was coarse and small, hesitant at first, picking up confidence at a smile from Vax. "—that you have to beat the stupid out of some people."

Scattered laughter made its way through the crowd. Vax nodded for her to continue.

"But . . . Well, no beating ever put anything useful into my head." She looked down at her hands, smiling at the next burst of laughter. "When I wanted to be a Smith, I found a gal who knew how and I did chores around the forge until she'd showed me all I wanted to know. So . . . Teaching or learning is how I would take care of not knowing what I wanted to know."

Magic lanterns drifted out over the assembly, spots of bright against the dim. In their luminance the colors of blood were muted. Breath of the living took on a touch of their light, lending a subtle glow to all beneath them. Bodies lay in astonishing numbers. Most lay where they had fallen.

"So you would combat a thing with its opposite?" Vax asked.

"I suppose," Lori answered.

"Ignorance with knowledge," Vax said, "Injustice with . . . ?" He looked up. "Anyone?"

"Justice," a few scattered voices proclaimed.

"Yes." He had a teacher's smile as he called out his bravest students. "Roan, Halsey, Brianna, Jim, Howard, and Katerine. Well said."

"And hunger with . . . ?" Vax scanned the crowd, "Everyone?"

"Food," more people answered.

"And darkness with?"

"Light." Most of them had answered that last one. Wylant knew where her son was leading them, but she wondered if the former followers of Dienox saw it, too.

"And fire with?"

"Water!"

"And hate with?"

He had asked the question too soon. Wylant heard a new hesitance in their reply. She would have tried a few more, maybe throw a silly one in there to get them smiling.

"What my son means—" Wylant raised her voice to not quite a full Thunder Speaker's boom, "—is that war is not an end unto itself. All conflict must have a purpose beyond the continuation of more conflict. Conflicts should occur in the service of a desired resolution."

"The aim of war," Vax interrupted her. "I know what it should be. I suspect you deduce my opinion on the matter. What I ask all of you is, do you agree? While you think about it, Mother, if you wouldn't mind?"

Something must be done about these bodies, Vax thought to her. *I want us to take care of them, if that is okay with you.*

"It's fine, Vax. We can consider it a part of their final resolution." Wylant rose into the air and poured forth her flames unto the dead, reducing the bodies to ash with such care and precision that her son's new followers were left staring in awe as the fire and smoke passed harmlessly around without singeing a single hair she did not intend to singe.

*

I don't remember collecting that many souls from— Kholster started.

Not your job any longer, old friend, Vander teased, *and those particular departures have been comparatively recent.*

A moment. Kholster turned to face a sudden charge of the reptiles who had been tracking him. *You speak their language now, don't you?*

I speak everything. Vander laughed. *Even some languages which do not appear to be from this dimension. Apparently, I now know all the languages from the lands to which the dragons departed as well as those here. Why?*

I want to try something different, Kholster thought, *in honor of my son's birth.*

*

<<What do you want?>> Kholster tapped the words with Reaper, his most recent warpick. Heavier and less decorative than either Grudge or Testament, it felt brutish and angry in Kholster's hands, each curve and line betraying the grim focus of its forger. Rae'en had offered Grudge back, but Kholster preferred to leave it in her hands, leaving Hunger for Bloodmane's use: a gift of sorts, his first weapon for his first warsuit, and his most elegant weapon for his daughter.

Headlong charge dissolved into flanking maneuver as the reptilian warriors, six on two legs, six on four, spread their formation. More experienced than the last Zaur he'd fought, the ones he'd encountered on the way to Oot and the Grand Conjunction, these bore Skria and Skreel blades with subtle alterations to better fit the bearer's grip or fighting style: some blades a little more forward of the forearm, others flat against it. The look of Named reptiles, if ever he'd seen any.

"Die, scarback!" a few of them hissed.

<<Stand down, idiots,>> one of them tapped fervently.

One clever one, Kholster thought.

Try this pattern next, Vander sent.

<<How long have you been out of touch with your commanders?>> Kholster tapped and scratched the words in the hardening earth of coming winter, continuing to study their movements for openings, even

as he tried to talk some sense into them. Most wore bands of splint mail on their bellies with chain rings and straps of leather joining them to thicker plates: a modified brigandine on their backs. Thin enough to allow the supple movements required by combatants who shifted readily from bipedal to quadrupedal tactics, the armor had its share of vulnerabilities, especially for the precise fighter.

"No answer?" Kholster asked. "Then let me show you something."

Exploding into motion, Kholster reversed his warpick's head, then hurled Reaper over his shoulder, its tip piercing one quadrupedal Zaur's skull, bursting through its jaw to pin the corpse to the ground.

Well, Vander thought, *that's one way to make your point.*

There are others? Kholster teased.

I am sure you noticed, Vander thought, *but you've thrown your warpick away.*

I intend to cheat. Kholster did as he'd done after he'd first fought Torgrimm, when Kilke's little living shadow had found him. He allowed his body to revert to the steel and bone-steel construction he had been before Uled had awakened him, and once again the remembered shape of that iconic self forced his body to return to its desired uninjured state and rendered him immune to the sharp Skreel blades as they cut at him now.

That is definitely cheating, Vander thought.

I am a god now, Kholster replied, *we're good at it. Which is a big part of the problem.*

That one is still pretty smart, though. Vander indicated the solitary Zaur who had not charged. Black-scaled with amber-colored eyes, it sat still, eyeing the Zaur Kholster had slain. Its left Skreel knife twitched high at the ready to ward off any blow that might come from Kholster, but the rest of its body language told Kholster a different story. Eyes wide, gray forked tongue flicking in an out in the direction of its fallen companion.

<<Stop throwing yourselves at the Aern and look!>> It hissed, gesturing with the Skreel knife in its right paw. <<He's demonstrated his strength, now pay attention.>>

"Coward!" one of the others, its scales mottled brown and gray, shouted at the black-scaled Zaur.

"It would be cowardly not to fight General Bloodmane if he sought to fight us," the black-scaled Zaur snapped. "But this scarback is not interested in killing us. It questions. We are all of equal rank." He aimed his next sentence directly to Kholster. "We decided the one who killed you would rank highest and command the others. By this method, none of us will rank higher than the others."

I recognize this one, Kholster. Vander showed him the memory Teru and Whaar had shared. *It's the one smart enough not to fight two Armored Aern, Bone Finders or not.*

"Kreej," Kholster said, his skin still metal, but moving as skin. "You returned the ring I gave my daughter. I know you."

"Coward!" The brown-and-gray Zaur hissed again, then choked as Kholster punched it in the throat.

"It is not cowardice to listen to the demands of the strong when your orders do not disallow it," Kreej snorted. "We have no orders; the echo tubes are silent and the ground does not quiver with the secret languages of tail or tongue. His Secret Purpose is obscure for now."

That is, without error, the most reasonable Zaur I've ever heard of, much less met, Kholster thought.

I wonder if he knows that you're—, Vander thought.

"Kholster Bloodmane." Kreej bowed so low, his belly touched the brittle grass. "First of the scarbacks, we are no match for you, but we will fight and die if we must. No Zaur fears a good death, to fall to a superior foe, especially in service to His Secret Purpose—"

Kholster turned, still listening, and strode to the writhing reptile he'd slain, seizing Reaper's haft. He waited for the death throes to cease, then, stepping on the Zaur's neck with one boot to hold it in place, he jerked the head of his warpick free, trailing a spray of blood, which still hung in the air when he rammed the warpick with a crunch down on the thing's pelvis, splaying its hind legs wide, its hips dislocated.

"I perceive you are trying to make us understand something." Kreej did not flinch at the sight of Kholster kneeling to grasp the splayed Zaur by both forearms, letting his warpick fall to the side. "But I am unsure what you—" Kholster tore the right arm free and threw it to the south. He hurled the left arm after it when he'd wrenched it free as well.

"Watch." Taking the extra time needed to shatter the bones in the dead Zaur's legs above the knee, Kholster stepped back, grabbing up his warpick as he moved.

"I have no interest in standing here while a scarback mutilates our fallen in front of me," one of the other Zaur growled.

"Just keep watching." Kholster eyed the Zaur who had spoken, sizing him up and finding him unimpressive in the half glance before their eyes met.

They are getting slower to rise, Kholster thought at Vander. *Maybe—*

It died, Vander thought.

Am I out of—

You aren't out of range, Vander cut him off. *I can sense only the rough edges of Uled's influence because much of its effects lies within Kilke's realm, but its hold is weakening over the newly dead. That one appears to have stayed dead because you killed it.*

So reuniting birth and death did not stop them, Kholster thought, *but it does appear to have weakened the new ones.*

You could always go kill them all yourself, Vander teased.

Don't tempt me.

"Do you need another Zaur to demonstrate upon?" Kreej asked. "I sense this display did not convey what you wished. May I suggest—" He indicated the mottled Zaur who had been so vocal. "—Leng."

Kholster slowed his breath but did not stop it and halt the flow of time.

Are they all rising more slowly now? He wanted Vander's input on this one, not Harvester's.

It was a secret, but easily checked, Vander thought back. *It is a universal change. As far as I can see, each returns a few heartbeats more slowly than the last.*

"I wonder," he muttered. Who could confirm whether this was spiraling down to zero or—? Vander would know unless it was a secret, which so much of it clearly was, so who, other than Kilke, could tell him whether all of the dead were walking or rotting?

Rot.

Gromma's less-pleasant aspect as the goddess of growth and decay. She would know if no other deity did, but did he really want to seek her out?

Where is Gromma, now?

Everywhere anything is rotting, in theory. Vander's concentration bled across their link. *The bulk of her attention, however, her—*deific locus *is* *apparently the correct word for the concentration of deity's attention in a specific area without the actual creation of a physical avatar—is at Port Ammond.*

Is that what this body is? Kholster frowned down at his hands, gripping his warpick firmly. *An avatar?*

No, Vander thought. *You resumed the habitation of your physical form, having only temporarily surrendered it.*

But I am still a god, yes? Kholster's eyes narrowed to slits, his gaze shifting up along the length of the warpick to lock with Kreej's slit-pupiled stare.

You are become both, Aern and god, Vander thought back. *Mortal to the extent you ever were, yet divine. Dead, but returned to life. A first. Even Nomi, when she stole Dienox's flaming hair did not die; she ascended directly without passing into Torgrimm's hands.*

First again, eh? Kholster smiled, baring his upper and lower doubled canines in a way he felt certain the reptile would misinterpret as threatening. "I have to go. Other matters require my attention more urgently than you."

Where is Kilke? Kholster asked.

Vander's surprise hit Kholster in advance of the images filling the left half of his field of vision. One showed a two-headed deity observing Yavi and Dolvek from the shadows. The other showed a disembodied Kilke head in the clutches of a . . .

Is that dragon headed for Fort Sunder?

She certainly seems to be, Vander thought. *If you want, I could warn them.*

Kholster's gorge rose, chest pounding, and he resisted the urge to stop time. Given enough of it, he felt certain he could talk himself into ignoring what was right and going to her aid. *Rae'en can handle a dragon.*

Vander tried to cover his doubt, but the edges of it hit Kholster hard.

Kholster, even you never—

Can you see my daughter's back from here? Kholster asked, *even through her armor?*

Yes, but—

Whose scars are on it? Kholster cut Vander off before he could tempt him into doing what he wanted, as Rae'en's father, to do more than anything: to charge back to Fort Sunder and wipe away the army approaching her kingdom like so much blood from his warpick at the end of a battle.

But as the Aern who had kholstered her all of her life, he knew he could not do it. It was either her world or his, and he'd already done things his way. Her turn now.

Kreej and the other Zaur still stared at him expectantly.

"When you kill Leng," Kholster told the most rational Zaur he'd ever met, "he will rise again as a thing both dead and active." The words lingered in the air between them, the gaze of the young Zaur shifting from Kholster to the lifeless ruin that had recently been its comrade. "Precautions would be an excellent idea."

Leng leapt at Kreej, the sun on his scales like the dark water over which many Aern had sailed in ships of both Dwarven and Aern construction. Eyebrow raised at the alacrity possessed by Kreej, Kholster knew immediately who the victor would be. Stronger, but less skilled, Leng exuded overconfidence. Kreej's stance betrayed nothing of emotion, a simple approach to the world Kholster had seen kholster Malmung teach many Elevens.

Whether or not they knew it, it was one of the reasons so many Aern found Glayne disconcerting to be around. Kholster fought with intelligence and skill, but his emotions lay atop his armor, plain for all to see. Neither method was by its nature superior to the other, but the emotional fighter always had to temper that emotion with skill to compensate for the cold, hard calculus of the more restrained style.

He's not bad, Vander thought.

Not a coward, Kholster agreed, *merely unwilling to take up a losing fight if he has no need to do so.*

Understanding dawned too slowly in Lieutenant Leng, and he lay with Kreej at his back, a Skreel blade severing the nerves at the point where spine became tail, his forearms pinioned at his back, and Kreej's forepaw gripping his neck to keep it from biting.

"You give me a secret, then?" Kreej had not even begun breathing hard.

"So it would seem," Kholster answered. "Be careful with it. The risen dead are very difficult to stop. I have other things which require my attentions."

"Do you know where General Tsan may be found?" Kreej asked. "Does the General live?"

Does she? Kholster asked.

Remember that dragon you saw? Vander thought, indicating the direction.

"Yes," Kholster said. "Tsan is that way, and *she* is now the leader of your people."

"Thank you." Kreej prostrated himself. "May we depart in peace?"

"You may."

Well, Vander's thoughts filled with mirth, *I think they've decided who is in charge now.* He watched Kholster head for Port Ammond for a little while before turning his gaze in three directions at once.

CHAPTER 17

SCALES IN THE GAME

In a great mass of bodies, the Zaur and Sri'Zaur lay huddled to preserve warmth. Tsan found repugnant their superficial resemblance to lesser evolved serpents gathered together as if in some perverse open air hibernaculum, no matter how necessary it was, with the scarcity of prey outside of their tunnels, to let their metabolisms slow while they rested briefly. Crouched at the center of her assembled kingdom, with the bodies of her subjects spread out around her as far as the eye could see, she resisted the urge to scream, focusing her mind on the raw mathematics of her realm's reduced population.

Scarcely a quarter of a million . . .

Others, she was sure, had escaped, fled the risen dead—but they would have headed to the northern side of the Sri'Zauran Mountains, to the lands of the humans. Would there be war when the humans realized the Zaur were on the run? Knowing that answer was a luxury Tsan did not possess.

A little pain slipped through, breaking her concentration. It took a supreme effort of will not to snatch up a nearby Zaur and bite down to muffle the discomfort and feed her growing hunger. But no. Such weakness was for warmbloods and scarbacks.

Tsan's muscles burned, pulsing with the changes Kilke's gift was working within her. Jun's fire was a tempestuous itinerant, and where it settled, she felt stronger than she had ever been. The term Tsan'Zaur had been heard among her people. . . . An attempt, she had no doubt, at explaining what their Warleader was becoming. Not Sri'Zaur or Zaur, but a species unique unto herself: Tsan'Zaur.

She would have to think up a better term, but it would serve for now. Her scales, already a bright crimson from her long-term use of Dragon Venom to stave off her gender switch, lit from within like the flickering light of a festival lantern in Na'shie. Tsan blazed with the inner fire, steam, kettle-like hissing from her nostrils in bursts that stank of blood and sizzling fat.

You will make a magnificent dragon, Kilke, his decapitated head still in the magical sack clutched in her foreclaws, whispered in her mind. *With your might, your army, your nation may even have a chance at destroying Uled.*

Poor Kilke, she mused. *He has failed to reassess.*

Destroy Uled? Tsan focused her thoughts at the god, chortling softly at the deity's naiveté. *Why would I march the remnant of my people against the abomination that struck such fear into even your . . . deific heart?*

There it was, a corner of his mind, quickly hidden, but as unmistakable as a foe's last breath: fear. Such a satisfying aroma.

If you don't intend to fight him— Kilke growled, covering panic with anger, his thoughts delightfully distrusting and confused. Had he expected her to trust in him forever? Follow his every word and suggestion once he'd proven himself to be weak?

True, he had once been the god of power, and, yes, he had ignited the metamorphosis that was transforming her into a dragon. His knowledge was vast, his cunning impressive, but he had been unable even to carry himself away from his enemies. No, Kilke needed Tsan'Zaur far more than she needed him. Having escaped the tunnels, her path was clear and his usefulness? No longer a requirement.

You're thinking you don't need me anymore, Kilke's thoughts seethed with shock. *I can—*

Be thrown back into the tunnels? she purred.

I am your god! His protestations were so pitiful to her ears.

Tsan's laughter rang out into the night. Those nearest her opened their eyes but, seeing she had no commands to give, let them nictate shut, shifting to grant their leader additional space to accommodate her increasing size. A sound like wet sailcloth snapping as it caught the breeze broke the night as her wings burst forth from her back, the pain so exquisite it temporarily robbed Tsan of the gift of speech, rolling her eyes up and generating an uncontrollable spate of spasms from her neck to the tip of her tail.

"Jun's fire," she purred to the ram-horned head as she withdrew it carefully from the bag and clutched it to her breast as a warm-blooded child might treat a favored doll, "not Kilke's. You referred to unusual circumstances having arisen that allowed the birth of a new dragon."

A gift which I—

I believe, she continued telepathically, *we both know that you cannot take this gift back.*

Lightning crackled in the god's eyes, and Tsan rolled hers in response.

We are still allies, Lord Kilke, Tsan chided. *I will fight you if I must, but it is a waste of time, if not effort. My people will always venerate you, as will I, but do not expect me to adhere to a previous relational paradigm that has become outdated.*

Allies? Kilke thought. *Outdated?*

Such things are fluid, Tsan purred, *in the absence of binding contracts or treaties, and in the haste to—*

I was saving you from Uled!

You provided invaluable aid and assistance, Kilke, but we both know who saved whom. Tsan shivered as her muzzle shifted and stretched.

You still need me!

Well. Tsan rolled her neck, the scales snapping, popping, and flying away to reveal new scales of an even more luminescent shade as her neck elongated, the muscles tight as cords around wet logs, swelling. *I still want you, but need . . .*

You're going to need to make contact with the Aern.

A painful thought. Mutual avoidance was unpleasant enough, but if the destruction of this new threat and the eradication of Uled's race required an alliance of sorts, it was a price Tsan was willing to pay whether or not Warlord Xastix would have condoned her actions. Xastix was dead, undone by Uled, through magic Tsan did not understand and Kilke had not felt the need to explain. She loathed the available choices, but at the very least the scarbacks were an undeniably strong ally. Their role as the only credible, if unnatural, predatory competitor made them very viable assets to the Sri'Zauran cause. Dietary quandaries notwithstanding, of course.

A light rain broke out, spattering Tsan's scales with brief splashes of water that turned quickly to steam, wreathing her in a layer of personal fog that glowed from within. Her subjects writhed more closely together in response to the cold, a cold she felt, but only in the casual way she might note the color of the grass or the clouds in the sky. In the depths of her, a tear opened somewhere, the pain bright and sharp then dull and at last quiet. She felt the heat of the bodies around her and realized she could take it if she wanted.

She could fill herself up with it. Wanted to do so.

Go ahead, Kilke whispered. *They are only mortals. We can—*

"They are my mortals." Tsan drew herself up to her full height, momentarily astonished by the sheer size she had attained in so short a span. Her metamorphosis had seized the armor of Warlord Rykk, melding it to her breast and her claws, a cool burning blue in contrast to the crimson that covered the rest of her. Sliding the tip of one claw into the base of his neck, Tsan drew the disembodied head of one-headed Kilke up to eye level.

Yes. Yes. I'm threatened beyond all measure. Had I the appropriate plumbing, I'm certain I would soil myself. The god, long presumed dead by the others of his pantheon except perhaps for the two who must have known, smiled, basking in the light of Tsan's scales. His golden skin reflected and amplified that light, his curved horns glowing brighter than the rest of him. *Do you treat all of your advisors with such discourtesy?*

"What changed?" Tsan narrowed her gaze, the focus pinpointing Kilke with twin beams of yellow-white from her eyes.

Nothing changed. Kilke frowned. *You still need to make an alliance with the Aern, but you'll want someone to make the initial contact. You could go, your-self, but if you prefer to avoid your presence starting its own little conflict, I suggest a messenger of lesser stature.*

He thought he was being clever, but Tsan saw through it. There were different sorts of power, and in the absence of raw superiority, Kilke intended to explore other avenues. *Such admirable adaptability. No doubt this facile grasp of shifting dynamics explained the deity's long survival beyond his decapitation.*

Had it been the lack of familiarity with draconic powers that led him to tem-porarily misjudge her, or was it possible that the feeling of superiority she now felt was exactly what he wanted her to feel?

Either seems likely, Kilke replied, *but if it is amenable to your draconic immensity, let's presume my current behavior to be genuine. Shall we?*

I hope—Tsan caught the thoughts of the deity very dimly, as if he had not meant for her to overhear—*my other heads have chosen more tractable pawns.*

*

Silhouetted against the noonday suns, the two flying companions passed over a Holsvenian border town. Dolvek felt it before he saw it, a pull of raw magic as disturbing as the army that had left it in its wake. Small and deserted, a modest temple to Jun the Builder stood at the town's center. A broken statue of Jun lay in pieces not far from the temple, its roughhewn head farthest from the steps, as if it had been pulled off and dragged. Mining equipment littered the streets, broken and bloodied.

Yavi's air spirit deposited her at the entrance to the mine, where grooves had been dug into the dirt by several heavy objects that had been dragged from the depths.

"An old spirit was disturbed here," Yavi called up to him. "I don't know what kind of stone it was, but it dripped so much power, I can see the trail stretching off that way."

She squinted at the furrowed earth and sighed.

"But that's kind of obvious even to you non-spirity types, huh?"

"Yes." Dolvek landed nearby, taking care not to kick up any dust when he did so. "But can you tell me anything more about the spirit? How can you tell it was old?"

"Just a feeling, I guess." Yavi coughed. "Blech! It is enough to make my eyes water. I can only imagine how uncomfortable it must be for the spirit, to be stretched out like this."

Dolvek closed his eyes and cursed, a sinking feeling in the pit of his stomach.

"What do you mean?"

"Part of the spirit is still here." Yavi pointed as if that would make everything clearer, but Dolvek saw nothing unusual. "It flows from the depths, drawn tight along the road. But it doesn't look like the spirit is trying to hold on . . ."

Yavi vanished into the mine entrance, and Dolvek summoned a glowing bead of magic flame to light the way as he ran in after her. Warmer air left Dolvek feeling clammy and wet a few yards inside the tunnel. Rot and reptile stink mixed with a smell that alarmed Dolvek, even though he could not readily place it. Touching the elemental realms of water and air, he lifted off the mine floor protected by a wall of air and ice.

A second-level ward against atmospheric poisons, Dolvek wondered. *What sort of mineral requires that? I don't think I've used one of those since Hasimak took Rivvek and me to the old quarry and . . .*

"Yavi," Dolvek called. "Come back! The rocks are dangerous here!"

Flying after her, Dolvek widened his elemental connection, ice forming on the rocky walls, spreading down the shaft ahead of him. Increasing the brightness of his globe of fire, Dolvek spotted veins of red Dragon's Blood and dagger-sharp formations like a mixture of silver and steel. Yellowish veins of sulfur marked the walls as well. Dragon's Blood alone was a forbidden mineral because of the silvery poison contained within, but together . . .

"Yavi!" Dolvek shouted. "We need to get—"

He found her standing before a pool of quicksilver, coughing and wiping at her eyes.

"Look," Yavi said between coughs, "they cut big chunks out of the walls farther back."

"It's dangerous to even stand on the stone here." Spreading his ward to protect her, too, Dolvek held out his arms. "I can hold you, or if you prefer to climb on my back or maybe an air spirit could . . . ?"

"They won't come down here." Yavi let him lift her in his open arms, her forehead against his shoulder. "Too afraid of the spirits in the stone. They aren't mean spirits, but they pollute what they touch and this one is angry because they deliberately tied part of it here."

Cut into the walls with the smooth precision only Geomancy or Dwarven ingenuity could accomplish, three ring-shaped sections of stone had been excised and, if the marks outside were any indication, hauled away. Exactly three times, Dolvek had been in the presence of objects that would have fit those indentations. He'd been a young man the first time. Hasimak had brought him into the chamber of High Elementals, where thirteen of them stood, one broken by Kholster in the Demon Wars.

The last time had been when General Bloodmane led mixed groups of Eldrennai and warsuits through the Port Gates in an attempt to stop the Zaur. Dolvek had never been as adept at perceiving magic as Rivvek, but he closed his right eye, squinting at the granite with his left.

Residual traces of magic, etched in violet and chased with red, told the prince a story he did not wish to hear or believe. Yavi's spiritual observations were not a component of construction Dolvek recalled, but it also was not an aspect of which the Eldrennai elemancers and artificers of old would have been familiar. Not even Hasimak.

"Dolvek?" Yavi looked up at him. "I trust you and all, but I thought we were flying out of here."

"We are—" A shadow fell over the mine entrance, light passing through the semitranslucent obstruction, casting a red tint over the two of them. "—I hope."

CHAPTER 18
SETTING DOWN ROOTS

Yavi perched on Dolvek's back, feathering their pursuer with arrows from her heartbow as the prince flew deeper into the depths of the abandoned mine. Most arrows glanced off the hide of the thing (golem?), but three arrows stuck firm in its carven face.

Made from a red stone mixed with a crystal of a similar hue, the thing was roughly people-shaped and obviously intended to be a boy-type person. Light from Dolvek's mystic flames reflected imperfectly in its quicksilver eyes. Gaping and filled with broad flat teeth, its mouth opened wide enough to take in her entire head. Hands ending in thick, badger-like claws pulled at the walls of the shaft, taking every effort to hurl itself faster.

"Can't you break through—fly us up and out, like you did back in the warlord's throne room?" Yavi shouted.

"These minerals are poison," Dolvek said. "When I reach out to shift them, I can feel more dangerous veins in the surrounding stone: metals that sicken and kill long after exposure, and seeded with a dark magic I've never encountered. I'll keep trying, but if I get it hot enough to break the golem, the gas it would release would kill me. Possibly you, too."

"Can't you hold it back with Aeromancy?" Yavi asked.

"No, but if I'm careful and focus all my strength into Pyromancy, maybe I *can* do enough damage make it withdraw unbroken."

"But it's made of rock, can't you use Geomancy and—?"

"It has a will now that Uled has awakened it," Dolvek said. "I tried, but it's mixed with magic stronger than mine."

Yavi concentrated her fire on the crystalline veins running through the monster, hoping to crack loose a leg or break an arm. With more arrows and more time, she imagined it would eventually work, but who knew how deep the mine was?

"Think you can make it past if we turn around?" Yavi asked. "This isn't working."

"Y-yes."

A quick thump to the back of the head made Dolvek yelp in surprise.

"You don't get to lie to me!" She thumped him two more times in quick succession. "*We* need to get past. If I wanted to leave you behind, I would have."

"Don't mines usually go down?" Dolvek slowed.

"Dwarves would know, but I don't." Yavi frowned at the creature's accelerated approach. "Why are you stopping?"

"Not much mine left." Dolvek hovered. "I was hoping to find a safe section to bull through, but we're going to have to make it past Uled's construct."

"I thought you couldn't," Yavi said.

"If I overlay my armor with magic crystal and drop all my magic except for Aeromancy," Dolvek said, "I think I can get past if you coax it even a little out of center."

"Are you sure?" Yavi asked.

"We don't have time to debate it." The monster charged on, light from Dolvek's bead of flame lending an eerie leer to its mercurial eyes. "Are you going left or right?"

Plates of crystal descended over Dolvek's hybrid suit of demi-plate. In the dark, a warm, candlelike glow suffused it, casting light even when Dolvek dropped his Pyromantic illumination.

"Left!" Yavi shouted as she rushed the thing, firing a final volley of arrows at the seams in its legs. Slick under her feet, the thin layer of ice Dolvek had been laying down came close to killing her as she spun wildly against the wall of the cave into another patch of ice. Claws the size of a warsuit's lower vambrace struck the wall above her shoulder, spraying her back with shards of red.

That got him out of position, Yavi thought with a smirk.

"Dolvek," she called over her shoulder, "are you—?"

Light so bright it blinded her filled the mineshaft. Even the creature's silhouette was lost in a brilliance that was like staring directly at one of the suns. Water and melting ice rained down from the ceiling. The floor turned to slush.

"Run, Yavi!" Dolvek bellowed. "The gas will be poison!"

"You were supposed to—" Eyes adjusting, Yavi saw that Dolvek had attempted to make it around the golem and failed. Crystal armor shattered, and breastplate bent by a blow from the golem's other hand, the Eldrennai prince was pinned to the wall by the red-stone monster, blood trickling from his nose and mouth.

Blazing fire, Dolvek's gauntlets shone red- then white-hot as he forced his hands toward the crystalline flaws in the death trap of a creature Uled had left behind.

"Please, make me some laughing salve, if you can," Dolvek said through gritted teeth. "If I make it out of this, I'm going to need it."

A roar filled the tunnel as prince fought construct. Crystalline plates of armor formed and shattered as the creature battered Dolvek, fumes hissing free of its stone body as Dolvek unleashed his inferno. Flaws in the golem turned red then orange, flecks of stone falling away.

Laughing salve, Yavi thought as she turned back toward the mine entrance and broke into a run. *I have no idea how to make that, but maybe I can find some.*

*

When nearing the more well-traveled paths, Kholburran became accustomed to other Vael steering his Root Guard and him in one direction or another, routing them around areas of thickest fighting or danger. Smoke marked places in the distance where bodies of the dead were burning in order to keep them dead, or where trees burned as the dead overtook the defenses of the living. He could not always tell which.

Not even sure which way the Twin Trees lay at this point, Kholburran eyed a column of smoke to the west. Faulina handed him a heavy cut of wild boar wrapped in wild lettuce and topped with mushrooms: one of his favorite trail meals. Though he nodded his appreciation, asked after the hunter, and thanked her directly as was expected and appropriate, he could not concentrate on the meal and savor it properly.

"So." Gilly, one of the newest members of his Root Guard, and the one who'd provided the night's dinner, sidled up next to him as he forced himself to chew the food he wasn't tasting. "Arri said you aren't like other princes and that this Root Taking isn't likely to have the same sorts of . . . benefits others have, but . . . if you fancy a bit of fun while you're still mobile . . ."

"You flatter me, Gilly, but I have eyes only for Malli." Kholburran brushed away the hand she placed on his thigh, and tried not to let his anger show. "My apologies."

Gilly stepped away, flustered but polite. Why was it so hard for girl-type persons to understand a boy-type person who only wanted one mate? Crossing to a more isolated branch with a better view of the dark funnel of smoke, he tried to place it.

Trees or corpses?

"That's a group of the dead," Arri glided toward him, dropping onto the end of his branch. It was broad enough for three, but she landed up branch from him, leaving him the trunk to retreat to, should he so desire it.

"Thanks." He tried not to stare at the lambent amber whorls at her neck and on her right forearm, but it was hard not to see them and feel guilty.

"Mind if I join you?" Arri pulled her own meal out of her pack.

"Sure."

Arri ate as if she tasted nothing, merely fueling herself in as efficient a manner as possible, remaining silent until she had picked the last scrap of oily lettuce from her fingers.

"I could stop them doing that," Arri whispered, watching him. "What you and Malli have is something I don't think I can fully understand, but I respect it now in a way I did not before."

"Before what?" Kholburran set his half-eaten meal on the bark before him.

"Yours had mushrooms?" Arri smiled. "Gilly must be quite fond of you."

"Everyone's didn't?"

"She didn't find many, so, since it was her hunt, she got to decide what to do with them."

"Oh."

"Don't feel bad, Kholburran." Arri indicated a spot next to him. He nodded and she took a seat on the branch. "You're the one Taking Root. She should have given them to you whether she hoped to curry favor and share your bed or not. On a mission like this, we are at your disposal, not the other way around."

"Thanks for letting me know," Kholburran said. "I think I have a jaded view of how all this is supposed to work."

"Your interpretation is far closer than I might like to admit," Arri said.

"How much longer to Fort Sunder?" Kholburran kept his gaze low, focused on her feet.

"We'll pass through Silver Leaf tomorrow and reach Fort Sunder the day after, if all goes well."

"Thanks, Arri." Kholburran caught himself trying to decipher the expression on her face, but the inexpressiveness of her thicker winter bark stymied him, leaving all but the most exaggerated expressions frustratingly neutral.

"If . . ." she began, then stopped. "I'll make sure to let Gilly and the others know how much you enjoyed the mushrooms. Maybe I can even get them to understand why you aren't interested in some of the more intimate encounters they have in mind."

"I don't want to hurt anyone's feelings," Kholburran said, but Arri was already walking away.

*

The dragon stretched her wings, scales glittering like liquid rubies, as Tsan grunted with the effort of trying to fly. Smoke poured from her nostrils, her eyes shimmering with inner light, but no matter how hard she flapped, her massive bulk remained firmly ground bound.

I will not roar, she thought before unleashing a mighty roar.

"Problems?" One-headed Kilke's disembodied head dangled at her throat like a pendant, secured with a braided harness she'd had her soldiers construct from strips of her own shed skin. It may have been the precariousness of his situation that caused the deity to ask the question cheerfully, yet in a tone quiet enough that the Zaur and Sri'Zaur of her army were unlikely to hear.

Foolish deity, Tsan thought, *you forget yourself.*

No more than you fail to recall—

"Out!" Tsan shouted aloud and in her mind, casting the deity free of her thoughts.

"You'll never fly that way," Kilke tutted. "You are thinking like the Zaur you have ceased to be."

She forced her way into his thoughts. Unguided, Tsan found instances of dragons flying, of two twins: one dark and one light, of Coal when he answered to another name, of other dragons being born and dying, but the secret of their flight eluded her. It was effortless to them, but also . . . She studied the wing length, noting that even newly hatched dragons with stubby little wings could fly. A nonsensical act from a purely physical approach, which meant . . .

Ah, I see. A fundamental lack of mystical experience. I have been altered by magical means, but never felt what it is like to actually use magic.

Stay out of my head, if I am not allowed in yours, Warleader, Kilke thought.

"I am no longer interested in an imprecise exchange of information, Kilke." Tsan rolled her neck, feeling the strength of her new form. Finished. Muscles finally stable. Reliable. Fixed. Flying should be a simple exercise for an adult dragon.

Foolish for assuming it was a purely mechanical process. Lofting a foreclaw, feeling its heft, made it clear her bones were not hollow. Such weight could only be shifted with non-muscular aid. Assuming the assist would be purely chemical had been gross zoological prejudice. Even so, she felt it ought to work that way, and so she had tried. Finding her center of balance had been easy. Rapid though it had been, the metamorphosis from Sri'Zaur to dragon had felt gradual enough to allow Tsan to adjust, a previously undiscovered benefit of having gone through so many different breeds of Sri'Zaur . . . All the types of specialization, size, and weight shifting, membranes allowing her to fly, new toxins and strains of venom, the ways her paws hurt for a year after she could no longer glide.

She unhooked Kilke's head from the single shed-claw hook holding him tight to her chest, and brought him up to eye level.

"Tell me what you want in exchange for the required information."

"To formally cement our allegiance," Kilke purred. "You acknowledged the change in our relationship when you became a dragon, and I must admit to a certain defensiveness on my part." He paused for an apology that did not come. "Having given the matter further consideration, I accept your premise.

"You are quite correct, Tsan, to say dragons do not worship the gods, but your people are not dragons, and you are not a god. The Zaur are your people, true, but they are my worshippers. I wish your assurance that that arrangement will remain the unaltered state of things. In exchange, I will continue to protect and assist as I can, and your empire will continue to serve His Secret Purpose."

"Why not grant me the knowledge first?" Tsan smiled, wondering in the moment what a smile looked like on the maw of a dragon. "A gesture of goodwill."

"You live, walk, and breathe in all the true evidence of my goodwill you require, my dear." Kilke clucked his tongue at her. "That you continue to be surrounded by your subjects, who also yet live . . . Need I continue?"

"I could swallow you whole and chew you to bits . . ." Tsan narrowed her gaze.

"And would not life—" Kilke's eyes and horns crackled with lightning, "—be ever so much more difficult for a dragon whose eyes had been burned out by the lightning of an angry deity in his final dying act of spite?"

Tsan's laughter boomed across the plains, sending her empire scurrying away from her in all directions until they realized the disturbing sound was a sign of amusement.

"Yes." Tsan nodded. "That is the sign I needed. You are still a worthy ally, Kilke. You have my formal agreement. My ally and," she indicated casually with her snout, "their god."

Returning him to the hanging clasp at her throat, she rose to all fours, letting her tail whip out over the heads of her adoring subjects.

"Now," she whispered, "flight."

"Of course, my friend." Kilke's horns began to glow, and as they did, Tsan felt what it was to fly, the magic in it, the freedom; and this time, with a single flap of her wings, she flew.

*

The dragon came in from the northwest, weaving in and out of the second sun's rubicund corona, vanishing then reappearing as the center of the blazing orb painted it black in contrast. Rae'en stared as only an Aern in a warsuit could, directly into the sun, relying on Bloodmane to keep her eyes free of afterimages and blind spots.

Kazan cursed in her mind, using the data from the scouts and war-suits Rae'en had dispatched to get a better view at the ground-bound mass following in the great wyrm's shadow. The true picture of the enemy rendered itself in the upper half of Rae'en's field of vision.

Not just thousands, Kazan thought. *Hundreds of thousands.*

"How many can we hold off?" Rae'en whispered. Her defenses were strong, stronger than Fort Sunder had ever been, except perhaps during the Demon Wars, but it had never been under attack by a dragon. For the whole of its existence, the only dragon had been Coal, and he far off to the south, harmlessly (for the most part) slumbering in the lava, stirring to hunt or stretch his wings, but not to wage any sort of war.

I liked it better, Bloodmane intoned, **when we were the ones with the dragon.**

How many can we hold off? Rae'en thought at her Overwatches.

I . . . Dragon wings and fire tinted Kazan's thoughts. *I . . .*

Amber or Glayne, Rae'en prodded.

The dragon is a problem, Glayne sent. *It doesn't have to close with us unless it wants to, and the Aiannai elemancers are tired. Let me think, but while I do, Amber, I can feel you working the other problem, so—*

Without a Zaurruk, the Sri'Zauran army is more manageable. Scaled-up versions of their existing strategies flowed freely from Amber's mind, accompanying her words. Rae'en watched the plans, the formations, shift and evolve, but it felt insufficient. *If they reanimate, then we need to know if they are in league with Uled or—*

They aren't, Joose and Rae'en thought together.

Joose, go. Amber thought, Glayne's token turning gold to show his approval.

We've been watching them fight, Rae'en, Joose continued. *Kazan and the others can correct me if I'm wrong, but this looks like a display of strength to me.*

He's right, M'jynn cut in. *That's how they work. If they attack by surprise, it means they want to send a message or to conquer, but look at the way they're approaching—in ranks.*

No, Kazan sent. *That's not all of it. Every interaction with the Sri'Zaur is like an audition. Joose is right; this is a whole power thing, but it is more than that. They aren't trying to hide the army. They are trying to hide the dragon. That part is a test. We have to react to the dragon as if we are prepared to kill it.*

I can't kill it, Rae'en growled.

We can fight the Sri'Zaur and the Zaur, with our Makers dying over and over again, only to be stripped and dipped or held safe within us until that can be accomplished, Eyes of Vengeance thought. Unless they all have shards of the Life Forge, we would eventually win through attrition, even if it took one hundred years and we lost every non-Aern ally, but such a victory is suboptimal.

What do you suggest, Eyes? Bloodmane asked.

"We have to deploy the Aiannai in a convincing defense against the—" Rae'en shifted from a whisper to transmitted thoughts. *I have to get Queen Bash to deploy her elemancers in a convincing dragon defense.*

Rae'en ran down the bone-steel-coated wall of the keep, heading for Bhaeshal.

CHAPTER 19

ARMORED

Kazan leapt out of the tree in which he had been stationed. His leg bones flexed from the impact, springing forward as they snapped back to their normal shape. It hurt like hells, which he took as a sign all would be well. Stumbling for a few steps before he regained his balance, he charged into the newest clash between Zaur, Vael, and the dead.

Following the map in his head, Kazan scanned for the undead reptile named Kuort but could not find him.

Where did Kuort go? he thought at the others.

Off with Cadence and Captain Tyree, M'jynn thought back, showing direction with a silver arrow. *They took the horse and a small escort of Vael.*

They wanted to test a theory about Kuort. Joose backed up the icons on Kazan's battle map to indicate when they'd left the dead Zaur, and exactly where. *Why he's still him even though he's dead. Long Speaker stuff.*

Thanks.

In Kuort's absence, that meant the Flamefang, Brazz, would be in charge. Kazan worked his way to where Brazz stood, flanked by black-scaled guards, directing his fellow yellow-scaled Sri'Zaur. Orange zigzag markings went dark as Flamefangs exhausted their alchemical fuel and rotated out of the fighting, a fresh soldier with blazing orange markings stepping in to vomit gouts of liquid flame at the dead.

What do we need to know from the Flamefang? Joose asked.

More information about how the Sri'Zaur make overtures of alliance.

You think that's what is going on with the dragon? M'jynn asked.

Warpick at the ready, Kazan sent an acquiescent token flash but ran on, tracking the local engagement through the eyes of his fellow Over-watches, each positioned in a tree at a cardinal point of the envisioned battle map with a few Vael warriors nearby to assist or help relocate them as the battle moved. Being in an armed conflict himself did not stop the rest of the Aernese Army from needing strategic information.

"What are you doing, Overwatch?" One of the frond-headed Vael who had been assigned to him dropped into the fray nearby.

He wished he could think it at her rather than explaining, but the Vael were allies and they'd come to the rescue. Kazan hated to think what would have happened to his small group of Overwatches if they had run into the Zaur absent an alliance between the Vael and the reptilian empire.

"I need to consult an expert." Kazan dodged a pair of mounted Zaur, moving in to help corral the burning corpses and herd them together until they had been reduced to charred ineffective combatants. Similar in form from an external perspective to the Jun beasts Kazan had seen in the deeper shafts of South Number Nine, the stony hides of the mounts showed no effect from the heat or fire, not even those with shaggy braids running from the place where the head on a normal creature would have been, which led Kazan to suspect it to be more like wire or horn than proper hair.

Intuiting his destination, the Vael sped ahead of Kazan, leading him skipping over a section of still-wriggling Zaurruk corpses, bulling through the groups of gray-scaled Zaur working in tandem with Vael to cut the downed serpent into smaller and smaller pieces, which they pinned down with fragments of the creature's spine to keep them in place long enough for a Flamefang to burn them to ash.

"Fair hunting at Fort Sunder?" the Vael asked.

"A dragon showed up with half a million reptilian soldiers." Kazan swung at a hissing Zaur, realized at the last possible instant that it was injured and not one of the dead, turning his overhand swing into a flip to avoid killing the unknown fighter. Twin arrows thunked into the skull of an animated corpse as Kazan stumbled into it. Trying to stand quickly, he found himself seized roughly and hurled back by two hulking black-scaled Sri'Zaur. Landing gracelessly on his rump, Kazan watched them grab the corpse and hurl it over the line of mounted Zaur and into the blaze beyond.

"Which dragon?" the Vael asked, a name he could not pronounce appearing over her head in gold, courtesy of Joose.

Oh-ar-HAR-wa, Joose thought at him, *is the way you pronounce it, though how you get that from O-R-H-R-Y-A is beyond me. My own fault for asking how to spell it, I guess.*

It does seem to be missing a few vowels while possessing at least one poorly chosen consonant, Kazan thought.

A blink later, and Kazan had found the interaction in Joose's memory and replayed it for himself. *How did I miss Joose flirting so shamelessly? Lack of tactical importance?* Applying those words to the actions of one of his closest friends disturbed Kazan.

"No one knows, Orhrya," Kazan said. "I need to know if they managed to keep one secret for several thousand years or what?"

"Tell Joose I said 'Hi,'" Orhrya said.

Quick on the track, M'jynn thought, *even if she does have a weird name.*

"He heard," Kazan said.

"Maybe the dragons are coming back?" Her violet eyes opened wide at the idea. Or he presumed that was what it was, until he saw the symbol for Eyes of Vengeance, a stylized *2* with an empty center where Kazan's new symbol, Vander's, fit perfectly, leave the world map Kazan was maintaining and arrive on the edge of the local map that bounded the current battle.

"Warsuits," Orhrya whispered. Kazan smiled, baring his doubled canines and sharing in a little of the Vael's awe. He had seen warsuits through the eyes of other Aern, but being in the presence of a warsuit for the first time was like standing exposed before an unflinching incarnate of battle, an ancient and relentless force. He'd heard Eyes of Vengeance in his head, but the idea that the armor was near, that he might soon don the warsuit for the first time, left Kazan speechless, all thoughts, even of the dragon, momentarily purged from his mind.

*

Why, Bloodmane asked, **did we run from one side of Scarsguard to the other?**

Rae'en vaulted the last of the steps leading up to the fortress, seizing the bone-metal-coated wall of Fort Sunder and latching onto it with the same force that let the Aern hang their chosen implements on their backs. Sunslight picked out the detail-work on her armor, her father's scars in a stylized union of engraving and enamel, leaving the curved lines smooth and flat with the illusion of depth. She snorted once, the sound of metal on metal clinking as she climbed, anchoring her knees, toes, elbows, and hands.

"I need to add this to the training regimen," Rae'en whispered.

Why, Rae'en countered, *did you wait until I was already at Fort Sunder before asking that question?*

It is a hard thing to question one's rightful occupant, Bloodmane thought.

The memory of her father's bridge test on the way from South Number Nine to the Guild Cities, Bridgeland, and to Oot beyond. Kholster had seemed out of his head, clearly wrong about the sturdiness of the stone bridge, but even so she had found it hard to question her father. Maybe it was the same sometimes for the warsuits. They bent their entire existences to the will of their "occupants," so much so that they had willingly stood in an abandoned hallway for several centuries because the Aern had agreed that they would.

Fair point, Rae'en thought.

I am getting better at it, Bloodmane thought.

Don't get too good, Rae'en teased.

A healthy balance?

Sure. Rae'en started to ask Kazan a question, but Glayne intercepted it, updating the queen's location on her map before she could tell him what she wanted.

Kazan will be occupied for the next candlemark or so, Glayne thought at her. *Unless you require him specifically.*

Do I want to know? Rae'en asked.

Eyes of Vengeance has arrived and Kazan is going to don him for the first time.

It didn't take us an hour, Rae'en thought at Bloodmane.

Kholster valued expedience, Bloodmane thought, **but Eyes of Vengeance is more traditional.**

Fine, Rae'en thought. *Keep me up to date.*

*

Bhaeshal stood on the roof of the keep, watching as an artificer in apprentice robes slotted lenses of varying shades into the end of a brass telescope mounted to a tripod. Checking the scope, the apprentice waved his queen over, and she peered into the eyepiece. She looked up, acknowledging Rae'en as she climbed over the edge of the parapet. The queen furrowed her eyes in an expression made unfathomable by the way her elemental focus banded across her eyes like a mask.

"You've seen the dragon?" Bhaeshal asked.

"Yes." Rae'en took a deep breath, expecting to be a little winded after her mad dash from the exterior walls to the top of the keep. Bloodmane had declined to allow it, however. "What do you think it means?"

"Could you make out the object adorning the dragon's neck?"

"*What object?*" Rae'en asked and thought.

And how did she find out about the dragon in time to get a telescope set up?

Her people are watching the borders, too, Bloodmane thought. **Let me check with Hunter . . .**

Hunter?

Glayne's warsuit.

I'm aware, Rae'en thought. *Everyone knows Glayne sees through Hunter and his—*

"Mazik saw the dragon, kholster Rae'en." Queen Bhaeshal stepped away from the telescope to offer Rae'en a chance at the eyepiece, but Amber already had a good view. Standing on the exterior wall next to Glinfolgo, holding the Dwarf's own spyglass, Amber focused on the golden-hued object. Between the amplification from the telescope and Scale Fist's ability to enhance his rightful occupant's senses, all it took was a few wingbeats for Amber to study the approaching dragon closely enough to transmit the crystal-clear image of a disembodied head with curling ram's horns and scales the color of gold.

What is that? Rae'en asked.

It is Kilke's central head, Bloodmane answered. **The one Shidarva cut off and cast down from the sky.**

"Well?" Bhaeshal asked. "Can your Overwatches get a clear view?"

"Yes." A strong wind whipped around them, lessening in intensity so suddenly that Rae'en was certain the queen had adjusted it with her Aeromancy. "It's Kilke's third head."

As she spoke, the eyes of the god's head shifted, looking straight at Amber, making eye contact. Kilke grinned, sending Rae'en's heart racing in panic.

"Is it alive, or—?" Bhaeshal asked.

"Very much alive," Rae'en said.

Amber raked the oncoming force with her eyes, taking them all in, and relaying scope and size of the threat.

Outnumbered.

Out-dragoned.

With a long-missing deity thrown in for good matter.

Bird squirt, Rae'en thought. *I want all available Aern and warsuits at the walls. If we have to fight this battle, it isn't going to be an easy win, so let's put on an impressive show and hope they want an alliance, not a fight.*

If I comprehend what the Vael have relayed about their practices, Bloodmane thought, **the latter may serve as preamble to the former.**

*

How did you sneak up on me like that? Kazan turned to face Eyes of Vengeance, the pull of their connection taking his breath away.

You are failing to allocate sufficient attention to your physical surroundings, Kazan. Eyes of Vengeance strode through the battlefield with ten other warsuits at his back. Five of them broke off to help gather the dead, escaping the edges of the living barricade that encompassed the bulk of the remaining dead. A flaming corpse sprang over a mounted Zaur, carrying the rider to the ground next to the warsuit, the corpse's skin sloughing off to land on Eyes of Vengeance's armored boot.

Seizing the offending corpse, Eyes hurled it one-gauntleted over the spooked mount, then scooped up the rider and returned him to his seat.

"You will want to chain yourself in properly this time," Eyes intoned. The remaining five warsuits altered course for the locations of Joose, M'jynn, Arbokk, Cadence, and Tyree. **We will address that flaw as we learn to work together.**

"Thank you for watching over my rightful occupant." Eyes stopped next to Kazan, his eyes of crimson crystal and the tilt of his helm indicating that he was watching Orhrya. He offered her the back of his gauntlet and lower vambrace in greeting.

"Any time." Orhrya returned the gesture, marveling at Kazan. "You're one of the Armored?"

"Second of One Hundred," Kazan said.

"Vander?" Orhrya asked.

"My maker has ascended." Eyes of Vengeance turned to Kazan. **Are you ready, sir?**

Ready?

Rae'en sent me to collect you and your fellow Overwatches.

When Rae'en entered Bloodmane, the warsuit opened to accept her, wrapping around her body in an effortless opening and enfolding. Eyes of Vengeance peered down at his new rightful occupant. No emotions flowed off of him as a hint. Assuming he wanted Kazan to don him, Kazan could not think of how to go about starting such a process without point-blank asking, and that was an irkanth's trail down which Kazan was not certain he wanted to track.

I shall continue aloud for the benefit of the Vael, if you are amenable, Eyes thought.

Sure.

"I am your warsuit," Eyes said, as if he could sense Kazan's thoughts—and it was possible the armor had done so. "You must begin to think of me that way. When you want to don me, I should know, through our bond. But, in hope that it may aid you to see our relationship as I do—" Eyes removed one of his gauntlets, slapping it into Kazan's hand. "If you find it acceptable, sir, I would prefer that we become one the way Vander did upon the first donning."

"Of . . . of course, Eyes. However you like."

"Would you be so kind as to assist me, Orhrya." Eyes gestured with an empty arm at the warsuits reinforcing the Zaur barricade. "My brother warsuits are occupied by other tasks."

"I'd be honored." Orhrya bowed deeply and, rising, began to disassemble Eyes of Vengeance in accordance with the warsuit's personal instruction. Though, to Kazan, it looked like she already knew what she was doing.

"You don't have—" Kazan said.

"Hush." Orhrya stopped his mouth with a light touch of the back of her hand, turning herself to the work before her without further instruction or guidance from Kazan or Eyes of Vengeance. Piece by piece, Eyes of Vengeance came apart under the Vael's hands, each section lying still, quiet, unassuming on the scorched and turf-torn forest floor. If any component held the semblance of life, it was the helm, crystals alight, pulsing to the beat of Kazan's heart.

She drew the last piece, the gauntlet Eyes had handed Kazan, and set it in place before turning to Kazan himself, her hands gliding across his mail, tugging it up over his head and dropping it to the ground. Taking a canteen from her belt, she poured the water over him, rubbing his skin clean with her hands, the winter bark was abrasive to most races but pleasantly textured to an Aern. Her scent, like a fir tree high on a mountain ledge, wreathed him, quickening his breath, stirring in him feelings he had not allowed himself the time to feel before, when he had been busy being Second.

He saw Orhrya as the sensuous being she was, made all the more alluring by her skills as a warrior, her strength, her confidence. Laughing wryly, Orhrya smiled, the expression catching his gaze as it spread all the way to Orhrya's eyes. Harsh and pure, her laugh cut through the tension between them, bringing the world back in and letting his attention return to the larger world, but not all of it. He would never be able to be in her presence without noticing again.

"We can mate later," Orhrya told him, "or we could if you were still going to be here. My guess is you are needed elsewhere, Second of One Hundred."

Mate?! Kazan knew the stories of how shocking a Vael's casual approach to physical intimacy, particularly with the Aern, could be. Licentious tales relating exactly that seemed to be a rite of passage among Sixteens. Joose had even managed to talk one of the Armored into sharing a memory that, even thinking about it, made Kazan blush. Vael were known to have very flirtatious humors, too, though, so did Orhrya mean that she wanted to be with him, or was she just being polite?

What if she did mean it and he spurned the offer? Would he be offending her? What if the queen found out and took—?

"Ahem." Eyes of Vengeance's voice and thoughts lost none of their deep reverberation outside despite the warsuit's current state of disassembly.

"Sorry," Orhrya and Kazan said together. She laughed again. Kazan flushed a deeper bronze in embarrassment.

Orhrya bent to her work, handling the armor with reverence similar to a God Speaker handling a shard of their deity's crystal. Kazan started as the warsuit molded to his form, as if it had been forged for him.

"I thought all Aern were used to the ways of warsuits." Orhrya chuckled.

"Only around five percent of us have ever been in the presence of a warsuit." Kazan held his breath as Orhrya leaned close, arms reaching around him to fasten straps that would vanish once the warsuit was whole.

"Care to guess how many of my people have met an Aern, much less a warsuit?"

"Then how do you—?"

"This?" She smiled. "Oh, my great-to-some-degree grandmother was one of Vander's wives. Every generation of her descendants has at least one sproutling who looks just like her. I have always known how Eyes of Vengeance likes to be taken on and off when there is time to do things properly. It is not coincidence that I'm here. I thought the memories were passed down, too, when an Aern took the place of an Armored."

"Not this time."

A warsuit had preferences like that? They were alive, with their own personalities, and Kazan knew that, but that they might have habits and quirks like beings with bone metal and blood was new to him. How much about the warsuits was taken for granted?

Orhrya's scent grew stronger with each piece of Eyes fastened into place, as if it carried her smell. Another thing he'd taken for granted popped into his head and out of his mouth. "I thought all Vael smelled like Royal Hedge Roses."

"The more floral of us smell like that all of the time." Orhrya paused, letting her palm rest against his breastplate, the sensation no different than if her hand were bare upon his chest. Did she know that? Battlefield forgotten, Overwatches forgotten, the world had narrowed to three beings: Kazan and Eyes of Vengeance, two beings who had become truly become one gestalt entity for the first time, and Orhrya, the Vael warrior whom they (both?) desired.

Veins and synapses pulsed with an electrical jolt of spirit as Orhrya lowered the helm into place.

Whole, Eyes of Vengeance thought to him. **I feared I would never feel this way again.**

I have never felt this comfortable in my own skin before, Kazan thought to his armor.

You've never worn *me* before.

Before them stood the same Orhrya he had met so briefly before, but now a thousand memories washed over him, Eyes of Vengeance's memories, of a long-withered Vael so kind and loving, the first female that Vander, and therefore, Eyes, had ever loved in a pure emotional way. A tear ran down Kazan's cheek when the first Orhrya died in his mind, killed by an Eldrennai with whom she refused to—

Do not focus on that emotion. Eyes of Vengeance wove calming thoughts in with the words. **She died long before the Sundering, and we paid that debt.**

Show me, Kazan thought.

*

It was less than a candlemark after the king freed the Aern with his careless breach of promise. Vander directed the battle, sending instructions, updating maps, fighting when he had to, reaching through other Aern to assist as needed. Then he'd seen the knight who'd slain Orhrya.

Gravand, one of the few non-royals who held mastery over two branches of elemancy, Geomancy and Aeromancy, led his lance in charge after charge, never touching the ground, hurling rocks and lightning, even gusts of gale-force wind.

Vander, Kholster had thought, *I can't see Wylant. Is she—?*

Flew for Fort Sunder, from what I saw, Vander thought. *Okkust and Scout had a go at her, but she threw her horse at them with a blast of wind and took their arms off while they were pinned.*

Their arms? Kholster laughed. *Where'd she put them?*

She dropped them atop the Tower of Elementals when she flew past. Vander had hoped he sounded like he cared, but instead, he was switching through the viewpoints of soldiers nearest Gravand, looking for an opportunity to strike.

He found it three times, sending unArmored Aern to their deaths for a chance at the Eldrennai knight before taking direct control of the fourth. Fourth was Aster, one of Kholster's daughters. He touched her mind and hesitated. She could do it, Vander had had no doubt of that, but was risking a female worth revenge?

Don't be stupid, Second, Aster thought at him. *You have a target in mind, point me at it.*

He painted Gravand in orange, reaching out to take control, but Aster rebuffed him. *Don't kholster a kholster, Overwatch. Keep my battle map up to date and stay out of my way.*

Warpick on her back, Aster grabbed two dead Eldrennai, pulling the heads from the corpses with a sound like a wet rag ripping.

Silently observing her orders to the rest of her kholstering, Vander tracked the assignments she gave to her Aern. Making themselves easy targets at one point, then hard ones at another, they guided Gravand near the edge of the western tower. The first head hurled at him from the tower parapet. He batted it aside with the wind, sending a lightning bolt along the route it had traveled. The second head made him angry, but right behind it came Aster's warpick.

Gravand dropped to avoid the weapon, cursing as he flew further back, his back scraping across the Central tower.

"Kill her," Gravand shouted, dispatching three of his lance at the tower from which the projectiles had been thrown. He noticed the shadow, eyes looking up, mouth open, as Aster fell on him, head-butting his nose, breaking both it and his concentration in one move.

Within the tower, two of Aster's kholstering slaughtered the three elven knights. Vander knew it, tracked it, but he only had eyes for Kholster's daughter as she rode the elf down, Gravand dead and bleeding before he came close to the ground. Aster terribly wounded, unable to move after impact.

Wylant's destruction of the Life Forge had ended the life of Aster and every Aern she had kholstered, but Vander then and Eyes of Vengeance now, wondered how Kholster would have viewed the sequence of events if the unArmored had survived and Aster's eventual death had been on Vander's hands. Both felt they knew what he would have thought, but what exactly would he have whispered to himself in those quiet hours when he remembered?

*

All of that took two blinks to pass through Kazan's mind's eye. He felt lost, out of place, disconnected from the battle, from the Vael before him, from the present.

You were flirting with Orhrya, Eyes prompted. **You had mentioned your misconception regarding the predominant scent of all Vael.**

"We arboreal types," Orhrya stood on her tiptoes and kissed him on the helm, "smell like roses sometimes, too. If you're lucky, you'll find out when."

The kiss brought with it the image of an Aern infant, presenting her in stages, an infant morphing into an Eleven then a full-grown female, a twin of Rae'en, undeniable Incarna.

"A girl-type person *and* an Incarna." Orhrya thumped him on the forehelm. "We ought to make that one, but not today and . . ." Moving backward in series of quicksteps, the Vael retreated from the Armored and his warsuit. " . . . and not when we both have fighting to do. You don't need my protection any longer, so my work is done here. When the fighting is over, come visit me at the Twins."

A shrill whistle signaled the withdrawal of the group of Root Guard.

"But . . ." Kazan scanned the layout of the battle. Fighting all but over, Zaur and Vael alike had untangled their forces. Brazz and the lead Vael stood off to one side of the battle, huddled over one of the Vael's living maps. Tyree and Cadence stood near them, advising, Cadence about her knowledge of recent news from Castleguard and Tyree about which tunnels he knew to be impassable now or compromised. Waves of a contradictory sets of data flowed at him from Captain Tyree. All appeared to be well, but it was not.

Eyes, Kazan thought, *how long were we, um . . . ?*

Occupied with ourselves and a beautiful Vael warrior?

Yes.

Half a candlemark, Eyes of Vengeance told him. **Scout has just brought me up to date on what we missed.**

Data shot through Kazan in rapid succession, absorbed, annotated, and disseminated as needed:

1. Rae'en's novel ascent approach: The strength of an unArmored Aern could limit the length of such uses, but it was a tactic to keep in the sheath for those patrolling Scarsguard. Note: Could strips of bone metal be embedded into the exterior surface of the newly built fortifications to allow rapid ascent and descent for those outside the wall in the case of a siege? He calculated the amount of bone metal required, dropping a request into the queue for Rae'en's future review and the Ossuary's approval.
2. Queen Bash: Her people had conveyed information to her rapidly and without alerting the Aern to the communication. Knowing Mazik had been the first to spot the new dragon gave him the data point to review. Triangulating the location of all Aiannai in the vicinity using the viewpoints of all relevant Overwatches showed him the sequence of flashes Mazik had sent as well as the Aiannai who had been watching for the signal. He dropped it into the minds of Rae'en's personal Overwatches to be decoded.
3. The telescope: Design noted, he guessed its relative magnification from the detail level Queen Bhaeshal appeared to possess.
4. Amber's view of the dragon and the god's head: Bird squirt!

Batting his eyelashes at him from his spot near Brazz, Tyree widened his eyes and nodded as if to comment on the thoughts and agree. Kazan opened his mouth to speak to Brazz, but then it was Cadence's turn to lock gazes with him. A subtle shake of her head warned him off. But why? What had the humans sensed that he had not?

He studied Brazz again and reversed his decision about asking the Flamefang for advice. Warleader Tsan had produced a threat display the Aern could not match. Telling the Sri'Zaur about it now . . . Kazan could not be sure they'd give advice rather than attack him and his fellow Overwatches.

Even with the eleven warsuits present, it was an avoidable risk.

He located Joose, M'jynn, and Arbokk on his map. Two of them had gone far enough away that he had to zoom out to find them. M'jynn and Joose were off to the north with Kuort and the horse, Alberta.

Guys?

Tyree says we need to go, M'jynn thought, *and take Kuort with us.*

Why?

They stood around, staring at the dead lizard, Joose thought, *and then Cadence jumped away from him like he was on fire and made of spiders.*

"Nice talking to you, flame belly," Tyree purred, "but it looks like my current employer wants a word or two with me and the missus."

Cadence glared at him for that, but any irregularity seemed lost on the old Flame Tongue. Kazan felt a murmuring at the base of his neck. Tyree and Cadence were talking to each other with some form of Long Speech, but it was not clear enough for Kazan to make out. With a muttered, "Fine, but hurry," Cadence walked away in the general direction of Joose, M'jynn, Alberta, and Kuort.

"You are, of course," Brazz said, drawing near, "welcome to stay with us as we continue to clear the dead from the forest, but this mint-breathed human claims you are needed elsewhere. A claim . . ." Brazz spat at Tyree's feet, the ground hissing and popping where his expectorant fell, "made more believable by the presence of warsuits."

"Duty calls, doesn't it, boss?" Smile plastered on his face, but warning clear as day in his eyes, the human clapped Kazan on the shoulder so hard Eye of Vengeance's bone-steel surely had to have injured the human's hand.

Cadence saw something, Tyree's thoughts came faint, but clear.

Kazan stopped himself from replying aloud and tipping their hand to the Sri'Zaur. What could she see? The woman had known he and the others would be in trouble and camped there ahead of time to aid them. Discounting her abilities was as stupid as the way the Eldrennai had underestimated the Vael for so long, just because they were pretty to look at.

Round everyone up and let's head to Fort Sunder, Kazan thought to his local Overwatches.

"Fine. Lead the way," he said to Tyree. "I don't like the idea of you skulking around behind me."

Brazz chuckled, a sound like a rasping bellows, as he walked back to the Vael and her living map.

"Well?" Kazan asked.

"Don't put on too good of an act." Eyes positively glimmering with mischief, the human steepled his hands and bowed before leading the way.

CHAPTER 20
SOMETIMES YOU DIE

Gray and overcast with cloud cover so thick midmorning felt indistinguishable from the edge of night, the day filled itself with cold and damp as if it knew what dark work was being done and could not but comment upon the horror covering the once-peaceful land of Holsven. Air spirits dropped Yavi without warning not because of a heavy heart, but because they had become mean and spiteful, winter gusts emboldened by the many deaths and the walking corpses resulting from them. Her current escort tossed her skyward and vanished with a cruel look in its translucent eyes.

"Dol—" she began, but he was already below, waiting to catch her like a faithful steed ready to be mounted.

I don't think I'll share that analogy with him, she thought, her ears twitching involuntarily as she cringed in expectation of Dolvek's ruined voice.

"Are winter's air spirits usually this capricious?" Dolvek asked hoarsely, like air wheezing from a poorly mended bellows.

"Not the ones I know." Yavi found it troubling. Events in the physical world affected the spirits, but it often took time and repetition, the passing of many years before they began to reflect tragedy. Beings of water and stone behaved properly, but the wind acted as if it were angry with her personally. Cold bit more deeply than it should have, too, chilling her so obviously that Dolvek insisted she accept his cloak, claiming that he could warm himself his Pyromancy, but that he could not safely keep her warm in the same way.

With her on his back, Dolvek flew lower, bringing the devastated land below into greater focus. Yavi had lost count of the towns they'd overflown, all apparently emptied, the inhabitants who did not lie in still-burning pits or chopped into pieces too small to be useful all marching with their dead master. Fields declared their passing with trampled crops and ruined pastureland, some burning, some ash. Yavi remembered thinking earlier when they had been forced to stop to let Dolvek recover that it might be hard to track them over the hard-packed barrens that dotted some portions of Holsven, but the trail was impossible to lose. Even a blind human could have tracked the army by the sound and the smell.

"I think he's taking them to the Sisters," Yavi spoke into Dolvek's ear. Yavi had never been north of the Sri'Zauran Mountains or south of the Parliament of Ages before the Grand Conjunction, but Queen Kari had told her stories of the two ports that were one in all but name, where the borders of Holsven and Zaliz touched at the Great Northern Gulf and combined to make the only port larger than Na'shie in the whole of the Northern Human Kingdoms.

"Makes sense," Dolvek said, before a coughing fit took him. His face and hands were mostly healed, the skin pink and new, but laughing salve was not a potion one could drink, and Yavi could hear a crackle and hiss in the prince's lungs, though he tried to hide it. What would Kholster think of him now if the Aern could see the way the once-complaining prince ignored his own injuries, suffering in silence?

"Why don't we walk for a little while?" Yavi asked.

He looked back at her as best he could, a request for clarification clear in his eyes.

"I wanted to soak up some more minerals," Yavi said. "If you don't mind the break."

He scoffed, seeing the excuse for what it was, but Dolvek set them down on one of the few good roads, two tracks of rough pavement cutting from the Holsven side of the Rin'Saen Gorge toward the Sisters, where invisible political lines between nations divided the humans' second-largest port city between Holsven and Zaliz.

"Uled is still dragging the huge chunks of stone he carved out of the mine," Yavi said. She took her boots off and walked barefoot along the edge of the road, drawing in what minerals she could without stopping. No sense in making the excuse a complete lie.

All that got her was a nod.

"We could take a break . . ." Yavi offered.

"If Uled is attempting to create and open new Port Gates—" Dolvek took long rasping breaths in between every four or five words, his voice more growling and ragged each time he spoke. "—then I am the only living being north of King's Watch who has any idea how to close them."

"Why don't we take a short break and you can give me my first lesson, silly?" Yavi waggled her ears at him, but his eyes were closed as he tried to slow his breathing and avert a coughing fit. Breathing around it, he called it. "Then there will be two 'beings' who know how it's done?"

"Excellent . . ." Dolvek dropped where he was, eyes still closed. ". . . plan."

Pebbles rose up from the ground, flowing toward him in orderly lines and sorting themselves by size and shape until he had the ones he wanted. With a shaking hand he dismissed the rest to roll away back to the spots from which they'd come.

He put them back, Yavi thought. *I approve, but why——?*

"Because," Dolvek answered. He gazed at her through rheumy, bloodshot eyes. "Because I could tell it was what you thought ought to be done with them. Would you please ask any spirits in the rocks if they mind being marked with fire?"

"They're really small." Yavi squinted. "Barely sentient. If they aren't going to be put back where they were, they don't care what happens next."

Eyes rolling up in his head, Dolvek teetered on the edge of a faint, before jerking himself straight and conscious again. One by one, he ran his fingers over the stones, shaping them further. Once they were a uniform shape and size, he scorched symbols onto each with elemental flame. "Uled may change the order of their arrangement on the Port Gates, but the runic sequence for destroying a Port Gate is always the same . . ."

*

Barren as a looted tomb, Silver Leaf City's current inhabitants reminded Kholburran of carrion birds picking at the leftovers of a once-vibrant animal. The thorn-fanged prince followed Arri's lead as they crept across the invisible border between forest and town, hugging the shadows, as Arri gestured for two less-senior Root Guard who vanished more silently than the cold blowing wind to scout ahead. One flew over the rooftops in the grasp of a friendly spirit, and the other dashed around the edge of an empty storage shed.

"Where is everybody?" Kholburran whispered.

"Our last scout said lots of elves and humans were leaving the out-lying areas and moving to be close to Fort Sunder," Arri said even more quietly, making Kholburran feel too loud. "But they said nothing about Silver Leaf being this empty."

As they moved along, the excellent night vision of the Vael showed Kholburran more than he wanted to see. Sickly or seedy-looking vagrants crept in and out of abandoned homes, thinking themselves concealed by the night. In the front room of one empty abode, two humans scuffled over a horse blanket, only to grow still and scared at the sound of a peg leg tapping on the scant porch.

"You have choices," spoke a one-legged man. He leaned on his good knee, fingering a crutch of stained walnut idly as he addressed the strug-gling humans. Kholburran noted the way the wood had been carefully wrapped at a point halfway down the crutch, as if it were meant to serve as a grip. "You can come to the Briar and Bramble, tell me who you are and what you are about, and have a hot, filling meal. I can find a use for you, maybe assign you a steading. That—" He smote the air with a wave of the crutch. "—is your best and most pleasant option, because at the very worst it leaves you with a full belly and a warm place by my fire 'til morning."

"What are you going to do if we don't, fat man?" It was a thin and angry voice, but unafraid.

Kholburran's head petals prickled as the fat innkeeper turned and locked eyes with him in the dark, offering a gesture and shrug that con-veyed some mixture of "I'll be with you a moment," "Glad to see you," and "I'm sorry you have to see this."

"Well then, lad." The innkeeper turned his attention back to the porch. "If you force my hand, we'll come in and have it out with you the hard way."

"'We'?" The thin man laughed. "Who is—?"

"I'm Wallace, the Baker of Castleguard," the fatter man in the aban-doned home said with a cough. "My wife and three boys are upstairs, and I was taking them a blanket when this man objected."

"Good to know you, Wallace," the innkeeper said. "I am Jorum of the Briar and Bramble, and I may have use for a baker. If not, I'll feed you and yours and set you on the path for Fort Sunder. It's the capitol of

Scarsguard, which is what the Grudgers and the elves they saw fit not to eat have decided to call their new kingdom. They might have a place for a man with your skill, and, failing that, it may be safe enough for you to head back home before long. Dienox is dead. Slain by the child of Kholster and Wylant, the Aiannai who slew Nomi and took her hair."

"You lie," said the first voice.

"Only to myself, and I'm trying to mend my ways there, too." Jorum patted his abbreviated knee. "I even have a nice little reminder of what seeing the world through tinted lenses can earn a fellow."

"But, Torgrimm," Wallace began.

"Kholster put him back in his old job after his Prime Overwatch . . ." Jorum closed his eyes, trying to think of the name. "Is it Vunder, Kirsten?"

"Vander." The correction came from inside the darkened home. Light bloomed within as someone unhooded a bullseye lantern, picking out a bloodied man in a coat of plates, still trying to pull the worn blanket from Wallace's grip. He held up his hands to shield his eyes, and the woman chopped into his neck with a woodman's axe. Kholburran only saw her for a moment, short and stocky with graying hair, flowers on her apron. "Jim, leave that lantern and help me get him into pieces before he comes back angry."

At a nod, Arri sent two Root Guard toward the house to aid Kirsten.

"You have Vael help on the way, Kirsten," Jorum called out. "Don't go trying to chop any of them."

"I'll chop you, if you don't get back to the inn and check my stew," Kirsten called. Her voice sounded harsh, but with an edge of affection. "And you just take Mr. Wallace and his family with you, while the ladies handle the women's work."

"Come on, lad," Jorum smiled the words, patting Kholburran with the back on his hand. "We have goat that you won't eat—it's farm-raised—but I might be able to scrounge up a little something I was saving for one of your scouts, Miss Ella, on her way back through."

"Was that all true?" Kholburran asked. "What you said about the gods?"

"True?" Jorum laughed. "I have to send a runner out to Oot noon and midnight just to make sure I don't need to build a shrine to Kirsten. The fate of the world is twisting and turning, son. I just hope it's like a kite on a string, getting ready to soar and not a fish on a line, heading for the pot."

Jorum led them inside, out of the dark, and Kholburran tried to pretend he couldn't still hear the sounds of the nameless man who'd died over a horse blanket being hacked to pieces across the street.

*

Dolvek stopped breathing deep in the middle of the next night. Unable to sleep, Yavi listened to the labored gristmill grind of his lungs and watched the air spirits swoop and dive. Angry and free, the spirits glared at her with blaming eyes, whispering to each other too galefully for her to understand. She felt the small pouch she'd made of her samir, which held the stones Dolvek had produced for her, and drew them out one at a time, trying to call out their order in the pattern of destruction without checking the numbers she'd scratched into the backs of them.

The symbols did not make sense, even with the mnemonic images Dolvek had taught her to aid in memorization. When his breath stopped, Yavi froze mid-pebble-check—the one that looked kind of like a little irkanth was fourth, wasn't it?—head cocked and ears listening as hard as they could.

"Dolvek?"

Nothing.

As she leaned over him, a soft whisper told her to back away. She scrambled back, trusting the voice, eyes widening in shock when the body burst into flame, burning hot and fast, guttering black smoke and flame, consuming the body so swiftly the smell was more like ash than burning meat.

"Sorry," the small whisper said. "I couldn't let it get up and possibly harm you."

Twirling toward the sound, Yavi spied the translucent spirit of Dolvek standing a few steps away, his eyes ablaze with flame. Behind and through him, Yavi saw a startled lizard inching away.

Looking back and forth from corpse ash to spirit, Yavi opened her mouth to ask a question, but could not find the words.

"Um . . ." Yavi hunted the right words or questions and settled on "How?"

"It does not matter," Dolvek whispered. "Sleep if you want, and I will watch over you."

"No." Yavi rubbed her eyes. "I am so awake right now I might never sleep again."

*

It should have been impossible for Yavi to appear more beautiful to Dolvek's eyes now than she had before his death, such was the strength of his attraction to the young Vael. The purely physical and pheromone-enhanced desire he had felt upon first exposure had grown over the time they had spent together to a deeper appreciation, gratitude, and love he did not expect for her to ever return, especially now. He had stopped seeing her features and begun seeing more of her true self, the caring princess who endeavored to spare his feelings, his pride, even when he had been filled beyond bursting with baseless self-aggrandizements and willful ignorance.

Her bravery, her talent, the way she smiled at a person with more than her lips . . . The kindness of her voice, when it had not been earned . . .

Now he saw the spirit that matched such a person, her essence bright, beautiful, and overflowing with joy, the excess of which burst out from her, attempting to share itself with others, overflowing to refill their cups and banish sorrow.

"Can you hear me?" Yavi asked.

Above them, the tendrils of Uled speared the air, stretching past and through the Sri'Zauran Mountains, staining the sky. Ahead, a miasma of purple and black writhed and pulsed. Nothing good would greet them there, but it was the center of Uled's power, and, like hints of silver, Dolvek found the tracks of the three great stones, the echoing images of their passage, echoes that could have only been present if someone were attempting to enchant them en route to their final destination.

"I can." He nodded, conscious of being watched. Spinning to look behind him, a coldness touched him, the very edge of an enraged force trailing them from the south. Not Uled, but still dangerous and bent on death and inflicting harm, revenge. "I . . ."

"Dolvek." Yavi's voice, gentle and light, drew his attention back to her.

"May we travel as we talk?" Dolvek asked. "With my new senses, I can see the worlds of the insubstantial much more clearly than the material one. We are stalked from one direction and head toward doom in the other. If we hurry, the doom may only be mine . . . or ours."

"Ours?" Yavi laughed. "Don't you mean *mine*? You're already dead, from the looks of it."

"Yes." Dolvek eyed Uled's tendrils and shuddered. "But there are worse things . . . by declining Torgrimm's collection, I am no longer granted his protection."

CHAPTER 21

HOW TO GREET A DRAGON

The Tsan'Zaur, as her people had begun calling her, drifted in lazy circles as she spiraled down toward the newly expanded city below. Each orbit described a deliberate circle through the air, designed to display the sapphire expanse of her armored undercarriage and the shimmering red of her scales to any onlookers who had not run for cover at the mere sight of her. She roared once, twice, and let them dread the third even more by denying it to them.

Still miles away, her army marched on. It was larger than it had once been, as stragglers who had managed their own escapes felt the periodic call pounded out in Zaurtol as they traveled. Asvrin's Shades, with their splinters of the Life Forge, had been a particular boon, but the Warleader presumed she would not require them . . . yet. Most valuable had been the news they had brought with them: the fall of Port Ammond, and the death of Coal. Asvrin, ever the clever the little agent, had even thought to visit Oot and verify things his assassins had spied out before their attack.

Even now, a pair of Shades lurked near the black mirror of the divine, sending out updates through echo tunnels on the third hour of every second day. A Sri'Zaur had become a dragon, yet two Aern, an elf, and an impossible half-breed had all become gods, with Two-headed Kilke an apparent member of their cabal. It was enough to make a mother proud. Even the backstabbing Dryga appeared to have risen to further prominence in his death atop the moving corpse of a once-great wyrm.

The world was in flux, crystalizing into a new structure with new opportunities for those who could work themselves into prominence within the new patterns as they solidified.

Even Fort Sunder had changed so much as to become nearly as unrecognizable to the dragon as she had become to it. The keep itself remained a brooding edifice of stone looming at the top of a tiered plateau, lording its presence over the Eldren Plains. Built up around it was a city proper bounded by walls of thick granite from the Rin'Saen Gorge and one of the Dwarven building materials about which the Zaur and Sri'Zaur were supposed to be ignorant: concrete.

Ha.

While reinforcing the relatively simple mixture with steel was quite clever, Tsan failed to understand why the mundane chemistry of it escaped the other races. Admittedly, getting the substance to set underwater had felt counterintuitive back in Tsan's newly remembered time as one of the more water-dwelling breeds of Sri'Zaur, but what impressed her now was the rudimentary aquaculture she saw taking place.

Small manufactured ponds stocked with fish marked sections of the earth dedicated to farmland. Improved drainage systems crossed what, from the odor of churned soil, seemed to be farmland whose winter crops were still going into the ground or had just been planted. It had been many years since Tsan had worked the mushroom fields or gone on farmland raids to the north of the Sri'Zauran Mountains, but she could identify rows of potatoes, spinach, onions, radishes, and peas being planted even now, in soil she suspected of being transplanted by industrious Geomancers.

Irrigation. Sewage pipes. All the intricate signs of Dwarven plumbing being set into the ground and run from foundation to foundation of buildings under construction and others merely planned, their future locations demarcated with little cloth flags and twine. Yes, the Aern had elves helping them, but they had a Dwarf doing the architectural design work. She spotted him waving a length of bent pipe at a distracted human farmer, who appeared to have plowed into it, because he could not take his eyes from Tsan.

"Why is the Dwarf so unaffected?" Tsan hissed to Kilke.

"Dragons do not attack Dwarves," answered the disembodied head harnessed at her neck like a brooch or a talisman.

"Why not?" Tsan asked.

"One of my other heads would likely remember," Kilke said, "but I do not."

In less than a month, the Aern had established the bones of an impressive city. More permanent structures were still going up; tents of all shapes and sizes formed the bulk of the shelter within the newly encompassed area. The bones of the thing filled in and took shape in Tsan's mind's eye as she followed the natural course to what would eventually be the first monument to the death of the war between the Eldrennai and the Aern, if not the extermination of the elves themselves.

I can tear this down around their pointed ears or stake my claim and estab-lish my people's part in it, Tsan mused. *What would it be like to bask in the sun again, as a free people united with the other races Uled made? More importantly, who could stand against us if we did form a permanent alliance, an alliance opening a corridor for a relationship with the Dwarves . . .*

Will we be getting Jun cannons, too? she wondered. *And lining the Fortress proper with bone-steel? How had they had the time for that?*

She chuckled lightly at the thought.

"You are impressed," One-Headed Kilke observed.

"Imagine what we would have found in another year," Tsan answered. "The Aern would have always made valuable allies, but their loyalty was, alas, never securable, due to our maker's enslavement of their race."

"I agree," Kilke said, "but free will won't change their taste for Zaur flesh. What makes you so willing to trust them and—?"

"The Aern were always trustworthy. Now, however, we have a common foe and the excuse of an ancient enemy's obvious defeat to seek alliance without losing status." Tsan sighed. "But then you knew that, or you should have. A little unsure of yourself now that my mind is off limits?"

Kilke did not answer.

Drawing nearer, the new dragon smiled as an arrangement of elves rose into the air in glittering breast plates over Aeromancer robes, bat-talions of dragonflies on parade. Fewer of them than she had expected. The Aern truly had slain a prodigious number of the pesky elves. Another excellent reason to have expanded the walls far enough beyond the dis-rupted area that had caused so much trouble for the cursed pointy-eared things and their precious magic.

Someone saw through our reasons for forcing them here and made impres-sive adjustments. Tsan considered Warlord Xastix's original timetable and growled. *We would not have been ready to launch the full attack for another few weeks. These walls would have already been up and, far from the decimated downtrodden wretches we had expected to encounter, they would have been ready and waiting.*

"We still would have won," she hissed.

"Of course," Kilke's cooed soothingly. "Of course you would have won."

Each branch of elemancy made its presence known by deployment of its practitioners . . . Very uneven numbers, Tsan noted. Between the ranks of elemancers, the warsuits and their Aern moved in unison: side by side as distinct combatants, then united together as one Armored, then side by side again.

The sight that made her chortle, however, was two females: an Aern and an elf, both of some import, sitting together on a large blanket well outside the walls. Walls whose gates stood wide open.

They were chatting happily together, one eating a plate of grilled vegetables, the other consuming large quantities of steak prepared in various manners: raw, grilled, steamed, smoked, and boiled (perhaps?). A human attendant stood at a respectful distance, dashing forward to refill the elf's cup or replace a dirty plate with a clean one.

Clever little things, Tsan thought. *Now if only—*

Curious, she came in for a landing, her claws rending the earth. She resisted the urge to scorch it as well, settling for an impressive plume of smoke from her nostrils. Raising herself up to her full height, she spread her wings and stared.

"Warleader Tsan," the Aern said, standing, "I am pleased we have this opportunity to speak. I am Rae'en by Kholster out of Helg, First of One Hundred; and this," she indicated the elf with the curious facial anomaly, "is Queen Bhaeshal, leader of the Aiannai. Would you care to join us? Bash and I were not sure whether you would prefer beef or pork, so we've arranged for both."

*

Is she sniffing us? Rae'en held still despite her natural urge to unsling her warpick and drive the sharp end as deep as she could get it into the dragon's throat. Warleader Tsan loomed over her, throat coated in blued metal, with the severed head of Kilke dangling over the center of the carpet.

"Zaur glean an impressive amount of information from scent and vibration." Queen Bhaeshal rose in genteel fashion, turning about once for the dragon to study her. "Is it the same with dragons?"

"My sense of smell is indeed keen," the dragon said, "but I can only speak for myself. I have met no other dragons."

This is crazy, Amber, Rae'en thought at her Overwatch. *I don't know why I let you and Bash talk me into this plan of attack.*

Because you knew it would work, Amber thought.

Well, the dragon certainly seems surprised, Joose thought. *You have to give Amber that much.*

Just because it is a good plan, M'jynn thought, *doesn't mean it is a sane plan.*

"Would you like to meet one?" Bhaeshal asked.

"Is that a polite way of asking me to leave this world?" Settling down on her haunches, the dragon drew back her head, peering down at the queen with half-lidded eyes. "Or are you merely attempting to determine the extent of my knowledge regarding Coal's demise?"

"Did you say you preferred beef or pork?" Bhaeshal asked through a smile.

*

Moving like a unit, eleven warsuits jogged across the expanse of purple myrrh grass. Four of the empty warsuits (they all had names, but Cadence had not asked what they were) ran farther out from the others: one to the relative northwest, another the northeast, their partners taking up matching positions to the south. Six others ran in a uniform circle of protection around the three young Overwatches, and the young Armored Aern now known as Kazan Eyes of Vengeance (as Cadence understood it).

At the center of the group, both Cadence and Randall Tyree rode on Alberta, Tyree's horse; two of the Overwatches were running alongside as Alberta alternated between a rack and a trot. Of the three of them, Cadence was certain Alberta was having the most fun. Her saddle bags and the provisions the Zaur and Vael had provided were being carried by the warsuits, and Cadence could have sworn the horse thought riding at the center, under escort, was her just due . . . as if this were all a parade for Tyree and his noble steed.

They'd left the forest behind in the early morning, eschewing the opportunity to stop by Silver Leaf City and heading by a more direct route, stopping only to rest Alberta. Kuort, their dead rescuer from back at the tunnels, did not rest when they did, continuing at a steady four-legged lope. They would pass him, then, while they rested Alberta, he would overtake them again.

He did camp with them whenever they camped for the night, but even then, he did not sleep but sat a stone's throw downwind of them, keeping watch.

"We need to hurry," Cadence said into Tyree's ear.

"Why?" Tyree asked, turning his head toward her. "Do you think we'll make any difference if they wind up fighting the dragon?"

"I don't know that it has anything to do with the dragon," Cadence answered. "All I know is that we have to be there to protect something."

"You mean you know-know," Tyree asked, "or you just have a hunch?"

"It's more than a hunch." Her head still hurt, had ever since she had incinerated the dead and held back the smoke with her power. Master Sedric was unreachable, so she could not even ask how Caius was doing. What was he learning? Was he talking yet? Crawling? Master Sedric could have answered those questions, but when she tried to sense him . . .

Closing her eyes, Cadence let her head rest on Tyree's shoulder. All around her, the only thing she could feel with her Long Speaking ability was the edge of the crazed dead thing whose mind drove the restless corpses. A day ago, she had been convinced it was Kuort's presence that threw things off, but when he was far away, the suffocating pall of Uled hung like a curtain, blocking out other minds. It was almost as if one or more of the Long Speaker's Spires had been destroyed. Pushing harder, she yelped as a vision cut through the static.

Wave after wave of dead Zaur poured out of a stone ring engraved in symbols she had never before seen. They overran warsuits, Aern, humans, and elves . . . all who opposed them. Villagers ran, but none escaped the crawling mass of rot that spread across the world, engulfing everything, even the mighty Junland Bridge. Head throbbing with intensifying pain, Cadence attempted to pull away from the vision, but it held her tight, a fist clenching her hair forcing her head under into to the pool of foretelling.

A tree. Small. Humanoid, but rooted—a topiary? Clouds of energy parted at its will . . . and it had a strong will; she could feel it riding alongside her mind.

When clouds parted, the tide turned, but only for a moment. A dead thing, unlike any Cadence had thus far beheld, flew through the stone ring, its skin a mess of scales and flesh slopped together by a mad artist. It smiled a rictus grin, revealing the teeth of an Aern. A tiny force tried to hold it back but could only slow its advance. Fire, ice, and shards of deadly red-and-green rock filled the air, pulping the tree and its ineffectual defenders.

"I don't know how to stop it," she whispered. "I don't even know how to describe it."

"You don't have to," Tyree said, his voiced strained, his skin damp with sweat. "I think I caught most of it."

"Do we really have to protect a tree?" Cadence asked.

"Somebody certainly does," Tyree said.

PART THREE

THE PORT GATE DILEMMA

"In the time before the Aern or the Zaur served the Eldrennai, Port Gates enabled elven dominance throughout the known world. Even Dwarves were wary of the devices that enabled the chosen elemancers of the king to reach out, establishing a foothold in every corner of the Last World, until it seemed a new age with a united empire that would reign forever, turning the tide against the spread of the splintered human kingdoms and breaking the hold of the Issic-Gnoss upon the frozen wastes.

How must it have felt then, when the first curious beings of the Never Dark forced their way through, igniting the Demon Wars and rendering the use of the gates a dangerous proposition at best . . . knowledge of the close-held secret of a Port Gate's destruction transmuted to a necessity for all elemancers. From that moment to this, the number of gates in the Last World dwindled, increasing again only on one notable and terrifying day that came close to destroying all. Even in death, my father seemed intent upon shaping the world in his own distorted likeness."

From the preface to *When the World Was Small* by Sargus

CHAPTER 22
THE FORGOTTEN GENERAL: BORDERLANDS OF THE NEVER DARK

Stretched out along the border between the edge of one world and the next, the Eldrennai Army formed a line of battalions and companies impressive in both their numbers and general lack of supplies. Deployed in a show of force unseen since the Demon War centuries before, they drilled and practiced, learning through trial and error the way magic responded in this strange world of rapidly shifting temperatures and landscapes. The Never Dark's few constants, the ever-present light and the mountain range beyond which, somewhere high and far, the illumination's source seemed to lie, felt like falsehoods, too, but they were not.

Foul Beak sniffed and adjusted his position. Clad in his Ghaiattri leathers, hooded, and crouching at the edge of an outcrop of rocks along the mountain ridge, with cave mouth at his back, the elf breathed in a long, deep breath, testing the air and catching only the faintly sweet scent of nearby demons. Scoffing, he set his right hand on the hilt of his rough-hewn blade of bone, keeping his left hand free to cast, but he did not shift his gaze from the foolish assembly in the distance below.

An Eldrennai army of this size had never before been seen on this side of the Port Gates, which served as tenuous doorways between Foul Beak's home and the place in which he now dwelled. Near thirty thousand elves were arrayed in a series of regimented camp blocks, each sleeping roll regulation distance from its neighbor, as if a tent were in place. Some had the skill to work crystalline shelters, using the same magic that let Crystal Knights summon the armored coating which was their namesake, but geomancers would have no luck working with the ground here, as close to the Gates as they were keeping.

Along edges of the Never Dark, the Mountains of Shade created a wide swath of land called the Darkening Mile. Grass and proper trees grew there in full eternal bloom when viewed from the mountains—which betrayed the falsehood of their existence. The first few hundred yards around each Port Gate were barren and cracked, the ground a thin layer of gray-brown dirt above a layer of stone the color of obsidian and as hard to work as an Aern's bone-steel. From that perspective, they might see the eternal bloom occasionally, but terrain that close to the space between dimensions was, strictly speaking, more material than that which lay in farther lightward in the heart of the Bright.

There the fully grown Ghaiattri, shimmering beings of light long having abandoned the violence and folly of their material youth, lived in company with a truly insane dragon. It was more comfortable out here in the physical, but it was dreary beyond endurance to dwell so close to the illusions of home: the trees, the grass, even the air held a proper scent here. Why the leader in his Ghaiattri hide plate (crowned helm, he noted) kept his army close to the more familiar geometries of the Darkening Mile made a certain sense to Foul Beak, but if they didn't move farther in, they'd never accomplish whatever it was they wanted to accomplish. Not unless all they wanted was to guard the Port Gate.

Further in, the erratic temperature, weather, and terrain changes they surely saw and felt from their perspective were less easily handled with magic. It was the gates that were to blame. Hasimak had introduced immutable alien stone to a place where the physical was meant to be fluid and ephemeral. He hadn't known it, of course, but he'd discovered his error in time, Foul Beak was certain of it. He'd likely faced the same moral dilemma himself. To destroy the Port Gates would be the more sensible course of action, but Foul Beak needed them as surely as the army in the Darkening Mile did.

They were the only way home. Without them, future demon wars couldn't happen. The Ghaiattri would no longer be able to play merry hells with mortals who stumbled across a piece of the world crystal. No invasion route to Barrone would exist. And yet . . . they were the only way home. He felt so close after all these years.

True, Ghaiattri had tried to force the gates before, even managed brute breaches of them at times, but the demons had quieted since the destruction of several Port Gates, so Foul Beak discounted that one. The demons, if one wanted to persist in calling them something they clearly weren't, were content, for the moment, to observe the newcomers, following Foul Beak's suit.

Well, except for a few of them.

Bones still vibrating from his most recent visit into the Bright, Foul Beak removed his Ghaiattri leather gloves and squinted at his hands. The bones still luminesced through the skin, but the flesh itself had grown opaque once more. With his thumbs, he popped in unison the third knuckles on the fingers of each hand, from index to baby finger.

"Noise and sensation instead of sparks," he murmured to himself in High Eldrennaic. "Physical enough for all sorts of things again."

"Stay here much longer, and it will have to feed," squawked a nearby voice.

Offering a habitual rude gesture, Foul Beak did not look in the spy's direction. The cursed Ghaiax were impossible to avoid in the mountains. More advanced along the path to eventual enlightenment than their larger brothers, the Ghaiattri, the Ghaiax were less obviously aggressive, less, well, evil. Farther along the path to understanding the light and abandoning their physical forms and becoming true Ghaia, the Ghaiax were nonetheless not to be underestimated.

I spy on them, he thought. *They spy on me. And we all spy on the new arrivals. We should start a quilting circle and be done with it. At least then we'd have something useful to show for our efforts.*

Spying was the favorite pastime of the winged pests.

At first, Foul Beak had surveilled his fellow elves in measured lengths of time to see how long they would survive. If he were to be honest with himself, he would have had to admit he was impressed at their ingenuity. They were faring much better than the brash young prince he'd had to rescue . . . however long ago it had been.

Well . . . not **had** to rescue. Almost hadn't. But the stamp of Villok had been so clear on the youth, he hadn't been able to watch him die.

Still, after the prince had killed three of the Ghaiattri, it had not felt just to let him fall prey to the remaining five . . . and with Shidarva's power lacking in this godless realm, who else was there to be the hands of justice and retribution?

"No one, but me," Foul Beak whispered.

He had been sorely tempted to nurse the boy back to health in the

Never Dark, rather than returning him insensate to the Dying Light via the Port Gate, but . . . the Ghaiattri flame seemed to have caught within him. Keeping him here could have been . . . dangerous . . . or transformative. Foul Beak did not know which would have been worse, but a complete transition had proved nigh-impossible to reverse, so he'd erred on the side of keeping the prince an elf.

On the shifting terrain below, the Eldrennai broke camp again. The scouts they'd sent out to explore the surrounding area had not come back. Foul Beak nudged with his boot the unconscious form of the one he'd rescued, eliciting a change in breathing but not consciousness. The stupid soldier had burns from Ghaiattri fire across his back, but he would likely live. Sniffing the wounds revealed no sign of taint, so there was that in the lad's favor, too. This close to the Dying Light, what the foolhardy Ghaiattri called Barrone, and Lambent called the Last World, things were dim enough for him to remove the smoked-glass lenses that shielded his eyes on forays further into Lambent's domain. The Bright.

Lambent . . .

What kind of name was that for a dragon? Or its realm? As if anyone could see the beast and fail to recognize him by his true name. No, Lambent was no name for a dragon. Zohar was a better name, a majestic name. If Zohar's dark twin, Abyssimus, were to play such games, people would call him Void.)

Not that Foul Beak is my true name either . . .

A breeze, sharp and hard and brief, spat comingled freezing and blazing hot winds across his back, but it had been many moons indeed since this place could catch him unawares. A casual flare of elemantic might shielded him from the worst of it, and he channeled what he couldn't block completely into twin bursts of ice and fire, which he hurled at one of the nearby Ghaiax watching him. Curled horns dimmed their usual light to express displeasure, but the crystal-scaled creature with its sharp-angled wings didn't bother going through too much of a display, merely snapping its beak in disgust.

"Not fair, Foul Beak," the wolf-sized Ghaiax croaked in Low Tongue.

"Oh, fair am I?" Foul Beak pulled back his Ghaiattri leather hood to reveal short-cropped black hair and the vaguely pointed ears of an Eldrennai. He glared over his lenses, revealing sapphire-colored eyes that caught the light and seemed to shine, amplifying that which it took in and reflecting it back. "Fair in appearance if not in deed or word. My tongue, though, of itself is attractive enough, yet the sounds it makes are no more fair than you." It took a little magic to allow Elven lips to produce the correct trills and squawks of the Never Dark's primary languages, but it was worth it to watch them tremble with rage as he insulted them in High Tongue, giving any polite messages he was grudgingly forced to relay only in Low Tongue. "I find, in fact, that you serve no purpose useful to any being other than to block the light which should so freely shine. Why do you yet thrive? Does death not crave your company more than I? He surely does, for anyone must, by definition, be said to crave it with greater appetite when compared to my own desire for the continuance of your presence."

Insults were a little forced in High Tongue, but it was one of the few true pleasures left to Foul Beak since he had gathered all but the last of his sheep together. Even now he could feel the Ghaiax's kin probing his cache and seeking a way into the cave, but once he'd managed to master enough of the dimensional magic with which Hasimak had forged the Port Gates, shielding the cave had been easy . . . And it had only taken a hundred years. Or was it two?

"No!" He barked the thought away. Keeping track of time, thinking about it, had proven dangerous. Too dangerous in this timeless place, where the light neither dimmed nor moved except as it approached the border between worlds. Beyond the edges of the Darkening Mile, the sway of time held but loose rein upon any elf.

One hundred years. He drove his palm into his temple. *Today. Tomorrow. Even the next. It will always have been one hundred years. Time has no reckoning until we return.*

"Foul Beak's thoughts are jumbled," the Ghaiax croaked.

"Yet his magic—" Foul Beak lashed out with a thin plane of violet power, bisecting, then quartering, the beast. "—remains sharp—" He killed another of the beasts clinging to the rocks of the Shade Mountains about him. "—and bright—" Another fell, this time into unequal pieces. "—and perilous."

As one, the remainder of the flock took wing, providing blessed solitude (the injured elf scarcely counted) if but for a scattered handful of moments. Drumming the fingers of his left hand on the stone outcropping of his overlook, Foul Beak used two small rings of purple magic like the ends of a telescope to magnify his view of the army below.

"Not a Bone Finder among them," he spat. "How the hells does King Villok expect me to reach the last one without one of Zhan's Ossuarians?"

You will find a way, General Kyland, the memory of the king's reassurance echoed in his mind. *You always do.*

"I haven't failed yet, my king." Taking a moment to straighten his armor and clean his smoked lenses, the Eldrennai called Foul Beak by the denizens of the Never Dark and General Kyland by the elves and Aern who had served under his command (including, to his simultaneous pride and chagrin, his daughter, Wylant) rose into the air on a wave of dimensional magic and arced toward those assembled below. It was clear enough they were no trick of the Ghaiattri or the light-bending Velli-ahnt. So what in Aldo's name did they think they were doing here?

"Time," he muttered to himself, "to see what the king has sent me."

*

Sweat ran down Rivvek's back underneath his Ghaiattri hide plate as he listened to another report telling him what he already knew. They had been there for days and Rivvek was no closer to finding the Lost Command than he'd been before he'd marched through the Port Gate. They weren't coming back. Not even when he'd sent a group hand-picked by Jolsit, himself a veteran of the Demon Wars, an elf who had been brave enough to tackle a Ghaiattri back through a Port Gate at Port Ammond what seemed like years ago now, but which could only have been a matter of weeks.

Jolsit's near self-sacrifice had averted the beginning of another demon war when, to transport the Aernese warsuits under General Bloodmane's command to multiple striking positions at once, they had risked opening the Port Gates within the Tower of Elementals.

Suddenly the blazing heat beating down on them from, well, from no suns Rivvek could see, was swept away. In its place, a frigid chill settled over them as the grass beyond the barren areas surrounding the Port Gate wavered and shifted, becoming a field of snow with columns of ice and stands of evergreens replacing what had been there only moments before.

He'd expected an army of the curly-horned demons to swoop down on them, wielding Ghaiattri Fire to burn them all to cinders, a swarm of unescapable death, in retaliation for their incursion in the Never Dark. But . . . nothing. Nothing close. Around him Pyromancers swapped out with Aeromancers and Hydromancers who'd been doing their best to ablate the heat, but there were fewer of them. He wondered why it was that Pyromancers and Geomancers appeared to have been more likely to be accepted as Aiannai by the Aern than Aeromancers or Hydromancers. Pyromancers tended to fight toward the front of the battle, as did Geomancers. Was there some inherent advantage for Aeromancers and Hydromancers when it came to command that meant an elf wielding fire or earth was more likely to have fought alongside rather than be in command over Aern?

It was worth taking time to do a full review of the matter with Sargus, if they ever made it back. Back. How were things going back there? He had been forced to take more than half of the trained soldiers and elemancers with him through the Port Gate. For every elf he'd taken with him who did not possess the power of elemancy, there were two who did. And only seven Artificers. It seemed those who shared Sargus's discipline were even less likely to have been in a position to offend the Aern by "holding the leash."

"We've tried scouting—" Jolsit began as he approached.

"But you've found nothing resembling what I saw when I went the Port Gate a century ago," Rivvek cut him off. "And the scouts haven't returned and we are still sitting on the doorstep counting down the hours to doom."

"Sorry," he said in response to Jolsit's silence. "I didn't think it would look this different. I—" —*didn't expect to still be alive.*

"If it helps, Highness," Jolsit offered, "the combat training is going better than expected for those lacking recent martial experience, and the landscape is definitely an incentive for the veterans to knock the dust off their skills as well."

"Did . . ." Rivvek tried to concentrate, to bring the mind that had been able to see a strategy to save the bulk of his people from the Aern and implement it to bear, but he was so tired. He had been so used to stacking up the trignoms on the game board of his mind, to running things through the probability matrix that was the collection of mathematical constructs the Gnomes worshipped as the Great Destiny Machine, but . . . "Did you get the organization issue sorted out?"

"Yes, sire." Rivvek could hear the elf's smile in his voice even with the horrible helm in place. "We've settled on forty-two battalions of approximately six hundred and fifty elves. I'd hoped to—"

"A moment." Rivvek cut him off, gesturing to a figure in the sky. But it was unnecessary. Rivvek had seen the approaching creature only a few heartbeats before Jolsit spotted it, a possible benefit of the Ghaiattri plate armor they both wore and the way its crystal lenses distorted the images around them. Back home, it allowed glimpses through the barriers between dimensions, illuminating the use of magic as well. Here, it also allowed glimpses of the world they'd left behind. Jolsit looked back toward the Port Gate at the ghostly image of Fort Sunder, hoping for a glimpse of Sargus in the hallway, working furiously on plan after plan at the desk he had moved out into the hallway, or building works of artifice to assist in the coming battle. Sargus had not been there for a day or so.

Rivvek turned his attention toward the incoming figure once more. It was wreathed in lines of purple, blue, and red. The slight demonic-looking thing glided on wings of amaranthine light. Light that bore more than a passing resemblance to the magic Rivvek had seen Hasimak use back at Port Ammond when he attempted to hold off an entire invasion force of Zaur . . . and succeeded.

"Pyromancers—" Rivvek began.

"I think it's an elf, highness," Jolsit hissed. "That's not its hide. That's armor."

"Elementalists hold," Jolsit ordered at a nod from Rivvek. Echoing cries of "Hold" went down the line in both directions. At a further gesture from their king, the troops parted to make way for the new arrival.

Draped in armor that was to a scout's leathers what the king's own armor was to a Castleguard Knight's suit of plate, the elf landed lithely, the surroundings shifting as his boots touched the ground. Replacing the icy landscape, an idyllic scene of tall grass and trees with leaves a vibrant green erupted, flowing out from the new arrival's position and bringing with it a cool breeze that smelled of spring and approaching rain.

Over the toe of his boots and at the tips of each gloved finger, demon claws were affixed with processes Rivvek could not readily determine, as if the under edge of each threatening talon were fused with the leather. Short bone spurs curved up from a thicker ridge of pad-like plating at the knees and elbows. Bone weapons hung belted at the elf's waist, but what caught the king's eye the most was the symbol etched into its broad chest plate: three towers lined in amber-hued resin. It pulsed with red, blue, and purple in sequence as if in response to his gaze.

The elf smirked beneath smoked lenses made not of proper glass, but some type of clear crystal, held in place with frames of Ghaiattri bone, worked thin like wires. Pulling back his hood to reveal close-cropped raven-black hair, the elf sniffed deeply, as if trying to catch the scents of those assembled.

His laugh took all assembled by surprise.

"He's gone mad." Jolsit stepped forward interposing himself between the elf and his king. "Stand back, sire."

"Mad, Lieutenant Jolsit? No," the elf barked. "Impatient, perhaps. Fatigued beyond measure, I assure you, but I am in complete command of my faculties, just as, one presumes will be imminently evident, I am of this army."

"I don't know how you know my name, but how dare—?" Jolsit drew his blade. The oddly outfitted Eldrennai smiled, baring his teeth in a very Aern-like manner, to reveal a mouth full of bone-steel dental replacements, not the haphazard sort of thing that sometimes happened on the battlefield when a soldier lost a handful of teeth and ordered an Aern to replace them, but a fitted affair . . .

On the trignom board in Rivvek's head, a handful of the three-sided tiles settled into their places for this variant. A new game. Those teeth were a very rare decoration, a military one, one of the most intimate the Aern could, as slaves, bestow.

Rivvek brushed aside Jolsit's blade with a one gauntleted hand.

"What," he asked as he removed his helm, "can you tell us about the state of the mission, General Kyland?"

CHAPTER 23
CONJUNCTION

Irkanth roars echoed against the distant butte upon which Fort Sunder sat. Shrieking shade-beast cries told the story of a hunt underway. Kholburran could not tell who hunted whom, but lay back on the cold ground, myrr grass tickling his bark, and tried to puzzle it out. Anything to block the sounds of the girl-type persons arguing felt a worthwhile pursuit. All had seemed fine; they had been approaching Fort Sunder and then Gilly, the advance scout, had come running back to make them crouch at the base of the butte instead of walking on around the main entrance. He wanted to go inside, see where real Aern had fought demons and won, where real warsuits walked and talked, beings who had predated the Vael, the Twin Trees. If there was a dragon, he wanted to see it, too. Besides, he could barely make out the fortress through the fog or clouds, or whatever they were, ringing the top of the butte.

"What makes the clouds so thick?" he asked, but the others ignored him.

"There is a dragon, Arri!" Gilly thrust her palm toward the senior Root Guard's chest, a mimed push emphasizing the strength of her opinion. "A dragon no one has ever seen before is leading an army of Zaur. We should go back to Silver Leaf and wait to see whether or not there will be a Fort Sunder to visit when the Zaur are done with it."

"The Zaur are now our allies." Arri's gaze flicked to Gilly's open palm, and she thrust her fist into it, daring the other Root Guard to close her fingers around it. "And the prince may go where the prince wishes."

How could so many people be both staring intently at and pretending to ignore the same spot? Kholburran held his breath. Surely Gilly wouldn't go so far as to challenge—

Gilly jerked her hand away, growling like an Aern.

Kholburran felt Arri's eyes fall on him, the heat of her gaze making him sap. He could end the argument, but he did not want to do it. If Gilly did not listen to him, if she was angry enough to oppose him directly, she would leave Arri little choice but to strip her rank and eject her from the prince's guard. Being kicked out of the Root Guard did not mean the end of a Vael's life or career, unless it happened during a Root Taking . . . then it was banishment at best, mulching at worst.

Refuse to serve the Root Tree in life and you could nourish his growth. So he looked at the fortress, looming silent over the plains, and tried to count the plumes of smoke rising from forges or cooking fires.

Another hundred count, he told himself, *maybe a thousand count, and then I'm going to run for the rock face and scale straight up to the fortress. Then they can either help me or stand back and gawp. Maybe that will keep Gilly out of trouble.*

"Arri," Gilly said, "you have to listen to reason. Ancient custom doesn't get to lead the hunt in wartime."

The whorls of green on Arri's bark lit up bright enough to blind even in the daylight. Her newly regrown arm lanced out, fingers splayed, grasping, just short of Gilly's chest.

"LISTEN?" Arri's trembling wood formed the sounds without need of her throat lips or vocal cord. "NO. YOU MUST HEAR THE ONE WHO TAKES ROOT."

Twitching ever so slightly, Gilly's Heartbow slipped its string.

Gilly dropped in supplication, and the trembling of Arri's bark ceased. Arri caught herself, stumbling, but not falling. Was that a smile?

"Prince," Arri's said, her voice sharp and fierce, "are we going back or going forward?"

*

You are never going to believe this, Kazan thought to Rae'en. *Look who the warsuits spotted on the trail to the main gate.*

A group of Flower Girls and a Flower Boy popped into her mind's eye. Zooming in more closely on the boy, she hesitated. Eyes a solid and startling jade peeked out from a face that was her father's wrought in bark and leaves. Were there such things as Vael Incarna? Yavi had looked similar to Wylant, but a younger version, with head petals. Her demeanor had felt like such a long spear's throw from the real Wylant that Rae'en had scarcely felt the need to make note of it.

Rae'en smiled at the approaching Flower Boy. He had fang-like thorns where an Aern would have doubled upper and lower canines. His head petals grew short and spiky, the floral equivalent of a Hulsite mercenary's haircut. No beard, though.

She squinted. A warpick—a wooden one—hung from his back in the Aern fashion. With a few facial tattoos, he might have passed for Irka from a distance. Her brother was forever messing about with his hair, so much so that the head petals could have been an affectation.

Why does that one have whorls and such? Joose asked.

None of us have ever seen anything like them, Amber thought. *I have to say I like the looks of the male, though.*

"News from afar?" Warleader Tsan looked up from her light meal, the half-crushed head of a pig visible at the rear of her maw.

"Guests." Rae'en nodded in the general direction of the newcomers. "Vael."

"How wonderful." Tsan shifted her bulk, settling lower to the ground but not following Rae'en's gaze. "Have you met the young prince before? He is quite charming."

How did—? Rae'en started. *Oh, Zaurtol. Can you spot the scouts?*

Found them, Amber shot the images to Rae'en, highlighting their outlines in silver. Scales changed colors as the trio of scouts moved. Rae'en started at the sight of the breed that had killed Vander, Okkust, and the others. *They're keeping pace, but just watching.*

Rae'en growled.

CHAPTER 24
THE PRINCESS
AND THE GHOST

Two spots of ash, reptilian smears of carbon and bone, marked the concrete steps of the Little Sister Lighthouse roughly thirty miles from the mine where they had faced the golem and hundreds of miles from home. The centuries-old structure stood squat and inelegant on the Dwarf-made isle due north of the conjoined port cities where Holsven and Zaliz met. Long ago, both cities had no doubt had separate names, but if there had been any living residents who remembered them, they now marched to the beat of Uled's mad drum. Only one living sentient existed within the fallen port. Below Yavi, impossible to miss from her vantage at the edge of the lighthouse's widows' walk, corpses lurked. Dead Sri'Zaur with gills and webbed paws swam laps around the scant isle and the bulwark against the dead Dolvek had created. His Geomancy had shifted stone around the lip of the isle, forcing it to billow out like a mushroom cap, creating an overhang the dead could not climb.

Wind stirred her head petals, freeing two that tumbled light and slow toward the sea. False Spring could not last forever, and each gust took a toll in yellow from Yavi's head. This was a time for hard bark and inner sap, if she had ever lived through one.

She peered out at all of those human and elven corpses intermingled with the reptiles, relieved to see no Aern or Vael among them. Did their dead not walk? Yavi hoped not.

Behind her, a mistlike apparition kept silent watch.

"Lucky that fell where it did." Yavi pointed down at long and fractured ruin. Fragments of the Long Speaker's Spire that had once stood high above the cities lay broken across the spillways, the very tip only a hundred yards or so from the where the Little Sister Dock had stood before Dolvek had rolled up the rock, sealing the way.

"Yes."

Yavi gripped the edge of the widows' walk, the watch room at her back, with the bright-white glow of the lantern shining behind her like a diamond in the sunlight. Would her bow be strong enough to punch through the Port Gates' surface, destroying the runes? She'd slipped a chunk of stone from the fallen spire into her pack just in case, but if it came down to that . . .

Gull cries split the air as brave, or incredibly desperate, birds swept down to tear loose flaps of skin from the moving corpses that lining the three main docks and the spillways, queuing up at the foot of three Port Gates upon which the thing which Warlord Xastix had become worked its spells. Yavi felt sorry for the warlord, to have been overcome by Uled, the Sri'Zaur's body torn apart to build Uled's grotesque current form.

"Now." Dolvek's susurrant voice cut through her thoughts. Several stones whirled past Yavi's eyes like evasive flies fleeing a flailing hand.

"Fourth, twenty-third, eleventh, second, eighteenth, and thrive," Yavi said as quickly as she could get the words out.

"Thrive?" Dolvek's voice, quiet but disturbing, like the noise of rats chewing at the attic walls, made her uneasy even though she did not understand why. Was it because the sound of the waves should have washed it away, blocked it out, but did not? His voice operated on a different range than other sounds, something Yavi didn't think she heard with her ears at all.

A smile broke the grim lines of his mouth, but he was still waiting for an answer.

"It was three or five," Yavi said. "I didn't get a good look at it, but I can do this, Dolvek. Can we just go already?"

"At your command, Yavi." He offered a smile and an abbreviated bow. "Give the order and I am at your disposal."

Dolvek shimmered, moving from standing to sitting next to her at the edge in one jerky transitionless motion. Up close, he looked pale, despite his translucent form, and Yavi wondered what his continuous use of elemancy was doing to his spirit. Where did he draw his power from?

His spirit was no more terrifying than any nature spirit, except for the disquieting feeling that he ought not be here. Torgrimm should have taken him. Dolvek said nothing more, but she sensed his impatience, borne not of a personal sense of importance but because they were running out of time.

Yavi's focus shifted back to the army visible through him, across the port. Uled's army was vast . . . and looking that way made her chest ache. Rank upon rank of the once-living inhabitants mixed with reptilian, human, and elven recruits had ceased their wandering, standing motionless in three large groups awaiting their master's bidding, each prong ready to charge through one of the three Port Gates before them once they were operational. Three Port Gates.

"What if we can't take out all three Port Gates?" Yavi asked.

"The Aern will think of something," Dolvek said, "or my brother will."

Below, the water looked stark and mysterious. The amphibious Sri'Zaur had swum away to take their positions with the rest of the army, abandoning their halfhearted attempts at seizing Yavi. She had not noticed when they left. That scared her, knowing such monsters could become so normal that she forgot about them, however momentarily.

A wave of sound echoed across the water with a thrum so deep the vibration left Yavi dazed for a five-count.

"What was that?" she asked.

"The beginning of the end of the ritual," Dolvek said. "The Port Gates are nearly complete."

*

Over the rise, close to the spot where the tower at North Watch had once stood, Zhan smelled the sweet-rot of the recently dead mixed with the salty tang of the sea, all overlaying the fire-pit aftertaste of a tower long since burned. Atop, of course, the reek of dragon and Zaur. The Zaur had tunneled under North Watch and destroyed it, as they had so many of the watch towers back when Warlord Xastix had been the enemy, before Uled's distasteful magicks stirred the dead to his call. A vibration twin to the bone metal pin of Glayne's which marked his spot amid the web of scars on Zhan's back pulled at him in a straight line through the hill, a taut fishing line of awareness. More than two hundred warsuit-clad Ossuarians stood ready to take back those bones, but Zhan hesitated.

Keeper's thoughts, silent, yet expectant, rang louder than words in Zhan's mind.

"You think I should have accepted Kholster's Rae'en's offer of aid?"

Zhan whispered, too softly for his troops to fail to understand the question was a private one, either to himself or his warsuit.

There are thousands of them, Keeper intoned. We seek the bones, not the battles. It feels as if, here, you seek both.

And you disapprove? Some communications were too sensitive to expect the troops to ignore. Their kholster . . . their Ossuarian should be certain of what he must do, presenting an unfaltering front of strength and guidance.

I would never disapprove of my rightful occupant so long as he seeks the bones and keeps them. Keeper's thoughts came strong and unambiguous.

Then what—?

But you are questioning your own actions, Keeper thought back. You have done so ever since you misjudged the First of One Hundred. You feel you are not seeking the bones, but proving a point about the relationship between the Ossuary and the Army.

I am resolved in this, Keeper. Zhan fought the urge to glance about at his troops. He knew where they were, could feel them as acutely as he did the pins in his scars. They did not question. Not aloud. But . . .

I would submit that you are not at all resolved in this, maker. Keeper's tone held no judgment, merely cold, calm, reflective observation. That is not, however, a requirement. Charge or stand. Swing or block. I will keep you as safe as I can, for your bones are my flesh and your flesh, my bones. I am yours to kholster. You are my rightful occupant. That which you bid me, I will do without hesitation, as have I always done.

Maybe . . . Zhan stood, knowing a single step would bring him within the enemy's possible range of detection, his helm visible via their field of vision, estimated using the direction of a fragment of Glayne's bone metal, the spot in Coal's chest in which Zhan felt the metal, the terrain . . .

"Zhan," roared the voice of a bellowing dragon, "are you going to hide behind that hill until the suns set, or are you coming for your precious bones?"

To Zhan's left, Alysaundra cursed.

Tell the First of One Hundred that it is possible the Ossuary has erred.

*

Three new points of contact erupted in the half light, stirring the ancient elf from his torpor. Like all Port Gates, they sought their terminus. Once, Hasimak had thought of himself as the engine that drove the portals he created, but after long millennia he had learned the truth of things. Perhaps at first he had been the source, but a balance had tipped, maybe during the demon wars, maybe long before, when the gates had begun to sustain him. Beginning had become end.

Without thinking, Hasimak caught the miswrought strands reaching through the void between the Dying Light and the Never Dark, threading them through his mental map of vertices and connections, and realigned them with their brother and sister gates before it occurred to him that they were not his gates. Like a parent thrilled to see the return of a child thought lost beyond all hope of return, he had presumed older gates had been brought into alignment once again. But, no, this was . . . else. Foreign. False.

A red line of barbed energy grabbed at his core, some crude trap of a lesser practitioner—*Ah. Of course. Uled*—and he discarded the nasty little things and the others hiding within before he understood the trick of them.

"A distraction," he chuckled to himself. "Needless, but clever in your way, aren't you, lad?"

Was it wrong to be pleased at his pupil's achievement? To view the beauty in the architecture of a mad elf even as he saw that it was evil and destructive?

New energy brought with it a rush of restoration, and within moments Hasimak stood whole and hale upon his floating refuge.

"Will you intervene?" Appearing after the voice, a Dwarf in shining armor manifested.

"Foreman Jun." Hasimak acknowledged the deity's presence with a slight nod. "I find your presence unexpectedly pleasant."

"That was all—" Jun started.

"Unforgivable?" the wizened elf asked.

"I was going to say it was long ago." Jun looked away.

"Not so long as all that." Hasimak wrapped himself in lines of purple magic, using them to alter the remnant of the Tower of Elementals within which he stood, rendering it a proper balcony (if one ignored the fact that it was floating in nothingness) surrounding a modest one-room house with mage lighting both inside and out, the fixtures in the likeness of Coal breathing out.

Changing size and shape until it pleased him, the abode cemented itself when it had become a long rectangle, with square home in the middle, a fountain in the likeness of his last apprentices, the Elemental Nobles: Zerris, Klerris, Lord Stone, and Hollis, the Sea Lord, each holding a floating sphere representing the appropriate elements.

My poor students, he thought. *My children.*

Jun nodded sagely, examining the new isle.

"May I?" he asked.

At a nod from Hasimak, the deity added a dome of black on the underside of the island. Atop the isle, at what Hasimak now deemed the prow, Jun wrought a simple orb of the same black material inset on a white pedestal. Hasimak sensed the magic with both the dome and the orb. The dome could draw on the currents of dimensional energies within the Betwixt. The orb acted as steering wheel, guiding the island's course with the touch of a hand and the will of an elemancer.

"I was not planning on travel," Hasimak said, frowning at the Builder's new additions. A means of propulsion created options Hasimak would have preferred to be without.

"You might change your mind."

"I shan't interfere, you know." Hasimak summoned a tunnel and reached through it, drawing out his mattress and his books. They had been destroyed, yes, but not truly, because no matter ever is. "Not unless they truly need me."

"They don't?" Jun asked.

"The Last World has no further need of its sole surviving mortal immigrant," Hasimak said. "My gifts are too destructive in their hands and, unlike the Dwarves, my knowledge cannot be so easily repossessed, should it fall into unexpected hands or be turned toward ends of which I disapprove; I decline to kill."

Jun bowed his head.

"I do," Hasimak said softly, "forgive you, however."

Jun looked up, eyes brightening, tears streaming.

"My mistake with the Port Gates," Hasimak continued, "though not as pronounced as yours with the dragons, has opened my eyes. We all fall prey to the call of fire to one degree or another. The only difference is the scope of our mistakes: the scale."

"The dragons—"

Hasimak arched an eyebrow.

"After everything they did," Jun said, "I still love every last one of them."

"That's a father's job." Hasimak peered into the void between worlds, his thoughts unknowable, his past untold.

CHAPTER 25

WE ALL HAVE SCARS

Three of the most powerful rulers in the entire world stared at Kholburran expectantly: Rae'en, First of One Hundred; Bhaeshal, Queen of the Aiannai; and Tsan, dragon and Warleader of the Zaur and Sri'Zaur. Kholburran swallowed hard. As he and his Root Guard had approached the main entrance to Scarsguard, the city that had sprung up around Fort Sunder seemingly overnight, two warsuits had escorted Kholburran and company to the picnic (was that the right word, for a meal in which a dragon was devouring an entire cow, al fresco?). Fifty yards away, the warsuits had instructed the Root Guard to wait at a remove from the three rulers, though, after some debate, Arri had been allowed to accompany him as guardian of his virtue. Even though Kholburran had known it to be a polite fiction on Arri's part, it still stung a little. A boy-type person could not possibly be expected to take care of himself. Ugh.

"You'd think the Aeromancers would keep the sky clear so we could have a good view," Kholburran remarked to Arri, noting periodic gusts of clouds or fog that obscured the elven elemancers as they performed impressive maneuvers in the air. Arri acted as if she had not heard him, however. She couldn't take her eyes off the dragon.

And the dragon was impressive.

Nothing Kholburran had ever seen could match the liquid red of the dragon's scales, the sheer size of her, the heat that emanated from her.

"Pleased to see you again, little prince."

The SAME Tsan?! The voice was deeper, but definitely the same. *Even so. How?*

"You're a dragon now?" Kholburran asked. "How did that happen?"

"Ahem." Tsan blinked twice with exquisite slowness. "We are allies and so I shall make allowances. Do not inquire again. Have you met the First of One Hundred or Queen Bhaeshal?"

"No."

"Rae'en." The female Aern offered to shake his hand, altering the gesture at the last possible moment to be an appropriately nonrestrictive Vael-style hand shake. "You look a lot like my father, Prince . . . ?"

"Snapdragon—" Why?! Why had he said that? Kholburran fought the urge to slap his palm into his forehead and die of embarrassment.

"Prince Kholburran," Arri corrected swiftly. "The other is a little nickname, referring to the way his dental ridges have thorns mimicking the canines of an Aern. I'm Arri."

"And I," said the third ruler, an Aiannai with an elemental foci like a mask across her features, "am Bhaeshal, but Bash is my nickname. You can use it if you like, prince, but then I shall avail myself of your nickname, as well."

"Does everyone else have a nickname?" Rae'en asked.

"The Tsan'Zaur," the dragon said, chortling. "My subjects think I have not heard them using the term to describe my unique metamorphosis, but they underestimate a dragon's hearing."

"I—" Rae'en gave Kholburran the strangest look he had ever received, like she was seeing him and seeing through him at the same time, her eyes tightly focused and then completely unfocused in the space of a heartbeat. "I must make our excuses, prince."

"Make Prince Kholburran and his Flower Girls comfortable . . . clear them some space near the pond or something. You like dirt, right?" Rae'en waited a beat, but started talking again while Kholburran was still busy being stunned by the question and her casual use of the epithet 'Flower Girls.' "Get some tarps or something put up around them for privacy and so they don't have to be gawked at unless they want to be."

The warsuits who had escorted them, move forward to lead them away. As they did, Kholburran heard the three leaders speaking in hushed tones. He could have sworn Rae'en asked, "Don't be offended by this, Tsan, but how fast can you fly?"

*

Two forms rode upon the wind, the ocean below reflecting one, blind to the other. As they split formation, Dolvek wove in and around snapping violet tendrils as Uled reached out to stop him. The dead prince did not know exactly what would happen if Uled got a tendril on him, but he presumed it would be unpleasant and final.

He fought the urge to look across the port and find Yavi, to follow her progress. They both had jobs to do, and she would not thank him if he came to her rescue but failed in his appointed task. Assuming he could actually manage it.

Dolvek had assured her he could, that he would have no more trouble destroying the stones than she would, but he could sense his physical presence diminish, the greater the distance between them grew. Within a few feet of her, he felt solid enough to do whatever he wished. His senses, though altered, could interpret the physical world effortlessly.

Yards away, the world became a twilight place, the corpses, the ground, the sky, all of one material, difficult to distinguish. Fortunately, magic and spirit shone more clearly. The Port Gates became radiant beacons, twice as bright as Yavi's resplendent spirit at this range, Uled's spirit and tendrils transforming into fluid shapes of atramentous shadow arcing through the liquid air.

Ahead, as if Uled knew Dolvek's final destination, swarms of black surrounded the Port Gate. The message was clear: *come near my Port Gate and I will end you.*

How fortunate, Dolvek mused, *that I no longer fear endings.*

Three tendrils struck him in unison when he reached the Port Gate. Pain blinded him as he fought the ripping, tearing things, then, realizing his mistake, Dolvek reached out to the planes of elemental magic. He could not touch fire or earth, but air and water still heard him.

He stopped fighting, turning all of his concentration to the spears of ice he hurled at the Port Gate, reading the symbols in order and destroying them one at time, even as Uled shredded his soul. He did not falter or cry out; there was no time for either.

*

At North Watch, Alysaundra kept both eyes on the fight she was in, relying on Bone Harvest to track Zhan and let her know if he needed assistance. It felt great not having to keep such a close watch on Teru and Whaar. Battle was the one time she was convinced they could take care of themselves. In the upper right quadrant of her field of vision, Bone Harvest displayed Zhan's position and status overlain with Keeper's point of view. Surrounding her field of vision, gold symbols and minute directional arrows indicated the positions and distances of the other Bone Finders.

She imagined Zhan did that sort of thing on pure instinct, letting the draw of bone metal and bone-steel call to him, processing the information without effort.

Well, Alysaundra thought at Bone Harvest, *is anyone else having any better luck than I am? They keep getting back up until the pieces are too small to bother with.*

She seized one of the surrounding Zaur, trying to pull her down, and used it as a club, spinning in a stumbling turn, knocking down enough of the dead to grant a moment to reach down and find her warpick. Unlike her first warpick, Sally, which lay in her berth back in North Number Three, Daisy was a sleek, minimalistic weapon, bearing little decoration other than the care that had been taken in forging it and in wrapping the handle. Skinning and tanning her own skin to produce the leather had been an awkward process, but after going through the trouble of producing a pick without apparent seams or joins—the handle curving scythelike into a pick head—Alysaundra had not wanted to skimp on any part of Daisy.

In a moment between crouching and standing, one arm outstretched as she pushed herself upright, a dark-scaled Zaur with a mouth full of broken fangs lunged at Alysaundra from the right, forcing her to strike out with her armored fist. Bits of bone and brain spattered her warsuit as the thing sprawled back into the arms of its fellow dead. Clamoring over the battered corpse, the others advanced. A normal battle of Aern became a ballet of seemingly solo combatants forming up, dispersing, and reforming in complete order under the direct supervision of an Overwatch.

Bone Finder missions tended toward singles, pairs, and the occasional triple, each trained in the standard tactics of the army proper, but with their own specialization based on how they worked best. In larger-scale engagements, they, in theory, borrowed Overwatches from the Aernese Army, but in practice, Armored Bone Finders let their warsuits stand in as Overwatches or the army took things over and battered down the defenses of whatever stronghold held the bones the Ossuary was after . . . Assuming they could not be acquired by means of stealth alone.

This isn't working, Harv, Alysaundra thought at her warsuit. *We're being overrun.*

None of these beings are capable of breaching us if we turtle up properly, but I will concede that this is not going to be the victory for which one might have hoped.

You aren't impervious. Alysaundra spun loose again, fighting against the crush and running through breaks in the enemies' rough formations.

Why, I wonder, thought Bone Harvest, pointedly ignoring the comment, is the enemy using formations at all? With the resilience of their targets and their own unceasing ability to continue fighting, combined with the extreme numerical superiority they enjoy, they should have mobbed us like swarming insects.

Three of the gold symbols at the periphery turned from golden to white in quick succession, denoting Bone Finders who had been overwhelmed and forced to turtle, letting their warsuits become rigid and unmoving, joints, eye slots, and other openings sealed and seamless until it was safe to move again. A fourth went red, then gray. Aern down. As she watched, the symbol vanished from her sight, replaced by a symbol representing the fallen Aern wrought in bones, to show his bone metal needed to be collected.

I am unsure what just—

"Hells," Alysaundra breathed. *Some of these dead things have shards of the Life Forge. Tell the others.*

*

Yavi's first two arrows broke against the stone of the Port Gate. Shot through with the red mineral Dolvek had called Dragon's blood and a greenish crystal she did not know, the stone possessed a poisonous spirit, like an underwater serpent traversing all the secret paths in a coral reef.

Destroying the Port Gate would unmake the magnificent creature, but it had to be done. Shouldering her bow, Yavi pulled the chunk of rock she had picked up at the lighthouse from her pack and located the first rune. She lined up the first string of runes in her mind, mapping the way she would turn and move. Gritting her dental ridges, she launched, and the wind carrying her turned cold and biting.

Die! Chill talons of scouring air scraped against her bark. Even as it slammed her against the dock, pinning her amid the moving corpses, she recognized its hate.

The winter wind, she thought. *Just as it promised.*

It felt like years had passed since she had been at Oot and called upon the cold angry spirit, promising to kill with it, knowing it craved violence. Then the situation had changed and there had been no need for killing. It had sworn revenge, and as inconvenient as its timing had been, she now found herself impressed at its tenacity.

"Wow!" she said as the dead bit and clawed. "Nice." She pulled free, leaping at the Port Gate and marring the first rune. "Follow through." Clinging to the top of the gate, she defaced the second and third runes.

The fourth rune, lower than the rest, proved her downfall. Dead things grabbed at her feet, and she threw herself down, hoping to roll between the legs of a large Sri'Zaur then scrabble up the back. The fourth rune crumbled, but the dead dragged her free of the Port Gate, pulling her down again to the bare wood of the pier.

Xalistan, she prayed, *if you help me get out of this one, I promise . . .*

Her mind went blank. Promise. Promise. Promise. What could she promise that she did not already do? She only ate meat which had been properly hunted. She respected the freedom of beasts and spirits alike. She . . . felt a spirit watching her. It was old and it was put upon. It was tired of the weight of cargo and the endless march of feet. Maybe she did not need Xalistan's direct intervention.

Maybe . . .

"Hey," she said to the wood beneath her, fighting not to let pain or fear into her voice, "want to help me get all these heavy dead guys off of you? What say we get rid of that big old rock circle while we're at it?"

A group of dead battered Yavi's arm, trying to break through the wooden core, splinter it, and tear it loose.

"What do I have to do?" the spirit asked.

"Break!" Yavi shouted.

CHAPTER 26
REINFORCEMENTS ALL AROUND

Rae'en felt the wind blowing through her hair, even though she knew it could not actually touch her, as she was wrapped within Bloodmane's bone-steel embrace. Below her, the rippling, radiant scales of the dragon's ruby hide pulsed with strength. Her massive wings snapped like sailcloth catching the wind. Down and farther to the southwest, Rae'en could make out the charging warsuits, the Aiannai lancers intermingled with their ranks, and even farther back, the reinforcing company of Zaur and Sri'Zaur doing their best to keep pace.

She hoped the Aiannai and Zaur would not be needed at all in the upcoming fight. Aern did not rise from the dead the way Zaur, humans, and . . . well . . . dragons did, so ending the conflict without the need to expose those most subject to Uled's perverse magic felt like the optimal condition for a clean victory.

"This feels wonderful!" Rae'en shouted to the dragon upon which she rode, nestled at the back of the neck, between the wings.

"Do not grow accustomed to the sensation," Tsan called back, flapping a lazy circle around Scarsguard before heading off to the northeast toward North Watch. "This serves the dual purpose of getting you the best view of the North Watch battle in the most expedient manner and providing a useful visual cue for both our peoples."

"What do you mean?" Rae'en asked. "My people—"

"Are not the issue," Tsan chortled, the sound appearing to come as much a surprise to the dragon as it did Rae'en. "Or rather, your Aern aren't. The humans, elves, and Vael of Scarsguard need to be able to see the leaders of our two empires working in unison so they can trust in the words that bind us together. The majority will never read the document itself, but all of them will hear of the day the Dragon Warleader of the Sri'Zaur and the First of One Hundred Aern flew into battle as one."

"I hadn't thought of that," Rae'en admitted.

"You are woefully ignorant in many lessons of power," Tsan told her. "Fortunately, you have allied yourself with an expert."

She's awfully sure of herself, Joose thought.

That's like saying, "Have you noticed the leader of the Zaur is a dragon now?" Amber thought. *When Coal was alive, did he ever strike you as less than supremely confident in himself above all others?*

All of Rae'en's Overwatches laughed at that. Rae'en could not help but join them, making sure to let her laughter ring out audibly as well to let Tsan think she had been amused by her statement. Rae'en could feel Kazan and Glayne about to shush the others, but she sent them each a gentle, *Let them chatter—they need this*, before they managed to say anything.

*

Another Port Gate came apart in hunks of flash-frozen stone, its fragments whirling about the diminishing specter of Dolvek, tearing through corpses already turning to march for the middle Port Gate. His mind was a burning parchment, the lines of his memory, his essential self, vanishing as the relentless abomination that was Uled consumed him.

He no longer remembered why he was destroying the Port Gates, only that it had to be done.

I only need one, you foolish prince, Uled's mind crowed. Dolvek ignored the voice. Uled was unimportant to him now, his voice the wailing of a tempest as incomprehensible as the rain.

It took a thirty-count for the Port Gate's residual magic to dim, and when that light winked out, Dolvek turned to face the other lights. The central Port Gate flared brightly, but the one beyond it was falling out of alignment, its magic dimming to a glow unperceivable by eyes which did not see the realm of spirits and magic.

Two lights remained. One, a great circle of magic, a passage to another place through which the dead army marched. The other light lay beneath the waves . . . dark shapes difficult for Dolvek to see, outlined only by the light cast beneath the waves, tore at it.

Gliding over the surface of the water, the ghostly prince slid toward the two lights, not sure which to choose. Closing the Port Gate was important, but the other light . . . the smaller light, was precious to him, though he could not recall why or what exactly it was.

Uled ripped and tore at him, shouting curses and epithets the ragged outline of an elf felt certain it would have once recognized. Along the way, it forgot the sequence of runes it needed to end whatever the glowing ring was, so it hurried for the fainter light, each footstep making it clearer and clearer that the last light was important, the most valuable light in all the world, a light which could never be allowed to go out.

*

Once the pier agreed to break itself, Yavi felt the sudden splash of cold seawater. Kicking and wriggling, she tore loose of most of her attackers, but most appeared to lose interest in her, only the several that already had their claws on her continued to follow her down.

We got two of them, she told herself. *That's is pretty darned fabtacular work if you ask me.*

Dying beneath the waves was a rough bit of gristle though. She had always assumed she would go to be with Xalistan, the Hunter, when she died. And she was certain she was dying. She'd stopped feeling pain partway through her dismemberment, but she knew she was missing an arm and most of her legs below the knees.

One eye was gone, too, and even though these were injuries she felt a Vael might be remotely capable of surviving if one made it safely and quickly to a healing temple and Gromma favored them, she was thousands of miles from the nearest Root Tree.

Ice began to form around her in the water. No, not around her, around the dead still clinging to or trying to attack her. One by one they froze and bobbed to the surface, unable to fight their newfound buoyancy.

She clung with her free hand to the base of a nearby pier support as best she could, eye widening at the gray and twisted thing gliding toward her through the water. It looked like a ragged cloak, torn, and flapping in an unseen wind. There were the rudiments of a shape, but what Yavi recognized were the eyes.

Dolvek? she thought. *What did he do to you?*

We . . . Go . . . the shattered soul said, its words echoing through her.

Dolvek? she thought at him again, but it showed no sign of hearing. As they broke the surface, she gasped in air and tried again.

"Dolvek," Yavi croaked, "we have to destroy the last Gate!"

Who?

They flew toward it, and Yavi realized she'd dropped her rock in the struggle.

"Use me as battering ram," she told him. "With enough force my core, my heartwood should be strong enough to . . ."

We . . . Go . . . Dolvek's mind howled.

"Dolvek!" Yavi had time enough for one last shout as they flew past rather than into the runes, then they were through the Port Gate and headed she knew not where.

*

"Don't breathe fire unless you can be sure not to hit any of your allies," Rae'en ordered, adding a "please" to the end only when Bloodmane played back for her the way Tsan's head had reacted to the command, a subtle yet precise twitch which reminded Rae'en of a horse reacting poorly to the kick of a rider's spurs.

"I had not intended otherwise," Tsan purred, "and, at present, my intentions remain unaltered."

Doesn't like to be ordered about, does she? Rae'en thought.

She may not be a dragon by birth, Bloodmane thought, **but I suspect the very nature of becoming one, of possessing the sheer power she now does, confers a certain level of resultant superiority.**

And the Zaur, Kazan added, *have a more than ample portion of that already.*

*

Sargus held a huge tome open with one hand, trying, as best Kholster could determine, not to seem intimidated by the once-mortal Aern's gaze. Using a series of crystal lenses, adjusting them like a musician tuning his instrument, the Aiannai artificer examined the work the two of them had performed upon the living body of the Proto-Aern, which lay stretched out upon its slab of marble. Peering back and forth between the diagrams in the secret volume of Uled's notes and the work itself, Sargus compared the two, his own steady hand having annotated Uled's spidery script and drawings.

It looks to me like it will work, Vander thought at him, examining the work more closely than Kholster, *but, though I have access to a large portion of the information, I have yet to master much of it, so Sargus is the real expert. As long as he hasn't made any errors . . .*

Your scars are already on his back, Kholster chided. *Too late to second-guess him now.*

Blood, more iron-rich and therefore a proper red rather than the typical Aern's extremely anemic orange, ran from the multiple surgical incisions Kholster had, under Sargus's direction, made into the Proto-Aern's flesh. Tools not unlike those Kholster recalled from his own forging—etheric hooks, soul anvils, and the like—lay bloodied and ready to be used again for adjustments, should Sargus find additional areas requiring refinement. Looking upon the work they were doing left Kholster with the uncomfortable feeling that he and Sargus were engaged in an act of desecration rather than the disarming of a trap set by Uled.

That discomfort more than the imagery itself sent him back repeatedly to the memory of his own forging. Sharing the memory with the rest of the Aern had been the start of his thirteen-year effort to awaken their hatred of the Eldrennai, to make more palatable the act of genocide he felt they must commit if they were to ever to fully cast off the shadow of their former slavery. Now, as he saw the memory again in fits and starts, felt the pain of a soul being altered to match a body by which it would be trapped, as he recalled the exchange he'd had with Aldo and with Tor-grimm, he wondered if portions of this could have all been avoided if he had been able to find it in himself to forgive the Oathbreakers.

That cow's already dead, Kholster, Vander thought, sensing the gist of his dilemma. *Might as well eat it. If you feel bad, polish the bones and make good leather of the hide.*

Kholster grunted, drawing a raised eyebrow from Sargus.

"Sir?" The artificer laid aside his lenses to eye Kholster clearly.

"Something Vander thought to me," Kholster said. "How does it look?"

"Well." Sargus closed the tome he'd been consulting, muttering a sequence of words and making a few arcane motions to return the book to its intradimensional shelving (a concept which he'd tried and failed to explain to Kholster in a way that made sense—it all sounded like magic to the Aern.) "You were right to have me examine it. If, and I stress that though I am presently the foremost mortal expert, my—our—father's usual methods apply, he may still have a counter for this of which I am unaware."

"If he does—" Kholster folded his arms, leaning back against the abnormally warm stone walls of the hidden space Uled's minions had prepared for the Proto-Aern, "—then he does, but assuming I am correct?"

"Assuming you are correct—" Sargus produced a fountain pen from some hidden pocket, and wherever he aimed it, the blood from the Proto-Aern's cuts flowed toward it, entering through the feed as Sargus twisted a small cap at the base of the barrel. "—then once the body is occupied, the soul should be trapped within it much in the same way you were, but . . . well, a bit more securely."

"Securely enough to suit my needs?" Kholster asked.

"You know my feeling on the subject?" Sargus asked.

"'Reckless, risky, needlessly dangerous, and rather inhumane,' I believe you said."

"Exactly."

"And?" Kholster closed his eyes and held his breath, using the stillness to check the location of all those he loved, then those few he feared. Satisfied with what he saw, he resumed the flow of time to allow Sargus to answer.

"It will work, Kholster." Sargus sniffed, pocketing the fountain pen and wiping his nose with the sleeve of his robes. "He—" A loud buzzing as of an immense hornet in flight stilled Sargus's tongue. "The Port Gate at Fort Sunder is activating." Sargus clasped his hands together, hope clear in his voice. "It could be—"

"It isn't Rivvek," Kholster frowned. "Not yet."

"Then who?"

CHAPTER 27
PORT GATE PROBLEMS

Each rune surrounding the gate of stone lit up in sequence, their light a blazing white so bright the stationed Aiannai elemancer had to look away. He felt a sharp pain in his neck, and then one of the Armored was helping him up. He did not recognize this one immediately. The bone-like design of its warsuit was reminiscent more of a Bone Finder's.

Around him, the docks of Port Ammond as they had been when he'd been a child were in full bustle of a delivery. Fishmongers were yelling. Aeromancers sent the more unpleasant smells away with gusts of magic, while Aern patrolled methodically. Lamps blazed with mystic light even during the day, and the scent of each shop matched the desired odor for which its owners paid the schools of elemancy.

Veiled Vaelsilyn flitted to and fro, running errands for their masters; and, as he turned his head to check them, he saw the three royal towers shimmering white, sparkling in the light of the suns.

"Oh." He looked more closely at the warsuit that held his hand. It was as if Bloodmane had been reforged in a skeletal likeness of its former self. "Kholster?"

"He has taken up other, more rarefied duties." The being removed its helm, revealing smiling elf-like eyes so ancient and kind, the guard felt no one could look into them and fail to recognize the deity with whom they were being confronted.

"But I thought he'd killed you, Lord Torgrimm."

"Nothing so final." Torgrimm smiled. "There was a fundamental imbalance in the heavens. Righting it was far from comfortable, but—" he touched a faint scar at his throat "—it had to be resolved or it would only have gotten worse. There are very few mortals to whom the gods may turn when their own affairs need sorting. Kholster was one of them."

"Was?"

"Was mortal," Torgrimm clarified, "but remains a being to whom gods and mortals alike may turn."

"So I'm dead then?" The guard looked around. All the hustle and bustle had ceased shortly after he'd turned his attention from it, his surroundings fading to a hazy blur as if to indicate they should no longer concern him. He turned back to Torgrimm.

"Yes, Rasternat, son of . . . Ah . . ." Torgrimm looked down and away, breathing out softly, before meeting the elf's eyes again. "Sore subject there. Apologies." He held out his hand. The elf looked at it as if it might crush him. In one smooth motion, Torgrimm stepped completely clear of his armor, the warsuit gliding free of the god—or the god of the warsuit, the elf could not determine which. Hand held out in welcome, Torgrimm looked down at the hand then back up at the elf.

"Sorry," Rasternat muttered, then took the god's hand. It felt warm and calloused.

"That was not so bad now, was it?" asked Torgrimm as he lead the soul away. "Tell me. When you were younger, you dreamt of the White Towers, but at school you had thoughts of your soul flitting off to become one with the elemental realm. Did you ever come to a firm decision on which one suited you more?"

"I get to pick?" Rasternat asked.

"Not exactly." Torgrimm's chuckle came warm and reassuring, washing away all worry. "But I am married to the goddess who makes those decisions, and while she keeps her own council on such matters, I can always put in a word, if it eases your mind."

*

Clad in curdled flesh, part scale and part elf, the scar-skulled abomination with bone metal teeth clapped its twisted hands, with claws clipped short on one hand but ragged, elongated nails on the other. Uled's army measured in the hundreds of thousands, but Vander noted the fretful desperation with which he strove to push his influence farther abroad, touching as many of the dead as he could. Animals, Vael, and Aern did not rise, yet humans, Zaur, and elves did.

He's raised a Port Gate of his own devising, Vander thought to Kholster. *I missed it until he activated it. I'm sorry—*

You aren't the god of secrets, Vander, Kholster thought back. *Besides, my daughter is capable of handling Uled's army, if anyone is.*

But she's not at Fort Sunder.

The First of One Hundred is anywhere there are Overwatches, old friend, Kholster told him. *Where is she physically?*

Vander transmitted the sight of Rae'en on dragonback, approaching North Watch from the southwest. Bloodmane's mane of red trailed wind-blown behind her, the awakened embodiment of wrath. Testament glowed with the light of the suns and the iridescent luster of Tsan's scales.

Poor Zhan. Kholster sighed.

Because she's coming to his rescue?

Because he wishes he were better than she is at kholstering. . . . And he may have been, for a few days, but Rae'en is her mother's daughter. She has no equal. I doubt even I would have thought to mount the dragon. It's an image neither the Army nor the Ossuary will ever forget.

Her triumph, Vander thought, *and his misstep. I hadn't looked at it that way.*

Of course you didn't hunt down that trail, Kholster taunted. *You're nicer than me and Zhan, and you have never felt the burden of authority in quite the same way as either of us.*

I kholstered the Overwatches, Vander objected.

And if they dared argue with you, to whom did you refer them?

Ah. Vander did not like that analogy, but he could not disagree with it.

*

Arri's ears twitched up, pinnae widening at a sound Kholburran did not hear. Silhouetted by the second sun, eyes wide and mouth open to increase the range of her hearing, she reminded him of the little animals they'd seen when cutting cross-country to Fort Sunder. She lacked the fur and the black nose, but the concentration and attentiveness were much the same.

Kholburran sat at the center of a small patch of ground, which had been cleared for them by the Aern, wiggling his toes in the dirt. There had been a different kind of grass here once, myrr grass, bright and lively, but it had been trodden to death by the refugees and construction crews. They had seeded some other grass in its place, some domesticated variety an elf from Port Ammond had brought with her. It was hardy and would thrive, but its light green did not belong here. It should have been purple or a deep red.

While the enclosed space the Aern had provided was open to the sky and the soil, it had four thick cloth walls, practically tarps, that hid Kholburran and company from view of the humans and Aiannai, though scent and clamor passed through. Was this supposed courtesy at all dissimilar from making his Root Guard wear *samir*? Walling them off completely was just a really big version of the traditional beaded veils used by girl-type Vael when visiting Eldrennai . . . Aiannai . . . to avoid any unfortunate complications their attractiveness could facilitate, wasn't it? It was made even more ineffective by the way the Root Guard perched atop the scaffolding that held the tarps, clearly visible to any who looked up as they passed.

He understood how attractive girl-types were to elven men, but his own resemblance to Kholster had brought him an odd combination of pleased, amorous, forlorn, dismayed, and even angered looks. Rae'en's reaction . . . He'd only met her briefly before she and the dragon dismissed him to deal with some emergency, but, at the sight of him, she'd had a combination of emotions he could not read. Bemusement? Nostalgia? He put it out of his head and concentrated on the soil. There were good minerals in it, but traces of an enigmatic other substance that he had never before encountered. He knew he could draw it into himself but worried whether it was safe.

A fish leapt, striking the water of a newly dug pond nearby. They'd put his little enclosure close to water. Kholburran could sense the fish . . . they felt far from home, but life was resilient. Life had to be resilient, lest Gromma turn her growing and green aspect from it, leaving it to rot, her second realm of influence.

Perched atop scaffolds the Aern had placed as bunks along three of the four walls in order to accommodate both Kholburran and his Root Guard in the small enclosure, other Root Guard kept watch (against what, he had no idea, what with so many Aern, warsuits, and elemancers about). The wood had been chopped recently enough that the girl-type-persons had been able to coax it back to life, but it would only die once they left. If they left. This place . . .

"I don't see how you can touch that soil with your bare bark," Faulina said as she came in through the flap of the one wall that had no bunks, a brace of rabbit dangling from her wrist. "It feels sick and dead."

"It feels alive to me," Kholburran said. "Just a little overwhelmed, I think. There is a . . . a magic in it I can almost see." He nodded toward the dirt. "I can most certainly taste it."

"Taste it?! It is a broken and twisted magic," Faulina said. "It—"

"Hsst!" Arri glared at them.

"I was just thinking, Arri, you look like one of those—" Kholburran began. He looked up as he spoke, intending to say more, but the look in her eyes stopped his tongue.

"Xalistan guide me," Arri breathed, more whisper than shout. Eyes widening even farther, Arri unslung her Heartbow, the whorls of Warrune at her throat and on her arm growing in illumination. "This is bad. Weapons at the ready, Root Guard."

"What is it?" Faulina drew her weapon, as did the others. "I don't—" Her voice stopped, ears flaring wide.

"We've got to go, Kholburran!" Arri snapped. "Now!"

"Why?" He made no move to leave, pricking up his ears in the same way Arri had in hope of an explanation. Kholburran could not hear it yet, whatever it was, but he felt a dark pressure pushing in at him, a virtual scream from the very soil at the soles of his feet. Leaving felt wrong. This place . . . it needed him. Not only in the short term, like helping a sick Vael hunt for a few days until she recovered, but a true setting down of roots and tending to the land. Repairing what ill had befallen this place and left such a stain. The Vael prince dug his toes into the dirt.

*

Screams became the natural currency of breathing for the untrained and unprepared of Scarsguard. Rae'en, en route to North Watch, watched through eyes of her Overwatches and cursed.

If we turn back, Bloodmane thought at her, we will merely ensure that we have failed the Ossuary AND the Aern at Fort Sunder.

Maybe not. Rae'en unslung Testament. *On dragon-back, North Watch and Fort Sunder are not more than a few candlemarks apart.*

Are we turning back, then?

No. We save Zhan and his Bone Finders as intended, then head back to Fort Sunder if they need us.

She growled, angry at the indecisiveness she felt.

"Problem?" Tsan-Zaur asked, massive head tilting so a single immense eye could focus on her.

It may be unwise, to share with her—

Because they only respect the strong, Bloodmane, Rae'en thought. *Yes. I know that, too.*

Had that been too harsh?

But thanks for bringing it up, Rae'en added. *If I hadn't known, we'd have struck bad stone for certain.*

"Fort Sunder is under attack," Rae'en told the dragon. "It's under control, but I wanted to be there to face Uled myself."

"Queen Bhaeshal can see to them. She seemed moderately competent. We left her plenty of troops. Let the drones earn their meat, kholster Rae'en," the dragon said with a laugh. "It makes them feel as if they are useful. We can't seize *all* of the glory for ourselves."

*

At Fort Sunder, the dead issued forth from the newly reopened Port Gate. New recruits in the form of human corpses from the cities north of the Sri'Zauran Mountains led the charge, wielding weapons of the northern militia and clad in armor marked by mortal-wound-dependent levels of repair. Spreading along predetermined courses, the fort's repurposed layout slowed them, but the dead knew no sense of impatience, basking as Uled was in the warmth of superiority.

Having surrendered most of the housing within the fort proper to those who were less used to sleeping in the shelf-like berths to which the Aern were so accustomed, no warsuits stood immediately to hand to stop them, no Aern to stem the initial flood. Aiannai and humans joined the ranks of Uled's army in quick succession, the fallen rising up to accompany their recycled comrades, swelling the ranks of the deadly and decaying. Weapons in better repair than their wielders recruited eagerly, and hidden amid those who slashed with steel were a handful who wore rotting scale, their foreclaws gripping shards of the Life Forge.

*

Breathing heavily, Hasimak, the former High Elementalist, floated between dimensions as he draped across a padded chaise, half-propped up on his right elbow, with his pale skin bathed in the violet light of the place betwixt. Even refreshed, the ache of consciousness weighed on him. Sleep called him with a volume it had never possessed in his youth.

"He's sending them through," Jun told him. "Uled is."

Eyes rimmed with etheric dust and crusted with sleep examined the structure of the newly opened Port Gate with a critical eye. He traced the pathway Uled had fashioned with his hasty gate, the gate Hasimak himself had rendered functional without thinking. Even so, it had not been made well enough to long withstand what Uled was doing.

Why use one Port Gate to connect directly with another when one could—

He saw the logic then. Flawed, but functional, he could not help but wonder if the design flaws within Uled's newest gates could truly have been so purposeful or— But they had been. He saw it all, saw the unthinkable, which no doubt had seemed natural as breathing to Uled.

Made from stone improperly tempered and possessed of trace impurities, the foreign gate could not last more than one or two openings, but then again Uled might only need it to survive a single protracted use.

"What are you thinking, child?" the tired voice asked the student who could not hear him. "Why this? And why do you think no one will arrive with writ of debt in hand, an expectant glare in their eyes?"

"You think he has not thought this through?" Jun asked.

"He has, but he has underestimated."

"Whom?"

Hasimak's eyes pored over the ravaged ghost cities Uled had left in his wake, from little mining towns like Immar to the Sister Ports of Essingway and Saraj. Whole populations lined the streets leading up to the already crowded docks, ready to enter Uled's final gate and vent his wrath upon the surviving elves.

The most intact dead were first, but Hasimak choked at the sight of juvenile corpses and less intact elder ones waiting near the back. He had seen too much in his many millennia of life to feel the kind of outrage appropriate to the matter, only sadness that his former student could have sunk to such a low. The creation of this aberrant step, neither life nor death but life-in-death . . . it had merit as an intellectual exercise, but to have acted upon it? Uled never had understood the sometimes subtle difference between *could* and *should*.

"This should never have been more than a theory, Artificer," Hasimak prayed. "Why have you allowed it? Why not intercede?"

"Don't call me that." Jun's voice came husky and low.

Hasimak's eyes narrowed.

Steps have been taken, a gruff sad voice spoke in the elf's mind.

"Steps?" Stirred by the unexpected reply, Hasimak felt a surge of will rise up from deep within. With eyes ablaze in mystic light, he rose from his reclined position, banishing the sleep from his eyes and mind. "Am I one of those steps? Do not tell me that once more you expect me, to—"

Jun laid a calloused hand on the elf's robe-covered shoulder.

"Rest, Hasimak." The Dwarf sighed, looking at his feet. "I expect nothing. I only build now. That and only that."

"Then what steps—?"

"They weren't mine," Jun said.

"Even so." Hasimak seized upon the wild instability of the new Port Gate and channeled a stream of its energy into himself, altered it and fed it back.

"Meddling?"

"Stopping him and closing the gate would be meddling." Hasimak tweaked the Port Gate at Fort Sunder, leaving it reinforced, but the flawed gate even more prone to collapse. It would last while open, but once closed, Uled's Port Gate would crumble . . . possibly explode. "I am merely acting as a natural limit."

"What do you think of your student?"

"Clever. Fascinating. Wholly devoid of conscience." Hasimak narrowed his eyes. He knew how he sounded, but he could only bring himself to judge the magic itself, not its originator. *We are too much alike.* "Monstrous and abhorrent."

He glanced casually at the Dwarven god but did not let his gaze linger. A Dwarf in shining armor, over-sized hammer in his left hand. Nothing had changed. With a snap of his fingers and a small expenditure of magic, the ancient elf created a crystalline lens the size of a small carriage, using it to view Uled more clearly.

"And even the closest kept of your secrets, my old teacher, has surrendered itself unto me!" Uled's mad cries echoed through the crystal. "Beyond death. Beyond gates. Beyond bounds! I am your superior, Hasimak! I have existed beyond you and beyond my beast."

Hasimak frowned.

"Disappointed?" Jun asked.

"In whom?"

"Your student."

"I pity him," Hasimak said.

Jun raised a bushy eyebrow and snorted at that.

"How tortured he must be," Hasimak said eventually. "It pains me to know he will never understand his failure of morality."

"Some would say he should be punished," Jun said.

"Understanding would be eternal punishment, Jun." Hasimak banished the lens with a wave of his hands. "Trust one who did and does and always shall."

CHAPTER 28
ROOT ROT REBELLION

Kholburran sprang up on one of the scaffolds, warpick in hand, and looked out.

"We must leave now, Snapdragon!" Faulina shouted.

"No." Where elves ran for the central fortress, the fog parted before them, sparse wisps catching here and there on the forms of the elves. A small few were caught in the midst of their own personal clouds, wreathed in the stuff and, as they cast their spells, rolling tendrils of fog reached out from cloud to target, connecting the two long enough for the spell to take effect, then trailing away like suns-banished mist.

"To arms!" an elf with an elemental foci like a silver mask across her eyes shouted using Aeromancy.

"A Thunder Speaker," Kholburran said. "Like Wylant!" He recognized Queen Bhaeshal, who flew toward a bare patch of sky. Kholburran winced, certain she would fall . . . but she did not.

Energy arced from the elemental focus that had replaced her eyes. Coursing lighting-like from Bhaeshal to the cloud and back, this secondary force maintained the connection she had to the clouds with only a brief interruption. Others who flew into the clear spaces experienced a similar reaction between their foci and the clouds or fell, their magic too unreliable to continue, until they hit another section of the nebulous cloud.

Sighing, Kholburran lowered himself back to the ground, digging his toes into the dirt again.

"What do you mean you aren't going?" Faulina reached out to try to physically pull him away from his spot on the soil. Arri, on the other side of the small open-topped enclosure from Faulina, easily made it across in time to block her, literally leaping across from her perch atop the opposite scaffolding that the Aern had placed along three of the four cloth walls.

Arri swept aside the grasp, shoving Faulina back with a palm to the chest. The other Root Guards stood back, torn between the confrontation between the two highest ranking girl-type persons and the oncoming danger from higher up at the keep.

"He can't stay here, Arri!"

"A prince on his Root Taking goes where he pleases!"

"Not if it gets him killed!" Faulina drew her Heartbow back, ready to fire, and held it. "He's going back south. You should never have let him come here, you—"

"We will enforce his right of choosing." Arri and another, deeper voice that came from the whorls on her body spoke in unison. Light bloomed brighter from the whorls of Warrune at Arri's throat and on her arm. The upper and lower limbs of Faulina's Heartbow bent inward, string slipping from the notches at either end before returning to its usual shape.

"You don't get to just—"

"The magic of this place is broken," the voice of Warrune thrummed. "It is different than the flaws in me, the rot that corrupts me, but you may find I recognize it enough to turn it to my will."

The magic of this place. Kholburran, only superficially cognizant of their actions, focused on the enigmatic clouds (What were they? Elemental power? Were they related to the words his father spoke?) he could see, but the others appeared to not see at all, to ignore, or to understand but not feel the need to explain. *I am not seeing spirits*, he thought. *This is . . . magic itself? The magic of this place?*

If the clouds he had seen, scattered and broken, represented the magic upon which spell casters drew, what would it look like if it was unbroken? He remembered walking through a morning mist and wondering at the way it was more visible when viewed at a distance than it was from within. Inside the mist, if it was thin enough, it filtered sight but was hard to discern as a distinct object. Was it that, rather than being unable to see magic like the girl-type persons, he saw the raw foundations upon which others drew, able to notice it only if it were broken up?

"Prince?" Arri asked, noticing his gasp even in the midst of her own exchange with Faulina. "What is it?"

Closing his eyes, he reached out for the living wood of the scaffolding. He could sense it just as he sensed his own warpick, and the Heartbows of his Root Guard, the other Vael, and his father's presence, connected by a long, thin strand of magic that wound its way through the soil from where Arri stood all the way back, he presumed, to the Twin Trees themselves.

"We who Take Root are not blind to magic," Warrune thrummed. "We see on a larger scale. Places like this are the exception. Broken. Unrooted, you are too close to see."

"Can it be fixed?" Kholburran asked.

"To fix this tiny fortress would be the work of a moment for one who took root here." Warrune's whorls began to smolder as he continued, and Kholburran wondered whether the frail wood could contain the intensity of his presence without failing. "But the damage spreads far and wide, and that would be the work of long life and, perhaps, more than one tree. Many trees, to spread the forest to these shattered plains and restore what the one who made us wrought upon it."

"Why can you speak to me and not Hashan?"

"I am insane," Warrune responded.

Arri's arm caught fire, but she did not scream, could not scream in Warrune's grasp.

Warrune continued, "My brothers can see the larger frame and love their work, but I have always longed for the life I left behind, not only to care for you and abide, but to be one of you."

"You're hurting Arri."

"I am killing Arri."

"What?! Why?!"

Warrune's thrumming grew louder, Arri's bark vibrating as her throat began to smoke. The Heartbows of the Root Guard sprang to life, writhing tendrils wrapping themselves around the neck and shoulders of Kholburran's Root Guard. "She acted against my seed. All of them have. After all I sacrificed, they dared!"

"Stop."

"No." Warrune's voice grew in volume until it seemed there was no other sound, would never be another sound in the whole of the Last World, until it cracked and broke under the strain. "You are my seed, my beloved sproutling, but a sprout may not question one who has Taken Root!"

No one gave instructions on how a Vael Took Root. There existed no books or scrolls, no ancient songs. The stories all told about the circumstances surrounding or resulting from a Root Taking, not the activity itself. Everyone assumed that Kholburran would know how to do it when the time came. For once, they were right.

"Then I will also Take Root, father." Kholburran's toes sank into the dirt and surged forth, drawing nourishment from the minerals therein and from the clouds of magic that billowed nearby. "And we will continue this discussion."

*

"Magic seems to work on them," Bhaeshal shouted above the din, her voice booming with Thunder Speaker magic. Civilians kept getting in the way, and there weren't enough elemancers to go around. Those there were kept hitting areas of Fort Sunder in which their magic did not work at all or where using it caused their elemental foci to grow at a debilitating rate. Several of her most experienced elemancers with more prominent foci looked more like automata than proper elves.

Younger elemancers, like Kam, found that their elemental familiars would not follow them into some areas at all, while others vanished upon doing so, leaving their masters powerless until they could find a stable enough location to summon them once more.

"Pyromancers, target the dead closest to the keep. Geomancers, try to keep them back, but do not try to affect the ground too deeply, or you risk focusing out before you realize what is happening." Bhaeshal spotted one Geomancer standing in the midst of a flow of fleeing refugees, a statue of brass and steel, his elemental focus having consumed him utterly.

Warsuits struggled to make it past the crush of humans and elves heading for the main gate, to the presumed safety (*Please let Tsan's army camped so conveniently around Scarsguard be innocent of any collusion with the undead*) outside the walls of Scarsguard, but many found themselves bogged down or halted if they opted not to injure the panicked refugees.

I wish the Aern weren't being so blasted careful about it, Bhaeshal thought. *If we don't keep this contained . . .*

Able to remain aloft and casting, the numbness accompanying her mask-like focus spread across her forehead and down along the sides of her face, but a queen could not abandon her people, not when they had already lost so much.

Dead poured out of the keep and down the steps of Fort Sunder toward the populated sections of Scarsguard. Fire worked best, but the closer they got to the hastily constructed tents and barracks, the bones of the new construction, the more dangerous flame became to the refugees.

A new front broke out in the middle of Scarsguard as those humans trampled in the first crush rose with jerky movements to fight their former allies. Warsuits echoed orders that passed unheard from Aern to Aern, allowing Bhaeshal and her people to coordinate their efforts. Elemancers with enough power to do so transported warsuits as close to the keep as possible. Too many of them spent their lives doing so. Ringing the walls, Overwatches, the crimson crystalline eyes of their warsuits flashing, stepped free of the animated armor, sending their skins into battle below, while they kept watch above, relaying what they saw, directing the efforts of the army below.

Still the dead came on.

Killing.

Recruiting.

Unstopping.

"Bash!" Kam shouted, his elemental familiar vanishing as they delivered warsuits into battle, using his Aeromancy to transport a cart holding three Armored Aern. The young Aiannai hit one of the dead spots in the magic and fell. Bhaeshal reached out for him, but he dropped with the Aern, landing amid the crawling, clawing dead.

Walls of ice generated with Hydromancy blocked some areas, providing defense where they could, but too often the walls were riddled with massive flaws where creations of elemancy would not hold.

A wave of magic sent Bhaeshal tumbling through the air, and she struck the side of Fort Sunder.

CHAPTER 29
GAME CHANGERS

"Come on Kreej," the human-who-no-longer-smelled-human argued. "You need to send in reinforcements."

"In support of whom?" Kreej snapped. He hated the cold and the way the air this close to Fort Sunder made his fangs ache. "Scarback corpses may not join the ranks of the Maker's dead army, but Zaur and Sri'Zaur do. We hold out here."

At the abandoned hamlet south of Scarsguard, the remnant of the Sri'Zauran Empire, camped like a besieging enemy, pulled back and prepared its next assault. Huge bonfires burned in the center of a series of rough stone dwellings erected by borrowed Geomancers. Each dome-like structure was built around a central hearth, feeding smoke up and out through inelegant yet functional chimneys. Bracing himself for contact with the cold wind outside, Kreej padded out onto the grass and stood on his hind legs, pointing a spyglass at the walls to the north and the chaos that could be seen: the fires, the smoke, the Aeromancers falling from the sky.

Raising a foreclaw, Kreej pointed to the lines of troops that escorted a few hundred yellow- and red-scaled Flamefangs, flanked by four Zaurruk and the required black-scaled handlers with the white rings and pattern on their backs matching the patterns painted on the back of the Zaurruk each group controlled.

"Flamefangs will be at the ready to burn the dead as they leave." Kreej handed the spyglass to Captain Tyree. "The Zaurruk will be on hand to seal the gates and ring the entire fortress city with a trench to slow the advance of any that make it through. I'm sending the bulk of both specialized troops, even assigned Brazz to the Flamefangs. . . . What more would you have me do?"

Kreej glared at the human, annoyed with him even before he began to speak. He understood why the scaleless warmbloods wrapped themselves in so many layers of cloth: they were fragile, sickly things that needed protection from the world around them—even from simple things like rocky ground or rain—but why this human needed so many variations of clothing, so many sets, to so often dilute his scent . . . It was maddening having to check for the bright-white teeth and dented chin then get close enough to smell the mint leaves it . . . he . . . carried.

"You could send Flamefangs to the walls with Gliders to get them the top. Even rank-and-file troops armed with bows or crossbows would help. Fight from the walls if you are too afraid to fight in the general melee."

Trust me. Trust me. Trust me. Having been exposed to him on multiple occasions and then spent time apart, Kreej's membranes nictated, nostrils flaring in shock at how obvious the human's method, whatever form of Long Speaking it happened to be, was to one who suspected it. A need to trust the human all the same squirreled its way into Kreej's core. *Trust me. Trust me. Trust me. Trust—*

"Stop attempting to influence me with your desperate little warm-blood thoughts, human." Kreej caught Tyree by both wrists with his forepaws, being sure to trap the bracelets the human wore. One need not know how magic worked to recognize enchanted objects. These carried the scent of elves and blood. Weapons of some kind. "You have received all of the assistance the Sri'Zauran Empire is willing to offer you. We are allied with the scarbacks by the will of Tsan'Zaur and He Who Rules in Secret and in Shadow. We have a similar arrangement with the Weeds. Unless you—"

Tyree bared his teeth in what Kreej assumed to be a warmblood attempt at a smile.

"What about the prince?" Tyree made no effort to free himself of Kreej's grasp, leaning in closer instead, throat exposed, but mouth close to the Zaur auditory receptors.

"What prince?" Kreej hissed the last word, his forked tongue touching lightly on the human's skin.

"Kholster-Face. Snappy Trap," Tyree purred. "The son of Queen Kari? Fresh out on his sacred self-planting party?"

"What of him?" Kreej released the captain's wrists but drew his Skreel blades to parry any incoming attack.

"Guess where he is." He nodded toward the chaos of Fort Sunder. "I know you wouldn't go out of your way to protect an average Sproutling, but the queen's own son . . ." Tyree let that thought sit with him for a few breaths. "You already cost her one Root Tree, to prove a point. How happy do you think your Imperial Dragonosity would be to find out you could have scampered in there and saved a Root Tree . . . and didn't? Think of the advantage it would give you in terms of your alliance. Think of the political and personal debt it would force Queen Kari to incur . . ."

<<I want Gliders, Shades, and a reserve Flamefang to take this human-like creature into Scarsguard on a mission to protect, preferably rescue, the Weed Prince.>> Kreej tapped the words instead of speaking them, but from the look on Captain Tyree's face, the human knew exactly what it meant: Tyree had won.

*

I need to get an Aern inside Fort Sunder to close the Port Gate, Kazan ordered. He stood along the newly constructed walls, wearing bone-steel chain and scorched jeans that he believed would never stop smelling of smoke. Spread along the optimal arch for accruing maximal battle data, he felt as naked as he was certain the other Armored did in the absence of their warsuits. He'd hated to give the command, but it made sense. The soldiers and kholsters in the fight below needed every weapon they could deploy. They needed accurate intelligence, too, so . . . compromise.

M'jynn, Joose, and Arbokk stood nearby, pretending they were not on guard duty, but it was impossible not to notice that they had assigned themselves to protect their Prime Overwatch and Second of One Hundred.

There are too many opponents to manage this with any alacrity, Eyes of Vengeance thought.

En route, Amber and Glayne thought as one.

Want to run the plan by me? Kazan asked. He found them on his mental map, but their locations looked odd.

It's what you already said, Amber thought back. *We get in there and we close the Port Gate.*

That's the whole plan?! Kazan asked. They were running along a wall, but there was a peculiarity . . .

We have to test a theory and then there might be more plan, Amber thought, *but if it doesn't work, I don't want to feel stupid.*

It will work, Glayne thought. *You are brilliant and your idea is elegant, inspired, and impressive.*

Was that a compliment? Amber and several of the other Overwatches asked Glayne.

Glayne's token, wherever it was positioned in each Overwatch's mind's eye, flashed gold: affirmative.

There. Eyes of Vengeance enhanced Kazan's vision, zooming in on a pair of figures climbing up the walls of Fort Sunder like spiders.

How are they——? Joose started.

The whole fortress is plated in bone-steel. M'jynn held out his warpick, fingers unfurled and palm down. It began to drop then snapped back against his palm, held there by the same connection that allowed Aern to sling their implements on their backs and hold them without the need for a manufactured sheath. Older Aern used the same trick to move without their mail clinking, by holding it against their skin, still and quiet.

Climbing a bone-steel wall using the same principle had never occurred to Kazan . . . not that there had ever been a wall plated entirely in bone-steel before Kholster's ascension to godhood. Amber had seen it, though.

"Maybe she should be Second," he whispered.

Have faith in yourself, Eyes of Vengeance intoned. **Rae'en and Amber do. Even Glayne does, or he would still be second-guessing you instead of scouting out ways to help your plans work.**

Shouldn't Rae'en be kholstering all of this? Kazan asked.

You are here and she is busy elsewhere, Eyes of Vengeance told him.

Just make sure I have an army to come back to, yeah? Rae'en thought at him.

I didn't know you heard that, I'm——

Heard what? Rae'en asked. *Things look bad there. You're sending me the battle data upper left, remember? Did I miss something vital?*

No, kholster, Kazan thought. *We've got it under control. As soon as Amber and Glayne destroy the gate and stop the flood of them, we'll be in better shape.*

*

"How can it already be in use?" King Rivvek asked.

He was not ready for another challenge. His ears still rang with the dying cries of the dragon at the center of the Never Dark. He still saw the fight in his mind's eye whenever he closed his eyes, even to blink, but he could not spare the time to question what he had done to complete Kyland's mission and to fulfill his own oath. Now, he had to make it through the Port Gate, then he could rest, collapse, die, or whatever the gods had in mind. With his oath fulfilled, it would not matter. But until then . . .

If the Port Gate is closed, that means what? Rivvek cleared his mind, forced the frustration and the exhaustion away. *Another party is accessing the Port Gate at Fort Sunder either locally or from another Port Gate.*

"Right?" He murmured.

Yes, he thought. *That would have to be it, but who and why and where?*

Were the forces at Fort Sunder using it themselves? With the Port Gate active, the energy had succeeded in blocking all of their combined attempts to see through the veil between dimensions and view the Port Gate at Fort Sunder.

Kyland, father of Wylant and longtime survivor of the Never Dark, laughed long and loud, the beads and bones of his Ghaiattri-hide armor adding a percussive music to his vocalizations. Rivvek opened his mouth to scold the general but could not bring himself to do so. Left on his own for centuries, the older elf had not only kept his sanity but also learned how to manipulate the ever-shifting realm as the demons did. He had been instrumental to the survival of Rivvek's rescue force, effectively rescuing the would-be rescuers.

Rivvek could not bring himself to join the general in his laughter, but he managed a genuine smile. Thanks to Kyland's expertise, instead of an ever-changing hodge-podge of seasons and terrain with violent weather patterns, they stood on a spring-like field of grasses shot through with wild flowers and the occasional Royal Hedge Rose. A sweet-smelling breeze blew steadily over them. At the edge of the field, a blizzard raged, filled with lightning and fire holding—for the time being—the Ghaiattri army at bay.

Rivvek may have mastered usage of Ghaiattric flame, even slain a dragon with it, but Kyland's control of the very substance of the Never Dark astounded the prince. How a lone elf had managed to thrive and become an object of fear for the demons . . . It boggled Rivvek's mind. For a breath, a heartbeat, he lost his concentration, and he was in the

Bright, at the center of the Never Dark, battling Lambent. It burned before him, first with its own light and then with the horror of Rivvek's magic. He opened his eyes with a start, not having meant to close them, and concentrated at the task before him. The Never Dark, the way time worked there, was especially dangerous for mortals. Even an elf, as long-lived as elves are, is meant to live in a world where each candlemark lasts the same length of time, never shorter or longer and definitely not stretching onward into infinity or passing in a heartbeat.

Task at hand, Rivvek, he berated himself again. He took a long look at the assembled army. They still needed him, and there were still plenty of soldiers to take home alive. Of the twenty-seven thousand two hundred thirty-seven Oathbreakers who had crossed with him from the world that was their home into the Demon Realm, nineteen thousand and four battle-scarred and weary elves stood in formation, and leading defenses at the rear were eight hundred and ninety-two Aern of the Lost Command, the complete remains of the other one hundred and eight Aern packed up neatly in wagons made of demon bone.

When King Rivvek's Oathbreakers had crossed over an unknown number (Rivvek had an estimate, but per Kyland's instructions, he did not allow himself to concentrate on it too fiercely) of subjective years ago, they had each had a blanket, a bedroll, two canteens, and whatever personal belongings, arms, and armor they could carry. Now every elven soldier wore demon hide armor best suited to their preference in fighting style: some wore thick, platelike affairs resembling that worn by King Rivvek upon their arrival; others, the more flexible leather-and-plate hybrid style Kyland preferred; and every possible permutation in between. Some carried weapons they'd brought with them, while others wielded flame-cured crystalline or demon-bone weapons.

Rivvek flexed his new dragon-scale gloves, the movement causing the unusual semi-translucent material to shift from dull gray to luminous light, drawing his gaze. He was still getting used to it, but Lambent's hide had proven the only substance in the Never Dark that could fully defend against the soul-burning flame of the Ghaiattri; and without protection, setting oneself alight with the devastating flames was easier than turning it on the enemy.

After the battle, there had been enough unspoiled hide to equip a score of elves with armor, but it had proven so hard to work with that they had only managed to turn out one usable suit, a combination of scales and bone approximating the full-plate Ghaiattri armor to which Rivvek had become accustomed. Lighter and harder, comparing the armor to his old was the same as going from an iron longsword to a bone-steel blade . . . like the one he wore in the sheath at his side, courtesy of Vodayr.

Kholster's scars. What wonders they worked in the hearts of the Aern. The sight and feel of them had been all it took to gain the loyalty of a thousand Armored Aern. Slaying the dragon had not harmed the awe in which they held him, either.

"Do not become too impressed with yourself, my liege," Kyland chided.

"As glorious as I am," Rivvek teased, the newly healed scars at the edge of his lips showing white against flushed skin, "how would such a thing be possible, Foul Beak?"

"As you say." Kyland scoffed at Rivvek's use of the name bestowed upon him by the denizens of the Never Dark. He had learned both of their major tongues, misusing them with deliberate malice to throw insult in the polite tongue, using the vulgar tongue for most other conversations.

"Tell me there is another way through," Rivvek said.

"There are other Port Gates, but they are watched with greater zealousness by the Ghaiattri horde. The shattering of the Life Forge rendered the terrain around this one more malleable to me, less so to them. Traveling to another gate on this side might grant us egress, but it would not resolve whatever obstructs the Port Gate at Fort Sunder."

"And if the gate was being used by the Aern . . . ?"

"If it were being used by someone to leave Fort Sunder . . ." Kyland rested a claw-gloved hand upon the smooth, glowing surface that marked the Port Gate's current state of activation. " . . . we should be able to see them moving through the gate. They would pass into this world, and be momentarily here, before the Port Gate sensed their desired destination and thrust them forth."

"Then do they need to fear a Ghaiattri at the gate?" Rivvek asked. "If they cannot interact with—"

"Anyone waiting at this side of the departure gate can interfere with a traveler. In the old days, we'd send in several Aern to secure the Port

Gate before using it." Kyland shook his head. "The Demon Wars made even that too dangerous most days. We'd open a gate, use it, try to close it, and then they'd try to force the gate."

"I want to come back to that, but first . . . If we found the departure gate in use by whomever is porting to the Fort Sunder Port Gate," Rivvek asked, trying to arrange it all in his mind, "they would be visible and vulnerable, however briefly, as they pass through the Never Dark, right?"

"Yes, but—" Kyland frowned, the terrain shifting underfoot from grass to gravel to snow-covered and back. "Odd."

"What?"

"The damage done by the Life Forge's destruction—it is being repaired."

For the first time since he'd stepped through the Port Gate, after ensuring the survival of as many of his people as possible, Rivvek felt the trignoms being shaken around in their box in his mind. The board was being dusted off, and as Kyland spoke, he imagined his hand hovering over the box of tiles, choosing two most important tiles: the last one, the objective, and the first one, the tile that once played would lead inevitably to the final desired tile.

"Interesting. We can worry about that in moment, but first . . ." Rivvek already had one of the tiles, a short-term goal: get the survivors back to Fort Sunder so that kholster Rae'en would be forced to forgive them and change their name from Oathbreakers, from Eldrennai to one the Aern would not feel oathbound to eradicate. "What happens to the departure gate if we force the arrival gate?"

"Force it?" Kyland asked. "You can't force a Port Gate."

"Ghaiattri can," Jolsit spoke up. "When General Bloodmane had us—"

"I apologize," Rivvek said, holding up a hand, "but that's all I needed. Thank you, Jolsit." He looked at Kyland. "And how easy would it be to find the departure gate?"

"Hasimak could do it, but while the gates map easily on the Dying Light side, this side has only one gate with a stable location, and that's it." He kicked the side of the gate before them.

"What would happen if we forced it open?"

"If it could be done, I don't know," Kyland said. "I know that they open if destroyed improperly, but even then, there is a cutoff. Once beings stop moving through them, they close."

Rivvek asked several other questions in quick succession, moving from Kyland to Jolsit as each told him what they knew. When he was finished, all of the trignoms were not yet in place, but he had enough to start.

The Port Gate stood glowing and impenetrable. Rivvek held out his hands, the scars old and new on his body flowing with heat and bright, sharp, burning agony. Ghaiattric flame rolled over him in waves. Harmless as long as he kept them under control. Breathe and focus. The new scars marring his cheeks and brow, a curling expanse flowing from throat to shoulder and encompassing the whole of his left arm and hand, had been caused by a simple lapse in concentration that had come close to ending him. He hoped his new armor would prevent similar recoil from recurring. Hurling the flame against the stone outlining the barrier, he called over his shoulder for Jolsit.

"Yes, highness?"

"See if the Aern can put together a battering ram for us, would you?"

Jolsit ran off to do just that. Unable to watch him go, Rivvek narrowed his focus on the stone, smiling as, with inexorable slowness, it began to show subtle signs of strain.

Kyland laughed, stepping well clear of the conflagration of purple fire that guttered and danced in a frantic corona about Rivvek, then narrowed into a roaring blast no wider than a spread palm.

CHAPTER 30

UNTANGLED MAGIC

Spirits flowed through and around Kholburran, creatures of the air, the earth, growing grass, the water in the fish pond, and the fish within it. At long last, the young prince saw them all. Luminous auras radiated from his Root Guard, their spirits bright and beautiful, glowing with life and years and strength.

Tender shoots of natural magic sprouted from the edges of the scaffolding around them, a sign of the fleeting, fragile nature of the wood his Root Guard had coaxed back to life, reawakened really, after its rough treatment by the Aern. He drew out the ends of those roots, coaxing an additional eight from the edges, helping them find purchase in the rich soil, a long-term solution replacing the crude workings of his companions, in the process strengthening his own connection to the spot upon which he stood, anchoring himself not just here, but to Scarsguard, the city, and to Fort Sunder within, the ethereal roots of his essence spreading far in advance of his physical body.

He laughed at the sight of the Aern, their spirits so similar to their physical forms, but blazing like tiny stars from the links which bound them together, strengthening them, protecting them from the tendrils of black that extended from the Port Gate uphill in the fortress.

Wrongness stood out in dark contrast to his green and golden light.

The suffocating will of Uled showed clearly, but older corruptions lurked in this soil, in this air. Kholburran's eyes burst free of his skull on strong new limbs, opening like buds to reveal crimson leaves, red and hooked like the those of a blood oak.

Absent his eyes, Kholburran saw even more clearly the twists and tears, old and frayed, that had been wrought by the destruction of the Life Forge so many centuries ago. Thin mists of magic usable only by those of specific bloodlines remained, but even those were like drought-parched limbs rather than well-watered boughs. The damage originated near this spot, flowing outward as far as he could sense.

Even as his toes grew long and his legs thickened and joined together, he sensed that the damage could be repaired in time so long as the source was put right. It would take many seasons to fix it all, but he looked forward to the work, to being of real use at last.

"Kholburran!" Nearby, hard to focus on as his thoughts and body expanded, a familiar spirit pulled at his attention. Turning his view this close to himself already took a tremendous force of will, and he frowned even as his face stretched beyond its previous boundaries, becoming unrecognizable.

Arri? Mouth gone, he could not speak the thought, but when he spied her, he doubted she could have answered, trapped as she was by a tenuous tendril, thin, rotted, and smoldering, which stretched from the Root Guard and off into the lands beyond his lands; for these plains were now his—he claimed and changed and renewed them. He had sworn in his heartwood to restore them and make this hostile land right.

It would always be dangerous, but that was because the irkanth and the shadebeast hunted here, with the amaranthine viper that so loved the myrr grass, the scaled wolves, all but extinct, but within Kholburran's ability to coax back to their natural state. Other animals were gone, forever, but he could rebalance the delicate system the demon wars and the Sundering had tossed out of balance—

"Khol . . . burr . . . an," Faulina said, the rot having spread its tendrils to her and to others. The Aern could not help them, but he could.

Those tendrils . . . they led back to a foreign Root Tree. With its rot, it had tapped into pockets of deformed magic, using them to burn and strike instead of gently untwisting and restoring them as he should.

Father, Kholburran thought. *Oh. I remember now.* Thinking as he once had grew more difficult by the moment, but he recalled his father's presence, his father's anger, his father's madness. Once, when Kholburran had been smaller and thought only of himself, Warrune's madness had felt special and brave, had comforted him, but now it felt only sorrowful and selfish.

Help me kill them. Warrune laughed in his mind. *They do not—*

I believe my wishes were clear on this point, father. Kholburran reached out to Faulina and the others, where the tendrils were new and weak, depriving them of connection, withering what needed such great energy and focus to maintain, saving all but Arri, whose connection to Warrune was strongest. Warrune reached out for other pockets of oversaturated magic, with Kholburran struggling to reach each one first and restore the magic to its proper ratio, spreading it out, restitching one patch of magic to another.

Wordless growls of frustration echoed out at Kholburran from the rotted tendrils, sinking deeper into Arri, through her throat and into her heartwood.

Stop, father. Kholburran sent waves of calm at the other Root Tree, trying to work in all the careful gardening Queen Kari had used in raising him. *Go home and rest. You got me here safely. I Took Root in a place of my own choosing. It's done. You—*

"*Traitor!*" One word relayed through the lips of Arri and the essence of Warrune struck Kholburran like a physical blow. *You weren't supposed to be happy. You were to be miserable, not content and siding against me!*

Fire licked Arri's bark.

Her spirit struggled against Warrune's, but tendril after tendril seized her limbs, working her like a puppet on a string. Her arms wrapped around Kholburran's trunk, her chest pressed against the organic scars upon his back.

Help, Arri's spirit mouthed.

*

"Idiots." Cadence watched her fellow humans screaming and running like stampeding cattle, those elves who possessed no magic mixed in with them. Her mind's eye pulled her from death to death, tragedy to tragedy, too many to stop. Every floor of Fort Sunder was filled with the dead and those combating them.

"Kazan, you need to protect the Vael."

"I can't even tell what exactly is happening there," Kazan said, his voice distant, distracted. "One of them has gone crazy and the others are all struggling with their Heartbows. I have Aern there, and they are helping where they can, but this is magic, whatever it is."

"Get me over there then."

"Cadence—"

There was no time to argue, nor truly time to get there. If only she could do what Master Sedric could and appear via smoke and . . .

Don't be a fool, girl, Hap's false voice rang in her mind. *You're a weak, pathetic little bit of fluff, good for nothing but a candlemark's fun in the dark.*

She smiled. If she had learned anything about that twisted, doubting part of herself that gave voice to the sort of poison Hap had so often spewed, it was that the voice was wrong about her. So wrong, she suspected that if Hap's voice said she could not do something, then she most definitely could.

How would it work? she thought to herself.

You can't think you have a chance. Hap laughed. *Why not stop wasting your time and do something you're good at? I'm sure there are a few soldiers here who could use a—*

Folding her legs beneath her, Cadence closed her eyes, letting her mind drift, seeking the mind that—

And there it was.

She'd felt him before, this prince, helped him escape the fall of Tranduvallu. His mind was changing, expanding, but it was still a mind. She smiled, sweat beading on her forehead.

Let's see if I can get his attention . . .

*

Kholburran had a momentary vision of the future, as if seen from on high by someone else. The Root Guard tearing Arri apart to protect him, the dead rushing in and wiping out the Root Guard. Uled laughing as he stepped through the Port Gate and tore the newly rooted prince out of the ground by his roots, rending him to mulch. The elves falling as Uled drove the dead forward to corner them in spots absent of magic, areas Kholburran had yet to heal. He could not work fast enough, could not restore the state of this place to properly claim it as his own domain, regulating the magic within. Not without help.

And then he was back in the moment, a woman, a crystal twist with tricolored hair hovering before him, a figure in the thin smoke rising from Ari's bark.

"I'm not all that good at this yet," she said. "Master Sedric never taught me how he did it, but I needed to reach you. You can't beat that other Tree Guy on your own, and if you don't dispense with him quickly, you can't help the elves stop the dead."

Then help me, he thought at her.

"I'm not a plant, idiot, just a Long Speaker." Her image was fading, smoke blowing out of shape. "You must take advantage of the help you're ignoring."

What help? he thought, but the smoke had become formless and she was gone.

Help, Arri mouthed again. Or was that right? Her spirit's hands were splayed out toward him, but not in supplication. An offer? He concentrated on her lips. *I'll help.* He read this time.

Oh.

Hashan and Warrune were so powerful not just because they were joined but because they were one with Queen Kari, their Root Wife, who helped to ground them in the physical world, serving as their conduit. The three together were stronger and more capable than the three unjoined.

Arri? He looked into her eyes even as his spirit reached for hers. As their spirits touched, he could hear her. She had seen what the crystal twist had seen without the benefit of Long Speaking, not in the same exact way, but she still she knew what needed to be done. *But Malli—*

They need our help, Arri thought at him. *Not mine. Not yours. Ours.*

A memory hit him, not from his point of view, but from Arri's:

"From this day . . ." Arri looked up at him, seeing in him the strength growing, the first signs of a true Root Tree and marveling at it. She took his grip and rose, in that moment wanting more, but pushing that thought aside. He needs me to help him, not to bed him, she thought. "I am your Root Guard, Kholburran. I pledge myself to the service of the new Root Tree you will become until the day the Harvester takes my spirit, Gromma reclaims my body, and Xalistan sees fit that I hunt no more."

Back in the present moment, a thousand different arguments and objections ran rampant through Kholburran's mind, and they were all correct. It wasn't fair. It wasn't the romantic overture he'd imagined. But had it been that for Queen Kari? She'd tied herself to Hashan and Warrune not because she wanted to but because it was required so that Warrune would Take Root and do his duty to his people.

You don't have to do this alone, Snapdragon, Arri thought, their minds already close, close enough for him to feel the edge of her sense of duty, her love for her people, her own willingness not just to die, but to live for her people, whichever they needed. Whichever he needed. He experienced the discomfort of Warrune's touch, the way it plagued and had plagued Arri for every moment since the Root Tree had spliced a portion of his wood onto her own. And she had never complained, never uttered a word about Warrune's mad whispers. She had endured. Much as Kholburran realized his mother must endure . . . all for the good of her people.

Kholburran looked into the mad rot of his father and knew that his own sacrifice was a pittance in comparison to Arri's and Kari's. Being tied to Arri was far from a punishment. They could work well together. They had done so all along, and though he did not love her, he trusted her.

And she was right.

One moment of mutual acceptance was all it took. Arri sank into his trunk, foreign wood falling from her body, burning, falling to ash. Arri's Heartbow crumbled, but Kholburran's warpick flew into her outstretched hand like an old friend.

I've got my hand on your warpick, she thought at him lewdly.

Just like a girl-type person to make jokes about mating at a time like this, but he felt the intent behind the words. She wanted him at ease, was trying to comfort him with her humor, and that made it okay.

Feel free to kill a few people with it, Kholburran thought.

Did you have anyone in mind?

Two spirits joined and turned their essence against the dark.

We can hunt down that trail in a moment, Kholburran thought. *First, my father.* That was all it took.

Warrune screamed, the sound of it retreating across the distant horizon. Arri stepped free of Kholburran's trunk. His wood had replaced Warrune's and his scars, the scars matching Kholster's, the scars with which Kholburran had been born, were on her bark. A warm, golden light pulsed from her eyes. As one, they reached out to work in the soil, the air, the water, to heal this most sacred of places, their new home.

*

Blood ran freely from a busted lip where Bhaeshal's face had struck the bone-steel plating despite the blast of wind she'd spoken to break her fall. Vision blurry, she reached out to the elemental air and felt a lightning bolt on her tongue. Speaking it at a nearby group of the dead, she found another waiting and another. Her connection to the magic was suddenly as strong as she had ever felt it.

Her ears rang, and the tiny hairs on her arm stood up. Her elemental focus was suffused with warmth in way it had not been for years. She had gotten used to the chill of the silver mask on her skin.

Time to suss out the eccentricities of my focus later.

Dead advanced toward her, and she took to the air; not just flying, soaring. Her elves were panicking. Hydromancers no longer worked in concert with Pyromancers and Geomancers, having been diverted to preventing fires from spreading rather than helping to delay and control the movement of the dead with walls of ice.

Shouting with the voice of command at Thunder Speaker volume, she called out instructions to soldiers, calling each by name.

"Queen Bhaeshal," a nearby warsuit shouted. "Kazan requests you reinforce the Vael encampment by the new pond. He says the prince has taken root and is correcting the flow of this place. Your magic will become increasingly stable, but—"

"—only if the prince himself is safe."

"Mazik!" Queen Bhaeshal shouted. "Have the Royal Lance protect the Vael and their new Root Tree at all costs. This new mystic stability is his doing."

"What about the Port Gate?" Bhaeshal turned back to the warsuit who had spoken.

"We are working on it now," the warsuit said. "You may have our oath on it. The gate will close."

CHAPTER 31
TSAN'ZAUR

Frost crept over Bloodmane's surface as Warleader Tsan prepared to Breathe. Within him, Rae'en showed no sign of fear, and her trust thrilled the warsuit. Relaying target intelligence as best he could, Bloodmane watched as Eyes of Vengeance established a best guess at the location where the dragon intended to breathe fire. A red circle appeared atop his image of the ground, painted by the Overwatches to delineate a very substantial swath of the landscape where they suggested any Armored who did not wish to be melted into slag make themselves not be.

Rae'en. In Rae'en's mind's eye, Bloodmane enhanced the information she was being given with flashing white auras, outlining the Bone Finders and warsuits who were within or close to the danger zone.

Thanks, she thought at him, then, "Tsan, I still have about fifteen Bone Finders in your targeted area, can you . . . please . . . try to—" Bloodmane filtered out the sudden glare as quickly as possible, but the blaze of red from the dragon's ruby scales blinded her anyway, forcing her to close her physical eyes and see only with Bloodmane's. "—focus mainly on the other dragon?"

White and too bright to look at with mortal eyes, the newly minted dragon's fire became a column of death, a beam that evaporated the flesh it touched, converting muscle, bone, even metal to a gaseous state. An eternity of inferno stretched, destruction writ in a bold italic hand scorching, melting, and hardening the earth as it passed. One breath reduced the thousands of the dead by a full third.

Rae'en's shock and awe echoed the warsuit's own. He had seen Coal breathe fire before, even a first breath, but either Tsan was far more powerful or a younger dragon's flame burned brighter, hotter . . .

Forty-one Bone Finders will need to be stripped and dipped before they can function outside of their warsuits, Bloodmane relayed to Rae'en. **Eleven warsuits will need substantial reshaping before they can—**

Then they were falling.

"Tsan!" Rae'en shouted. "What are you doing?!"

Wings limply flapping, shifted by the rush of air, but through no effort of the dragon's, Tsan plummeted. Bloodmane, and thus Rae'en, gripped Tsan's neck, holding on as the ground grew closer by the heartbeat.

Bloodmane, Rae'en thought. *What hit Tsan?*

Nothing I could discern, Bloodmane answered.

Then what happened?

Perhaps a breath weapon is more taxing on younger dragons?

Jump free of the dragon., Keeper, Zhan's warsuit, thought at Bloodmane, as he flashed in Bloodmane's personal viewpoint his own position below, among the intact and still-fighting dead. **Aim for us.**

But—!

There is no time! Now or not at all, Bloodmane!

Trusting his fellow warsuit, time too short to ask permission or discuss it even with Rae'en, Bloodmane stood up, overrode Rae'en's instinctive attempts to keep clinging to the dragon's neck, and jumped.

"What are you doing?!" Rae'en thought and shouted simultaneously.

Do you think, Keeper asked, **you will hit with a thud, a crack, or a bounce—**

*

Aly, Bone Harvest thought at Alysaundra. **Aly, are you there?**

Don't call me Aly, Harv. Alysaundra tried to blink and failed. Her fingers flexed when she ordered them to close, but the motion lacked . . . substance. Her skin felt as it should, as it always did when inside her warsuit, but . . .

Oh. Flesh peeling. Eyes boiling in their sockets as her organs burst. *Not a memory I'm going to be calling up on purpose very often.*

Aern aren't supposed to burn, Bone Harvest told her.

We're only immune to **most** *extremes of heat and cold, Harv.* Alysaundra knew her body had been reduced to a lifeless mass of charred flesh and bones, no use to anyone until she had time to strip the meat off the bones and fill her warsuit with blood, but body death was no excuse for one of the Armored to stop fighting.

On one level, riding a warsuit entailed the same sorts of interactions as wearing one, only even when worn, Bone Harvest was in touch with himself, able to make decisions, override her movements for her own protection, make subtle alterations to his form to accommodate combat maneuvers or provide greater protection as the situation required: turtling to defend against ranged weapons, a stampede, or a mob-like army of corpses. They worked seamlessly together, the line between control and controller unimportant.

When housing Alysaundra's spirit such actions became a total hand off; either she was completely in control and Bone Harvest was a passenger in his own bone metal, or she was. She winced mentally at the casualties she saw in Bone Harvest's field of vision, denoted by shades of red (body dead, but warsuit functional), white (warsuit forced to turtle to protect its wearer), purple (warsuit damaged, body dead, movement impaired, repair achievable), blue (warsuit damaged, but body alive, movement impaired), and gray (warsuit and occupant both dead).

Gray! She replayed each death in rapid succession, letting Bone Harvest handle the fighting, wielding Sally one handed and using his left gauntlet to batter the dead, grab them and send them flying, or—

Some of the deceased Armored had been slain by corpses wielding shards of the Life Forge. These were two types of undead Sri'Zaur: one with mottled scales that helped camouflage it and the other with scales a shade of black so dark that focusing on it made her head hurt.

All of this processing passed in a mere moments.

Can you send these images out, please? Alysaundra thought to her warsuit. *We need to target these two kinds of Zaur and weed them out of the rank and file, then—*

A shadow fell over the warsuit. Alysaundra watched and Bone Harvest looked up, running as fast as he could, bulling through lines of the dead in an effort to get clear of the most beautiful dragon either of them had ever seen. Scales like liquid rubies flashed with inner light as the creature fell . . . right toward them.

Make sure to get all that sent out before the dragon crushes us. Okay, Harv?

PART FOUR

A FATHER SLAIN

My Prince,

Incalculable are the times I have been tempted to reveal one of the many secrets I have gleaned from the work of my father and from my own delvings into secrets esoteric and forbidden. I have gazed into the discoveries of Uled and comprehended them. Worse, I have deduced the cure for death for which he sought so long.

Immortality, however, is not for elves or men, dear Rivvek . . . though I have met one human who acquired the trait somewhat accidentally. I write this letter because the idea of withholding knowledge, even dangerous knowledge, from you is repugnant to me. It feels a lie. You will not find the secret to eternal life in the missive, only my confession that, having discovered it, I have not used it for my own ends or yours, but rather have destroyed all my notes. I have also altered my existing texts to mislead all who may use them to seek what I have found.

With apologies,

Sargus

An unsent letter

CHAPTER 32

BETRAYER

"How inconvenient." Uled strutted and cursed, hovering to and fro above the Port Gate. He let one scaled, misshapen hand rest on the stone surface of the gate, tracing a poison-riddled declivity with one nail-less finger. A change was being wrought in the place beyond the Port Gate, one Uled had not expected, or so Vander gathered from the abomination's ranting. The god of knowledge kept losing the trail of thought, so he could have missed a thread or two; Uled's babbling covered many topics. Vander's attention was drawn over and over again to Uled's double-pupiled eye.

At first he thought it a trick of the light, but no, the pupils flowed together and through one another, changing color and properties. The pupils shaded from brown to black to gold, and only the subtle way their focus altered gave him warning that Uled had at last detected his presence.

Smiling, biting, and clawing all as one motion, Uled's touch fell on empty air, Vander having stepped back, not just away, but to the pocket dimension he thought of as his library. Uled's image, smaller, and more distant, glared at him through a scrying mirror hovering in front of Vander. Running one hand over his bald head, the newly deific Aern felt the eyes of Uled staring back at him, as if the mad elf thing could actually—

"I see you, Vander," Uled said. "Why has my beast's right eye become Aldo's chosen form? Come back and let me see you more closely."

With a wave, Vander banished the view of Uled.

Did you see that? Vander asked, sending the memory to Kholster even as he asked the question.

I have seen it now. Kholster stood on the bluff where the royal tower at Port Ammond had once stood. He had bathed in the sea and stood dripping, his jeans sodden, his boots dark with moisture. The dark warpick, Reaper, hung on his back, bone-steel on bronze skin. *You forgot you were tracking an irkanth and almost got mauled.*

Not mauled, but . . . That maw, full of bone metal teeth from Kholster's own jaw loomed in memory, and he left the sentence half finished. *Are things all prepped down below?*

You don't know?

I could know, but I left it a secret per Vax's request.

Good. Kholster closed his eyes. *Sargus?*

Vander found the elf on the road to Fort Sunder, pack disguised as a hump, head seemingly distorted by some ailment of birth, all to hide his true appearance and conceal the resemblance, slight though it was, to his father.

Making good time for an elf without Aeromancy, Vander thought. *Are you certain it is wise to send him away? You might need him.*

No. Kholster's lips drew into a pressed line. *Wylant will deal with him if he is one of Uled's contingencies.*

You really think——?

No. Kholster sat down, eyes studying the waves, watching Sea Hawk strike in the distance. *But . . .*

"With Uled," Vander whispered, "you can never be too cautious."

*

Amber and her group of Overwatches scuttled across the bone-steel-plated ceiling of Fort Sunder, dodging the occasional blow from corpses that wielded weapons long enough to reach them. Joose and Arbokk had to hang back, but Glayne still crawled with Amber through the smoke, each letting their warsuits breathe for them. Up ahead and also down below, a Pyromancer, a Geomancer, and a Hydromancer were back to back, attempting to clear a way to the Port Gate. Glayne indicated a dead elf in Aeromancer's robes, not yet risen, resting among the mass of dead.

The elves moved in step with the Geomancer using a floating chunk of wall to shield their backs, the Hydromancer leaving walls of ice on either side, and the Pyromancer shooting flame from her palms to clear the dead.

Someone had the same idea we did, Amber thought to the others.

Smoke billowing around them, Glayne and Amber had to slow, hanging closer to the ceiling despite the smoke, as the ceilings grew lower down the stairs to the level on which the Port Gate stood. The elves' progress slowed, then stopped, as it looked like the Pyromancer was running out of steam.

"We're nearly there," the Geomancer growled. "Keep going!" But then the Pyro was down and the dead were upon them.

Glayne caught a thin, shard-like dagger as one of the dead hurled it through the air.

Was that—? Amber asked.

A shard of the Life Forge, Glayne agreed. *We're getting close. Be careful.*

Even as he said the words, Amber swatted away a thin, needle-like spike the length of a quill, but with the weight of a dagger. It shot away, embedding itself the stone to her right, before she recognized it too was a shard of the Life Forge.

She snatched it free, pausing to slide it safely into her oversized side pouch; Aernese saddlebags, the Dwarves called them. As she packed it away, a trio of Sri'Zaur, their scales torn, camouflage broken by gaps of red flesh or white exposed bone, appeared in the upper quadrant of her display.

Glayne had spotted them clambering along the ceiling toward the two of them, claws scratching and scraping along the minute irregularities in the ceiling that survived the bone-steel plating.

Amber repaid the favor by detecting a fourth and a fifth sliding up the walls behind them. Subtle as ever, Glayne, though they were within earshot, showed his appreciation with a green aura around his symbol on her mental map and a matching aura around her own.

He was nothing if not old guard to the bone metal.

Glayne held the shard he'd caught in his palm, testing its weight, its balance.

What? Amber thought at him.

Wondering what, if any, effect these would have on the dead.

The Life Forge was devastatingly effective against Aern, because they had been forged upon it. Amber did not see the link.

It was called the Life Forge, Glayne thought at her. *These enemies are dead. I'm going to test it.*

Turning for the nearest of the wall-crawling corpses, the two behind them, Glayne did a somersault along the ceiling and came up on one knee, shard plunged into the skull of his target. It fell lifeless, without any signs of further animation, to the floor, knocking over a few dead beneath it.

Glayne, Amber thought, *that's—*

Promising and interesting, but largely immaterial unless we find more shards. What if it works on Uled? Amber asked.

*

Zhan, Rae'en growled as she plummeted toward the ground, *I thought we were past this.*

He laughed in her mind, a single, dry cough of a laugh. It did not sound like the laughter of a mad Aern, but more friendly, like a . . . joke?

Does Zhan even have a sense of humor? Joose had asked, so long ago.

Halfway down, teeth bared, doubled-canines ready to rip into Zhan if she and Bloodmane could even move after a fall from this height, the First of One Hundred felt a sudden pain, as if an iron mitt had seized her right shoulder, the thumb biting into her skin, then a matching impact connected unseen with her left shoulder, and she was . . . slowing.

Half expecting to see Tsan'Zaur awake and flapping, gaining altitude, having grabbed her shoulders with one huge talon, Rae'en had glanced up and back, but there was nothing there.

The dragon had fallen past Rae'en in the air.

Bloodmane, what in Torgrimm's name?

Keeper apologizes on behalf of the Ossuarian, the warsuit thought. **Many fail to share Zhan's sense of humor, possibly because it only appears to rear its head in dire situations.**

Stepping out onto the molten earth, Zhan had run to take up a position as close as he could get to Rae'en's most likely point of impact. Tsan'Zaur struck the ground nearby, with an unearthly crack, gouts of flaming bile vomited forth from her unconscious maw.

How did he do that? Rae'en had stopped in the air, Zhan's arms upraised, holding her a few hundred feet aloft. *I can pull my warpick to me from a few feet away, but this . . .*

Every Aern is best at something. Bloodmane had never sounded more like her father than he did with that single sentence.

A low laugh so deep it rattled the bones in her chest erupted from the other, very conscious dragon. Tsan had frozen in a blast of cold. Rae'en plummeted again, wind whistling past, striking the ground a hand past the lines of molten earth and fused glass. She struggled to her feet quickly, bruised and battered but not broken.

*

Coal loomed over kholster Rae'en, his chest open, ribs splayed, the cavity within ablaze with crawling blue light, ghoulish and pale, refracted by icicles descending from his scales.

"Kill her," the parboiled Sri'Zaur on his back roared.

"Shut up, Dryga," Coal drawled, slinging the Sri'Zaur from his back with the flick of a hind leg, like a dog scratching at a flea. "You can try to kill her if you like. I have more important things to do; it seems there is a lady dragon present."

"Daughter of Kholster." Coal bobbled his head at her in rough approximation of a nod. His eyes raked over Zhan. "Talk amongst yourselves." Then he was moving past, clawed paws steaming where his path crossed the trail cut by Tsan'Zaur's breath.

What is Coal going to do? Joose asked.

From the carnage, M'jynn thought, *I would venture to guess nothing good.*

Dryga sprang up, fire licking up his back. He charged, Skreel knife in either hand, as if summoned there by magic. In death, he was fast. In life, he may have been fast enough. As it was, Bloodmane struck the Sri'Zaur once in the head with his right gauntlet, catching his throat with the other and separating the brain box from the trunk with workman-like disdain. Rae'en's attention never left the dragon. Unlike Coal's chest, the expanse of his back scales were a wall of unbroken armor, the edges ice-rimmed and flickering with an inconstant blue.

I'm searching every Aern's memory for something about how dragons interact, Kazan thought, *but Coal has been the only one alive since before Kholster was forged.*

Not strictly true, Glayne thought to the group, *but the memory would not help you.*

"You should have slain me with your First Breath, Little Firestarter," Coal cooed. "To come flying into my presence with my spark of Jun's fire burning in your breast and not consider me—ME—your first priority . . .

I have borne many indignities, biding my time until I could get to Uled and show him face to maw why I was called the Betrayer, but this . . ." Coal spread his wings, one broken and frayed, the other marked by a massive hole in the dark membrane. "THIS I cannot ignore and yet consider myself a dragon!"

Coal drew in a deep breath, lungs whining like dying bellows, a wave of heat pouring off of him in all directions, the blue on his scales a bright, piercing azure, steady and flaring.

Corpses caught like matchsticks, drying, steaming, and bursting alight in an uneven gyre as Coal expelled heat to make ice.

Warmth coursed over Rae'en's skin, evaporating as Bloodmane cut off the sensation from his exterior, then finding her again as it worked through the warsuit's metal. Skin began to cook, searing through, pulling away from the flesh beneath.

Do you want me to let you out, or— Bloodmane's thought, worry, and fear hit her, the edges colored by the panic of a memory, of Bloodmane acting as unintentional conduit for Ghaiattri fire, the flames burning Kholster, driving him into the water, too late . . . too late.

No, she thought, *keep me safe. This is only normal fire—*

Pain blanked her mind. No data. No input. No mental field of vision. No Overwatches, but . . . wait . . . not completely alone. Never completely alone. Never again.

Bloodmane?

A strip and dip will be required, kholster Rae'en, he thought.

"Blast," Rae'en whispered, the words deeper than if they'd come from fleshly lips.

So many Aern.

So much blood needed to restore them.

On the other hand, most of the dead were burning, their bodies weakened. Given time, they would all burn down to ash if the strange wave of heat acted anything like normal dragon's fire.

To her left, Coal loomed over Tsan'Zaur, the prone dragon's scales shimmering brightly. Making sure she had a good grip on her warpick, Rae'en ran toward the dragons. Bounding over the patches of heat Bloodmane thought hot enough to melt or scorch bone-steel, Rae'en charged at Coal's back.

Bloodmane, Rae'en thought, *tell Keeper I thought Zhan said his Bone Finders came for the bones.*

Bone Harvest would like—

Quick thoughts.

Bone Harvest. Alysaundra. Right.

Put her through.

Zhan didn't die, but he's unconscious, Alysaundra's voice hit her mind, *which means, for the moment, I'm the Ossuarian.*

And?

Are you going to help me end this dead dragon or not? Alysaundra Bone Harvest shot past Rae'en Bloodmane, running backward and waggling the little finger of her right gauntlet at Rae'en like she was some inexperienced Eleven on her first outing, still hacking her little fingers off for the extra bone metal.

Bone Harvest's crystal eyes shone a twinkling red, but even through the faceted eyes, Rae'en saw the lifeless body behind them . . . loose, dead, eyes boiled in their sockets.

Were I not Armored, I'd be dead now, Rae'en thought to no one beyond her own mind. Riding in Bloodmane, however, her thoughts were too close to go unheard. He tried to lean clear of them, but she was his occupant in a way a physical being could never be. Like two dogs in a one-dog kennel, there was only so much space they could cede to one another.

I will not let you die, Bloodmane thought. You need no longer concern yourself with—

You let Dad die.

No. Bloodmane's thoughts were iron. True, I made a mistake . . . but he chose to die rather than make me pay the price for it. He should have destroyed me, kholster Rae'en. He should have torn my consciousness out of my bone-steel hide and inhabited it himself . . . leaving a new piece of his spirit behind when he was stripped and dipped.

He could have done that?

Yes.

Could I?

You are not yet strong enough to force me to depart, but I would allow it.

Why?

Armor may be reforged to suit its wearer many times, Blood-mane thought, but a warsuit does not attempt to reforge its occupant.

Another flash of remembrance clicked in place, a quick sensation of Bloodmane molding his shape to accommodate the differences in size between Rae'en and her father. She briefly pondered what would have happened if the warsuit had merely pulled her taller, stretched or bent her body until she fit instead.

Gruesome thought, Alysaundra sent. *Stop dwelling on it and fight, unless you want your brand new-shiny dragon to get eaten by the old stinky one.*

Rae'en blinked, or felt like she had—her eyelids were totally gone—before centering herself, committing to the battle, shoving aside the concerns at Fort Sunder, the worries about Bloodmane's willingness to sacrifice himself, her father's sacrifice, his godhood, Wylant, Vax, even Zhan and the relationship between the main army and the Bone Finders.

Left or right? Alysaundra asked.

You're already on the right, Rae'en sent back, *so I'll go left.*

Bone Harvest sent an image of two warpicks swinging at opposite sides of a melon.

Meet you in the middle, Rae'en agreed. Then she was running up a dead dragon's back, its scales slick and black beneath her feet. A pull came from Alysaundra, and Rae'en matched it, the two of them pulling on each other's bone-steel, opposite gauntlets extended toward one another as if they were attempting to draw a weapon to them that lay only a few inches away. It was enough to keep them from sliding off of the dragon, enough to give them purchase as they sped straight up Coal's back on their way to his massive head.

*

Warleader Tsan stirred, her body slow and cold, thoughts fuzzy. A sharp stab from her ribs told her they were broken, her left foreleg, too. Her ears thrummed. Surely they should have been ringing, should they not? And why did the thrums sounds so much like words?

Wake up, One-Headed Kilke hissed in her thoughts.

Fool. Did he not realize she was awake already? Had been for several heartbeats. *Ah*, she thought, *the thrumming. Of course.*

Great warmth had made her stir, and she had sucked at it greedily, wanting more, yet it had all but run out. Why not just lie here until there was more heat? The suns emitted enough that, given a good, hot noon, she might want to start thinking about trying to stand . . .

A sound like rippling sailcloth. A smell like . . . dragon.

Tsan, Kilke thought, *you have to wake up.*

Did you know that would happen with the Breath? Tsan rose with grace despite her injury, keeping all of the weight on her three good— No, the rear left leg felt weak and shaky, the pain deep and sharp—two good legs and as much as she could tolerate on the rear left. *Did you?* Her thoughts slid cold and calm toward One-Headed Kilke as she tested her wings. They felt intact, but she'd wrenched the muscle—left side again—and doubted she could stay aloft long.

I did, Kilke thought, *but I had not expected you to—*

Give me power.

Tsan, Kilke purred, *it is not that simple. I need—*

Are we two allies or enemies? Tsan's massive head turned toward the scent of the other dragon. *Because allies can have little misunderstandings, missteps requiring amercement, yes, but excusable at the end of the day. Penalty paid; no need to discuss it further.*

She felt a trickle of power, eyelids closing for a few beats of her tremendous heart as the world spun tail over tongue. A head injury, too, then.

More, she demanded.

You're a dragon already, Tsan, Kilke said. *Once your metamorphosis was complete, there was little that I could offer. You will heal more quickly, but even Gromma would have—*

Blast and damn then, Tsan thought.

I—

My enemies, Tsan directed.

What? the god asked.

A tinge of fear set off the train of instinctive reevaluation Tsan could not help but entertain whenever she detected it in an ally. Kilke feared Coal. By extension then, did he now fear Tsan herself? Her mind muzzy, she tabled the equations until a later date . . . a date, for example, when she was the only dragon remaining on the Last World.

My words were a call to action, not a curse, Kilke, Tsan thought at him. *What?*

Coal loomed closer, babbling about something Tsan could not understand, the words metallic and echoing. Kilke's fear stained the air, seeping into Tsan's thoughts unbidden. Fear? No. Tsan declined to share such a useless emotion. She forced her calm into the disembodied god, explanation twinned with it: *You have magic, and as power is your purview, you demonstrated the ability to enhance my army, keep them refreshed. Said magic obviously functions on those with some measure of immunity to magic. Given your previous threat to blind me, unless that was an empty threat, you must possess some offensive capability.*

Now, rather than forcing to me explain at length . . . Tsan tracked the path of two warsuits as they vaulted the dead wyrm's shoulders. They blinked from one spot to the next and the world winked, Tsan hovering on the edge of unconsciousness. Breathing deeply despite her ribs, the dragon leaned into the pain, riding it back to full alertness. *Use your magic to blast the dead and the dragon. Send them to one of the hells or rejuvenate our allies if you can, but whatever you do, do it now, because—*

Because you need me, Kilke purred.

Because otherwise, I will eat you and see if that makes me a god, helps me regenerate, or merely puts a grin on my maw.

CHAPTER 33
BETRAYED

Prismatic sparks became Yavi's entire world beyond the gentle yet unyielding embrace of Dolvek's spirit. An old panic woke in her core, not the instinctive fear of being entrapped itself, but a shadow of it. She'd lost an eye, her arms, and most of her legs below the knee, but none of those injuries held the terror for Yavi that being held against her will did.

Come on, Yavi, she thought. *Act like a girl-type person, not some scared sproutling.*

If she asked Dolvek to let her go and he refused, the panic would take over, but if she declined to ask, the illusion that she was in control could be maintained and the panic kept at bay.

I will not scream.

A series of pops sounded in her ears as the wind vanished, leaving behind a tepid atmosphere like stepping into a cave whose temperature defied the chill without, ever warm.

Sparks faded, gray void replacing them. Nothing in all directions. How could such a place exist?

Where are we?

Combined confusion and physical restraint opened the doorway to instinctive panic.

"Let me go!" Yavi shouted and was instantly falling.

He let me go. Even if she fell forever through whatever this place was, Yavi knew her gratitude for the spirit's compliance would be eternal, that at least that much of the prince remained even when he no longer knew his own name.

More opaque and solid-looking in this place, Dolvek's ghost was painted in violet hues. He plummeted alongside her, brow furrowed as if trying to work out a complex equation, one he would not give up on but knew he would never solve.

"Where are we?" Yavi asked. "Where did you bring us?"

"I meant to take you home," the ghost replied, "but then . . ." his eyes unfocused, form flickering, then regaining stability.

"But then . . . ?" she asked. "No. Before that. Would you catch me, please?" She looked down, seeing the same gray in that direction. "I don't seem likely to hit anything, but it's . . ." And his arms were around her waist. " . . . disconcerting to fall like that, through endless nothing."

"Not endless." Dolvek's voice was stronger in this place, too, less whisper than soft-spoken.

"No?"

"No?"

"Dolvek." Yavi closed her eye. "Are you saying there is somewhere else here, a way out, or—?"

"Some. One." Dolvek's image wavered. "Some. Thing. A . . . life." Her sense-dulled bark registered a cold wetness where his spectral fingers touched her, had indeed begun to slide through her, his fingers losing more substance as he faded.

"Dolvek?" Jaw slack, eyes vacant, color washed out of his image. She drifted deeper, his arms poking through her, too insubstantial to keep his grip. "Don't go!"

Desperate, Yavi looked around with her remaining eye, casting wildly about for another spirit, but there was only Dolvek, his spirit torn and frayed. He reminded her of the spirit she'd met at the White Road on her way to meet with the Eldrennai, so downtrodden and worn thin, she had been hard-pressed to tell much about what it might once have looked like.

With Dolvek, though, she knew what he had been like, remembered the look of his face and his spirit. Could she help him regain a portion of his old self? Hadn't she already? When she called him Dolvek, he answered, but before passing through the Port Gate, he had no longer known to whom that name belonged.

The fingers of her lone remaining hand trailed along the ephemeral outline of his jaw. Her brows knit in concentration as she touched his spirit with her magic. Torn down, battered, and reduced to his core, Dolvek's energy hummed liked an air spirit.

Maybe . . .

Conjuring thoughts of him, the arrogant prince who had been overstimulated by her scent, discombobulated by the sight of her unveiled face, the wiser prince who had seen through his own blinders and accepted that he had been wrong, then moved to change himself, the resolute and heroic prince who had decided not to allow Uled's Port Gates to remain standing even in death. A sweet and foolish spirit who valued Yavi's life more than his own life, his own sanity, or the whole of The Last World.

*

Silent by choice, by injury, and by name, Caz stalked amid the flow of animated corpses. Bone-steel gauntlets traced with skeletal filigree struck out, serpent-like, bringing quiet to the restless dead courtesy of the thin, golden-hued spikes tightly clutched within. A mob of opponents this thick could overwhelm a lone Aern, even in a warsuit, if they were possessed of comparable strength or they were exceptionally hard to kill, but they fell before the Bone Finder as easily as the angry nobles or petulant farmers who had foolishly stood between him and his quarry over the centuries.

He came for the bones and, save for a single time in living memory, no opponent had ever thwarted him for long. A burst of the memory struck at his mind, sinking its images deep, fang-like, into his concentration. The new warsuit. Wylant. Vax, thinning into a wire strangling cord, cutting through Caz's warsuit, then his neck, his spine . . .

Caz banished the memory, haunting the present. Now his purpose was rekindled.

We come for the bones, Silence thought.

Caz sent a mental nod, but even his thoughts were sparse, clear of everything but the mission and the bones.

What a wonderful difference a few assassins could make.

He had been standing at his post in the room where Wylant had slain him, the same room where the Life Forge had once been housed, as ordered by Zhan, the one member of the Armored Ossuary not allowed to pursue the lump of bone metal withheld by the dead dragon, Coal, when the influx of the dead had begun. Invasion had been meaningless to him. Only the bones, the bones and his oaths, truly mattered. Then he had felt the tug of uniqueness.

Twice a shard of the Life Forge had pinged his senses, not bone-steel, but close enough when a proper Bone Finder was alert for it. Not a concern, as such, but he had been obligated to leave his post. After that, it had been easy to snatch the warsuit-slaying implements from the claws of would-be assassins. They would not have been his equal even when alive . . .

Surprise and numbers were the only edges the undead reptiles (he was noticing a few humans now, too) had when facing an Aern; Silence, Caz's warsuit, negated the one and his own sense for metal obviated the other. He had fought his way down the corridor, tracking the source of them. Clearly the Port Gate, but he felt a deeper tug, too. From beyond the gate, perhaps?

Farther down the hallway, Caz saw the Sixth of One Hundred, Glayne, testing the hypothesis Caz the Silent had already confirmed to his own satisfaction: the shard of the Life Forge slew warsuits and Aern, but also ended the unquiet dead.

We could tell them, Silence thought.

Caz sent a mental head shake in reply. Glayne would know soon enough and would disseminate the information more efficiently. Long Knives and Warpick (his first soul-bonded weapon, forged before he'd discovered and taken a liking to dual blades) hung from his back. With a shard of the Life Forge in either hand, Caz waded through the dead, stilling more dead with each step.

The Third and Sixth of One Hundred were going through the Port Gate to find the source of the dead and end it. A mission of complete unimportance to Caz, except . . . who knew where their bones would lay if they died? What easier way to ensure their bone metal would not be lost to the Ossuary than to follow them himself?

Besides, the tug he felt, unusual and distant, but clear enough to track prey by, grew stronger with each step toward the grand circle of stone through which the dead still poured. Another step or two and he knew would be able to identify the Aern from whom . . .

First Bones.

Kholster had metal beyond that Port Gate.

We come for the bones, Silence intoned.

Kholster . . .

Caz flushed with embarrassment at the situation Kholster (and to no small extent Caz himself) had allowed to develop between Wylant and himself. She had fought well. Word among the warsuits now held that Vax had been properly born, freeing Caz from his oath to Kholster himself to ensure the child's eventual full awakening. But . . . to have been to so blinded . . . so unwilling to hear what Wylant was saying . . . so intent on finally having his oath fulfilled . . . Caz could not help but feel he had deserved the thrashing she and Vax had given him.

Memory rushed him again, the feel of Vax decapitating him, the embarrassing necessity of a strip and dip to restore his body . . . now finally his honor would be restored. Habit preventing him from growling in his throat, but he did the equivalent in his mind.

I come for the bones.

He waited, spying with Silence's assistance on the Third and Sixth until they were through the gate. Then, with a hiss and a heroic burst of strength, Caz performed a twisting flip, landing toes and knuckles on the ceiling before darting through the Port Gate after them.

*

Coal reeled back, lightning from the talisman at the female dragon's neck burning his eyes, making them smoke, hiss, and sizzle. Savage blows raked his neck scales, heavy metal footsteps skidding down its length.

Warsuits? A wet splash signaled the end of his eyes, but Coal could still see . . . vision cloudy and dim, like a mist, images defined by an inner light. *Souls?* Muzzy and wearied by the attack rather than feeling its true impact, Coal sensed the mad elf thing that Uled had become gaining a foothold at the edge of his mind.

That is the head of a god at her throat, Uled's screeching voice wailed. *Seize it!*

"So . . . One-Headed Kilke sided with the Zaur after all," Coal muttered. Chromatic sprays of light popped at the edges of his vision, remnants of the meat body's optics—nerves misfired by the raw magic of an angry, disembodied god. "I would be irate, too, if I were only a head."

Clawing absently at the Aern on his back, Coal could not believe it when they dodged his massive claws. *I was that nimble once*, Coal mused as he noted a marked change in his emotional state. From rage to introspection. *Ah. Brain damage.*

Dissociative concern coated his mind. Uled's hooks sinking deeper. Coal's tail twitched, controlled by a mind that was not his own.

"You will need to lay me to rest more quickly than this," Coal drawled, his words slurred, his jaws slow to respond. "He gains purchase in my . . ." He searched for the word, could not find it, and approximated. " . . . head."

"Stop fighting, then," the young dragon replied. "Logic would seem to—"

Coal struck the foolish thing a mighty blow across the face, claws drawing blood, marking the scales and the flesh below deeply enough that it might scar. Dazed, the female fell back, eyes unfocused, a loud crack sounding from one of the bones in her forelegs as she landed.

"Dragons never stop fighting!" Coal bellowed. "We end fights or we die."

He loomed over her, reaching for heat but unable to grab it. Cold flowed through him instead, a sure sign Gromma's order had been turned on its snout.

*

"You have to concentrate!" Coal's voice boomed, reverberating in Bloodmane's warsuit. "You will never win this unless you can manage a Second Breath."

Rae'en mapped out a second run on the great wyrm's head, Bone Harvest relaying Alysaundra's agreement. They had lost ground dodging Coal's claws, moving all the way back to his shoulders.

Amber and Glayne just went through the Port Gate. Kazan flashed their new location on an updated map.

Where is that? Rae'en caught the tip of her heavy boots and might have gone tumbling if she and Alysaundra had not been working together, the bone-steel bond between bracing them against each other to increase traction.

The Sisters, Amber thought. *Northern Ports where the borders of—*

I know where the Sisters are, Rae'en interrupted. *Bloodmane was there when the Dwarves . . .*

Sorry, kholster Rae'en, Bloodmane thought. **Memory seep can**

happen when we both share the bone metal this intimately. Our minds are pressed close.

Rae'en Bloodmane, they thought together.

She missed what Coal said to Warleader Tsan at first, but Kazan had not missed a thing.

He's giving Tsan'Zaur instructions on how to use Jun's fire to kill him, Kazan thought. *But he's attacking her at the same time.*

Rae'en lost her balance, stumbling over the side of Coal's neck. A certainty that she would fall sent trills of fear plucking at her spine, her stomach light and trembly, but she felt Alysaundra's pull and kept moving.

Together they kept going, orbiting Coal's scaly neck in a counterbalancing rotation until they reached a steady balance again.

Kazan, time the strike for us.

*

Many jun away, Kazan sat on the edge of Scarsguard's extended boundary walls, an Armored Overwatch within his warsuit's reassuring embrace. He shunted all of his other responsibilities to the minds of his fellow Overwatches, sending most to Joose, Arbokk, and M'jynn, but not stopping there. A mind that could see the whole of the Aern narrowed its attention to two single Aern: kholster of the Aernese Army and the Acting Ossuarian. They were already in close sync, both warriors of like spirit and strategic leaning.

Since both were in need of a strip and dip to coat their bone metal in new flesh, he provided the touchstone for their physicality. His heart set the internal rhythm they lacked. His lungs simulated the steady pump of their breath. He painted the world for them in traces and arcs, each step outlined and glowing. Hands outstretched, his left to form Rae'en's strike and his right Alysaundra's, he lost all sensation of body, leaving that to Eyes of Vengeance, becoming an extension, a bridge between the weapons.

Every conversation any Aern had ever had concerning dragons, Coal or others, flooded his mind as he pinpointed the most likely spot to crack the wyrm's colossal skull.

On a level below conscious thought, where instinct and autonomic function live, he felt connected, his motions appearing to guide theirs, but in the core of him, he knew the truth: They were the initiators, the attackers, the true talent, and he was little more than a clever metronome.

They brought his arms together, hands clapping in the middle, echoing the twin strikes to the dragon's temples. Leaping and spinning, they flew through the air like soaring sea hawks, bone metal striking once, twice, three times, and over and over, though the lightning of a decapitated god lit them up, flaring the crystalline eyes of their warsuits until, with a solid clink of metal on metal, their warpicks met in the center of the dragon's brainpan.

Then the cold hit them, freezing the ground, but not as solidly as before. Frost rimmed their joints and as they saw what Kazan saw, Rae'en and Alysaundra, Bloodmane and Bone Harvest released their unseen tethers and fell away from Coal just before the Last World's final dragon breathed her Second Breath for the first time.

*

Even as Coal blew apart, becoming ash and molten scale before her, Tsan could hear the thumping of his mighty tail. She would never be sure, as no one seemed to know whether Coal spoke Zaurtol or not, but his tail seemed to tap, <<Betrayed by my own fire. Well done, little red one. Well done.>>

CHAPTER 34

THE MAD ELF

Wretched beasts of his own design, long since beyond his control, burst through Uled's Port Gate, stilling his dead and claiming space on his docks. Uled recognized the warsuits and sneered. The Third and Sixth. He narrowed his eyes, the dual-pupiled mass in his left socket bulging beyond its ocular orbit, filling with a brown mixture of pus and dried blood. He lanced it with an impatient jab of the foreclaw on his left paw, the mixture running over the scales of the Zaur-elf hybridized appendage.

Grinding his bone metal teeth hard enough to make sparks, he flexed his right hand, its smooth skin close to that of a normal elf's, excepting the rips revealing bone and desiccated muscle that marked its back. His clothing shifted and flowed, becoming a long robe of red chased with silver thread. It would not do to allow his beasts to behold him in tattered rags.

A cold rain sprang up, soaking his robes through, unnoticed. Having addressed appearances, he had moved beyond them. Who cared what beasts thought?

The Sixth spun to face the Port Gate, his gauntleted fist obliterating the first rune without even pausing to take in his surroundings. The Third—was it inhabited by some . . . female?!—held off the dead as best she could, stabbing them with shards of the Life Forge. A third warsuit, a Bone Finder, and therefore of little concern other than to collect the bones of these two when Uled had finished with them, sprung out of the rear of the Port Gate, dropping off of the dock and into the water below.

I did not realize any of the beasts knew it was possible to control which section of the Port Gate they came through. Interesting enough to give him pause to ponder what else the beasts might have deduced about the workings of the Port Gates. The Sixth, however, did not pause, destroying the second, third, and fourth runes in swift succession.

Uled was unamused.

*

Lightning crackled over the mountainous boundary marking the passage toward the center of the Never Dark's diminished light. Demons gathered, their numbers growing. Craggy voices of true Ghaiattri rang out with increasing volume, a low rumble at the edge of the scarred elf's ears. The shifting of their leathery wings formed an audible susurrus illustrating that time had grown short.

He did not look at them, ignoring the clashing weather that mirrored their violent will. His troops faced outward, ready to defend the Aern and the wagons at the center of the massive formation. Even so, they were forced to tighten their formations as the Ghaiattri increased in numbers and their influence grew.

Clad in his dragon armor, Rivvek poured fire into the Port Gate, the purple conflagration of his Ghaiattric flame shining like a bonfire. He felt his skin burning despite the draconic armor he wore, but he did not stop. All around him, those elves who had followed him on his suicide mission stood ready to charge, and with them, the Aern they had come to claim.

Jolsit, Cambrish, Hevrt, Vodayr, and Kyland . . . he ran out of names then. He knew more but did not have the concentration to spare in summoning them. General Kyland stood at his back, Jolsit to his left. Each shifted nervously, stepping farther away from him as his nimbus of heat grew.

Kyland and the Lost Command, he thought. *Found, recovered, and ready to return, but for this truculent Port Gate that refuses to break open.*

Violently flickering between the seasons, the surrounding environs fought Kyland's will. Rivvek, who longer thought of himself as prince or king—titles had no meaning now—had considered himself dead. The idea that he might live, might be triumphant, could take only tenuous hold on his thoughts. Self had gone, replaced by that part of Rivvek that plotted and planned, setting out trignom tiles on the board of his mind.

He had learned to use them as a mental exercise when he had been sent to the gnomes of Rurnia to study and convalesce after his first ill-fated sojourn into the Never Dark. A mistake, he'd thought then, but time had proven otherwise. Without the scars his foolishness had won him then, Kholster would not have put his scars upon Rivvek's back, and without Kholster's scars, the Aern might never have listened to him, might never have spared the quarter million of his subjects who had been spared.

It was such a small population, but better than zero. Sufficient, according to the species formula the gnomish arithmeticians had drilled into his head. It was enough for the elves to survive and thrive and grow in number again—threatened, endangered, but not extinct. He had thought his quest over, his calculations completed, his projections and plans, what the gnomes called the Great Destiny Machine, all resolved, quiet, but Kyland's presence had brought his mind back to life. This Port Gate, forcing it, was required for any of his current projections to succeed. The crucial first step.

I have to get them back to the Last World.

As he poured all of his magic into the task at hand, his mind, without regard for his own feelings on the matter, could not help but continue his design. Portions of the equation, vital ones, lay still and dark, completed: Destroy the dragon. Retrieve the Aern.

Others shimmered in uncertain shades, needing completion: Get them home. See Sargus. Destroy Uled. Cement Bhaeshal's power. See Sargus. Ensure the continued safety of his people. See Sargus.

Stop looping, he thought, removing "See Sargus" from the equations, an optional subset that his subconscious mind kept shifting to the "required" permutation set.

Fine. He had two living friends, and the thought that he might see either of them again felt unreal to him.

"Whatever is being done on the homeward side of the Gate," Kyland said through gritted teeth, "may be fixing the ebb and flow of magic, but it is making the elements on this side as hard to control as the wind in a hurricane. If they get a few more Ghaiattri up there fighting me . . ."

Rivvek made no comment.

Flame rolled up his arms, the skin bubbling and popping, pain sinking into his shoulders, his back, his chest. If he had not had to use the Ghaiattric flame so much or so often, he felt he could have done this less painfully. If there had been more time . . . If there had been another with the skill to aid him. Instead, he pushed to his limits and beyond until the whole of him was a flaming knot of agony.

Break!

In the end, it was not the thought of Sargus or Bhaeshal or even of those elves already accepted as Aiannai by the Aern. Nor was it the desire to show kholster Rae'en what the elf whose father she had killed could accomplish. It was not the need to see the suns of his own sky that made him push on. It was the nineteen thousand and four Oathbreakers who would be counted forgiven by the Aern if he could only get them across the threshold of the gate. If he could only get them home, it would be nineteen thousand fewer deaths on his conscience.

Break! His heartbeat rang in his ears, the only sound penetrating the high-pitched whine of near deafness. Vision faded, then returned, brief instants of unconsciousness or blindness. He could not know which. His nostrils filled with the pork-crackling smell of his own flesh burning. *Break!*

"I am Rivvek," he whispered through parched and cracking lips, his tongue a thing of leather, "son of Grivvek, and I sat on a throne I did not want, to rule a kingdom I did not need, to save a people I must save, and you will break."

His breath became steam. He felt his hair ignite.

Break!

"King Rivvek," Kyland shouted, his voice carrying the hint that he had been shouting for a long time. But it was hard to hear, hard to make out the words over the sounds of someone screaming as if he was being torn apart. With a sense of mild disinterest, Rivvek discerned that he was one screaming. It would, he imagined, have been nice to know what Kyland was trying to tell him, but he would have needed to stop screaming to do that . . . Rivvek could not spare the effort of will that would have been required to stop his own cries.

Instead, he let the purple flames do to him what they would, so long as they also removed this one final barrier between the elves who had followed him in the depths of the Never Dark and the home they had left behind.

BREAK!

A crack, like the sound of an axe biting the wood of an ancient and long-forgotten door rang out, and Rivvek felt the world of his birth open up before him. Two Port Gates surrendered and one failed, its explosion echoing along the open portal, sending shrapnel into the Never Dark where it bounced harmlessly off armor or was caught up short by the geo-magnetic shields his elemancers had at the ready.

Energy hit him, bringing with it a dark and insane intellect, which screeched at him, but could not touch his soul. To do so, it would have had to brave the Ghaiattric flame, and it fled before him, before his conflagration, connected, yet distant.

First the Gate. He saw the burst of interdimensional energy, caught and grabbed it as easily as he worked the flame. So similar, but one cool, the other hot. He gathered it to him as the gates collapsed, surrendering his hold on the flame, letting the soothing flow of the Port Gate's magic reach out to his army, to the Aern, to the precious cargo of bone metal they brought with them; and as the failed gate burned away and closed, another door opened within him.

He could have gone anywhere. As energies of the shattered gate coursed through him, he saw the whole of his home world, the icy wastes and what lay beneath them, the ruins of Port Ammond, the Dwarven mines, Bridgeland, and many places and people he had heard of but never seen.

He saw Kholster standing over the Proto-Aern, saw the Overwatches battling the thing Uled had become, saw the newly rooted Vael prince and his Root Wife who had saved Fort Sunder, and his mind expanded to encompass the whole of what he saw. He understood, for one shining moment, the whole of the Last World, why the Ghaiattri called it that, and where the dragons had gone.

At the apex, he balanced on the edge of a blade. He could not hold it; to do so would rip him apart. Even if he had been Vander or Kazan, it would have been too much. Perhaps Hasimak or Aldo, but they were not here. He would have to use the energy, deplete it . . . or let it go.

Narrowing his focus, he sought the perfect place to send those with him. He considered Uled, and when he did, for the briefest of instants in the tenuous connection between them, linked by the destruction of Uled's gate and the forcing open of Hasimak's, Rivvek saw the terrible design of Uled's contingencies.

There was hate there and madness, but Rivvek's mind touched Uled's at their most common point: Uled's dizzying lattice of calculated plans.

He saw the ten thousand contingencies the mad elf had set in place to ensure his return from beyond the grave. As the contact broke, Rivvek seized the remaining vestiges of his complete understanding to see which contingencies would be the natural course for the horrific thing to take.

He marked the obvious way in which Uled's pathways to life had been restricted, an unknown agent forcing him along a set route where his plans dwindled to a point of failure, trapped or destroyed, and then, as his clarity failed, he saw the flaw in the effort, one point they had overlooked or simply not discovered.

Click. Rivvek smiled, feeling the edges of himself fray as he placed a single trignom tile and knocked the metaphorical tile over, his final calculation using the Great Destiny Machine completed and executing.

CHAPTER 35
FOR THE BONES . . .

Glayne swung at the next rune, ignoring his creator's panicked attempts at dissuasion. Uled hurled artifice and invectives in equal measure, pulling out a few of the more desperate physical countermeasures. A swarm of wasps wrought of stone and magic vomited forth from a hole Uled opened in the air, buzzing and stinging at the bone-steel of Hunter's sturdy plates.

They will not make it through, Hunter intoned.

I was unconcerned, Glayne thought back, irked by the suddenness of the encounter and Long Fang's unsuitability to the fight. Wielding shards of the Life Forge, as efficient as they may have been, did not carry with it the satisfaction of whirling Long Fang, his dagger and chain, in constant revolutions of death, simultaneously increasing his sphere of awareness. He consoled himself with the view Hindsight, the bone-steel garrote which hung behind him, showed him, using it keep watch on Amber's progress protecting his flank.

It was at the edge of his thoughts to warn her she was about to be overwhelmed, when she told him herself.

I'm going over, Amber thought to him. *You have as much of a bulwark as I could give you . . .*

You did better than I would have. Four sight lines filled his field of vision. Water to his left and right, Amber behind him and the Port Gate before him. Overlaying all of them, a map of the Port Gate, the location of each rune, numbered. Those he'd destroyed were a dull gray, his current target golden, his next target blue, the remaining runes a shimmering silver.

Amber, finally overcome by the horde of dead, was carried over the side of the pier and into the water.

Keep going, Amber thought at him. *He can't throw too much against you or he risks knocking the Port Gate over with you.*

Glayne signaled his acknowledgement via a token in her mind. It would be close, but he thought he had time. She had erected a barrier of stilled dead between him and the unquiet ones. Doing so bought him time but made her vulnerable.

She drowned in the harbor's dark water, her warsuit unable to breathe for her beneath the waves because it, too, was beneath them. Fighting on, riding her warsuit rather than the lifeless meat within it, she struggled to regain her place on the pier, to purchase every moment she could for Glayne to succeed.

He signaled his approval again, intent on showing her, once they were finished, the earlier point at which he would have lost the pier. With ten runes left, Glayne heard a scream echoing in the middle distance from the pulsing gate before him. Its shimmering portal changed to a purple he knew too well.

Ghaiattri fire, Hunter cursed. Panic stained the warsuit's thoughts; it tried to make him withdraw. Glayne relived the moment when he'd lost his eyes, the fire, the laughter, the death of the offending demons. He wrapped it in a shroud of will and set it aside. He could feel the terror later, if he failed.

We stay on mission, he chided Hunter.

But— Hunter's argument vanished, caught and covered by the explosion of the Port Gate. Green and red mineral seams flared, the stone coming apart, huge chunks of it flying off in all directions. Several of the sharpest, heaviest pieces struck Glayne point-blank.

Pain announced injuries to his chest, his lungs, hands, and head, and he was flung backward through the wall of dead. Hunter's words changed to a babble of pain. Glayne had clenched the two shards of the Life Forge he'd been wielding tightly in his gauntlets, but that had not been enough to stop him from stabbing himself in the shoulder with one of them.

He jerked it free, but the wound hurt worse than any demon fire.

Glayne! Amber shouted in his head. *What in Kholster's name?! I'm coming! Stay put!*

Glayne laughed, the sound hollow, coming from his warsuit and not his own lips. He plunged his shards of the Life Forge hard into the wood of the pier. They sank deep and solid, so deep he felt certain the dead could not quickly remove them. Hands free, he grabbed the edges of the largest piece of Port Gate, trying to shift it off of him. It pinned him to the pier, as unmovable as the shards he'd buried in them. Either it was too heavy or—

"It is too late, Sixth." Uled drifted into view, hovering over him, a twisted sneer on the twitching, scaled face. "I have too many of my dead through the gate and they have claimed so many more recruits. You have lost."

"Unlikely," Glayne Hunter said. "**Even if Fort Sunder falls, the Aern will win in the end. I will see the victory with Hunter's eyes.**"

"No." Uled's grin overstripped the edges of nature, showing tendons and ligaments black with rot. Descending upon Glayne's prone form, the dead seized his (Hunter's) arms, unfolding them with combined effort, leaving him exposed, arms splayed before his creator.

Slowly, tenderly, savoring the moment, Uled drew a shard of the Life Forge from his robes. He stabbed the spike into Glayne's left knee, then his right. "You will not see the morrow, nor even the next hour."

Uled rested his weight on the unresponsive lower extremities, and Glayne felt another stab. Leaning close, but just out of arm's reach, Uled bared his bone metal teeth in a grin far too similar to a normal Aernese one for Glayne's comfort. More dead piled on the Aern and his warsuit until some hung suspended over the edge of their pier, rotted tatterdemalion legs dangling above the water.

"Now, where shall I lance you next, you traitorous automaton?" Uled took the shard firmly in both hands. "I think I know a good spot."

He raised his arms, then jerked, once, twice, three times, each jerk punctuated by the stabbing sound of a blade piercing flesh all the way to the hilt and being jerked free again. *Shunk! Shunk! Shunk!*

Uled gaped, hands dropping to his sides, as the tiny pointed end of a shard of the Life Forge sprouted from his forehead.

Amber? Glayne asked.

Uled's head ripped free of his misshapen shoulders, gripped by bone-steel gauntlets worked in a skeletal likeness.

Silence's skull-like helm peered down at Glayne as the warsuit rotated Uled's head toward itself and began to unceremoniously jerk the teeth from its jaws.

"Caz?" Glayne Hunter asked, still startled. "**Where? How?**"

Helm cocked to the left, like a wolf puzzling over new prey, Caz the Silent said five words in a hoarse whisper, as if they were all the explanation anyone would ever need:

"I come for the bones."

*

Not as simple as that, Uled's soul shrieked. It plunged through the air, drawn by the inexorable pull of Uled's nearest contingency. *Never as simple as that.*

*

He's heading your way, Vander thought.

Acknowledgement in the form of a gold token blinked once, but timing was important on this one, and Wylant did not want to foul it up. If Vax was right, there were very few dead-end pathways in Uled's web of contingencies. The idea of stopping him, putting him out of her husband's path for all time appealed to her.

. . . Clemency transmitted something, or rather started to send it, then stopped.

What? Wylant asked.

. . . A long pause stretched into minutes, and Wylant let it. **Nothing, ma'am.**

Clad in her son's warsuit, an array of Dienox's weapons at her disposal, the unseen arsenal ringing her, unseen by all, save her, unless she wanted it seen.

Is Vax—? Wylant started.

He is well, Clemency said quickly. **It is not that. I cannot comment further.**

But you'd like to? As they spoke, Wylant selected a spiked shield and a utilitarian sword that matched Vax's most common sword-form to within an ounce of weight, its blade a match in length and sharpness.

I would.

Both items shifted from translucent blue to the dark, well-used hue many of Dienox's implements possessed. Hefting the blade, getting the feel of the subtle differences, Wylant took a deep breath, held it, then forced it out.

Maybe Jun could make a similar replacement, Vax thought. *He is the Builder, isn't he?*

"It would be a mere shadow," Wylant murmured. Invisible to mortal eyes, the goddess of resolution paced along the ancient road, her bait mere paces ahead, unseeing, but not necessarily unaware of her presence.

Stooped and with a shuffling walk, the elf went before her. His manner and mode told anyone who saw him he was malformed . . . hunchbacked, one haffet of his skull loomed large and distended.

All lies.

Sargus scratched at his travel robes, stopping to pick an occasional herb growing by the side of the highway, where a few spots of green had survived the passage of the great exodus from Port Ammond.

Vander painted the trail of the approaching spirit for Wylant, complementing it with a precise countdown at the lower left corner of her eye.

Wylant wished she could have told Sargus what was about to happen, but the consensus among her Aern was that doing so might set off some inner and unknown treachery worked deep into Sargus, a countermeasure activated only in the event of Uled's death and in such case as Sargus became aware of the potential for his body to be possessed by his monstrous sire.

Screeching over the rise, a blot of terror tainted the cold air. Sargus seemed to notice something, then let loose an "urk" sound and fell, muscles taut, to the ground, muttering unintelligible noises through locked jaws. The tips of Sargus's fingers began to twitch.

"You were prepared for me when I was mortal," Uled shouted, "but now I am—"

Wylant smashed the incoming spirit in the side with her shield, its spike piercing center mass. Recoiling with a pained wail, Uled fled up and to the West, and Wylant followed.

Clemency did not slow her flight at all. If anything, the warsuit lent her strength to the endeavor, allowing turns and maneuvers Wylant would have been hard-pressed to manage solo.

Each time Uled tried to slip past her to reach Sargus, Wylant met him with shield or blade.

"The beast's bride," Uled growled. "Then you know." He twirled and dodged, no longer attempting reach Sargus. "And if you know, then you think . . ." He looked in the rough direction of Port Ammond. "Or do you?"

"Come and be ended, Uled," Wylant tried to goad him. "I am the goddess of resolution. Come and be resolved."

"Stole Nomi's hair, did you?" Uled croaked an awful laugh. "It was impressive when Nomi did it. First is inspiration, second mere duplication."

The mass of dark energy coalesced into a more lifelike representation of the elf, but wrought all in black. Wylant could almost see the ideas turning behind Uled's eyes. He was weighing her and considering.

"No . . ." Uled laughed. "No, I don't think you do know, but as a matter of precaution . . ."

He zoomed off, and Wylant let him go in accordance with the plan, landing at Sargus's side. On the stone of the White Road, blood trailed along the pale surface of the stone, picking out tiny irregularities and web-like cracks.

"He's headed your way, Kholster." Wylant knelt next to Sargus, coming free of Clemency as she did. Two fingers to his throat revealed his pounding heart.

"Why does a lone elf deserve a goddess's direct intervention?" Sargus whispered, through jaws that appeared to be coming back under his control by degrees.

"You helped me kill him once." Wylant continued her exam, checking his pupils, his breath—a skilled Aeromancer could deduce a lot from such intimate air. Scowling, she applied pressure to the bridge of his nose to stop the bleeding, while checking his teeth for signs of cracking behind the bloodied lip.

"Vander says Uled is not headed for Port Ammond," Clemency said.

"Where?" Sargus barked.

Wylant nodded for Clemency to answer.

"The Parliament of Ages," the warsuit said. **"And there is something else."**

*

"All of them?" Kholster whispered, quickly repeating the question to Vander in his mind. He stood still as a statue, at the center of what had once been the Lane of Review. The bay was clearly visible from this vantage point now, and he found it hard to reconcile the new view with a lifetime of memories.

Vander repeated the news, transmitted the image, and despite the alarming update about Uled's unexpected course change, Kholster grinned from ear to ear.

*

Rae'en Bloodmane drudged her way out from under the layers of ash, dirt, and dragon that covered her. She had not known a warsuit could lose consciousness, however briefly, but then no one else had ever smashed their way to the center of a dragon's brain, then barely avoided being melted by dragon fire.

Patting herself to make sure she was all there, Rae'en was astonished to find the detailing on Bloodmane's right side had run like candle wax.

We can fix that, right? she asked.

In time, but— Bloodmane froze, the awe in his thoughts hitting her moments ahead of the relayed message.

Ordamar by Ordam out of Lilly, the unfamiliar Aern's voice spoke in her mind, *current kholster of the Lost Command, previously under General Kyland's kholstering, reporting for duty, First of One Hundred. All Aern accounted for, though a few of us will need a good strip and dip, before—*

Did you say all Aern? Rae'en choked. *The whole of the Lost Command?*

And about twenty seven thousand elves who say they don't want to be called Oathbreakers anymore, kholster Rae'en, Ordamar thought. *I suppose that is appropriate given that we are now more aptly called the Found Command.*

The warsuits of the Lost Command confirm they have regained contact with their rightful occupants, Bloodmane reported. **All Aern accounted for.**

How? Rae'en had never heard Bloodmane sound giddy before.

Rivvek, Bloodmane said. An image filled the center of Rae'en's field of vision. Rivvek in armor she'd never seen and covered in Ghaiattric fire, which rolled back on him even as it poured from his gauntlets, engulfing the Port Gate from the Never Dark side, doing something Rae'en had only heard of the demons themselves managing. An inelven scream poured out of the elf, as raw and disturbing as the magic he wielded.

Rae'en thought of her father emerging from the farmhouse where they had first encountered Cadence Vindalius and her son, Caius, the way he had looked before Bloodmane had managed to redirect most of the heat to himself, the way he had looked when the Ghaiattri fire had flowed along the link between Kholster and Bloodmane at Oot when they had had to hold off the invading Ghaiattri, the image of him burning and in such pain he threw himself into the sea to attempt to quench it.

His pain had not sounded anything like this Oathbre—like this elf's, this elf who had her father's scars on his back.

This explains what shattered Uled's Port Gate and stemmed the tide of the dead flowing through it into Scarsguard, Kazan sent.

Did he . . . Rae'en stopped to compose herself. *Is he still alive?*

A new image replaced her center view, a beautiful Vael (quickly labeled as Kari, then amended to Queen Kari by golden script over her head) clad in white, the same color as her head petals, kneeling over the charred, naked form of the elven king. He lay on a carpet of new spring grass, bathed into mingled sunlight tinted amber by crystalline sap glass overhead. Several female warriors stood guard. Other unarmored Vael stood by, holding containers of strange-looking unguents.

Rae'en recognized the translucent white of Laughing Salve, but the others—a small clay pot of amber liquid, a dust the color of ground brown leaves, two jars of differing shades of green—were all unknown to her.

Under Kari's instruction, the assistants tended the king's charred skin while she held her hands, one over his heart, the other over his head, and did . . . something. Amber and green light poured from her hands, and her eyes glowed white, but what she was doing—well, it was magic—but beyond that . . .

As Rae'en watched through the eyes of an Aern named Vodayr, Kari gasped, jerking her hand away from Rivvek's head. He stared with unseeing eyes open wide and milky, the whites an angry red.

"Gromma have mercy," Kari whispered.

Another elf stepped into view, and Rae'en knew he must be General Kyland, Wylant's father, because to have seen his daughter's face and know it was to know his, too.

Blinking, streaming with a liquid only partly composed of tears, Rivvek's eyes narrowed, appearing to focus on his surroundings. He stopped at a point between Kari and Kyland and wheezed.

"No," he croaked, "not until I am finished."

"You have finished, my king," Kyland said. "Your work is done. We are back in the Last World and—"

"Uled." Rivvek choked on the word. "He is not yet stopped."

"The Aern—" Kyland began.

"Have missed a contingency," Rivvek said, "and there is not much time."

CHAPTER 36
BETWIXT

"You will not be able to make him what he was."

Yavi sat, the stumps of her legs dangling over the edge of the stone island floating between dimensions, naked and more than half buried with mineral-rich topsoil against her back and covering all but her extremities. She looked down toward her absent toes and smiled.

I hope they grow back, she thought. *They feel like they will. They will. I'm almost sure they will.*

Dolvek's spirit, the shadow which remained of it, paced nearby, responding to her unease.

"I will be fine," she told it.

Yavi soaked up the nutrients, not even caring how or where Hasimak had gotten it all. She felt his eyes on her and returned the gaze. He did not look like he was an ages-old master of magic. Ancient, yes (*an elf with wrinkles!*), but in his clean robes, the way he held himself, the only sense of power she felt from him was one of wisdom and knowledge.

His spirit did not appear to match, until she caught sight of a—*seam* was not the right word, but it was the only one she had—seam in it, as if what she could see of him was only the surface, the first page in the book of him. A sense of depth, of vastness, hung there at the edge of awareness, flitting away from comprehension as if he had caught her looking and closed the book of himself.

"How do you do that?" Yavi asked, her voice cheerier than she had expected.

"I suspect you will never know," Hasimak told her. "May I get you anything else?"

"You're certain Uled's third Port Gate was destroyed?" Yavi asked.

"Yes."

"Then I'm okay for now." Yavi traced a thick cord of spirit that ran under the dirt. She did not have to uncover her chest to know the thread ran into her heartwood; it felt . . . like the juxtaposition of a cool breeze under warm summer suns . . . the relief of a melancholy soul.

Hasimak turned to walk back to his chair.

"Unless . . ."

"Unless?" The wizened elf walked nearer, sitting beside her, folding his legs up easily, like a morning flower at night, as he settled on the stone with a grace that surprised Yavi.

"You said, I could not fix him . . ."

"Correct."

"Can you?"

"Even I cannot make him what he once was." Hasimak frowned as if the words were bitter.

"But you can make him better?"

"I could, possibly." Hasimak's eyes lit within, examining the spirit of Dolvek in a way that made the prince cower. "Yes, I could do much, but . . ." Hasimak shook his head slowly from side to side. "No. I decline. But you, it would be safer for you to sever the bond between you, that which helps him cling to the mortal realm. Let Torgrimm take him."

"He can't. Dolvek said he forsook Torgrimm's protection. Surely you will help him some. Just a little?" Yavi waggled her ears at Hasimak as best she could despite the dirt and her prone position. "Please?"

"What can be done," Hasimak said softly, "I shall help you learn to do."

"Fabtacular!" Yavi chirped, as if she had not been wounded near to death as the world tried its best to fall apart around her.

*

Father? Vax asked.

Hold, Kholster's calming voice said.

But Uled— Vax thought again.

Hold.

*

The dead tide had ceased, but the fight still raged. Cadence's eyes snapped open, her pupils shining. She tried to rise in one smooth motion, stumbled, and growled when Tyree caught her. Expecting an errant grope from the man, Cadence furrowed her brow when it did not come.

"You holding it together?" he asked.

Zaur and Sri'Zaur still surrounded them, refusing to fully engage, but there were fewer of them than before.

"I thought you went—" Her eyes flicked towed the city walls.

"Went." Tyree showed her the stains on his sleeves. "Showed the scaly people where to go. Came back."

"Why back?"

"I'm not staying in there fighting angry dead guys." The smile left his eyes, but not his lips. "Nothing in it for me. I can't kill the dead. But I have been working on the reptiles in charge. We're coming to an understanding. I can be very—"

"I need to get to Kazan." Cadence gestured toward the wall. She could not make him out from where she was, but she knew he was there without needing to lay eyes on him. "They will win without me, but if I guide them, this will be faster." *And the faster I'm done here, the sooner I can get back to Caius.*

"Is that all?" Smiling brightly enough to light a room, Tyree patted her on the shoulder. "Let me go talk to my newest scaly admirers. Oh, and revise my previous answer. I came back in case you had any errands for me."

Gone in a wink and back in a trice, Tyree carried Cadence out onto the cold purple myrr grass where Kuort awaited on a Zaur mount.

"Point me where you need to go." The black-scaled corpse held out a rotted paw.

Nearby two reptiles argued: the old Flamefang Brazz and a Zaur who argued with both tongue and tail.

You have to love Kreej, Tyree thought to her. *Whether he winds up officially in charge or not, he can certainly read the moment. You'll make it to Kazan.*

The leather saddle creaked beneath her, and Kuort's ghastly stench filled her nostrils as Cadence was lifted up into place.

"What do I hold onto?" she asked. In answer, his tail curved about her waist.

"I have you," he said, and then they were off at a gallop straight for the wall of Scarsguard.

Her stomach churned, filled, it seemed, with tadpoles doing flips, but she forced herself not to vomit through sheer willpower. At the wall, the mount did not slow, lunging up onto the wall, its belly low against the stone, legs spread wide as it got its grip.

Gravity pulled back on Cadence, her body trying to slide backward, falling off even as she clenched her knees to the beast's rough sides. Kuort's tail drew tighter, vertebrae pressing through the scales.

She vomited once, over her shoulder, spattering their mount's tail with bile and effluvia, then once more, her abdomen wracked with tremors as the beast bumped and thumped its way up the wall.

"It takes some getting used to," Kuort said.

*

Kaze, Amber thought at him, and a part of him responded appropriately. He did not have the attention span to devote to knowing what he'd said. It was all he could manage to respond to her and to the others needing his attention. Flitting from mind to mind, building the maps needed by the army, combining the intel provided by each group of Overwatches at Fort Sunder (Scarsguard?), ensuring kholster Rae'en had what she needed for her local map (cobbled together from the vantage points of various warsuits though it was), and directing . . .

Devoting the whole of himself to the timing between Rae'en and Alysaundra had been such a relief, such focus . . .

Mind leaping from Aern to Aern, warsuit to warsuit, Kazan guided the battle against the dead. They had not fallen when Uled had. Not here.

Why?

It did not matter.

Dead fell. Newly dead rose to join the fight against the living.

A core guard of warsuits protected the still-growing Root Tree near the fish pond in a part of Scarsguard that lay beyond the former boundaries of Fort Sunder. It was safe for the time being, but the dead appeared to be drawn to it.

Distracted, Kazan directed a warsuit to kill a nearby Zaur as it prepared to strike, only to shift back in a split second later to countermand the order and redirect the attack.

Kazan, Eyes of Vengeance thought at him, and a portion of him answered Eyes as well. Embarrassing not to have the time to pay a substantive portion of his attention to his warsuit, but the battle . . .

Stop it, stupid. Cadence filled the whole of his vision, multicolored sparks twinkling in her hair and in her eyes, a frown on her face. She cut through his thoughts with her own, forcing his attention to focus on her, shoving the whole of him back into his own head like water into a bucket.

A cold like nothing he had experienced since he had been an Eleven shot along his neck and down his spine. Heat in equal measure ran from his belly button to his chest and settled there.

He attempted to ignore it, ignore her, but she was everywhere he looked and as his mind narrowed down to a single point of reference, he felt a sharp hard slap across his face, a heel grind into his foot . . . and then he was falling out of his warsuit, knees scraping on the ground as he fell.

"What in Kholster's name?" he started, before yarping wetly between his outstretched hands as he caught himself. Bones and scale peeked out at him from the loose pellet and he yarped a second time.

He smelled Cadence . . . her scent, her humanness, felt her hand on his back, patting him like she was burping a baby human. He did not hear her, though. Around him M'jynn, Arbokk, and Joose stood by, along with the rest of Rae'en's Core Overwatches aside from Amber and Glayne.

Cadence's lips moved as did those of Joose. Arbokk's eyes narrowed. His mouth moved, too, but Kazan's ears were filled with the noise of thousands of little battles, of the temperamental wind storm rising up out near North Watch where kholster Rae'en was.

He yelped, when Cadence slapped him again, shaking her hand afterward as if the blow hurt her more than him. He did not hear his own yelp either.

You're spread too thin and giving all of your attention to distant Aern, Cadence thought. *If you keep doing it, you're going to manage to lose this city in the process.*

What are you talking about? Kazan thought at her.

You are ignoring the humans and elves, Cadence thought. He felt an unseen hand on the back of his head as he saw the battlefield in a more nuanced sense. Elves fought, but Aern did not reinforce them. Humans, Vael, Zaur, and Sri'Zaur all fought, but there was no communication between the allies and the Aern. Diving deeper into the minds of the army gave them great maps, but it closed all external lines of communication.

"Bird squirt," Kazan said.

"**Bird squirt indeed.**" Eyes of Vengeance loomed behind him, gauntlet on his shoulder. "**May I suggest the others . . . ?**"

Joose, Arbokk, M'jynn, Glayne, and Amber, he thought, *you all run the battle, and I'll advise until my head is sorted. Amber, you take the Prime slot and swap off whenever you*—Kazan laughed. *Just handle it. You know what to do.*

They did.

CHAPTER 37

OVERWATCH

Vander stood at Jun's forge, the fires cold, the Builder absent. He imagined the place in full swing, the heat of it, the forge-lit shine of many metals. He had gone there on a whim, his flesh feeling exposed in Eyes of Vengeance's absence. Pale light from dim Dwarven lanterns painted his bald pate in skull-colored tones. His eyes gathered shadows beneath them, the effect enhanced by the black sclera of all Aern.

My Beast's right eye. Uled's earlier words sent a shiver down him, out of place for one who experienced only the most extreme edges of winter's spectrum. Smiling gap-toothed, he peered through the first of several tiny bone-steel disks, their edges sharp, serrated, at Kazan and Cadence.

So there was a limit to his replacement's capabilities. Vander presumed the new Prime Overwatch would learn in time how to control his perceptions, to chase the edge of a perception cast too far afield. As soon as he mastered that one skill, Kazan would truly be his superior. Knowing the Army was in good hands, that his friend's daughter would have the sort of Overwatch a good First deserved, lightened his heart.

"New ideas." Vander's whispered words echoed in the open space of Jun's workshop. "We all need to keep improving, to keep growing."

It had been worth a few teeth to test out his own version of Aldo's myriad scrying objects. Deity opened avenues of creativity with regard to that subject that he had only nicked the skin on. Inspired by Glayne and his soul-bound weapons, combined with the recent encounter with Uled, Vander had created a handful of his own new "eyes." Making them fly had been as simple as wanting them to be able to do it when he made them . . . and if something like Uled tried to seize one of them? Well, they were sharp for a reason, now, weren't they?

Moving more of his Scrying Discs through the embattled city, he observed a family of humans huddling behind the flaps of a small tent. Children screamed as dead Zaur ripped through the canvas, the screams changing timbre as Villain, Jae'lyn's Armor, a warsuit with a spiked surface, his helm a faceless thing of crystalline spikes, charged through the other side. An Aeromancer whipped the canvas away with her magic as a Geomancer raised a thin wall of stone between the humans and the dead.

Acting in sequence, a Flamefang ignited the invading corpses with huge bursts of vomited fire, even as Villain dismembered the corpses with precise strokes from bone-steel hand axes, hurling the engulfed limbs into thick knots of the dead beyond his normal reach where Jae'lyn herself, Villain's rightful occupant, her hair raised in a blood-spiked strip like a shark's dorsal fin, fought side by side with dark-scaled Zaur, forcing the dead into tight clogs for easier kindling.

A particularly intact corpse leapt up and over its fellows. A glint of golden Life Forge shard in its paws, it struck toward Jae'lyn as she shoved three dead before her, using the length of her warpick, two handed, to increase her area of effect. Vander considered intervening, only to see a black-scaled Sri'Zaur bat the thing aside, stripping the shard from its grip and tossing it to an Aeromancer overhead, who flew off to distribute it to Coming Spring, a warsuit whose bone-steel plate was worked with multicolored enamel depicting roses and blooming plants.

Overwatches and Thunder Speakers shouted back and forth, relaying commands and updated information. Zaur and Sri'Zaur pounded out instruction with their thick tails or by having Zaurruk Keepers pound them out when they had time as they drove their mighty serpents inward, using their scaly armored bodies as living walls to control the streaming corpses they all fought.

"There is nothing the get of Uled cannot do if we work toward a single purpose," Vander whispered, and he wondered how his Maker would feel to see the great unity his wretched divisiveness and evil had finally wrought: the birth of a new and brighter kingdom . . . in time, perhaps, an empire . . . with seven races working toward a single purpose.

Kholster, Vander thought, *Scarsguard looks okay now that they are all working together again, better than ever, but the Vael—*

Hold, Kholster thought. *They have this.*

And at Scarsguard, they did indeed have it handled. Vander could still see a hundred easy ways to make things work out more optimally for his former Overwatches and the army they served, but that was no longer his duty. At the center of the city, Kholburran, the new Root Tree of Scarsguard, had his roots sunk deep and strong, surrounded by guards of all races, no longer in danger.

Sections of the city cleared of the dead in arcs of safety spreading from the gates, the Root Tree, and Fort Sunder. Clean up would take a long time, but victory had become inevitable, and even if it had not, the Bone Finders, Rae'en, and Tsan'Zaur were en route from North Watch and would be regrouping at Scarsguard in the next few days as well.

Kreej led the remaining Zaur and Sri'Zaur in through the gates of Scarsguard, too, with Tyree and Alberta riding at the rear.

The fight raged on at Castleguard, but the war in the Guild Cities had sputtered and died, a swell of hope taking over as Vax's followers worked to stop the fighting, with violence if necessary, but more often with a display of arms and an exchange of words. Rebuilding there would take years, but Vander imagined he would see a stronger, more vital trade center arise from the ashes and soot.

I wasn't talking about the Vael at Scarsguard, Vander thought. He turned his gaze to the Twin Trees, his grin fading to a thin, grim line.

I am aware, Kholster said. *Nevertheless . . . hold.*

*

Rivvek swam in a sea of pain and fire. He had warned them, but he did not think he had explained. A seed of Uled. One remained.

One what? he thought, as his sense of the present fell away, replaced by fever dreams of the past. *So hot. Lambent?*

Semi-solid at the core of the Never Dark where all other matter became energy, the dragon had burned in eternal incandescence, luminous bones thrilled with white-blue forks of lighting. The dragon's scales were translucent teardrops of azure lined in gold and silver. Each eye roared with the gold-red fury of a star. Lambent's presence assaulted the physical, empowering the nonphysical, the source of all light, the heart of the Never Dark.

Awe had been the only word Rivvek had to describe what he felt in the face of such a creature. It was insufficient. Just as the definition of agony did not contain, could not come close to encompassing, Rivvek's pain as the dragon's existence burned him.

This pain, the now-pain, was close. Did that mean he was still fighting Lambent, and had only dreamed of victory? Were they still searching for the final Aern, the last of the Lost Command?

I found him, Rivvek thought. *I brought them back. All of them. Didn't I?*

Was this some function of the Never Dark? The Bright at the center, the material, could only exist as a transient state. Could that be tricking his mind? Turning dreams and plans into false realities?

He could see them in his mind, clouds of majestic beings, no longer Ghaiattri, but adults, full-grown Ghaia, purged of their youthful evil along with their horned and clawed bodies, beings of radiance and alien benevolence. They swooped and sang sweet melodies to the luminous dragon who lay sleeping at the center of the Bright . . . not quite physical, but neither wholly ethereal.

What had Kyland told him?

Is the dragon the center of the light, or does it emanate from a flaw at its core? He had wondered, his thoughts blending with General Kyland's, in a way he felt must be similar to the way one Aern could communicate with an Overwatch.

Perhaps, Kyland had answered, *but it matters little. Our quarry is there.*

Gesturing with a translucent finger of azure chased with gold, General Kyland pointed through shining halcyon mountains, over an argentate sea and fields of shimmering vermillion, to a dim shadow in the shape of an Aern, with the dragon itself curled around it.

The dragon took the Aern hostage? Rivvek had asked. At the edge of things, Rivvek's physical pain ebbed, his skin glowing. Every part of him yearned to let go of the physical and fly in ebullient freedom. A beautiful harmony rose within, echoing what it discerned without.

No. General Kyland swatted the back of Rivvek's hand, sending visible sparks of pain across the skin. *And don't let yourself get too enthralled with that sensation, highness. If you let yourself turn into one of those Ghaia, you'll never leave the Bright.*

Is such a thing possible? He could think of worse things than being all wings and light.

You wield their fire. General Kyland thumped Rivvek's scars, which shone the color of Ghaiattri flame, trails of the purple light leading to pendulous knot that hung like a bead of elemantic flame at the sight of each wound Rivvek had received from the Ghaiattri all those years ago. *I've never seen an elf do that. When I stay lightside too much, I feel as if I am spreading out, being absorbed into the surrounding scatter.*

With that in mind, Kyland continued, *we'd best be about it.*

Wait. Rivvek tapped the Ghaiattri hide armor the general wore. It kept its solidity even in the Bright. He wanted to ask questions about that, too, but there was too much to know, to learn, to ask, and they had a mission. Maybe when or if they ever made it home, there would be time for all of those questions. *You said the Aern is not a hostage. Then why is he still here?*

He wants to stay, General Kyland had answered, *but Kholster made me promise to bring them all back if I could. I know in my heart I can drag Astert back no matter how he feels on the subject. I am an elf of my word, highness. Maybe your own oath allows more flexibility, but mine is clear. Once I get him home, he can turn right around and come back, if his kholster allows it, but . . .*

Rivvek recalled his own promise, and it had allowed for no such ambiguity either. Bring back the Lost Command or die. If he had only been required to sacrifice himself, Rivvek liked to think he would have considered it.

If Kholster had still been First, he might have decided otherwise, but kholster Rae'en had struck down an old elf who had offered no resistance, who was no threat. When faced with Grivvek, she could have spared him, but she had murdered Rivvek's father, when no oath required it. Rivvek understood the act, even as he detested it. It spoke to him of an Aern who would not hesitate to kill every last one of the elves who had followed him into the Never Dark over some fabricated technicality. The capacity was in her to be magnanimous as well, to show mercy, he had seen that, but the emotional algebra was too complex to count on clemency.

One Aern's (perhaps temporary) grief against the lives of his elves? Easy math.

Very well, Rivvek said. *How do we get him out of there?*

We kill the dragon. General Kyland had grinned, revealing bone-steel teeth, a gift from Kholster from a time when it was the greatest honor an Aern could bestow upon a favored elf, a true friend.

One dragon. One Aern.

Still, if there were another way . . .

"Rivvek." A soft voice echoed at the edge of his attention, and the dreamed memory's hold weakened as he recalled the battle with Lambent, the dragon's rage, hurt, and confusion.

Kyland dragging Astert away.

Rivvek standing alone against the dragon and burning. Burning the dragon, himself, everything around him. Beings of light-blue and green flew at him, only to fuel his Ghaiattric flame.

"I have become the Bright," the dragon had spoken at the last, beaten, dying. "Destroy me and the Never Dark may not recover. Would you doom an entire realm to save your outcasts?"

One world. One dragon. One Aern.

All of the calculations, the algebra of his ethics, said the price was too high. Grivvek would have turned back. Even Villok, first king of the united elemantic bloodline, might have turned back.

But I can win . . . Rivvek had thought. *I can save them and go home.*

Rivvek would have liked to imagine he'd have apologized to the dragon as he murdered it, but in truth, he'd said nothing. Killing was his answer; and if something inside of him broke, he told himself he could live without it.

*

"I gave my oath," Rivvek groaned.

Rae'en stared at the injured elven king through the eyes of Ordamar. He looked . . . well, he looked like he needed a strip and dip, if she were to be honest with herself. He rolled in the grass, struggling against Kari and her assistants, raving as they applied salves and ointments Rae'en doubted would work.

Why don't they put him out of his misery? she asked Bloodmane.

He is a hero and a king, Bloodmane said. **The elves have their ways. In the days before the Sundering, it is possible that one of the Artificers would have found a way to save him, much as they managed to adapt to the—**

What is Kyland doing? Rae'en asked.

Ordamar shifted his gaze to the ancient Eldrennai veteran. Stripping off his claw-tipped gloves, Kyland was muttering something under his breath in a high, lilting tongue neither Rae'en nor any of the other Aern or warsuits spoke.

It's one of the demon tongues, Ordamar explained. *He speaks it on occasion, but I never had the time to . . .*

Kyland continued stripping out of his armor, his scars drawing a note of admiration from Rae'en. His back, neck, and arms were a network of scars it would take a century to read. They told the story of a being who had nearly died a thousand times a thousand times, but refused to succumb to Torgrimm's call.

"Roll him over," Kyland ordered. Not looking to see whether he was being obeyed or not, Kyland began to strip out the lining of his armor.

Two ghastly-looking beetle-like objects fell out of the material. One, a dark matte black, was so small it was momentarily lost among the blades of grass until it scuttled to the top, perching as if making itself easy to find. The other, large as her thumb and a pale bone-steel white, fell flat on its back, serrated mandibles unmoving as it lay there.

Rae'en had never seen their like before, but Bloodmane had, filling in the gap in knowledge even as her Overwatches labeled them in blocky script.

A bone-knitter and a blood-sifter.

"No broken bones then," Kyland muttered. "Blood sick already, though. Never good."

He seized the small beetle, jabbed its pincers into his own thumb, then threw it at Rivvek's throat, its mandibles a glistening red. Where it struck the elf's charred flesh, the insectoid piece of artificery quickly burrowed beneath the surface, but Kyland was no longer watching. He found the flat wide item for which he sought, still clinging to his side, a tan-colored thing resembling nothing so much as a squashed centipede of leech-like dimensions.

"Wish I had more of these things." Prizing it free of a raw wound where the flesh had been torn away in clawed strips, Kyland dropped it on the king's chest.

Flesh-weaver, Glayne's text labeled it.

"Best I have to offer," Kyland growled. "Let me check with the troops." He lifted off the grassy floor with a burst of Aeromancy, faltered and lost altitude, then regained control and darted out of the room and to the troops.

A map of the area unfolded for Rae'en, showing the layout of the Twin Trees, the nearby location of the troops, both elf and Aern.

"Can he live through that?" Rae'en asked. "Even with those artifacts?"

It is unlikely, Bloodmane told her, **but King Rivvek, as you may have noticed, is quite tenacious.**

*

Malli lay in the healing loam, drifting in and out of sleep. At times she did not remember what she was there for and tried to sit up, to brush the soil from her chest, before the pain, deep and sharp, woke at her movement. She got visitors, of course; she'd broken her core saving the prince, had helped the others get him out of Tranduvallu, which made her quite popular, a genuine hero.

Today, whatever day it was, she opened her eyes expecting to see the priestess applying more blue flower or changing the moss, even uncovering her to let redirected sun fall on her bark. Her head petals had been shed, ready for winter or because of the blue flower, she did not know.

Goumi was not there. In her place stood a thing in the shape of a person. Hair and head petals mixed with vines to cover her scalp. Her face was beautiful, but not a mortal beauty. One arm was fur-covered, the other bedecked with tiny yellow-and white-flowers and festooned with fruit-bearing vines from which hung ripe and succulent fruit and rotted matter in equal measure.

The skins of many animals flowed together to make her dress, and though this version of her was uncommon, Malli recognized Gromma, the goddess of growth and decay.

"Goddess," Malli croaked, her air bladder still weak as much from the treatment as from the fungal infection that had brought her closer to Torgrimm's door than to Gromma's. "I—"

Silencing her with a sharp look from two lupine eyes and a dismissive flick of one claw-tipped and thorn-covered hand, Gromma snorted.

"The twins were precious to me." The goddess's voice hurt Malli's ears, more like the howling of wolves or groaning of storm-tossed trees than a real voice.

"Were?"

"One hale and hearty, thriving, the other sick with rot." Gromma looked away, her movement carrying with it the smell of roses and death, of honey and heartbreak.

"And now?" Why was the goddess speaking to her? She kept thinking it might be some new ailment, some poison of the sap or root, but Gromma felt too real to be a hallucination.

"He has ruined my sacred Root Trees." Gromma's rage shook the earth, her size expanding then contracting.

"Who?" Malli asked.

"Uled." The breath carrying his name became a foul burst of corpse scent and fresh animal spoor.

"How?"

"No!" Gromma howled. "Wrong question!"

"What . . ." Malli waited, trying to moisten her lips with a tongue that was too dry and to give Gromma time to interrupt her if she was hunting after the wrong spoor again. The goddess eyed her expectantly. " . . . do you want me to do?"

"Become my champion." Gromma doubled in size, talon-like fingers digging into the dirt and lifting Malli out whole, her core ablaze with pain at the movement. "You will be well again. Rot will always be a part of you, but under your command. Uled seeks to destroy my twin trees. The one who can destroy him lies dying, with a foolish elf using inadequate tools to try and save him."

"But what about Kholburran?" The sentiment as much as the words themselves surprised Malli. She loved her little Snapdragon, but she had not understood how much until she spoke his name in the clutches of the Goddess of Rot and Decay.

"Who?" Gromma's voice was the hiss of steam and the crack of thunder. "The new Root Tree? I have no truck with Kari's sproutlings. He is more Xalistan's than mine, like his sister."

"He asked me to be his Root Wife," Malli said. "I thought—"

Had Gromma referred to Kholburran as a Root Tree?

"What does the little prince need with two Root Wives?" Gromma chuckled. "Surely Arri is sufficient. Xalistan is well-pleased with the pairing as it stands."

"Arri?" Malli's sap ran cold. "Are you saying that Kholburran Took Root and that he and Arri—?"

"None of that concerns me!" Gromma's voice rang so loud it banished all other senses except for pain. "Ask the happy couple yourself if you live to visit the Aern's new ruling perch. Though, I will admit, his is a nimble mind, quickly finding the wrongs in the land, seeking to return balance to his dominion. As such, I bear him no ill will and, perhaps, a grudging respect. Only the passage of seasons will reveal whether that sentiment will grow or wither."

He did not even say good-bye. Anger, slow to kindle but steadily growing, swelled Malli's chest.

"What would you have me do?" Malli asked again, eyes narrowed.

Gromma smiled. With a loud crack, Goumi, the priestess who had looked after Malli since her arrival, screamed, dropping to the ground as the outstretched hand of the goddess came to rest upon her torso. Dark vapor escaped from knots and pores in the goddess's hand and forearm, flowing over the prone form of Goumi, silencing her forever.

Malli's own pain vanished, a shifting of wood escaping her torso and sharp bite of citrus in the air around her preceding the return of strength to her limbs. Her orchid-petal hair flowed lush with new life, falling languidly about her shoulders. Her breasts swelled, her belly and biceps tightening.

Gromma released her, and rather than drop backward to the ground, Malli turned a backflip, landing lithely on all fours. Strong and fast, this was more than she had possessed before. She felt like an irkanth, prowling the forest, felt she could kill with her bare hands.

Even her breath came more easily, but as she drew in deep bladderfuls of air, a scent assailed her nostrils, not noxious as such, but sweet and earthy, the odor of fungus and rot.

Malli's head swam at the sensation of a darkness inside her, spores, she imagined, of some fell seed, the darker gift of Gromma. Her eyes fell on Goumi, and the brackish sap flowing from beneath her. Malli blinked, her eyes the red of a blood oak's leaf with blackening swirls rotating lazily within.

"Does all your healing come at such a price?" Malli asked.

"You must heal the scarred elf, King Rivvek." Gromma's voice sounded sweet and terrible to Malli now, as if she heard if with her whole body, her whole self. "Let him do what must be done."

"And after?" Malli took deep breaths as the goddess studied her. The scent was there, still, but she thought she could get used to it. Her eyes did not leave Goumi's lifeless trunk, her bark cold and bare, until she felt a sudden absence, as if the world itself could breathe again.

Gromma was gone. In her place, the soil was damp and rich, worms churning the surface, grass already starting to grow. A skittering and cracking gave her a start, turning her back toward the fallen priestess. Goumi's bark came apart like rotten wood, beetles erupting from the sagging corpse and flying in a swarm, once, twice around the temple of healing and then out into the forest.

Grinding her dental ridges, after a quick search, Malli found her Heartbow and spare leathers, donned them, and set out for the Garden of the Twins. If Kari and some foreign elf were trying to heal an elven king, Malli doubted they would have taken him anywhere else.

CHAPTER 38

MISSED CONTINGENCY

Redirected sunslight warm on her bark, Yavi blinked herself awake. She rubbed hardened sap from the corners of her eyes. It felt like seasons had changed six or more times, but Hasimak had assured her only a scattered handful of days had passed in the Last World.

Yavi thought she had never heard anyone refer to her home by that name before, but it sounded right on her tongue and in her mind.

The Last World, she thought. *Which, then, was the First World?*

Invisible fingers brushed the soil from her breasts and torso as she sat up. Her bark, smooth and silky from the hours of ideal conditions, felt a rush of cool air at the touch of her unseen caretaker. Gentle hands helped her to her feet. *So nice to have two of them again.*

Even though they were hands of spirit, Yavi felt the trace of familiar knuckles and the backs of hands against her bark, no grasping, no restrictive touches. Dolvek did not always remember his own name, but he knew how to treat a Vael, how to comfort her, and make her feel safe.

"How are you feeling this morning, Dolvek?" Yavi squinted so she could see him better, catching the rippling detail as Dolvek, sensing her focus, brought himself into better clarity. Unless he concentrated, Dolvek appeared like a shadowy cloak, his facial features a watercolor pastiche of the elf he had once been, the rest of his body a gray impression of form.

Trick question? He looked like his old self, wrought in a pale palette, but clear and fully featured. His crystal breastplate sparkled, his cloak a cape with the emblem of three towers on it. All of it shifted as he moved, becoming his hybrid demi-cuirass in one step, formal robes in the second, and lounging apparel in the next.

"Is that a trick question," she corrected. "No, I know you're still dead, but you're more . . . together than usual."

You look fabtacular today, Dolvek said, his lips curved as if he thought using one of her favorite adjectives was especially clever.

A deflection. Yavi struggled not to frown. He had three phrases he used when he did not know what else to say.

Can I get you anything? His smile faltered, seeing through her careful expression.

So hard to fool a being who sees your spirit more easily than your body, she thought.

"Some water, maybe?" Yavi said, more out of pity and to give Dolvek something to do than out of any real thirst.

I love you, he said, his form going fuzzy around the edges as he used his magic, summoning a crystalline goblet out of thin air, filling it the same way. Geomancy or Aeromancy carried the goblet to her open hand.

His magic was coming back so much more easily than his personality. There was a core essence of him, still there, but if Hasimak was correct, though he would become more complex in time, the more she worked with him, he would never be his old self. Dolvek had sacrificed that, let Uled destroy a large chunk of what made him Dolvek to preserve Yavi's spirit.

"I love you, too," she said warmly.

Bathe now? he asked as she drank the ice-cold water.

"Would you like me to bathe you?" Yavi corrected. "Or would you like a shower?"

You look fabtacular today. He smiled hopefully, eyebrows knitting together earnestly.

"Please try to ask it properly, Dolvek."

He glanced to the side, as if momentarily unsure to whom she was speaking, then asked the question a different way. *Shall I bathe you? Wash clothes, too, maybe?*

"Yes, please," Yavi said, genuinely thrilled to hear him string things together rather than echoing what she had said back to her. Partway through the shower, in the midst of hydromantic streams of pyromanticly water warm, he kissed her, a hesitant peck on the cheek.

I love you, Yavi, he whispered, a hunger in his voice that spoke of desire and longing, a question and purpose all in one. His eyes blazed with intelligence and self.

She placed her hand on the back of his neck, pulling him to her and kissing him deeply.

"I love you, too, Dolvek," she whispered back, and then they spoke to each other in more primal ways for a languid span.

*

Once she was dressed, Yavi walked to the small house on the little floating island to which Hasimak fled when he needed to sleep or when he thought Yavi and Dolvek needed privacy. Changes in the house marked the apparent passage of time on the isle, if not in the world beyond the Betwixt. A dome of stone stood where Yavi had seen a pyramid, a ramshackle shed, a floating orb, even an open-air domicile with lazy hammocks for beds.

Yavi smirked, remembering how quickly the open-air house had been replaced once she'd started feeling better enough to enjoy a few amorous endeavors with Dolvek.

Despite Hasimak's many years, or perhaps because of them, the elf did not seem to be able to adapt to the lack of modesty typical of Vael . . . the girl-type-persons, at least. Yavi's nose crinkled at the thought of how fussy Kholburran could be about such things.

Boys were silly that way. So were most races except Aern and Vael. She could not think of Aern now without the image of Kholster and the child that could have been theirs rising up in her mind's eye. When it did, a warm glow filled her chest, and she knew the child would never be. She was surprised at how fine with that she was.

"Going to tease my old teacher?" Dolvek's voice was stronger, more himself, an actual spoken thing rather than a whispering against her mind. It usually was after they had spent a little time being intimate. Hasimak said it had to do with the way Vael were in touch with the spirit realm. He'd been too embarrassed to elaborate, but Yavi thought she understood. Her spirit knew Dolvek better than her mind ever could. When spirit touched spirit, hers guided his, reminding Dolvek what he was supposed to be like through the mere act of expecting it . . . shaping him into a resemblance, an elemental core, of what he had once been.

It was fun, too.

"I'm going to ask him to show us how to get back home," Yavi told him.

"We don't live here?" the shade asked.

"We're only visiting," she said. "Healing."

"Fort Ammond?" Dolvek asked.

"Port Ammond," she corrected. "And no, you're going to come live with me, in the Parliament of Ages."

"Live?" Dolvek laughed. "I suspect one of us will be, at best, abiding."

He grimaced, a little of the focus going out of him at the thought of his own nebulous state. Dead, but not departed.

"I have not been hunting." Hasimak met them at the door to his dome, his robes clean and freshly pressed. "There are, however, fish in the pond. It's a doorway for them."

The pond had been constructed once Yavi had been well enough to start asking questions about the origin of some of the meat Hasimak had been providing for her meals.

"A Port Gate?" she asked. "I thought—"

"No." Hasimak walked past to indicate the pond. "Nothing so dramatic. A simple slip way. It's much easier to construct something through which only non-sentient animals may pass. No chance of an incursion from the Never Dark . . . or the Faltering Light, I suppose I should call it now, either. A simple connection through the plane of elemental water is all that is needed. Similar in concept to your ever-filling bed of earth."

"You've been very kind," Yavi said.

"But you need to go home," Hasimak finished for her. He nodded, his long, white hair bobbing with the motion of his head. She saw him then, saw how ancient he truly was, and how alone he must be.

"We could stay a little longer, if . . ."

"No. No." Hasimak waved the words away. "You are more right than you know. The two of you are my final touch of meddling in the Last World for the foreseeable future. When you leave, I will rest, close my eyes to what was once my home, and check in on it again when all the people and places I remember are long gone."

He touched her cheek. Dolvek's eyes darkened in response, lightning and fire whirling behind his ghostly eyes.

Can I get you anything? he thought menacingly.

"I'm fine, Dolvek," Yavi whispered.

"My apologies," Hasimak said, backing away. "I meant only to say that I shall remember you fondly when you are gone and that I hope, despite the perils to which I return you, that you are well."

"So you'll send us back?" Yavi waggled her ears at him. "I'd thought we might have to use more nefarious tactics to convince you."

"Not today." A portal of smoke and light opened in the air by a wave from Hasimak, its edges rimmed with purple. "Step through together and it will take you both to where Yavi should be."

"Where I should be, but not Dolvek?"

"He should be in one of the Hells," Hasimak told her with a sigh. "One heroic act does not often atone for all in the eyes of the Bone Queen."

I love you, Dolvek thought, once more a billowing cloak with the impression of his face.

"I know," she whispered back to him. "I know."

Taking his hand, the Vael and her ghost stepped through the portal and into . . .

*

Kholster, Harvester said in the Aern deity's mind, **Torgrimm asks if you are sure that we should not—**

Him, too? Kholster stood in the shadow of a maned beast of a god. Xalistan had chosen a humanoid torso terminating at the waist with the body of a horse-sized wolf, bushy tail bedecked with the bones of past prey. He loomed over Kholster, clawed hands hanging in a loose but threatening position. An irkanth's head topped his neck, the eyes sharp and angry, its mane the ebony of a shadebeast's.

"No wings?" Kholster asked.

I think it was a mistake for Xalistan to go through all of the trouble to weave bones into his tail, Vander thought to Kholster, *then skip decorating his mane.*

"This fight of yours encroaches on the territory sacred to me." Xalistan growled the words, spittle flying from the edges of his mouth.

"I did not make Uled." Kholster unslung Reaper, letting the weapon rest in a casual position, parallel to the broken ground of Port Ammond, gripped firmly in both hands. He did not bother to brush away the spittle from his cheek.

"Do not quibble with me," Xalistan roared. "You will—"

"You love her, don't you?" Kholster asked.

"What?" Xalistan asked.

"Surely you mean, 'Who?'" Kholster snorted. "I will give you a secret about wives—or, to be honest, I don't know if you and Gromma have gone that far, or—"

"My relationship with Gromma is none of your concern!"

"Wife then." Kholster nodded. That felt right. "I have had many of them. I have loved them all, but even so, it took me centuries of being married to Wylant to wrap my head around the idea that she wanted me to only be married to her and her alone, not just her alone among elves."

"Because it is unnatural," Xalistan began.

"This is not the time for you to talk," Kholster shushed the other god. "Gromma does not need your help. She is handling things even now and—"

"Do you realize what I do to those who dare lecture me, Kholster?"

Kholster's jade irises expanded to fill half the area of his eyes. He smiled his famous smile, baring all eight canines.

"I deny you permission to fight with me at this time." Kholster turned his gaze back to the rolling waves below to watch a sea hawk cry and dive. "When the mortal realm is no longer in peril, we can fight, if you like, but important things are happening now, and I do not have time to humor petulant beings who have failed to preserve those placed in their care."

"I am the Lord of Hunter and Hunted!" Xalistan bellowed the words directly in Kholster's face, his black-blue lips a hair from the Aern's nose. "You will—"

"I am the arbiter, the birth and death of gods." Kholster's voice was gentle, was firm, and came from all directions. "My family, my people, and those I have freed from tyranny you and yours allowed to exist are seeing to the matter. We can discuss it later, if you wish, but either leave me be, ask what you can do to help, or— There aren't any Vael deities yet, are there? Or would you prefer your replacement to be a manitou?"

Xalistan vanished with a roar.

Well spoken, Harvester said. **Even so, Torgrimm wonders if you might—**

Hold, Kholster thought to him. *The mortals have this under control for the moment. I will fight my father soon enough.*

But, sir . . .

Hold.

*

Kholburran's mind spread across the plains again, Arri moving at the edge of his thoughts; at times easier to hear than others, but ever a part of him. She gave him news and he reacted in ways he hoped she felt and recognized, but with the battle about him winding down, regarding it with concern became increasingly difficult in the face of the unbalance the Sundering, the demon wars, and Uled's magicks had wrought into the Eldren Plains.

To the Northeast, the ground had been frozen and burned where a live dragon fought a dead one and the Aern had silenced the dead. Their need clear, he guided a herd of escaped cattle toward them. There would not yet be enough grass, and the winter would not have been kind to them, so Kholburran sent them to their deaths. Slaughter would remove the animals, remove a portion of the instability, and lessen the impact of such a large number of Aern needing to be stripped and dipped to restore them to their proper, fleshy selves distinct from their warsuits.

Eastern currents carried the aftermath of the fall of Port Ammond, environmental echoes of the battle between Hasimak's apprentices and Coal, to Kholburran, provoking from him a series of small tweaks to repair. He diverted the residual dimensional magic from the destroyed or out-of-alignment Port Gates, trapping and isolating little patches of frightening sorcery seeping up from ruined underground chambers that stank of experimentation and artifice gone awry.

Hard to believe I feared this, he thought.

" . . ." Arri was saying words at the base of him, her breath easier to register than her words. The feel of the human, Tyree, distracted him, too. His life force did not flow as it should, did not move through and around him, mixing with his surroundings. Unnatural.

Kholburran wanted to send the human away or fix the flow, but it twisted and turned beneath his gaze, impossible to hold or untangle.

Death distracted him, pulling his attention back out over the plain to where the warsuits walled in the herd, slaughtering them, draining the blood to restore their the makers. What meat they could eat or carry, they did, burying the remains of the cattle. The white muscle of their own former bodies they tore to shreds, grinding it between their teeth to get the desired consistency, spreading it far and wide, mixed with their own blood and saliva, planting the fertilizer shallow with cuts from their bone-steel.

Warsuits marked off areas with cattle bones in signs Kholburran did not understand but the Aern knew well.

Kholburran felt the soil respond, starting the long process of reclaiming the nutrients locked within the Aern meal. How had Uled designed such amazing beings? He could not ask, nor did he think the ancient evil would have answered if he had.

Warsuits too damaged or melted by dragon fire to be fully functional turned to the southwest, making for Fort Sunder and the forges within. Another contingent arrayed themselves around the new dragon as an honor guard. A portion of the meat from the herd made its way back to the dragon, too. They set her broken bones and bound them with woven grass while they tanned their own skin to bind them tightly into place. She would fly again, and soon, but she had torn her wing muscles and they would need time to heal.

Two of the Aern set off together after the slaughter of the cattle, the bloody mane of one's warsuit blowing in the chill wind as she ran to the southeast and Port Ammond's desolate grave.

*

She would need to strip the flesh from her left leg and work it on an anvil, possibly amputate the whole limb at the hip to get the dratted thing to grow back straight, but Rae'en did not feel as if she had the time to spare.

He's this way? she asked Bloodmane.

According to Bone Harvest, Bloodmane thought.

Having a directional arrow rather than a detailed map showing Kholster's destination grated on Rae'en's nerves. Yes, it seemed to indicate her father was at Port Ammond, roughly ninety jun from North Watch, but without even a rough estimate of distance, he could be across the bay somewhere in the wilds of Gromm. An unlikely place to find her father, but who knew where his deific duties might take him? To the suns and beyond, as far as she knew.

Thinking mind to mind with Alysaundra and her warsuit would

have made things simpler in some ways, too, but when Kazan had linked them, Rae'en had gotten traces of thoughts unrelated to the laying to rest of Coal's animated corpse, the way Ossuarians felt about direct connections between anyone, but an Aern and her warsuit among them, so she honored the preference despite its inefficiency.

"Why are we seeking the former First?" Alysaundra asked aloud as they ran side by side.

"I have to see what he's doing there," Rae'en told her. "Something is going to happen."

Kholster's intuition? Amber asked.

Daughter's, Rae'en thought back.

"You're the First," Alysaundra said as she ran.

The agreement was balm to Rae'en's concerns. She enjoyed working with Alysaundra. She was glad Zhan was going to recover, but deep down she wished there had been a change of Ossuarians, too.

He might step down if you asked, Bloodmane thought.

I would not ask it even if he would, Bloodmane. No one needs to change the rules for me. I can handle Zhan and anyone else with whom I need to cooperate. Or did you fail to notice our new empire?

I noticed. Bloodmane beamed amusement alongside the words.

CHAPTER 39

QUEEN OF THE VAEL

A snowflake fell within the realm of Hashan and Warrune's eternal spring. Malli marked its passage as she strode with determination toward the sacred inner sanctum. Her back itched and crawled, bracket fungus scarring her bark with shelves of pink-and-yellow-edged semicircular conchs. The quickening of their spores ebbed with her breath.

Root Guard gasped when she passed them, stepping through the delicately patterned exterior portal into the trunk of Hashan, wending up the stair. One of the guards on duty outside the sacred chamber raised a hand in greeting, then drew a sword, stepping to block her path.

"I am Gromma's," Malli said. "Step aside."

"The queen—" the young Vael began.

Malli breathed her dark, heavy breath, filling the air with black and brown spores. She felt the mass of them in the air, grouped and aimed them with her new magic, covering the young Vael in spores that found purchase in unblighted bark. The Root Guard fell, still clutching her sword, free hand grabbing at her throat as her air bladder stilled with fungal bloom, her bark splitting and bursting with dark-red mushroom caps.

Inside the grass-carpeted chamber, Kari and her Vael attendants worked what healing they could. An Aern and an elf stood, attention focused on the scarred king. Unseen by most of those assembled, the spirits of the Root Trees looked on, too. A sting of poison struck the spirit of Warrune, turning his tainted heart bitter, dark, and alien.

The blow struck the very instant Malli's foot hit the sacred grass and her bark felt the twinned light filtered by the crystallized sap overhead.

Gromma's timing, she wondered, *or Uled's?*

A dark and evil thing touched Warrune. The Root Tree howled in pain, a sound only heard by his brother, their Root Wife, and Malli herself.

Kari's shock locked an image of the queen in Malli's memory, beautiful beyond words, her flowing head petals askew in a way that increased her loveliness. In a race of beings designed and bred to be desirous, Kari's features held the perfect balance of angle and curve.

Lips parted in the beginning of a moue of distaste that would in a flutter of heartbeats become abject horror, Kari's gown of diaphanous white clung to her form, pulled tight by the torsion as she looked away from the king and up toward the amber sap above.

Why, Malli thought, *did her eyes turn upward when the wash of pain and fear came from below them, in the heart of Warrune?*

Peering into the monocolored eyes of her queen, Malli wanted to explain, but the elf king was dying despite the efforts of the queen and her assistants. An Aern stood nearby, looking out-of-place and unsure. If Warrune lived, Uled would gain a foothold in the very soul of the Parliament of Ages, tainting the forest, its people, and their magic.

For Warrune to die, Hashan and Kari had to die with him. The three were inextricably linked. For Uled to die, the elf king had to live.

The pure logistics of it made sense to the part of her who was a Root Guard, who would have died for Kholburran without question. She had no thought of what would happen to her after it was done.

"I'm sorry, my queen," Malli said. "Stand back, Aern, I can save him."

The Aern stood back, and she knelt over the king. He was hot, his blood poisoned, his whole system overtaxed by a magic she had never known, but she knew how to fix him.

"How?" the Aern asked.

"It's the simplest thing in the world," Malli said. Her fingers glistened with new thorn-like nails sprouted just for the occasion. She sank one hand into the king's chest, the other into the bark of the queen's exposed leg.

Kari screamed as healing magic, growth magic, flowed from Malli into Rivvek. Rivvek gasped as hurt, in the form of rot, left him in dribs and drabs, then in a torrent of relief as all the wounds he had endured over the last few hours (Days? Months? Years, perhaps?) abandoned him like parasites before a mystical cleansing.

*

Layers of skin sloughed off in sheets of lightening shades until Rivvek was pink and unmarred except for his oldest scars, those from his first encounter with the Ghaiattri and those on his back, but even they were softened, smoother. He would never be handsome again, but less monstrous? Yes, he sensed that he had become a newer thing.

He wiped what he took to be tears from his eyes, his hands coming away thick with detached masses of yellow and brown and red. His scalp itched; he touched it absently to scratch, stopping at the sensation of new hair, silky and soft, surging beneath his fingertips.

The many elemental foci the various Artificers had implanted in his back popped free in a light patter upon the grass. An odor hit him, of waste and dead, wet grass the day after the scythes had done their work.

An unrecognizable thing jerked and thrashed near him, parts of it flying free and spattering the grass. A second mass lay still beside it, and a Vael lay dead with a warpick in her skull that Vodayr jerked free again even as Rivvek watched.

"Don't look, Elf King," said a Vael, her hand on his chest. "I am almost finished and then you have your own work to do."

"Thank you," he said, before he truly understood what had happened.

"This is as much a curse as a gift," Malli said, the scent of her breath at once intoxicating and repellant. "You have your own work to do, and you will do it or my sacrifice and Kari's will have been for nothing."

His heart sank as he turned to face the pile of refuse and death that had been Queen Kari, her screams a low gurgle as she slumped and spread into a mass of beetles and effluvia around a core that no longer resembled a living being.

Rot and regrowth, Rivvek thought. *Magic from Gromma's realm?* His lips curled into a snarl. The Vael's beauty, the mixed scent of her, the fungal growth. *A Justicar of the goddess then.*

"Reverse this," Rivvek snapped, trying to pull away from Malli, forgetting in his shock his own comprehension of Uled's contingency and what he must do. "You may think I am important, but I am finished. My work is done. I am not worth her."

"You are needed more than any of us for the next candlemark." Malli tightened her grip. "Worth more than half the lives on the Last World, because only you can drive Uled where he must be driven."

Uled! Realization and remembrance threaded Rivvek's mind with a cord of duty, sewing thought to action.

Rivvek pushed her away again, and this time, she let him go, the white skin of his chest marred only by the five marks her thorn-tipped fingers had left behind.

Unbidden, Rivvek felt the flow of heated water splashing over and around him, washing away the debris of his renewal.

Kyland, no doubt.

General Kyland emerged from a nearby stairs. His eyes pinioned Malli, weapons at the ready even as he worked his elemancy. Would Kyland and the Aern present be enough to subdue the Justicar? Rivvek thought they might be, but she was as trapped as he was, by the need to defeat Uled, to drive him toward the dead end the Aern had engineered to trap him and stop him with finality.

"Very well." Rivvek closed his eyes, breathing deeply in way he had presumed he never would again. "But this is the last harm I will ever do. Do you understand?"

"It is not harm to cut away the rot or to cull that which can be saved." Malli's voice, resolute, matched the determination in her eyes.

"Tell yourself that lie." Rivvek stood. Kyland rushed to support him in case he fell.

"Would you mind assisting the Vael in the evacuation?" he asked the Aern, Vodayr. "Kyland," Rivvek continued, "have my army assist the evacuation, but leave behind one of each elemental path to assist me, should I require them."

"Is there no way to separate the trees?" Rivvek asked as his subjects and his ally left to carry out his instructions.

"No," Malli said. "Would that there were."

"Then may my name be forever remembered in the Litany of the Vael." Picking his armor from the grass, he donned the reflective dragon scale. Taking in the whole of what needed to be done, he ran it all through the calculus of his personal Great Destiny Machine. In his mind's eye, the trignom tiles were cracked and charred, but he knew how to place them. His blessing was to know that which must be done; his curse was to be willing to see it through.

He saw many possible endings, but the paths leading to the most palatable of outcomes for the Last World ensured one more kingdom of its people would hate him. If all went well, the Vael would recite his Litany through the future generations, remembering the names of those he had wronged, but not what he'd done, whom he'd saved, or how.

"Leave me," he commanded, feeling the magic of the trees reaching out to quell his power, knowing they lacked the experience to prevent his use of the Ghaiattric flame.

They left him, as instructed, Malli studying his face for signs of he knew not what. His own resolve? Finding that which she sought, she too departed.

Though the trees had been stunned or unable to attack Gromma's champion, they now struck out at Rivvek, the crystallized sap overhead shattering as limbs twisted to reach him, to crush or strangle him. It did not matter which. He wanted to apologize, to explain, but knew it would not matter. Roots sprang up from the grass, clods of black soil falling from them in clumps.

Let Torgrimm take me and be done with it? If he wanted, he could stand there and wait for the Root Trees to kill him. It was that or commit one more horrendous act to protect his people from Uled. *To stop the monster, one must occasionally become a monster.* Had he read that somewhere, or had Sargus said it to him?

Speeding up with each beat of his heart, the tendrils of wood moved with greater agility, writing in the air like the fingers of an elf whose arm had fallen asleep, wriggling them to spur the flow of the blood and the return of sensation. *Give them a few hundred more heartbeats and we might die together. A few hundred more and they might be able to stop me.*

He imagined his people, fallen, overrun with various creations at Uled's command. Bhaeshal broken before the mad elf. Fort Sunder fallen. Sargus slain at the hands of his own father.

No, that could not be allowed.

A monster . . .

"Very well," he whispered, "I know how to be a monster." Rivvek held out a gauntleted hand and let the Ghaiattric flame come forth.

*

Beneath the wreck her body had become, Kari's core continued to regenerate. As long as her Root Trees stood, she would continue. Torgrimm frowned inside his warsuit.

We could . . . Harvester did not complete the thought.

Torgrimm ached to help Kari, to reap her or to ease her pain, but those moments, even at the end of the physical body were points of experience, life experience.

It was such a shame, too. Given time, Kari could recover, would be whole and fresh and hale. She would not have that time. Torgrimm felt that truth like a law of the universe . . . and so . . . he watched.

*

Outside, in the many rooms and walkways of the Twin Trees, elf, Vael, and Aern worked together to evacuate a city that was not yet burning. They shunned the fungus-ridden champion of Gromma, obeying the Aern without question or hesitation. Sap beaded and ran from the walls, as if a great forest fire were approaching, but Vander doubted Rivvek had any intention of burning the city.

A few of Vander's watch discs overflew the Parliament of Ages, noting Root Trees beginning to sap in other portions of the forest as far away as Little Tree, along the Southwestern border where Vael territory ended and touched, 000 by 127, the nearest of the Gnomish Universities, and to the far west at Overlook, where the Root Tree named Fambran balanced in what looked like a precarious perch forever leaning toward the Cerrullic Ocean he had so loved.

Along the foothills of the Sri'Zauran Mountains to the northwest, scarcely separated from Zaliz, a hardy group of Vael who had founded Shade Tree with the Root Tree Gumblin, the Shadow Rider, lived together with their shadebeast mounts (*Animal allies*, Vander corrected himself) calmed their companions who howled in the day and snapped at the ground.

Birds chattered madly, flying about in confused patterns. Deer ran into trees, and animals of all sizes bolted for their dens and barrows to wait out a storm they sensed but could not see or smell. All of this commotion in the Parliament of Ages announced the calamitous touch of Uled's soul to the dark seed within Warrune.

Elves, Aern, and Vael fled, not looking back. Only one mortal being did. Malli stood at the edge of the city, needing to see what she had wrought.

Malli wept.

Hashan, Warrune, and Kari screamed.

Uled laughed.

Rivvek burned the latter four of them together from soul to seed to soil until there was nothing left of the glorious Twin Trees than dead wood, dry moss, and rich soil without a touch of magic inside to nourish a new Root Tree, leaving nothing for even Torgrimm to reap.

*

"Queen Kari would have . . ." Malli let the words die.

Kari would have been happy to die so that Uled could be defeated? Malli thought. *Perhaps, but I did not give you a choice, did I?*

Uled's defeat weighed against the life of two Root Trees and their queen, but Malli could not feel good about the math. She looked down at the wash of fungus upon her breast and frowned. Her eyes went hot, but they did not sap.

Come to my continent, Justicar. The voice of her goddess filled her thoughts, seeming to echo through her core. *There are great works that await you.*

Great works.

Malli took one last look at the dead space where her queen had died and tried to feel triumph at the victory that had been won. In its place, she felt only despair. Without any further interaction, she walked deeper into the Parliament of Ages. She had no need of maps. The pull of Gromma was a hook in her soul, and she felt she knew what it was like to be a fish on a hook.

It was worth it, she thought. *It has to have been worth it.*

*

At the center of a jun empty of spirits, Rivvek stood, his dragon scale glimmering, caught his breath, and walked down the hollow stairs toward to the spiritually barren ground. The stairs creaked and groaned, holding strong but sounding like human- or elf-made things fashioned decades before and ill-maintained.

Outside, the air smelled dry and dusty, grass brittle, crunching under his boots. He followed the trail of bone-steel-laden wagons to where his army stood with the homeless Vael and the Aern of the Lost Command.

The air felt alive there, the humidity welcome, the earth ready and . . . Rivvek stifled a laugh, letting tears come in its stead. Let them think they were other than tears of joy. They should have been. Yet even grief has a bottom to it and from that lowest point, any glimmer of hope, any unexpected bright spot, any gift, whether it was a reward from the gods or simple happenstance, held the power to amaze.

He had doubted, in the moment of his final murders, if he would ever laugh again. Resignation had become his cloak, to surrender to the needs of the mission over all else, his shield. He imagined the names they would call him, the Vael, no different than what his own people had said when he'd helped the Aern divide the elves into Aiannai and Eldrennai. He expected to hear them begin jeering him at once.

Instead, he heard a call to which he had long been deaf. A sorcerous pulse thrummed alongside the more familiar tone, music from another sphere tickling a range he had not known he possessed. Dimensional magic, but not Uled's malformed work: Hasimak's.

Rivvek turned to face it, recognizing the Vael with Wylant's features, though he did not believe they had exchanged more than a word or two since she'd joined his brother in the Grand Conjunction.

I just killed your mother. The words blazed through his mind so plainly he feared Yavi might read them in his eyes. He considered explaining. Reconsidered. Did not.

"You are Queen of the Vael, now." Rivvek did not bow, did not greet her in any of the formal fashions. "Uled infected Warrune, and I had to destroy all three to stop him from spreading."

He expected a snarl, an attack, but Yavi, bred for peace by the mad elf who created the Vael, only frowned and cocked her head as if listening to some voice that was hers alone to hear.

"Your brother died helping me track Uled to the Sisters, where he'd erected three new Port Gates. I destroyed one. Dolvek another." Her voice wavered, lips drawing tight before continuing. "I would have destroyed the third Port Gate, but even in death, his ghost rescued me and carried me Betwixt."

Dolvek had died a hero, then. Rivvek sighed. *That must have made him happy.*

"Do you have anything you wish to say to him," Yavi asked, "before I exile you?"

Exile? Rivvek's heart swelled with relief's ugly opposite. *I would have preferred your rage.*

"He is here?" Rivvek asked.

"Bound to me in death." Yavi gestured and the elemental plane of fire yawned, lighting Dolvek's ghost to the eyes of any experienced elemancer.

"Your servant?" Rivvek regretted the question even as it left his lips.

"The Vael have no slaves, King Rivvek." She ran the end of one sentence into the next, giving him no natural break into which he could interject. "Until I understand what happened, your name will be added to the Litany."

His army murmured, even the Aern ready to take his side. Had an Aern ever wanted to take the side of an elven king before? Rivvek silenced the murmurs with a raised palm.

"Tell him I love him." Rivvek spoke over her. "Tell him I am proud. Tell him our father would be proud."

Yavi began to speak, but he cut her off this time. "If it is of any aid to the relationship between our kingdoms, there was no other way for me to stop Uled. You have my oath on that."

"The word of an Oathbreaker?" she asked.

"There are none left among my people," Rivvek said. "Those the Aern would not accept as Aiannai and insisted upon killing, I ordered slain. Those the Aern did not want to kill, but could not accept as Aiannai, I led into the Never Dark to retrieve the Lost Command in exchange for their lives and a new name for our people."

"What do you hope they will name you?"

"Kholster's scars are on my back," Rivvek said, "placed there by Bloodmane while Kholster was still First. I am already Aiannai, so when I give you my Oath, understand that it means something."

Yavi spoke again, but Rivvek was not listening, did not need to hear. Even if the Vael welcomed him back to the Parliament of Ages, absolved him of his Litany, what he had been forced to do stole all pleasure he might have taken in visiting. He was trying to stack the trignoms in his mind, to determine what he needed to do to best support his people, but the tiles crumbled beneath his touch, the fragments impossible to find or reassemble.

No, Rivvek thought, *I need not come here again. I have to get out of here.*

In his right hand, as the Vael spoke, he felt the pull of Hasimak's dimensional magic. He shifted it from one hand to the other unseen. New as it was, Rivvek did not pause to experiment. Doing so would have made him feel like a murderer who stands over his victim trying on a new set of clothes.

"Does anyone have a candle?" he asked, not meaning to speak. "A dragon-tallow candle would be best."

"I'll have one in a moment, highness." Jolsit turned to shout for one, but Rivvek stopped him.

"Never mind," Rivvek told General Kyland as he opened a connection to the elemental plane of air and used it to take flight. All of the elements answered his call as they had in his youth.

"Old friends," Rivvek whispered to his elemental magicks more than to any mortal being, "you come too late, but I am glad of your company."

"Majesty?" General Kyland shifted uncomfortably. "Would you like an escort?"

"If someone wants to kill me, General—" Rivvek allowed the Ghaiattri fire to glow in his eyes. "—they are welcome to do so."

"Surely you mean they are welcome to try," Queen Yavi asked.

"I'm going to Fort Sunder to find Sargus," Rivvek told them, "and to call in a final debt. The First of One Hundred owes my people a new name."

*

He looked fa . . . Dolvek appeared to search for the word. . . . *like a person I knew.*

"He is your brother," Yavi whispered. "He said he loves you and he is proud of you."

Confusion crossed the specter's face, then: *Can I get you something?*

CHAPTER 40

FIRST, LAST, AND ALWAYS

Kholster waited in the tomb-like dark, quiet . . . expectant.

A deep chill had settled in at the back of his eyes, a registered alteration in temperature completely lacking in discomfort, despite the thin layer of frost. Some portion of him processed the stream of information available to him via Vander, but mostly he focused on the still figure of the prototype Aern.

Slaying the dead Zaur that Uled had left behind to tend the body had been a calculated decision, one he was glad he had made. In response, secret panels disguised as pockmarks had opened, releasing the things that now cared for the body's needs.

Spiderlike automatons no larger than Kholster's palm scurried about, changing the bags of fluid attached to the larger creature's arms. Fixtures of steel, brass, and crystal pierced its skin, delivering fluid to its veins. A dim symphony of clicks and the being's own bellows-like breaths were the only sounds.

Seeing the panels open had allowed Kholster to locate other such portals, one leading out of the hidden chamber to a tunnel that led to a jun outside the former borders of Port Ammond.

Escape route. Reaper, Kholster's current warpick, rested silent on his back. He reached over his shoulder and held its haft. With his right hand, he turned a small, sharp piece of metal over and over again, careful not to prick himself. He practiced holding his breath, releasing the metal, watching it hang in the air.

Still holding his breath, he walked the circumference of the room, plucked the metal from the air and moved it, released it, moved it again.

This will work, he thought, allowing time and his breath to resume.

Rae'en headed toward him, her symbol a bright spot on his mental map. Uled's spiritual trek traced a line of gray, Vander indicating as best he could exactly where it was without getting too close.

Kholster wanted to go home. For years he'd thought of Fort Sunder as his true home, the Eldren Plain as his homeland, but standing in the cave-like blackness, surrounded by stone, he knew Helg had made South Number Nine his home. Raising Rae'en there had secured its spot in his heart in a way he did not think could be easily undone.

Where would Wylant want to live? She could, of course, pick anywhere she chose, but if she dwelt amongst the gods, Kholster did not think he could join her. Would Rae'en object to him sleeping in his old berth? Once this was all over again, he thought he would enjoy the mundane routine of sleeping and eating again. Would Vander?

Uled's coming, Vander thought. *He appears to be bypassing Sargus and heading straight for you. Are you sure you don't want me or Wylant to—*

I track your concern, old friend. Kholster took a step forward, resting his right hand against the Proto-Aern'd sternum. *But no. I will kholster this.*

Have I ever told you how weird it sounds when you use your name as a verb and I don't see it coming? Amusement painted Vander's thoughts like sunlight on a grave.

If you require assistance— Harvester began.

I will ask if I require it, but thank you, Kholster thought at the warsuit. *How is Torgrimm?*

I can connect you, if—

I would prefer that you refrain from doing so, Kholster thought.

Sir, if you would like to resume your post, I would eliminate Torgrimm . . .

That won't be necessary, Harvester.

Incoming, Vander sent.

Give me a moment to collect my thoughts, Kholster broadcast to the others. Instant compliance left him alone with his musings. Anger did not fill him. Not even anticipation, so much as profound understanding of the immensity of the next few candlemarks. He took a breath and held it, stopping the flow of time, the little automatons nearby frozen in place.

Loves.

Hopes.

Hatreds.

So much time . . .

So much life . . .

. . . and death . . .

. . . had led to this point.

Kholster tallied the exact number of the dead, weighing it in his mind as he knew few other beings could comprehend. . . . The sheer tonnage of those divided forcefully into meat and spirit, not just those lost in the current exchange, but over a span of years measured in millennia, far more of them than Kholster had seen with mortal eyes.

Vander thought he knew the price, but as Kholster saw it, there were only three beings in existence who could understand the ultimate cost of the final Aernese liberation.

He had wanted all of this to be decided by Rae'en, and he'd managed that. Rae'en had taken to her role as First with impressive skill. He had hoped she could deal with Uled as well, to strike the final blow, but as the saying went: Sometimes the kill is yours. Swing your pick or go home hungry.

There could be no later.

Uled had wrought a contingency plan into every single race he'd created. Each stay of execution he granted himself had cost the lives of others, often forever altering whole civilizations in the process. Who knew what the Zaur might have been without Uled's experiments, what sort of people they might have become? What would the world look like with no Aern or Vael in it? Kholster eyed the gray trail on his mind map. Once he allowed time to resume, Uled's arrival would be imminent.

Standing there, Kholster let himself relive the entirety of his mortal life. Human and elven memory were malleable, but Kholster's was not.

It is most distressing when you do this, sir, Harvester said.

"Sorry," Kholster said aloud.

Time resumed.

" . . . last one of you will be mine!" the Proto-Aern's mouth spewed, its eyes snapping open. "You will be mine once more and the planet, no, this dimension shall be mine!"

Kholster held his breath again and pushed the needle into place. It was so sharp he doubted his father would even feel the prick.

If he squinted, he could see in the rough structure of the Proto-Aern's facial features a shadow of Uled's own face. Slack and unconscious, it had been serene, but madness flowed into its expression, a frenzied energy to its stare as Uled's soul found purchase and took up residence. Shifting his vision to the spiritual realm, he examined the whorls, curves, and barbs his mad creator had wrought in his own soul, to match the receptors he'd installed in the eleven-foot-long mass of muscle, bone, and sinew.

Was this what had frightened Yavi when she'd seen the unawakened body? On some level had she perceived the sort of soul that would one day inhabit it, or had her horror truly been at the spiritual residue that had taken root there and tried to grow, the sad, mad thing Kholster had reaped?

Preparing himself, he conjured forth his own Litany of hate against Uled—the death of his children, his wives, the soul slavery, the oaths, the many wrongs the Eldrennai had committed—and one by one, he let them go.

"Hello, Father."

"I am your master, beast." Uled, clad in his new massive body jerked free of the tubes pumping fluids into his veins. Kholster took a casual step clear but did not run or unsling Reaper.

Uled stood much taller than Kholster. His snarling mouth held four pairs of canines instead of Kholster's two. Where Kholster was lithely muscled, Uled's new body was thick with corded muscle. "Not your father!"

"No." Kholster smiled sadly. "You are, have always been, will always be, my father. It is not a job you can quit or a title that can be altered. I have but one physical parent, and you are he."

"All obey!" Uled narrowed his gaze, amber pupils eyes ablaze with light, jade irises pulsing.

"They cannot hear you, Father." Kholster tapped the side of his head and then a point at the center of Uled's chest, where the tiny sliver of metal peeked out amid the flesh.

"I am now First," Uled growled. "Now you obey me and the first thing I will do is—"

"You are afraid of death." Kholster took a step toward the hulking Aern, unslinging Reaper, letting the warpick hang at his side. "I understand that. So many mortals fight to avoid dying, wanting to cling to life, to avoid the Horned Queen's judgment, or merely to spend more time with the ones they love, but you crave physical existence like a crystal twist hungers for god rock. You—"

"Kneel!" Uled screeched, spittle flying from his lips.

I don't think he understands what you did, Vander thought.

He will.

"—have developed plans within plans. Contingency after contingency, and all to extend your life and power at the expense of others."

"You—" Uled pawed at the metal in his chest, pulling it free with fingers that were significantly thicker than those to which he had been accustomed. "—think this is enough to stop me, Beast?"

"No, Father." Kholster studied the eyes of Uled . . . Circle of amber, ringed by jade, in a pool of black. Did Uled see the world the way he did with those eyes, so much like a proper Aern's, or was any difference beneath his notice, the way a "beast" saw the world?

Is he mortal? Kholster thought at Vander.

Secret, Vander growled.

Vax? Kholster thought. *Ask Kilke.*

My uncle says he is only as mortal as any Aern, Vax responded instantly. *He can only die if Torgrimm allows it.*

Harvester, Kholster thought, *are we still in agreement?*

Torgrimm objects, Harvester thought back, **but he is the Sower and I am the Harvester, if one is inclined to be technical in such a matter, sir. I assure you, I am so inclined.**

As Uled pounced, claws sprouted from beneath his nails, one set of fangs dropping lower, longer. Kholster let his skin become bone-steel, his eyes obsidian. Teeth and claws raked skin of the same material, raising sparks without marring the surface.

"I do not give you permission to fight me." Kholster swept the Proto-Aern's legs, following with a two-handed blow from the butt of his warpick, then swung again as he rolled to sit astride the Proto-Aern.

"I command you to—" Uled began.

Unwilling to let Uled finish speaking, Kholster struck Uled in the temple, skull fragmenting beneath his blow. A second strike hit Uled in the throat, a third below the side of his jaw. Uled hurled Kholster into the nearby stone.

"Stop!" Uled shouted. "I order you to—"

Kholster charged him again, and this time Uled was more prepared, striking a martial pose, ready, it seemed, for unarmed combat. But as they clashed, Kholster recognized the counters and attacks Uled used. They were the same set all Aern had come with, but they had not been updated since before the Sundering . . . and Aern practiced every day. Uled rained blows upon Kholster, with massive fists, hitting him whenever he could.

Any compulsion to—? Vander thought.

No.

Seeing that he was outmatched despite the advantage of size, Uled bolted. He touched the table upon which he had lain, jabbing the sliver of the Life Forge at Kholster's face when he drew near. It slid in deep at the corner of Kholster's eye. Then Kholster had his hands on Uled's, pulling, forcing it back and down, trapping it between the stone slab and his own weight.

"Sir!" Harvester's voice came from inside the room.

Uled's eyes found the warsuit, and he began to speak in a language Kholster had never heard.

What is that? Kholster demanded.

A secret, Vander thought. *I have no . . .*

Uncle Kilke says you shouldn't let him finish, Vax thought. *He is relatively certain it will not work, but . . .*

Kholster head-butted his father five times in quick succession. The Life Forge needle plunked as it struck the stone floor to Kholster's right. Bone-steel hands were on Uled's jaws, one at the top, the other gripping the lower. Kholster pried them apart. Muscle tore. Bone popped. Uled's lower jaw came free and was discarded. There was no blood. Apparently the Proto-Aern did not bleed now that it was occupied.

Uled tapped out something in Zaurtol, but Kholster did not bother to translate it. The words of the mad elf mattered less now than they had in the whole of recorded history, because Kholster knew what must be done and had resolved to do it.

"I wanted to explain it to you, Father." Kholster rolled the larger creature away from the slab and down onto the floor trapping the needle beneath the two of them. Straddling Uled, Kholster grabbed for Reaper, bringing the handle down on his father's throat, holding the implement there with both hands as Uled kicked and tried to roll from under him.

Tongue lolling from his ruined mouth, Uled gurgled and hissed.

"That would not have worked, Father." Kholster leaned in close, took Uled's tongue between his teeth, and ripped it free, spitting it out on the cold stone. Now Uled bled, an ichor of orange and black pouring from the wounds. "You may take it as a sign of respect, however, that I decline to allow you to test that theory."

"Torgrimm," Kholster snapped. "This is an Aern, subject to the rules governing the souls of the Aern, yes?"

"Kholster." Torgrimm stepped near, pulling back despite himself when Uled clawed for him, "please, this seems . . . too much."

Harvester, Kholster thought, *if he won't agree, reap him.*

You do not need his acquiescence, sir, Harvester thought, only mine . . . and you have it already. Upon death, the soul of Uled will be treated as all Aern. He may be added back to the Aern to strengthen them or he may remain in his body, to—

His soul, Kholster said, *joins the Aern. There is no option for him. Agreed?*

Of course, sir.

His soul has overwhelmed beings before, Kholster said. *Will he . . . ?*

Be a threat? Harvest asked. He will be but one soul among a flow of millions, all working together to strengthen the Aern. He may still manage some small harm at the personal level, but he will never threaten the larger world again.

"So be it." Kholster kept pressing until Harvester's dark metal cracked Uled's neck.

"I did not want to hurt you." Kholster released his grip on Reaper, gripped either side of Uled's head, and pulled.

An hour later, the bones of the Proto-Aern had been stripped clean.

He's still in there, Harvester said. He refuses to come out.

"I will handle that as well," Kholster whispered. Allowing himself a single sigh, Kholster rose and set his hands to work.

CHAPTER 41

DEBRIEFINGS

By the time Rae'en and Alysaundra arrived at Port Ammond, the suns hung low in the sky, lighting the bay with a purple-orange glow. Alysaundra left her at the outskirts, job done, and went running off to do the Ossuary's business. Rae'en watched her go, Bone Harvest's long strides carrying them quickly out of view.

Would you be offended, Rae'en began to ask, but Bloodmane was already releasing her. Outside of him, her leg hurt and she limped, but she wanted time alone with her father.

Go, Bloodmane said. **I will come if you call.**

"Thank you."

Rae'en found Kholster working shirtless at an open-air smithy. Blood, oil, fire, and metal all melded together with the briny tang of the ocean to form a scent she could taste as strongly as she could smell.

When did he have time to build a forge? Joose asked.

Benefits of being a god, Amber cut in. *A sexy god.*

I am with Amber on the former and will pretend I did not hear the latter. Rae'en half-expected Glayne to hush them or ask them to move to a level of discussion that excluded her, but they babbled on uninterrupted.

Kholster worked with a metal darker than normal bone-steel, more gray than white. It had a similar ring when he struck it with his hammer, but even the way the metal looked when heated was off, turning shades of blue where red hot and white hot were expected.

Magic, her Overwatches chimed.

"Dad?" Rae'en asked.

His smile lit up the world. Kholster faced her, lifting the smoked lenses Rae'en had bought him in Midian. They caught the light, resting in his newly trimmed hair, so short she could see his scalp. Clean-shaven, eyes sparkling. His jeans, spotted with burn marks and smudges of oil, made her laugh.

"A moment." He crossed to a rain barrel and washed the grime from himself, toweling off with a ratty-looking cotton cloth that hung on a bone-steel peg mounted to the barrel.

When they embraced, she recognized the scent of him. Solid and real. Hard to believe he was a god. Hard to believe she could decide to visit her father . . . who had died . . . and find him working at a forge as if it were any other day . . . as if they had not just defeated Uled's plans, defeated his army, defeated the Eldrennai, forged an alliance with the Zaur, Sri'Zaur, and Aiannai, and regained the Lost Command.

"How is the First of One Hundred today?" Kholster asked.

"We're still finding corpses that don't seem to know how to stay down." Rae'en looked around for a place to sit, since her leg pained her and she wanted to conceal her limp. She spotted a rough-hewn wooden stool and perched on it. "I have to send a group over the mountains into the human territories to help wipe them out. We want to repair the damage to the human settlements, restore trampled fields, gather more livestock. The Zaur think there may still be stragglers in their mountain tunnels, too."

"Sounds like a few long-term projects, then." He went back to his work, pausing to heat the metal more, to hammer it into the curved shape of a . . .

"Vambrace?" Rae'en asked.

Kholster nodded to an armor stand. Pieces of breast plate forged of an unusual blue-black bone-steel hung all but finished, waiting only for her father to begin any desired pattern work.

"A new warsuit?" Rae'en pursed her lips. "But the Life Forge . . ."

"That has a needle of the Life Forge in it." Kholster slapped the anvil.

"That works?"

"It does if you're a god." Vander's voice sounded in the air before he appeared, then Rae'en was up and hugging him, rubbing his bald pate with her palm as they both laughed.

"You look much better than you did the last time I saw you." Rae'en returned to her stool, feeling self-conscious about the grin she could not banish.

"Where's Bloodmane?" Kholster asked, as if he could not have Vander tell him.

"He'll be along," Rae'en said. "I wanted a little time for just us first."

"I could always go . . ." Vander teased.

"You don't count." Rae'en rolled her eyes.

Kholster had done a good job hiding his concern at her limp, but she caught him looking.

"It got partially melted," Rae'en said. "Dragon fire."

"I could take a look at it." Kholster tapped the anvil. "Straighten it back out for you if you don't want to lop it off and save the bone-steel."

"Well." Rae'en eyed the stack of unfamiliar bone-steel. Ingots of it made a tidy pile a few feet away from the anvil. "You look a little busy."

"Never too busy for the First of One Hundred," Kholster said.

"I wish you wouldn't call me that." Rae'en limped to the anvil, wincing as Kholster cut through her jeans, stripping away the denim, flesh, and muscle with practiced cuts, exposing a few handspans of bone.

"Never too busy for my daughter, then," Kholster amended.

"You ought to amputate and grow it back." Vander frowned, leaning in over the wound. "Too twisted, and it looks like the femur needs work as well."

You can stay in armor until they grow back, Bloodmane thought. **I think your right leg has a structural twist as well and—**

"*Fine*," she spoke and thought together.

*

Later she sat legless, clad in Bloodmane, his helm sitting next to her on a small table Vander had summoned. They ate meat from an animal she did not recognize, and she suspected her father of giving the thing two livers to help speed her regeneration.

"Half a year," Vander was saying.

"That long?" Kholster folding his arms in front of his chest. "It never took me that long for just a leg."

"You were First of All of us," Vander said, smiling. "It is not a fair comparison. You always healed faster than the rest of us, then acted confused that it took us longer."

"Did I?" Kholster asked in mock dismay.

"Shall I cite a few memorable examples?" Bloodmane asked.

"No. No." Kholster gestured with a haunch of the meat. "I believe it. I—" His gaze shifted to that inward look he got when a conversation started up inside his mind. Subtle, still aware of the outside world, but

Rae'en never missed it, awkwardly aware of any time she felt he was not wholly there.

"Vax—" Kholster looked to her. "—would like to know if it would be an intrusion if he were to join us."

Rae'en swallowed hard, tried to cover her emotion by covering her mouth, realizing belatedly that it only made her discomfort stand out more.

"You can say 'no.'"

"No." Rae'en coughed, clearing her throat. "No, it's fine. I want to meet him. Really."

The most beautiful being she had ever beheld stepped into the edge of the forgelight. Strawberry-blond hair fell past his shoulders, shaved close to the scalp on the right side of his face. His eyes, a blue as startling for their shade as for their unique nature, found Rae'en's and met them with mirth and welcome. He smiled, revealing the doubled canines she expected, but blunter than most, less pronounced. His ears were in the right spot, high up, like a wolf's, but they too were less pointed and a little shorter than normal. He wore a pair of dark-gray denim jeans with bone metal buttons and leather lacing up the sides and no shoes, his bare feet silent on the ground.

"Hello, Rae'en, First of One Hundred." Vax's voice was soft, but it cut the air in way that needed no increase in volume, as if the world around him muted itself so as not to be heard over him. "I am Vax by Kholster out of Wylant, Deity of Conflict."

"And you are my brother . . ." Not sure of what to do, Rae'en hugged him, and knew instantly that had been the correct course of action.

They chatted for hours, Rae'en not realizing how long until the first of the suns was coming up and Vax was telling her about killing Dienox and his approach to his deific role. Wylant had come in at some point, and the sight of her next to Kholster turned Rae'en's stomach, bringing thoughts of Helg to mind, stirring up dreams of might-have-beens, were her mother still alive and still Kholster's wife.

Kholster and Wylant discreetly vanished during part of Vax's tale, returning later looking a bit happier than they had before. Her father turned his attention back to the forging of his armor, and Wylant set about grilling herself a healthy portion of the remaining meat.

Being the only mortal among them, Rae'en slept after a bit, letting the sound of the waves, and the chatter of the gods—Vander, Kholster, Wylant, and Vax—lull her as much as the ringing of Kholster's hammer on the bone-steel.

*

Tyree and Cadence are leaving, Kazan thought to Rae'en. She woke with a start, expecting everyone to be off godding or whatever the appropriate verb (*deificating*, maybe?) was for doing whatever it was the gods did. And they *were* all gone except for Kholster and, of course, Bloodmane.

Where are they going? Rae'en asked Kazan.

Back to the Guild Cities to look for her son.

Did you offer them an escort or . . . ?

We offered to let them ride with the contingent Tsan wants to send to Castle-guard, to make sure they understand the new arrangements with regard to traffic to and from Scarsguard and our allies, but they opted to go it alone.

Tell them I wish them luck.

I will. Kazan hesitated.

Yarp it up, whatever it is, Rae'en prodded.

Captain Tyree has requested that "Sugar Bosom" be given his regrets. He says he must delay their marriage until Cadence is reunited with her son . . .

He probably thought he was being irascible, Rae'en thought.

I suppose, Kazan thought, *but I have no idea who Sugar Bosom is—*

Rae'en laughed long and hard at that one, rubbing the sleep out of her eyes. Without being called, Bloodmane walked over to engulf her. Vander and Kholster had both been knowledgeable about exactly how much stump one required to feel comfortable in a warsuit, and both were proven correct when she was inside Bloodmane and walking about as if she still had two whole legs.

Her father stood exactly where she had left him. Hammer on the ground now, Kholster moved to sit on the edge of a stool and began fiddling with the small work of fitting a gauntlet together. On the armor stand, a near-complete suit of plate armor hung, and the pile of ingots that lay next to the anvil was noticeably smaller.

"That's not normal bone-steel." Rae'en studied it, ran her fingers along its smooth surface.

"No," Kholster agreed. "I buried the remaining meat over that way to keep it cold enough, in case you wanted any. Regenerating legs . . . and all."

"Not yet," she said. "What kind of material is it?"

"Bone-steel." Kholster set the finished gauntlet down on the anvil, standing back to study it from a distance. "From Uled's first draft of an Aern. He inhabited it after Caz slew his animated corpse, Wylant and Vax prevented him from possessing Sargus, and Rivvek destroyed the Root Trees Uled had infected.

"Uled fled here and sought to use the body to wrest leadership of the Aern from you. He failed."

"What is Torgrimm going to do with him?" Rae'en eyed the gauntlet as if it might bite her. "One of the Horned Queen's hells?"

"I've asked him to let the Aern handle this," Kholster said. "Unless you object."

"Me?" Rae'en started to laugh, assuming it was a joke. He could do whatever he wanted, he was . . . but he wasn't First of One Hundred anymore. She was.

"You are First of One Hundred," Kholster said, "ruler of the Scars-guardian Empire. Sooner or later, we all have to move in a world our parents shaped and make our own decisions, leave our own impressions. I would like to give a gift to the Last World, remove a single threat. My will is that Uled be added to the souls of all Aern, one voice drowned out by millions, trapped in connection to a people who work no magic, but only if you agree."

"If I don't?"

"When Worldshaker is completed, I will hand the armor over to Minapsis, the Horned Queen, and ask that she place him in the deepest of her hells where he can never escape."

"If I do . . ." Rae'en eyed the armor stand, the plate armor upon it taking on a more-sinister gleam colored with the knowledge of who was trapped inside. "How would it work?"

"When I finish Worldshaker, I would bond with him in the way any Armored does. A piece of me would reside within, forcing Uled's spirit out of the bone-steel and into the clutches of Harvester, who is prepared to do as I have suggested."

"Worldshaker?"

"I have named my warsuit in honor of my father." Kholster picked up the gauntlet, carrying it over to the armor stand. "Uled was many things, committed great evils, but without him, there would be no Sri'Zaur, no Aern, and no Vael. He was evil, mad, and terrible, but he created me. After a fashion, any good we have done, therefore bears his mark as well."

Thoughts? Rae'en asked.

His soul versus the souls of every Aern who ever died and every Aern who lives? Amber asked. *We can take him, kholster. No question.*

Bloodmane? Rae'en asked. *You've been quiet.*

It is a mercy Uled does not deserve, the warsuit thought, **but mercy is always a gift that bestows more upon the giver than the receiver.**

We may have to start calling you a peacesuit, Rae'en teased.

I would give him to the Bone Queen, Glayne thought.

Me, too, M'jynn thought, the other Overwatches except for Kazan and Joose joining in.

Whatever you want to do, though, Joose thought. *You're the First.*

Just so long as there are no more armies of the dead, Kazan thought.

"Bloodmane votes for mercy," Rae'en told her father, "and since he hardly *ever* asks for anything . . ."

CHAPTER 42

THIRTEEN YEARS LATER: THE SCARSGUARDIAN EMPIRE

Nothing grew where Hashan and Warrune had once stood. A wild chitterer sniffed tentatively at the edge of desolation, fuzzy ears flat, wet nose snuffling, before it darted away to less-objectionable climes. Queen Yavi despised the empty, arid atmosphere of the char-scented place. She had ordered it burned in hopes the cycle of most forests could be restarted, but the ash had stayed ash with no wind to blow it away or rain to soak it in.

Rain did not fall on their graves.

Even a side-shoot donated by her brother, Kholburran, had withered and died when planted there, leaving him unable to attempt to repair the damage from afar. When asked, Arri explained that, as best she could tell—because though Kholburran was the most communicative of the Root Trees, his complete attention was hard to get or retain—he had lost touch with it when it entered the "deadened spot."

Standing in the center of the cracked and barren earth, soot and ash clinging to the ground rather than her feet, Yavi understood what Kholburran meant. Rivvek had killed a piece of the land, irrecoverably, to stop the seed Uled had planted in Warrune. Her head petals itched, drying rapidly in this zone that drained all life within it.

Dolvek, little more than a cloak with the rough impression of a face here, scowled and paced, bumping against her incessantly in attempts to nudge her toward the blossoming forest that lay without the ring of death.

I love you. His thoughts were tinged with urgent anxiety.

"Hush now," Yavi told him. "I won't be long."

Root Guard rimmed the border, their anxiousness as palpable as her husband's. No one wanted her to be here. They wanted to forget what had happened and let it be a name in the Litany. She touched the soil where she had found the foci that had fallen from Rivvek's back. She'd found them when recovering her mother's remains, what there had been of them.

Most of the foci had since been sent to Scarsguard's Capitol, Fort Sunder, except for a trio of them, two of which pierced the bark of her own back and a third the wood of her new Heartbow, made from Kholburran's living wood. Even now, she understood why Rivvek had done so, but she still wished there had been some other way to victory over Uled. Seeing all of the elemental dimensions exhilarated her but depressed her as well, when she saw the way elven elemancers shaped and controlled the spiritual inhabitants without any concept of the harm they often did.

She sometimes wondered why Dolvek, through Rivvek's abandoned foci, had seen fit to gift her with earth, wind, and water, but not fire. Maybe he knew it was not for the Vael. Too tempestuous to be wielded by beings made of wood.

"Queen Yavi." Droggan, the living image of Drokkust and the first of the male-type persons she'd allowed to join the Root Guard, spotted the artist she had summoned first. Irka arrived by air, escorted by a pair of attractive female Cavair, two dangerous-looking manitou, and an elven Aeromancer with one of the old-style elemental foci that had engulfed her right arm in a layer of metal painted like a mural.

After seven years of waiting, Yavi had given in to suggestions and commissioned a memorial. There had been, of course, only one candidate, since no living work of Vael could survive there.

Irka landed barefoot, leaning back to kiss both Cavair on their bat-like muzzles, his long, red hair falling to cover one side of his face, highlighting the multicolored patterns he'd inked onto the other. He wore loose-fitting tan trousers (which billowed when he moved) and nothing else, though his hair was bedecked with beads of many metals, but predominantly bone-steel.

"Queen Yavi," he boomed, moving to touch the back of her hands with his own. At the contact, a spark arced between the two of them, and she saw the child they could have made, the same Incarna she had envisioned when Kholster had kissed her years before.

"Irka," Yavi said, "by Kholster out of—"

"Just Irka," he interrupted. "And, regarding that spark, I have no real interest in having children. With the staggered waking of the unawakened Aern Kholster carried into exile after the Sundering, there are an astonishing number of Ones through Thirteens running about between South Number Nine and Scarsguard already without any contributions on my part."

"I was not going to suggest—" Yavi flushed.

"Don't worry about it." Irka touched the ground, bent down to touch his cheek to it. "Or my apologies; whichever would be appropriate. I am forward and presumptuous. There is simply no accounting for me."

She quirked a smile at him. Seeing a person with Kholster's body, so different, and yet as he studied the terrain, taking it all in, the set of his jaw, the concentration so exactly like Kholster's, cheered her in a way she had not thought possible.

"Wait beyond the perimeter, would you?" Irka asked. "This may take several candlemarks."

He walked every foot, taking in the angles and the light. As he moved, his companions broke camp, setting up easels and tents. One of the Cavair took a large bag of finely powdered bone-steel, spreading it first around the perimeter of the area, then working her way inward until she had emptied three more similar-sized bags.

Area examined, Irka spread his arms and retraced his steps, the layer of bone-steel dust following him like myriad minute soldiers, an army of sand, until the whole of the dead area bore an even coating.

"Now," he said with a tone of weary satisfaction, "I know what I have to work with. This place is problematic, you know?"

"We know things won't grow here." Yavi stepped back into the dead area and hesitated, staying put rather than disturb the bone-steel.

"Oh." Irka did another circuit of the area. This time, the bone-steel powder collected behind him, first as an amorphous mass, then a square, a ball, and finally, as roughly half of it had been gathered, it split into two balls, then three and, as he gathered the last of it, four.

He directed three of the balls into bags awaiting them at his camp, then the fourth rolled after him to Yavi.

"How do you do that?" Yavi asked.

"I'm sorry." Irka sat cross-legged in the grass, the ball of powdered bone-steel swinging around directly before him. "Did you say you wanted to take a look at some ideas I had about what to build here?"

Flowing nimbly from a sphere into a mass the same shape as the dead area in miniature, right down to the cracks and crevices, Irka sent the excess bone-steel through a series of rough shapes: a pyramid, a series of pyramids, an irkanth, two figures standing back to back, three figures holding hands in a line, the same three figures in a rough triangle.

"I like that one," Yavi said. "But I wish you could make them look like—"

"Kari, Hashan, and Warrune?" He closed his eyes, muttering words under his breath, eyes glowing brightly enough beneath his eyelids that the light shone through as the suns began to go down.

Kari changed first, one of the figures shrinking, features becoming more distinct, refined, then exact.

"You should see how discombobulated I make other Aern." Irka winked. "I did help kill the god of knowledge, and the new one is my uncle."

Shortly, Hashan and Warrune appeared as Vael rather than as trees, like tiny pearlescent statues, holding hands with their Root Wife-to-be.

"Fabtacular." Yavi's ears wiggled and tears welled in her eyes. As little details sprang to life, vanished, and reformed to suit the artist's eye, she felt the back of Dolvek's hand on her shoulder.

A fitting monument, Dolvek thought. *It will be . . . bigger, though. Won't it?*

"So, I'm thinking we'll make the whole thing out of metal and stone . . ." Irka said, oblivious to the ghost's confusion.

"Of course," Yavi said to both of them. "Of course."

*

Far from Fort Sunder, in the Sri'Zauran Mountains, a dragon's shadow fell across the white-capped peaks, announcing the arrival of guests. The three most powerful mortals (if an Aiannai, a dragon, and an Armored Aern could truly be called such) and the dragon's designated speaker (a Zaur named Kreej) circled a stone abode. From a distance, it blended in with the peaks around it, but the view from above shone true.

They are expecting guests, Bloodmane thought to Rae'en.

All well back at Fort Sunder? Rae'en asked.

I would have told you if it were not.

General Kyland did an excellent job on the place, Kazan cut in. In Rae'en's mind's eye, he highlighted cunningly concealed lookout spots manned by autonomous sentries of purely elven artifice.

Glinfolgo waved up at them from the back of the manse, as he closed the door to the pump house he'd come up to take a look at and help repair. Really, he'd just wanted to check if Sargus had been keeping up the maintenance on the place without any trouble.

A wide spot on the west side of the property had been cleared away, and they set down in the middle of it, Kreej scurrying down from his precarious perch at the dragon's breast. Rae'en wondered where the dismembered head of Kilke, which had hung there during the Battle against Coal, had gone, but she knew better than to ask Tsan'Zaur again. All answers on the topic had been met with baleful glances, disdainful snorts, or dismissive retorts.

Queen Bhaeshal waited for Rae'en to dismount the dragon before the two of them set out for the front door in unison, Kreej trailing along behind. Sargus met them halfway, wearing a warm coat that obscured anything else he might be wearing except for a pair of leather boots. He walked upright, without his disguised pack or the array of lenses that he had once worn camouflaged to make his skull appear distorted. He carried a massive tome under one arm.

He offered a brief bow to Bhaeshal and Rae'en, aiming a deeper one toward Tsan'Zaur, who gazed with half-lidded eyes in their general direction.

"Please tell Tsan'Zaur," Sargus said, "that, per her request, I have devoted my writing time to an account of the creation of the Sri'Zaur and the twisting of the Zaur to Uled's purposes."

Kreej tapped and scratched his words in Zaurtol, and, though the dragon plainly understood what Sargus had said, she waited politely for Kreej to finish before responding in a mixture of Zaurtol and Zaur to Kreej.

All a part of the Zaur need to appear superior, Joose thought.

She's a dragon, Glayne thought. *And Warleader of the Sri'Zauran empire. She has to maintain—*

It was the least-objectionable solution to resolve their perceived disrespect in her lowering herself to speak directly to those below her, Rae'en thought. *Stop hunting after that spoor!*

All of the Overwatch tokens in her head lit up gold in acquiescence.

"Tsan'Zaur honors you with the assurance that she will read it soon, noting the many errors she will no doubt find in the work." Kreej said.

Rae'en rolled her eyes.

"I am honored and grateful." Sargus bowed, handing the book to Kreej, who set off directly to his mistress to stow it in his seat or assemble her reading apparatus, if she so desired.

"How is he?" Bhaeshal asked, her metallic eyes making it unclear whether she was studying Sargus or watching Kreej struggle to assemble the mass of rods and gears that allowed the dragon to turn the pages of books too small or delicate to handle dragon claws.

"Not that way," Glinfolgo bellowed, stealing a quick kiss on the cheek from his niece as he passed. "Let me do it, you daft lizard."

"Your assistance would be quite acceptable, master Dwarf." Tsan'Zaur shifted into a more comfortable position to wait, shooing Kreej away with a wing.

"Much better, highness," Sargus answered Rae'en's earlier question.

"Well enough for visitors?" Rae'en asked.

"He had a rough night," Sargus warned, "screaming about trignoms not stacking, but he's been up for several hours now, and he'll likely be clear-headed until bedtime as long as we steer away from troublesome topics . . ."

*

Inside the house, Rae'en marveled at all the artwork. Re-creations of statues or paintings that had been lost in the destruction of Port Ammond were displayed next to other genuine objects that had been rescued by refugees when they fled to Fort Sunder. An oversized Dwarven Hearthstone poured heat into the room. Kreej promptly positioned himself next to it, hissing his pleasure. Rae'en recognized it as one of the fancier ones that cast light as well as heat, noting a rune that might allow it to mimic the appearance of flame. The Dwarves were grateful to the Aiannai whose plans had helped end the feuds between Zaur, Aern, elf, and Vael.

The former king, one of the few who bore both the names Oath-keeper and Bone Finder, sat in a chair before the hearthstone, stacking trignom tiles on a board.

"Your turn, Sargus," Rivvek called. "Did you know there is a Zaur in here?" He looked over his shoulder, eyes questing, and smiled when he spotted his guests.

"My queen." Rivvek hopped up and crossed to hug her, then, "First of One Hundred," he said to Rae'en, accompanied by formal nod.

"Bone Finder." Rae'en nodded back. "Or would you prefer Oathkeeper?"

"Rivvek." He laughed. "I prefer Rivvek."

"As you say, Bone Finder Rivvek," Rae'en said formally, a hint of mirth in her voice.

Bone Finder.

The solution still made her smile. What to call a group of elves who had trekked into the Never Dark and accomplished the impossible? The answer had seemed obvious, and Alysaundra had talked Zhan into accepting it, though that had been a near thing. Zhan did not appear to appreciate the irony of having elves as part of his Ossuary.

She studied Rivvek as he offered Bhaeshal some tea or soup. He'd lost weight. His eyes were hollow and ringed with the dark bruises of constant insomnia.

At least his hair looks like it is growing back, Amber thought to her.

Rae'en let Sargus lead her through the tour of improvements since the most recent of her annual visits, while Bhaeshal and Rivvek visited. Most of the house was taken up by a library that looked out onto an interior garden.

A pleasant enough place, Joose thought to her, *for an elven home.*

Not everyone loves combat drills and forge work like we do, Rae'en thought back.

"How are *you*, Sargus?" Rae'en asked. "Everyone who matters lauds Rivvek for his contributions. Being officially dead seemed to do a lot for public opinion of him, but you are the one who helped my father adjust the Proto-Aern so Uled could be trapped by it. Without you, Wylant may not have been able to slay him in the first place back at the Sundering."

"She would have found a way." Sargus led them to a cozy lab, handing her a thick square of bone-steel the size of her thumb. "I've inscribed another seven books and the one I wrote for Tsan'Zaur on it."

"Seven?" Rae'en slipped the tile into her saddlebags. "Last time it was only three."

"I'm getting better at it with Glinfolgo here to help me." Sargus shrugged. "Eventually, I hope to be able to create an automata to do the encoding for me."

"Your own pace is more than sufficient." Rae'en patted his shoulder.

"How are her subjects taking it?" Sargus asked.

"As much as some hated him, others loved him." Rae'en looked about the lab, recognizing some of the tools and equipment as elven or Dwarven. "General Kyland helped there, too, singing his praises. With the Lost Command backing him up . . . Well, I don't think they will ever come around completely, but most mourned his 'death,' and the monument only gets defaced about once a month now. Even so, his brother's is more popular."

"Thank you again for arranging all of this." Sargus gestured all around him. "He really is doing so much better. He eats. He reads. Some days he laughs. Maybe this will heal him."

"I hope it does." Rae'en clapped her hand on the elf's shoulder. "You both accomplished the impossible and kept your oaths in the process. We respect that."

Most beings are simply ill-suited for the level of death the former king encountered, Bloodmane thought. He did well to bear up under it until the task was completed. We saw elemancers suffer as he does after the Demon Wars.

Will he recover, do you think? Rae'en asked.

Your uncle might know, Bloodmane thought. I do not.

"Let me show you the gardens," Sargus said.

*

"It's not so much a secret." Three-Headed Kilke strode through the heavens in robes made of shadow and lightning, his strides so long, Vander had to double-time it to keep pace with him. "But I still cannot tell you. The Artificer could have, in the old days, but I am bound by time, as are we all—and, having given mortals the right to govern their own minds, no god may determine how any one of them may act in future with complete certainty."

"Is there anything we can do to help?" Vander asked.

"To repair a mortal mind? We could remove the troublesome memories, let Sedvinia massage the ones we leave behind," Kilke said.

Kilke led them into the Throne Room of the Gods. Vander had never been there before. He hated it on sight. Grand pillars and nonsensical physical laws made it the essence of everything he disliked about the way the old gods acted. "But Kholster objects to that sort of manipulation rather strenuously."

Gromma and Xalistan lounged in a shared bit of jungle that jutted into the room through a section of crumbled wall, as if time and decay had collapsed a portion of the hall, granting access to the wilds without. They chatted to each other in animal tongues, aloof as if the other gods were unimportant.

Sedvinia, goddess of joy and sadness, waved at Vander from her seat upon the edge of a marble fountain through and around which flowed the elemental deities of water and air.

Clemency stood casually next to Kholster, flaming helm giving evidence of Wylant's presence within. Vander sought about for Vax, covering his surprise with a cough when instead of an answer he hit the word: secret.

Jun's seat (a throne in the likeness of an anvil) sat empty, as did Shidarva's seat on the throne raised above all others, as befitted her station as Ruler of the Gods.

"Kill him." Minapsis spoke from a throne of the souls of her worshippers. "Give me his soul, and in time I will heal it. He will be punished as he feels he should be and then, once his guilty conscience is assuaged, he will be rewarded as befits his deeds."

"*When* in the natural course of events—" Torgrimm (in Harvester, helm clutched under one arm) shifted from foot to foot next to his wife's throne. "—Rivvek dies, *I* will decide whether his soul is to be placed into your capable hands, or reincarnated, Minapsis."

"No one suggested otherwise." Minapsis's second set of eyes opened a bare fraction, pure white light shining out from behind the lids. "And my congratulations on the return of your third head, brother. How did you arrange that?"

"Simple." Kilke grinned with all three mouths. "I won."

"Won what?" Wylant's voice asked from within Clemency.

"This game." Taking a position against the wall opposite Shidarva's throne, Kilke sat, the shadows gathering into a throne beneath him. Swelling with the swirling dark, he grew to over two kholsters, the deity's central head purring all the while. "Perhaps the final game we are allowed to play with the lives of mortals, given our dear Kholster's opinion on the topic."

"He's only one," Xalistan roared. "One voice against many. He—"

"—is the Arbiter, the birth and death of gods," Kholster said firmly, his voice commanding and loud. "I do not like the idea of gaming with mortals as if they are tokens or dice in some Guild City game room or Midian back alley."

"I. Regrettably. Agree." Each of Kilke's heads spoke one of the words, allowing the sentence to flow right to left then starting over with the rightmost head. "My time on the mortal plane has taught me much. Our new God of Knowledge has convinced me of things Aldo tried and failed to teach.

"The Artificer never meant for us to rule them." He kept speaking, lightning playing across his horns, arcing from head to head, jumping to his fingertips where he let it course from claw tip to claw tip, gathering it at last into ball of lighting that he set hovering above his shadow throne. "We were to look after them, council them, teach them. Protect the Last World when they could not. What were his last words to us, Vander?"

"Be kind." Vander folded his hands behind his back. "Love them. Care for them." Without pausing, he reached out to his bone-steel discs, drawing them near, but not inside the hall. "Be the parents to them that I could not be to you." He met each deity's gaze in turn as he paced the room. "Let them flourish and protect them from all exterior harm, even undue influence from yourselves or your fellow deities.

"Let them learn from their mistakes." Getting Xalistan to meet his gaze took longer than any of the others, but Vander got him, in the end, and by then he had all of their attention. "Guide, but never rule.

"Be stern, but never cruel. They have been through too much at my hands already." When he stopped, Vander stood in the center of the room, his back to Shidarva's throne. "Do not seek me, for I am already within you and you will not find me without."

"Nonsense," Xalistan barked. He drew himself up on his hind legs, tail swishing. "I have had enough of this. You mortals, taking the heavens by a quirk of fate and Torgrimm's foolishness. Someone should strike you down and throw your filthy carcasses back to the Last World or beyond the Outwork entirely and into the depths of the Dragon Waste!"

A spear, cruel and long, materialized in Xalistan's paws. Two sickles appeared in Gromma's grasp, one rusty, the other new, both sharp.

"I abstain," Minapsis drawled, vanishing with her husband and his armor, leaving only her own voice behind to complete the sentence. "I would fight only for my souls or for my husband."

"Then strike!" Behind Vander in the wavering air, Shidarva appeared, a blazing blue sword in each of her four arms. He ducked one blade, took another to the shoulder, and blocked the remaining two with the alacritous arrival of two of his bone-steel discs.

Vander cried out in pain but kept moving, rolling away, covering his retreat with disc after disc as she smote them from the air and existence, each with a single blow.

"Stop," Kholster said softly, no sense of real urgency or emotion in his voice, as if he merely wanted to be able to say he had tried. "Wait. Don't."

Gromma drew back, but Xalistan and Shidarva came on.

One step took Vander to ruins of Port Sunder, but Shidarva followed. A second step took him to the Isle of the Manitou. Shidarva followed.

Last chance for her to turn back, he thought at Kholster.

She won't.

A third step took Vander to the Sacred Arena at center of the city of Warfare in the Guild Cities. She followed. As planned, Vander rolled right. Head down, arms out, in a sign of submission.

"I yield!" he shouted.

"You die!" Shidarva roared, "And without you, so falls your—"

Her body fell to the arena floor next to Vander, sparks of power arcing from her severed neck toward the being who held her head aloft.

"Eventually you will all learn to see that coming." A second thrust from Wylant's blade severed Shidarva's spine. "If there are any of you left."

Methodically dismembering the body (because one could never tell about some deities), Wylant did not stop until she had consumed Shidarva's heart, and the blade Wylant had been holding turned blue with matching fire dancing along its edge.

"Kholster is a lucky Aern," Vander said from the floor. He'd rolled over and sat up, but he showed no sign of standing. Stripes of Shidarva's blood and his own marked his chest and his pants: red on orange. "How did he convince you to behead a second goddess?"

"Both times it was my idea, Overwatch." Wylant threw the head into the dirt, setting it aflame with her sword. "Kholster may have set my slaying of Nomi in motion, but this one was all mine."

I wanted to spare her, Kholster thought. *Shidarva meant well once, and I think I understand her better now than I did as a mortal. I called her Queen of Leeches, and I meant it, but she was still grieving the loss of her people, her continent. In time she could have been brought back into line. Wylant disagreed.*

Was that Vax inside Clemency? Vander asked.

Yes, Kholster answered. *Wylant gave him her flaming tresses this morning. Balance, you know.*

Smoke from the body worked its way across to Wylant in white clouds, which sank into her skin, giving it the slightest hint of blue. When Shidarva was ashes, Wylant pulled Vander to his feet, and they returned to the halls of the gods. Her hair flamed again, but it had gone azure.

*

"Where would you like to go now?" Kholster asked the soul of Shidarva in his best imitation of Torgrimm's gentle tones. Down below the surface of the sea, the two of them stood on the remnants of the ancient temple at Alt, its white marble flecked with underwater life and the soil of the seabed.

"Here is fine." She knelt on the spiral pattern of the temple floor, portions of it whole and unbroken, depicting the whirling flow of her blades and the balance between Justice and Retribution.

"I can make you mortal and hand you over to Torgrimm to be reincarnated," Kholster said. "Aldo opted to remain a colony of ants. More

orderly, I think he said. Nomi let him send her back as a human. Or . . .
you would make a good Aern . . ."

"Fine." That drew a bitter laugh. "Make me an Aern then, or an elf,
or even a manitou, but not a human. I want to last."

Kholster nodded, and she was gone, whisked away to wherever Torgrimm chose.

How does it feel to be king of the gods? Vander asked.

I would not know, old friend. Kholster brushed the algae from a statue
with Shidarva's face, her expression wise and aloof. *Wylant is the ruler of the
gods. I suppose that makes me her consort.*

Consort?

Females make better leaders than males, Kholster thought. *If I handed my
army to Rae'en, why would you think I would try to keep my wife from kholstering
my gods?*

Your gods?

Kholster only smiled.

What about Kilke? Vander asked. *He was our ally, our confidante, and
integral to our plan. Do you think—?*

I think we need to keep an eye on him, Kholster answered, *but of what deity
is that not already true?*

RED EYES, BLACK WINGS

Two blood-red eyes stared out into the torch-lit corridor and waited. The guards would, if his information was sound, soon be passing through this portion of the artisan gallery. The guard he was waiting for should be on this particular inspection as well.

An owl hooted; to Caius's surprise, a real owl. It seemed the nights of most cities, particularly the political ones, were always filled with the false cries of one animal or another as thieves, spies, and lackwit nobles went about their intrigues.

Several times as the boy crept his way through the maze of pathways in Duke Eobard's home at Castleguard, the desire to relieve the fine noble family of a few notable items had proved an unwanted temptation.

In a glass case on a corner table in the duke's private study, they had an inherited bone-steel mask that was of considerable interest. He loved the look of it, the pearlescence. Who had given such a thing to the duke? Why? He took it, examining the smooth blankness of the face. Who had made such a thing, and why did the duke have it?

He froze, lithe body flattening against the wall, the well-oiled leather of his armor silent as shadows. Bitterness filled his mouth, hackles rising. They hunted him. He slid the mask on and smiled at the feel of the metal against his skin.

Caius felt them, their minds, questing for his down dirty streets and bleak alleyways. Especially the sad woman with the tricolored hair. Father's taint stank, a presence in her mind the boy could not abide. Anyone who'd ever known Happrenzaltik Konstantine Vindalius, who had spent time with him long enough for his words to stick and take root, was worth avoiding.

Not now, he thought. Eyes closing to slits, he dropped further into himself, so deep, so still, his breath made no sound but the wind's, his boots on the stone noiseless, his wings tucked in, his eyes, if one thought they saw them, twin fireflies, flashes of inconsequential flare in the black. The mask did not obstruct his vision at all. . . . How had that been possible? It felt like it had been made for him.

He smiled, the feel of the questing minds even stronger. *You will not find me*, Caius crowed to himself. *No Long Speaker can.*

Tomorrow would be time to move again, as a precaution, slip out of Castleguard and back to the Guild Cities or even farther from Midian and the Dwarves' bridge to Scarsguard or the human lands on the other side of the Sri'Zauran Mountains.

This chill evening, however, he had a mark, and when he was on the hunt, his clients could always rely on his ability to focus, do as he was instructed . . . kill whoever he was sent for, and then leave.

The darkness called to him as he waited, breathing softly into his bone-steel mask. Maybe the Bone Finders would come after him, too, for stealing a relic of bone-steel. He relished the thought.

As the wind howled outside, Caius checked to ensure his long, black hair remained securely tied beneath his hood and that only a short braid of false red hair showed beyond the hood's silken confines. At the same time, he checked the tightness of his belt and looseness of the two slits of fabric in the rear of his tabard to make sure that his leathery wings could spring free very easily if he found himself in need of a swift escape.

A quick check of the more-mundane portions of his equipment helped him pass the time until muffled footsteps echoed down the passage. The guards were right on schedule.

The tension in his body palpable as he prepared, Caius focused on the sounds of their footsteps, hoping to learn something about the men he would momentarily be fighting through the cadence of their gait. It would be all he would ever likely learn about the way they fought.

Sliding deeper into the shadows as they passed, Caius fell into step behind them, the weighted iron hilt of his throwing dagger coming down hard on the base of one guard's neck where skull and spine met. That man was safe from him, but the other was the one whose death was a greeting on the tip of the Harvester's tongue.

Shalka, he believed the man's name was, drew his sword as he turned, freezing when he felt the cold steel of the assassin's blade drawing a thin line of blood at his throat.

"Not a word," the assassin spat. The man remained motionless as he considered his options, neither lowering his blade nor making any effort to close with his assassin.

"Sheathe the sword, then undo your sword belt."

For a moment, the guard hesitated. In that micro span of time, the hooded boy saw defiance light the man's eyes, could almost feel the sinews tense and muscles move as the sword stroke began.

"A waste," Caius whispered, slitting the man's throat and swatting away the guard's sword with a bat of one newly freed wing. As the body hit the ground, the crystal twist was already down the hallway on his route to the roof.

He'd wanted to know what the guard had done to inspire a duchess to pay for his death. Now all he had were guesses, but guesses were fine. Curiosity did not always need to be satisfied; it was okay to wonder.

His thoughts were interrupted by the surprised shouts of two guards who were definitely well behind schedule. Maybe if he had not been so involved with his own thoughts, he would have heard their voices up ahead.

There were three of them, meaning that somewhere a patrol was one man short, or perhaps they were a whole patrol short. Head cocked to one side, he ran through the possibilities, saw himself fighting the guards, saw himself flying away. He picked a third option.

His throwing knife took the first one through the throat, but somehow the man still managed to scream an impossibly intelligible "INTRUDER!" as he died. The other guard froze in his tracks and choked out one word, a simple whisper of terror. "Malvolio."

Where do they keep getting those names? Caius laughed, a dry rattle.

"You've heard of me?" Caius asked, leaning in close. The stench from the guard's trousers and the puddle forming at his feet answered the question well enough. Standing there in his studded leather and black, with the bone-steel skull mask and graceful black wings, it looked as if a Bone Finder had come to collect.

He disemboweled the man as an afterthought, then took wing, flapping toward the Garden of Divinity. If he was lucky, he would make it in time to see the Changing of the Gods.

*

From the shadows, Three-Headed Kilke watched Caius Vindalius fly, admiring the lad's capacity for death. The other gods could wash their hands of the games, but with his last piece still on the board, well . . . it would be rude not to continue.

Even as the boy flew overhead, Kilke saw Tyree and Cadence making their way through the streets after him.

Tyree called the assassin's name. The boy looped in the air, reversing direction, plunged toward them both. He caught Tyree in the throat with one dagger and the heart with another. The human fell to the street, blood welling through Tyree's fingers as he collapsed, clutching at his throat.

"Stop following me." The boy stood across from his mother, daggers drawn, blood-red eyes glaring at her from behind a mask. "Or you will die, too, next time."

"Wait!" Cadence shouted as the boy took wing. She reached for him with her Long Fist, trying to pull the boy back to her, but the power slid off, unable to grip him. She tried to reach him with Long Speaking, but it was as if his mind was not even there.

Sitting up blearily as his wounds closed, Tyree frowned at the blood on his newest shirt, "We'll get him next time," Tyree said.

"Next time?" Cadence peered out into night after her son. "This is best look I've gotten of my son since he was a baby, and you chirp, 'Next time'?"

"Would you rather I assume that we'll never find him?" He put a hand on her shoulder, and she fought the urge to pull away.

Please, she thought to her abilities more than to herself. *Show me whether we ever—*

Whatever powers her son possessed had made it harder to catch glimpses of his possible futures, but she caught an image of him smiling in the sun, wings outstretched, a hand in his. It was not much, but it was enough to keep Cadence going, to give her hope.

"If it helps," Tyree said, "I've been a paid killer before, and I turned out pretty well."

Cadence wished Tyree was joking but knew better.

"I just wish I knew what Hap did to him."

"I think I have an idea what the boy might have done to Hap." Tyree touched a hand to his throat, the wound already gone.

Had Caius killed his father? What had Hap done to the boy? She did not know, but she was determined to find him and undo whatever damage had been done, to give Caius the same chance at happiness and freedom she had been given by a pair of Aern who had not ever met her before that day, but who had looked into her eyes and known.

"Was that a bone-steel mask he was wearing?" Tyree asked.

Cadence nodded. She could not track her son's mind, but now that he had bone-steel, she knew who could track the mask.

"We're going back to Scarsguard," Cadence told him. "I need to borrow a Bone Finder."

*

On a berth in the cave-dark tunnels of the barracks at South Number Nine, Kholster slept soundly on the hard stone. Reaper lay along his right arm, his hand resting lightly on its haft. He wore freshly steam-washed jeans, his boots lined up neatly along the side of his berth, his shirt folded tightly atop them.

Worldshaker stood in a specially carved niche across from him, its blued surface covered in dynamic lines, enhancing its leonine appearance, the helm in the likeness of an irkanth, its mouth closed, its gaze impassive, its mane white and clean.

The clearing of a throat broke the silence of four hours. Blue, flickering light as if from a pure-gas flame accompanied the sound.

"Come to bed," Wylant told her husband.

"Yes, kholster," he teased, rolling off of his berth and taking her into his arms. They kissed, and then together they took a step and were gone.

ACKNOWLEDGMENTS

This was the hardest book I've ever written. During the writing of *Worldshaker*, my health issues became more prominent, limiting not only my writing time but also the time I have to spend as father, husband, and friend. It is exceedingly irksome to sit down to write and have nothing to show for it hours later and, on occasion, to not even have the memory of what I did while I was sitting there.

But all that aside, this book, more than any of the others, would not exist without the patience of my dear friends and family, my Overwatches: Mary Ann, Rob, Dan, Karen, and Richard (it is still all his fault).

My wife, Janet, spent hours on end, listening to me, consoling me, and generally keeping me alive and functioning, all while being a wonderful mother to our two boys and an excellent teacher. She is the love of my life, my best friend, Prime Overwatch, and personal grammarian with a dash of editor in chief. She, along with those listed above, had the mixed blessing of listening to all my bad ideas and helping turn them into good ones.

This series would not be the same without my sons, Jonathan and Justin, either. Kholster would not have been Kholster without them and the things they have taught me about love and fatherhood.

Thanks are also due to my long-suffering editor, Rene, who waited much longer than expected for the manuscript. She is aces.

And, as always, thanks to my Mom and Dad, Martha and Ferrell Lewis. Without you, there would have been no me.

Last, but never least, thanks to you, the reader. Without you, I am just a crazy old dude typing in the darkness. (Don't forget to post a review, okay?)

ABOUT THE AUTHOR

Alabama madman J. F. Lewis is the author of the Grudgebearer Trilogy and the Void City series. Jeremy is an internationally published author whose books occasionally get him into trouble. He doesn't eat people, but some of his characters do. After dark, he can usually be found typing into the wee hours of the morning while his wife, sons, and dogs sleep soundly.

Track him down at www.author atlarge.com.

Photo by Janet Lewis